FORGET
me not

USA TODAY BESTSELLING AUTHOR
RACHEL LEIGH

Cover designs by Lori Jackson

Photographer: Emma Jane Photography

Editing: Fairest Reviews Editing Service

Proofreading: Rumi Khan

www.rachelleighauthor.com

Light is easy to love. Show me your darkness.

-R. Queen

CONTENT WARNINGS

PLEASE NOTE:
THIS IS A DARK ROMANCE

FORGET ME NOT IS A DARK ROMANCE WITH DARK THEMES AND CONTENT THAT MAY BE TRIGGERING TO SOME. SOME POTENTIAL TRIGGERS INLUDE, BUT ARE NOT LIMITED TO...

Dubious consent, somnophilia, emotional scars, suicidal thoughts, graphic murder, obsessive stalking, trauma bonding.

Flashbacks of: drug use, sexual assault, loss of pregnancy, physical assault (not by H)

PLAYLIST
CLICK HERE TO LISTEN
https://spoti.fi/3Zgdyuq

Daylight by David Kushner
Fix Me by 10 Years
Lilith by Halsey
Just Pretend by Bad Omens
The World I Know by Collective Soul
Torn To Pieces by Pop Evil
Monsters By Shinedown
Feel Something by Pink
Death of Piece of Mind by Bad Omens
What Was I Made For? By Billie Eilish
Cradles by Sub Urban
Unbreakable by Fireflight
Done With Everything by Line So Thin
Wish You The Best by Lewis Capaldi
Ghost by Badflower
Deep End by I Prevail
Under Your Scars by Godsmack

CHECK OUT THE: PINTEREST BOARD
https://pin.it/4wZoKxV

PROLOGUE

RHEA

Savannah, Georgia
Fourteen Years Old

I'm TRYING to remember my earliest memory as my mind completely drowns out the reality of what is happening around me. The desperation in my mom's pleading eyes. The fear of what lies ahead for both of us.

It's all too much. So for just a moment in time, I let it be nothing at all.

Just me and my thoughts.

She doesn't exist.

Neither do I.

I'm pretty sure I was five years old—my earliest memory, I mean. It's a little spotty, but I remember sitting on a curb in a big city surrounded by people who passed me by like I was nobody—except for one person. Wearing only a torn tee shirt and one sock, I sat there freezing in the dead of winter. I remember sobbing uncontrollably just to gain the attention of a wealthy man. He was probably in his late sixties to early seventies. Sort of reminded me of Santa, save for the jolly belly. He scooped me up on his hip and said in the softest, most consoling voice, "You've got to be freezing. Are you lost, cutie pie?"

I nodded and cried out for my mom while pointing to the alley where I knew she was. And just as expected, he walked me into the darkness, holding me tightly. I felt safe. No harm could come to me—at least, not in that split second.

Our plan was timed out strategically. We watched that sweet old man for weeks while Mom trained me. I practiced crying, memorized the words she told me to repeat. Then I helped her lure him into that alley, only to watch her manipulate the situation and play victim. After roughing herself up and throwing out countless false accusations toward the man, including attempted kidnapping and sexual assault, she got what she wanted. To ensure her silence, he gave her all his cash. I'm not sure how much, but it was enough for us to eat dinner and get a room for the night.

I knew that man would never hurt me or my mom. But nobody else knew that.

Since that day, the only tears that ran down my cheeks were trained ones.

Like my mom has always said, *this is work and we can't allow emotion to interfere with what we have to do. It's nothing personal. It's a job, plain and simple.*

"Look at me, Rhea." Mom crouches in front of me as if I'm that five-year-old girl again, even though I'm nearly the same height as her. She cups my cheeks in her hands and the look in her eyes nearly crushes my soul. I don't like when she's nervous. It makes me nervous and there is no time for feelings when it comes to our line of business. And yes, this is business. Even this moment that will one day feel as if it was frozen in time.

Mom and I live on the run while bouncing from one hotel room to the next. I've never attended school or had friends. I learned to read from literature in the lobbies of the various hotels we've stayed at. Everything I know was taught to me by either my mom, or myself. I don't know how to form relationships because I've never had the opportunity. No sleepovers, dances, or talks about boys. I guess I can't miss something I've never had. Although, I do find myself wondering what it would be like to experience those monumental things in a girl's life.

She says this lifestyle is necessary to protect me from my biological father—a very wealthy and powerful man. Because of it, I've assumed other identities more than I have my own. We've survived off the accommodations of others and the money of strangers. We steal, lie, and cheat our way through life. But we *do* survive, and that's what matters.

"I need you to take this one for us, Rhea."

I stare back at her in a state of shock. All the air rushes out of my lungs as I gasp, "Me? But, Mom..." My eyes dart around the room, head shaking, no, because I can't. I won't. This wasn't the plan.

Her chest heaves and she tries to stifle the coughing fit that takes over. Fighting to clear her lungs of the virus she has been fighting for days, she hacks into a balled fist pressed firmly to her mouth. "I'm not well today, Rhea," she says, voice coarse as she weakly gasps for air. "I don't think I've got it in me."

I take her by the wrist, attempting to lift her to her feet when the realization hits me that she's not on her knees because of a failed attempt to console her child, but because she's weak. She has been for a while now. Instead of tugging her arm, I allow my fingers to graze softly over the tattoo on her wrist—flowers. Forget-me-not flowers, to be exact. Beautiful blue petals surrounded by blooming stems. I have the exact same one on the back of my shoulder.

My love for you is immortal. If something should ever happen to me, let these flowers be a reminder that near or far, we will never forget what we did to survive this life together.

That's what Mom said to me after she surprised me with the tattoos two months ago. Yes, I'm only fourteen. And no, it's not normal for a girl my age to get permanent ink tattooed on her skin. But I'm not normal, and what I'm being asked to do right now is proof that neither of us are.

And my response only confirms just how completely abnormal we really are. "Okay," I tell her on a whim. "I'll do it." Suddenly, the weight of the world lands on my shoulders, slowly drilling me into the hotel floor.

Mom's lips curve downward, and it's the response I expected. Neither of us are happy about this. There is no reason to smile or feel joy over what I'm about to do. It's not until the job is done that we can allow ourselves to feel relief. However short-lived it may be.

Two thousand dollars for a fifteen-minute task can bring us that joy back, and maybe even help my mother feel better. If I do this, it will be a moment worth celebrating. Two thousand might not sound like much, but to us, it's practically millions.

This job is a new one for me. I've never dealt with drugs before, let alone delivered them to a flock of middle-aged men who could scoop me up in a second and sell my body for more than they're making off the goods I'm bringing them. Sure, I've seen them, but my mom has always tried her best to protect me from that line of work.

We don't usually work like this, but desperate times call for desperate measures. Mom got an offer to deliver some goods on the east side of town where the heat runs hot. It was an offer she couldn't pass up, considering we're fleeing this state before dawn breaks and we've got no money to our names.

Am I scared? Hell yes. Will it stop me? Nope. Mom and I are

a team, and when one of us is down, the other stands tall. It's my turn to stand tall for her.

Mom manages to get on her feet, only to gasp for breath as she stumbles backward, allowing herself to fall on our shared bed. Getting herself comfortable takes every ounce of strength she has, but when she lies back, she's finally smiling. "Oh, Rhea. You are an angel."

Her words and smiles are meant to be a distraction because she doesn't want me to press on the fact that she can barely breathe right now.

"You need to see a doctor, Mom." My voice is stern, eyebrows pinned to my forehead.

She lifts her head off the bed, arms still lying on either side of her. "It's just a cold, Rhea. I'll be fine. I promise."

"The words of a promise mean nothing if they're drowned out by the loudness of our actions."

She smirks. "I've taught you well."

"That you have." I grab both of her hands and lift her until she's sitting. "But this isn't one of our schemes, Mom. This is real life and it's a life I won't survive without you. You need to see a doctor." I gently tuck a stray hair behind her ear and her body seems to give in a way I'm not used to seeing from the strong woman who raised me. So, I keep pushing. "Please. For me."

"Oh, Rhea." She grabs me by the waist and pulls me onto her lap. "I love you, my sweet girl, but you really are a pain in my ass sometimes."

"So you'll do it?"

"It's not like you've given me much of a choice in the matter."

Mom frowns. "You are so mature for your age, honey." She lets out a small laugh. "I blame myself for that. It won't always

5

be like this. And I promise I'm going to spend a lifetime making it up to you."

I'd like to believe her, but unless we hit big, I don't see us ever leaving this lifestyle behind. These promises are nothing new. Three years ago, it was a trip to Disney World. Two years ago, it was public school. Last year, we were supposed to get a home. Yet, here we are. I'm not even sure who I am today. Was it Jenny or Kate? Doesn't matter, as long as I'm anyone but me.

"Are you hungry?" Mom asks. "Let's celebrate."

"Aren't you being a little presumptuous in thinking I might actually pull this off?"

She picks up the hotel phone and brings it to her ear. She clears the phlegm from her throat and says in a clear but raspy voice, "You're my daughter, Rhea. I have not a single doubt in my mind that tonight will go flawlessly."

I listen as she orders room service on the card of another guest. A minute later, she sets the phone down, an artful smile playing on her lips. "Dinner is on its way."

"Look at this shit, Winton. They sent a toddler."

I drop the briefcase in my hand, letting it hit the pavement with a thunderous clap. "Very funny, asshole. Now, do you want the goods or not?"

The man I take to be Winton snaps his fingers, eyeing me. "You're Trixie's girl, ain't ya?"

Holding my composure, I keep my expression stoic. "Maybe I am. Maybe I'm not."

Trixie was my mom's stage name before I was born. She was a well-known stripper in Vegas whose name made the rounds. Her reputation precedes her as one of the most unscrupulous females in our line of work.

"A little Trixie," the man singsongs as he comes closer. Chills dance down my spine at his close proximity, but I don't show my fear.

Taking a step back, I seethe at him. "It'll do you good to keep in mind that if I am Trixie's daughter and you fuck with me, you fuck with her."

A new man steps out of the shadows. One of many I'm sure are watching from afar. This one with a lit cigarette hanging from his mouth. He's wearing a suit that tells me he's likely the one in charge.

He draws a long drag of the cigarette, then flicks it over my shoulder into the bay. "Open it up, little girl."

My knees knock as I crouch down in front of the briefcase. The newcomer shines a light down, watching intently as I flip it open, exposing clear sacks with different powders in a multitude of colors.

He brings his foot down hard on the top, forcing pressure with my fingers still inside. "Let up, asshole!" I screech.

A low chuckle rumbles from his chest before he finally shifts his grip enough for me to wiggle my fingers free. I give them a shake, then flip him off with my middle finger.

He grumbles at my gesture. "Cute."

"Wasn't meant to be." My lips curl in a snarl.

"Grab it," he tells Winton, before snapping his fingers twice, beckoning another man. "Give her the dough."

With a stern expression, clearly meant to intimidate me, the newcomer hands me a new case, this one full of cash. At least that better be what's in here.

They all turn as if they're just gonna walk away, but I straighten my back and call after them. "Whoa. Whoa. Whoa. Not so fast, boys."

Three pairs of eyes land on me while humor plays on their lips. I rest my hand on my hip, making it clear that I will retaliate if they don't give me the opportunity to check the contents inside. I might be fourteen years old and new to the drug world, but I'm no rookie. Not only that, Mom's already got me in eyesight, double-fisting pistols that are pointed at two of the three men.

The boss's henchmen glance sideways toward him, seeking silent permission to proceed. He slowly tilts his head in my direction, subtly giving them the green light.

I stiffen my posture and narrow my gaze, glaring at the boss as I kneel down and unlatch the briefcase. Sure enough, stacked neatly inside are bundles of cash—thousands, to be exact. I don't count it. Playing this game for long enough, I can easily tell it's all there.

"You can go now," I tell the men.

"You hear that, Winton," the annoying one says. "The toddler said we could go."

Winton knocks the dipshit upside the head, and I'm grateful he did the deed for all of us. Then in a split second, the henchmen disappear into the shadows, leaving me with their boss...alone.

I watch his sleek black shoes as they draw closer and closer. My heart races and my palms become slick with sweat as the toe of his boots touch the edge of the briefcase. He drops down to level his black eyes with mine.

"You've got balls, little Trixie. But a word of advice, don't do this shit again." He plucks an unlit cigarette from his ear and sticks it between his teeth. It hangs carelessly from his dry lips as he pulls a lighter out of his breast pocket. "Next time you might not be so lucky."

"I'm not scared, if that's what you think."

He chuckles, a smile forming that makes wrinkles gather on either side of his lips. "Oh, I can see you're not scared. That's the problem. We all need fear because it forces us to set boundaries for ourselves. Your lack of it will get you in some serious trouble one day."

I push down on the lid of the briefcase until it latches. Resting my palms on the cash that will no doubt get me and my mother out of this place, I look deep into this stranger's eyes. "Boundaries are for people who have the luxury of setting them. And fear is for the weak."

Sliding my fingers through the cold metal loop of the brief-case, I yank it up and straighten my back. The man's eyes follow my movements, but I refuse to acknowledge them. Without a backward glance, I leave the docks to meet up with my mom, so we can begin the process of setting our next plan in action. Starting a new life.

CHAPTER

ONE

RHEA

May 13, 2022
Charlotte, NC
Twenty Years Old

HOLY FUCK! He can't be. Can he?
Oh. My. God! He is.
He's...dead.

This is the second time one of my clients wound up dead in the last two weeks. Am I truly naive to think this is a coincidence? There are no common denominators with these two bastards, aside from them being rich, horny, and on the Siren's Call app. A handful of days ago, I had a client drop like a fly right at my feet in a hotel lobby outside of Tulsa. I fled before the paramedics even arrived. Fortunately, I got to keep the cash deposit I was given prior to his death, but still, I was out three hundred bucks.

I replay the last words of who was supposed to be my client, John. *"It's been so long since I've been with such a beautiful woman."* My stomach drops as my brain begins to process this. Could his excitement of what was coming literally have been the death of him? For *both* of them?

Unless, it's him. The man who's been following me for the last couple months. But, why? It doesn't make any sense why he'd end the lives of these innocent men, but allow me to run free.

Regardless of whether or not he's doing this, nothing has changed. I have to keep going. Just a little longer.

I step closer to the lifeless body on the bed. Bile rises in my throat and I gag, bringing up the lobster and steak dinner this stranger bought me before we came up to his hotel room. It definitely doesn't taste as good coming up as it did going down. I quickly force myself to get a grip. If I throw up in here, it'll be proof that someone was with him when he bit the dust.

With a trembling hand, I grasp the cold, bony shoulder of the naked man. Gently, I roll him over onto his back. For such a slender guy, he's heavier than I imagined he would be.

His face is gaunt and pale with a blanket of gray hair coating his chest. Fortunately, his eyes are closed. If it weren't for the lack of movement and sound coming from his body, I might actually believe he wasn't dead at all and possibly just sleeping. But there's no mistaking it; he's a goner.

Regardless, I have to be sure. "Mr. Denali," I whisper, giving him an impalpable shake. I hold my breath on the off chance he might suddenly come alive, but he doesn't move. I put a hand over his heart, searching for a beat, but one of my dollar store press-on nails gets caught in his chest hair. I blow out a puff of air in annoyance and rip my hand away. Biting my lip, I cross my arms over my bare breasts and look down at him. Then I see my damn nail lying there, caught in the hair on his chest.

"Oopsies," I mumble as I pluck the nail off him. "Sorry about this, Mr. Denali." I stick the nail back on my finger, holding it down with force so it'll stay in place.

My gaze trails along his body, landing on his limp dick and sagging ball sack. I'm not heartless by any means. I do have a heart, but I think it's acceptable to have the thought 'thank fuck I didn't have to touch that thing.'

You're probably thinking I have sex for money, and your assumption would be correct. Before I'm judged, you should know that I only do it when necessary. It's a way of surviving and times are tough right now. Who am I kidding? Times are always tough for me.

For what it's worth, I find my clients on an untraceable app that thoroughly vets users. Obviously, I hide my identity, and I also *always* use protection. There are rules I have in place to protect myself. That's not to say they haven't been broken by clients in the past.

This is a dangerous line of work and sometimes things go amok. When that happens, I pick the broken pieces of myself off the floor and stitch myself back together with the thread of willpower a girl like me is forced to conjure. There's no sense in living in the past; it's there for a reason.

A devilish grin creeps across my face, and for a second, I hate myself for it. There are times I wish I had more empathy toward others. Unfortunately, this is not one of those times.

My eyes flicker to the man's pants lying at my feet. The same pants he was wearing only minutes ago. I wonder what crossed his mind as he was taking them off—I'm certain it wasn't his imminent death. He was probably elated at the prospect of a girl my age getting into those pants. At least he died hopeful. For that, I'll pat myself on the back and leave this room without guilt.

After all, nothing is free in this world, and I deserve to be compensated for the final minutes of hope I gave this man. In any case, that's what I'll tell myself when I close my eyes to sleep tonight. If I look at this from any other angle, some remorse may creep inside me and feast on my insides, putting a damper on the future work I need to do. It's hard keeping my feelings in check, but it's necessary to survive. I'll leave here with a nice payout, even though I'll forgo the final payment I'd have received if I had the opportunity to carry out my job.

After quickly re-dressing, I stoop down and pinch his jeans with my index finger and thumb, pulling them back just enough to slide my hand into the back pocket until I feel the smoothness of his wallet.

I remove the soft, leather billfold. Not the cheap kind either. It's the real deal. One hundred percent genuine leather. I bring it to my nose to inhale the scent. Leather and money—two of my favorite fragrances. This man definitely has money. It's the sole reason I pulled him from the app. Well, that and his age. The elderly like to carry cash and I prefer the anonymity that comes with using it, while they prefer it as well, considering the majority of my clients are married men. Cash is the only way to guarantee my financial activities can't be tracked.

I flip open the flap on the wallet and grab all the cash from the back compartment. I remember to slide a single one-hundred-dollar bill back inside to make sure things don't appear suspicious. Then I close it and put it back in his pocket.

Without hesitation, I count my payout. Six hundred and twenty bucks. Definitely more than I would have gotten had he not croaked. Not too shabby for a single night's work.

This isn't my first rodeo. I've done this a time or fifty. I'm not proud of what I do by any means, but it's work, and I'm damn good at it.

I do my research on prospective clients. I chat with them briefly, learn their behaviors, and sometimes, ask about their families, too. In the case of Mr. Vincent Denali, there wasn't much to learn. He's a seventy-one-year-old widow with no children. He's also the president and owner of Denali Enterprise, a Fortune 500 pharmaceutical company that deals in some very shady activities.

I could have easily wormed my way into this man's life and made him fall in love with me. Eventually, he would have proposed and we would have gotten married. When he died, I'd get everything. However, I don't work like that. I don't attach myself, nor do I allow anyone to attach themselves to me. Matters of the heart are not my forte. Instead, my work is done rather quickly. Just not usually *this* quickly.

I know, I sound depraved. There's not much I can do about that, unfortunately. You try living my life with a shell of a heart inside your chest that only beats so it can take you from one day to the next, and tell me what you'd do differently.

In my depravity, I snatch up the old man's phone and use his face to gain entry. Hurriedly, I delete The Siren's Call app from his phone so there is no connection between us. Then I tap on the search bar and type in a popular porn site before placing the phone in his hand while resting the other on his lax dick.

Death by orgasm. It's a sad way to go. There will be no need for an investigation. The autopsy will show foul play was not a factor in his death and me being here was merely a coincidence. Doesn't matter, though. Come tomorrow morning, I'll be long gone, and there will be no trace of Charlotte Millis in Georgia because Charlotte Millis doesn't exist.

With a hurry in my steps, I snatch up my purse and give the room one last sweep. Then I blow Mr. Denali a kiss. "Rest in peace, babycakes."

On my way out, I reach into my purse to retrieve one of the many packets of flower seeds. Not just any seeds, forget-me-not seeds. I like to plant them in random states I visit, knowing that a few short weeks later, they will bloom into beautiful flowers in memory of my mom.

Before I step through the revolving door, I flip up the hood on my jacket and lower my face to hide from the outdoor cameras. Not that it matters, but I try to cover my tracks when I can. My feet hit the pavement in front of the hotel and I tear the top off the packet and let it flutter to my feet. I walk straight ahead, my eyes skimming my surroundings until I see a grassy area beside a beautiful stone water fountain.

He's here. There's no doubt in my mind. I can feel the burn of his gaze on me. Scouring the area, I stop when I see the sleek black Mercedes Maybach he conceals himself in. I'm not surprised he found me; he always does.

I don't know who he is or what he wants, but I can only derive he's a lackey sent by my father. Oddly enough, I'm not afraid of him. He only ingrains a small amount of assurance that my job here is complete. As with every other time I've seen that car in my neck of the woods, I'll flee, until he finds me again.

Soon enough, my follower's mission will end. He'll no longer need to hunt me, because I will no longer be his prey. I'm going to find my father, a man who sold my future to the devil, and I have every intention of taking my fate back into my own hands. Because once I find him, I'm going to kill him. Only then will I free him from the contract he signed. It's a favor for him as much as it is for me. At least, that's how I'll feel as I slide the blade across his wrinkly old throat.

With my hand held out, I sprinkle the seeds in memory of the only person I've ever loved in this entire world.

As they drift to the ground, landing on top of the grassy knoll, I'm reminded that I'm still here and she's not. I'll never forget. It's excruciating, but 'tis life. The reality is, nothing is permanent. Those who live will perish every time.

Don't you worry about me, Mom. I'm doing okay.

TWO

ALARIC

June 18, 2022
Hampton, SC

There she is. The thief of the air in my lungs. The sole reason I feel my heart beat in my chest. I've seen her countless times, but I swear each time is like the first.

Her caramel-colored hair cascades around her face as she bends forward and reaches into her purse that's hooked beneath the bar.

In a split second, her emerald eyes skim the large bay window in front of the bar, as if she's searching for me. I keep watching, knowing she can't see me behind the tinted windows of the car I'm in. The last thing I want is for the image of my face to be etched in her memory. She's aware of my presence. I make sure she is. But I keep my distance, just enough to make sure my identity stays hidden.

When we meet—and we will meet—I want it to be like the first time. An impromptu encounter. Maybe she'll bump into me and drop a stack of papers and we'll scramble to pick them up off the side of the road while our eyes lock and our movements freeze. I'll play hard to get at first, because I know my girl and she likes a challenge.

Or maybe she'll search a crowd and suddenly see me. I'll steal her breath with my gaze the same way she has stolen mine. Whatever the scenario, it will be unforgettable.

Sometimes I find myself wishing I didn't know her at all, because then I wouldn't have this agonizing feeling. As if I need to pull her close and melt her body into mine.

With the face and body of an angel, she's got a soul as dark as night. Lacking a moral compass, she does whatever the fuck she wants and pays no mind to the havoc she wreaks. We're alike in that way—going after what we want and not letting anyone stand in our way.

She's untamable and unhinged. It's become evident over the weeks of tracking her—and finding her—that my girl wasn't born to be caged, and I have no intention of trying to tame her. She's perfect exactly how she is. I just want to watch her wild ways, and when the time is right, I'll run with her.

For the last couple months, I've been on a mission to seize the girl of another man's dreams. It all started as a quest to find her—for him. He may want her, but he's not willing to put in the same work for her as I am.

The moment I saw Rhea, all grown up, my heart forced my plans to change as quickly as her location did. I made a deal, and now I have every intention of breaking it. Regardless of everything I will lose, he will not get what was so obviously meant to be mine.

Everywhere she goes, I find her. Because much like she will never forget me, I cannot forget her.

Until then, I'll sit back and wait. If I get too close, too soon, she could slip away somewhere I may never find her. But the clock is ticking and before long, my little wildcat is going to know exactly who I am and what I intend to do with her.

The older man she's sitting at the bar with leans in, a smile on his face that I wanna rip off and nail to the bedframe as I fuck some sense into Rhea. The veins in my neck protrude to the point of eruption. My fists clench the back passenger door handle, ready to tear it open and take what's mine.

If there's one thing I'm grateful for at this moment, it's the full-wall window inside the bar that allows me to track her every move. This isn't the first time I've watched Rhea throw herself at men. I keep my wits about me, though. I know it's a survival tactic. It's the only way she knows, because it's the only way she's been taught. Really, I blame the men she targets for being such ignorant bastards, actually believing a girl like her would be interested in guys like them. Then again, they only want one thing from her and that's to slide their dirty cocks into her tight cunt, and that thought knots my stomach in a white-hot ball of rage.

Lately, it's becoming almost too agonizing to watch and I've found myself intervening. As hard as I try not to, something snaps inside me and I lose all self-control. I keep reminding myself that it won't be long and the scams and tricks can end. She'll never want for anything because I will give her everything she could ever hope for.

I watch as the man's eyes travel from Rhea to another female passing by. My jaw clenches when I see his gaze land on her ass. How dare he look at another woman when he's got undeniable perfection sitting right in front of him. My fingers twitch while spit builds in the corner of my mouth.

When his attention returns to Rhea, she's unfazed, but I'm certainly not.

As the rich prick runs his grimy fingers down her bare leg, my patience begins to wear thin. I clear my throat and force myself to look away. He's going to live to regret touching her. Or rather, stop living altogether.

Stealing quick glances, I gnaw on my balled fist in an attempt to alleviate some of the rage I'm feeling. Minutes later, she spins her ass on the stool and steps down. I straighten my back, watching keenly.

Leaning into the man, she puts her hand on his shoulder and her lips brush his earlobe as she whispers something that delights him.

Rhea walks away to the restroom, I presume. I could go in and grab her right now, slap a hand over her mouth and drag her out the back entrance into the dark parking lot. She would be all mine. But she'd never stop fighting to be free. The harder I'd try to make her love me, the more she'd resent me. That's not the life I want for us.

Instead, I'll be patient. I'll wait. And I'll wait some more. Because an eternity with Rhea doesn't hold a candle to these short days we're apart.

My chest aches, knowing she's going to run again after this, and I'll have to track her down again on the app. It's the inevitable game we play.

Taking a moment to check my surroundings, I decide it's safe to make my move, though I need to be quick.

"Keep it running," I tell Leonard, my driver. I push open the car door and step out onto the sidewalk. With my hands in the front pockets of my black trench coat, and my ball cap dipped low, I enter the hotel bar, taking the seat she kept warm for me.

The old man looks in my direction, his guard down when it should be raised. "That's quite a looker you got on your arm tonight," I say, making small talk.

"She sure is a beauty." His voice is thick and coarse. If I had to guess, I'd say he's a former smoker, which only makes this next part easier. Everyone knows smoking can wear out your heart.

"That she is." I wave over the bartender. "Two of whatever 'he's having."

"Why, thank you, sir. That's very kind of you, but my date should be returning soon."

"No worries. You've got time," I say point-blankly.

Once the drinks are in front of us, I press my sleeve to his glass, sealing his fate with a deadly powder that will stop his heart. He's got thirty minutes, tops. It's much more humane than spooning his eyeballs out of their sockets the way I'd like to do, but that would only scare my little wildcat.

I push the glass toward him and raise mine. Our glasses clank and we down our drinks together. As I turn to leave, a very rare smile crosses my face.

Walking slowly, I listen for Rhea's voice. Once I hear it, I push open the door to exit, adjust my hat, and keep my chin down.

Good night, Rhea. I'll be seeing you.

CHAPTER
THREE
RHEA

September 2, 2022
Somewhere in Alabama
Twenty-One Years Old

"Morning, Heidi," I say, after reading the badge pinned to the blue button-up shirt. She has those kind eyes, the ones that look easy to manipulate. It only solidifies for me that I was meant to end up at this hotel. "I was wondering if y'all have any rooms available?" I sweep the hair of my blonde wig behind my shoulders and smack my battered, bright red lips together.

Curious eyes study my face, and while the bruises I'm covered in will definitely help my case, this wasn't at all the plan. "We...we do," the kind lady behind the customer service desk stutters in the same southern accent I've forced upon myself. "Are you looking for a specific room, my dear?"

"Just a single, Doll. I'm just passing through on my way to Texas. Caught my husband cheating on me, and the bastard had the nerve to kick me out. Can you believe that?"

"Aww," she gushes with pressed lips, "I'm so sorry to hear that. Did he...do that to you?" She's referring to the two black eyes I'm sporting and the handprint around my throat.

I drop my head, avoiding eye contact while forcing the waterworks. "I can't talk about it."

"Oh, honey. Don't you give up on men, though. There are good ones out there. My hubby is proof of that. You see those flowers?" She nods toward a beautiful bouquet of long-stemmed roses on the desk behind her. "Sent me them this morning."

"Wow!" I beam with genuine excitement for her. "Those are gorgeous. My Dexter never did a thing like that for me. Probably did for his mistress, though."

"You," she emphasizes with so much emotion, "deserve so much more than what that man gave to you."

She's wrong, but I don't tell her that.

"That son of a bitch gave me nothing. In fact," I reach into my faux leather crossbody, pulling out a single hundred-dollar bill, "this is all I've got to my name."

"Well, you're in luck." Her face lights up with a wide smile. "Our single rooms are only eighty-nine per night. And because you're so sweet, I'll even give you a discount so you can take yourself out for breakfast in the morning."

"Aren't you just the sweetest? Thanks, Doll."

"You're so welcome. Now, if I can just get a photo ID from ya, then I'll get your key and you can be on your way."

My shoulders slump and a pout morphs my features from the strong facade to the broken woman someone would expect after hearing my story. Then I bring on the waterworks for extra emphasis. "He took it. He took everything from me. My debit cards, my ID, even my damn social security card." I let out a shaky stutter, allowing my lips to quiver. "He'd have taken the clothes off my back if I hadn't run as fast as I did."

"Oh, sweetie. You need to report that. The theft and..." Her eyes skim my face again. "Everything else he did to you."

I nod while pulling a neon pink handkerchief out of my purse. "I'm going to the minute I get to my room." I cry harder. "I don't even have my cell phone. He's probably watching those dirty pornography videos on it as we speak."

It's a lie. I do have a cell phone, but she doesn't need to know that. My chest heaves and I keep up the facade, seeking more sympathy than I actually need. I mentioned I was good at my job, but did I also tell you that this is the fun bit? When I really get to sell the story, it feels more like winning an award than just doing my job.

Heidi hurries around the counter and comes to my aid. Her arm wraps around my shoulders and she pulls me in for a hug. It's uncomfortable, to say the least. "Keep your money," she whispers. "There's a room set aside for employees who work doubles or have to travel through bad weather after their shifts. Take that for the night and I'll put it in my name." She pats my back, attempting to help me calm down from my little bout of emotions.

I take a step back to look at her beautiful face. "You are the sweetest soul who has ever graced God's green earth, Heidi. Thank you." I pat her hand that's wrapped around me.

"It's my pleasure..."

"Savannah. But you can call me Savvy." I sniffle and wipe the tears from my burning eyes, knowing I just smeared the thick black mascara coating my lashes. It's a form of visual manipulation that works well on women. I've already secured the room, but keeping up my act is necessary to carry me through this night.

"Lemme go get you that room card so you can get some sleep. It's mighty late."

I steal a glance at the clock behind her and see that it is

much later than I thought it was—two o'clock in the morning, to be exact. The bus ride from Georgia to the middle of Alabama was only four hours, but bartering a ride from the bus station to the hotel took a little longer than anticipated.

Heidi taps some information into the computer while I pat my eyes with the corner of my handkerchief and pretend to take some steady breaths. A second later, she hands me the room card. "Room 322. And sleep in, Savvy. The room is empty until tomorrow night at the earliest. No need to check out. I'll handle that during my shift tomorrow."

"Thank you again, Doll. You have no idea what this means to me." I pat just over my heart in a grateful gesture.

"You're so welcome. And it was a pleasure meeting you."

I turn around, taking a breath that to her would seem like one of relief. In a way, it is. Just a different kind than she would expect. I walk to my free room with an ear-to-ear grin spread across my face.

It was a pleasure meeting you, too, Heidi.

As I press the button on the elevator to go up, I feel a strange sensation come over me. My chest tightens, a feeling of dread curling in my stomach like a snake. It's time to face facts—I need to get out of this line of work while I still can.

"I'm not paying you a fucking dime until you drop to your knees and suck my cock like we agreed. Understood?"

"Sir," I reply sternly. "I'm not so much as touching you until I get my deposit. Understood?" The sarcasm in my tone is uncanny and I'm probably being a little too cocky in this situation, but I don't trust anyone, and I certainly don't trust this man. I already broke my first rule of meeting in a private location before the deposit is received. I need the money, but I'll be damned if I continue to break my own rules just to appease a man. I'll die broke before my mouth is used without payment.

In a fleeting motion, the palm of his hand strikes across my face, taking me by complete surprise.

"I said, on your fucking knees."

An audible growl climbs up my throat as I baby my cheek with my palm. Pulling myself together, I charge at the two-hundred-and-fifty-pound man, knowing he could break me in half if he tried. And he might, but my stubbornness and pride will not allow me to go down without a fight.

Instead of my heart racing with excitement of playing Heidi like a fiddle, it's barely even noticeable. Part of the excitement of what I do is the thrill of playing a con. But this time, something is different. All I feel is a deep ache inside me.

Maybe...

No. It's not time. Is it?

It's only been three weeks since the news broke of my sperm donor's death. As suspected, I'm no longer being followed. The lurker is no longer lingering in alleyways or at every unexpected turn. My gut always told me he was hired by my dad to find me, and fortunately, I was faster than him. I always got away before he could take what he was after, whatever that was.

Now that Grayson is gone, the contracts that were never fulfilled are now void. There's really no reason for me to hide any longer.

I make it to my accommodations for the evening and pull out my phone to call the only person in the world I know I can trust.

Standing in front of the bathroom mirror, I dab at the bruise under my left eye, flinching at the pain. I hate the person who's looking back at me. The fact that she would allow anyone to treat her body this way is asinine. It's no way to live.

"It's me," I say into the speaker of my phone pressed firmly to my cheek as I turn away from the mirror.

"Where now?" Dexter replies sternly in a thick, southern accent. It's much stronger than the one I portrayed when I arrived at this hotel. Dexter is real, he's just not my cheating husband. He's got this gruff and masculine undertone, but it's coated with kindness. For some reason, hearing his voice always calms my anxieties. Maybe it's because he's the only constant in my life now.

"Somewhere different," I tell him. "Mountains. Maybe a small, cozy town."

Dexter chuckles glumly. "Ain't much money in those small towns, Doll." He always calls me Doll, hence the name I just plagued my new friend, Heidi, with.

"I was thinking again—"

"No. No. No," he repeats, making himself clear. "It's too soon. We said one year."

"It's been three weeks, Dex. I'm safe now."

"Exactly," he stammers. "Three weeks out of the three months we agreed was best. Until one of us gets a look at that contract, we don't know what addendums could be in place."

"I promise you, everything is going to be fine. I can feel it in my bones. I need a change. I'm starting to get...lonely. This game, it's not fun anymore."

"Get a damn cat if you're lonely. As for the game, it's not supposed to be fun, honey. It's a way of life, survival. Did something happen at this past location?"

"Cats are messy. They require care that I can't give." I ignore the question and he lets me. If I want to talk about it, I know Dex is there. But talking about it doesn't change what happened, so I have to force myself to move on.

"It's not safe, Rhea."

"Hey!" I snap at the sound of my name rolling off his tongue. "What's our number one rule?"

"If you're even considering settling down somewhere, then

the first step would be to eliminate your no-name rule. This just goes to show you're not ready. You're just bored."

Walking out of the bathroom, I pace the room as I talk. "I'm not bored."

"You didn't choose this life, Doll. It chose you, and it chose you for a reason. You're the strongest person I know and you're half my age. I've never met anyone so manipulative..."

"Wow. Thanks." I shrug as I sit down on the bed, huffing like an insolent teenager. I know I'm asking for him to take a risk, I know *I'm* taking a risk, but it feels like it's time. And if there's anything I've learned in this life it's to trust my feelings.

"It's a compliment. Take it and put it in your pocket for a rainy day when those ridiculous thoughts of settling down pop into your head."

"Maybe I don't wanna be manipulative anymore." My voice rises as my frustrations do the same. "Maybe I don't want any of this anymore."

My body is tired of being used and abused. Last night didn't go as planned and while, this time, I was able to get away before any sexual assault, he sure as hell tried. My heart longs for normalcy. My mind is demanding me to make a change...and fast.

"Says the girl who checked out of a weeklong stay at a five-star resort last week." He laughs as if it's funny and his words don't cut somewhere deep inside me.

"This isn't a joke, Dex. I really want this."

"You say you're lonely? You want a friend? You've got me. If you want love—"

"Absolutely not. Love is not in the cards for me and you know this. And you're not my friend, Dex. We deal in business together. Nothing more, nothing less."

"I'm your uncle. That's a hell of a lot more."

"Then prove it. Do this for me. For your only niece."

"What is it you want, Doll? Tell me."

I open my mouth to speak the words, but nothing comes out. I have no idea what I want. I've been on my own since I was fifteen years old. I'm a one-woman army, surviving in a line of work that generally requires a team of people to pull the shit off that I do. Dex is right. I'm cunning and manipulative and my heart is stone. But lately, I feel warmth flowing from it. There's a nagging urge inside me to do something different.

"I wanna be me, Dex. Make it happen." I end the call abruptly, wondering if I'm making the biggest mistake of my life.

Excitement ripples through me, mixed with a bout of nerves and nausea. I'm really doing this.

Holy shit, I'm really doing this!

Dexter is my mom's brother. It wasn't until my mom got really sick that I even knew he was my uncle. She said it was best not to form connections and put labels on the people we come in contact with. I haven't seen him since my mom passed away, but we talk often. Even before that, I only met him a handful of times. He's the best of the best when it comes to forging. He's handled every alias I've ever assumed, never leaving a single question mark on my identity. But he's always done it from afar.

Tomorrow morning I'll call him again and he'll argue some more. Try to give me a location with a form of identity that's not my own. When he does, I'll kindly refuse and threaten to go where I want to go so I can be who I want to be—twenty-one-year-old Rhea Thorn, born out of wedlock on July 15th to Viola Brooks and Grayson Thorn.

I don't know Grayson, and thank God, I never will, considering he died three weeks ago.

"Promise me, Rhea. You will never search for him, or stop running."

I carefully clasp my mom's hands. Her skin draped loosely over her frail bones. I can feel the tiny ridges of her veins, a painful reminder that the end is near. "How can I hide from him if I don't know who he is? Just tell me," I raise my voice a few octaves to show how serious my request is. "Tell me his name."

Silence engulfs us. The only sound is the faint rattling that follows each breath Mom takes. With her oxygen mask secured to her face, a white mist clouds around her nose with every exhale.

"Grayson," she manages to get out before bursting into a coughing fit. I squeeze her hand firmer in an attempt to coddle her. "Grayson," she says again. "Thorn."

Grayson Thorn. My last name is Thorn. A smile tugs at my lips, but I force it back down when I notice Mom side-eyeing me.

"He's a horrible person, Rhea. Horrible!" She gasps for air, but musters the strength to say, "If he finds you, your life will belong to him."

I can feel the prominent crease on my forehead as I squint at her in confusion. "But why?"

"He tried to take you from me. That's why I chose this life for us. I was so young when I had you, Rhea. Only seventeen years old, and I hung on to Grayson's word that he would protect us. When you were only a couple of months old, I overheard him strike a deal with a very wealthy family. That's all I needed to hear before I packed our bags and snuck out the back door." She pauses to catch her breath, but I'm too invested in this conversation to have patience.

"What sort of deal? Tell me, Mom!"

"You were the bargaining chip in a mutual agreement."

My heart is pounding out of fear that she'll slip away before I know the truth about my dad. I have to know! "I don't know what any of this means. Please, Mom. Tell me!"

"He gave away your hand in marriage to a boy a couple years older than you. He sold you, Rhea. He sold your future for his own gain."

A cold gust of disbelief sweeps through me, and the tiny hairs on my arms stand tall. "Who is this boy? This family?"

"A powerful one. Far more powerful than Grayson. I don't know much about them, but they came to an agreement on a marriage of convenience to form an alliance of sorts. They hold enough force to hide you away and keep you forever, and not a single soul will know you're gone—except for me, and I refuse to let that happen."

My stomach twists into a ball of knots. My entire life has been a lie. I always knew we were running from my dad for a reason, but I never anticipated the reason being this. "No," I blurt out. "That can't be."

"It's true, my love. That night, I took you away, and I've kept you away ever since. But as long as he lives, he will never stop trying to find you."

Losing my mom was the hardest thing I've ever had to face, and I've faced some pretty hard times. I never want to feel a pain so deep again. With God as my witness, I will never love, or be loved. I'm nothing but an invisible force, merely existing in a world where money is power, and power rules the world. I don't want it, but I need it. There is not a single desire in me to live a life of luxury. As for love—that's a burden I refuse to carry. I'd rather not love and lose anyone than love and lose them all.

Mom left me that night, in our hotel room after being cared for by an on-call doctor brought in by Dexter. I held her hand and watched her drift away into her eternal sleep, begging for God to take me too. I didn't let go until almost three hours later when Dexter came for her body. And when he did, I plagued him with questions about my dad. The only information he could share was that he was a very wealthy man who struck a deal with the devil to save his own ass.

The deal being me.

CHAPTER
FOUR
RHEA

Present Day: October 9, 2022
Lockhaven, VM

"Good morning," I say to the sweet elderly couple who seated themselves in my section. Their fingers are intertwined, resting on top of the table, and they're wearing matching white shirts, hers adorned with a gold chain holding a locket that rests against her delicate skin.

"Can I start you two off with something to drink?" I ask as my pen hovers over the notepad in my hand.

"Two coffees," the kind gentleman says. "Black. And ice water for my sweetheart, please." My chest fills with warmth at the way his soft blue eyes sparkle when he looks at his wife.

"You got it. I'll be right back with those."

As I turn away, the forced smile on my face slowly fades. My shoulders slump, and the warmth that radiated through moments ago is replaced with rawness. This job has been... different. It's not that I hate it, but there's just no thrill. Not a single bit of excitement. I'm not sure what I expected in this town that consists of one main road with buildings that are all attached like they're one big happy family. That's sort of how everything, and everyone, in Lockhaven behaves—like we're all family. Only, they're not my family, and I'm struggling hard to connect to a single person I've met thus far.

"I see you've met Mr. and Mrs. Hargrove," Taryn gushes as she places her hand over her heart. "Aren't they just the cutest couple ever? Did you know that they've been together since high school? Even got voted the cutest couple their senior year."

"Did not know that. But thank you for sharing." The lack of enthusiasm in my tone is apparent because I make no attempt to mask it. Grabbing the pot of coffee behind the waitress station, I pour the piping hot drink into a Michigan Wolverines coffee mug. Then I grab another. This one's got a panda bear on it.

All the plates, cups, and bowls in this place are mismatched. It's almost as if everything was donated, or purchased from a thrift store. Yet, no one cares. Taryn's Tavern is the one-stop shop where everyone goes. We serve breakfast, lunch, and dinner. There's a small gift shop attached to the 'back of the place that's run by a lady who rents the extra space. We also have a full-service bar—the only one in Lockhaven. On the weekends, it's the most popular hangout.

Dexter really stuck the fork in me when he picked this town. Then again, it's what I asked for. I suppose the saying is true, be careful what you wish for.

"Rhea," Taryn says with a bite of seriousness in her tone. It's odd hearing my name. Almost a surreal feeling. "I know you're still settling in, hun. But could you please try just a little harder to turn that frown upside down?" She sneaks up on me with a sly smile, then pokes my side with her index finger. I yelp and jump away from her. "Just smile, girl. It's not that hard."

Forcing the biggest, fakest smile on my face, I grind my teeth together until my lips nearly reach my ears. My eyebrows shoot up to meet my hairline, as I widen my eyes with false sincerity.

"Okay. It's a start. But maybe less forced." Her face pulls into a grimace.

My fingers braid through the handle of one mug, then the other. "Forced is all I've got today, Taryn. Take it or leave it."

A grumble climbs out of her mouth. "Fine. I'll take it. Just try harder. That's all I ask."

My boss, Taryn, is a twenty-seven-year-old bombshell with curly gold locks and eyes as bright as the sky. Her legs run for days and she towers over me a good three inches, save for the heels that add another three. Her lips always match the shade of eye shadow she's wearing and her lashes are crow black and as long as her blood-red nails. I still have yet to figure out if they're fake—the lashes, the nails, and her ginormous tits.

Taryn is also the owner of Taryn's Tavern, no surprise there. From what I've heard, she inherited the place when she was only twenty-five after her grandfather, who raised her, passed away. It was in jeopardy of being shut down due to the debt her grandfather accumulated, but the town rallied together and helped save it.

It's a cute place, no doubt. It's certainly no Eleven Madison Park, but a restaurant like that would be out of place in this quaint town. It's got appeal, and the townsfolk are loyal customers. It's also the only job I could get that pays me enough to rent a room at the bed-and-breakfast next door. Shitty part is, that's all it pays for.

"Here you are." I set the Wolverines mug down in front of Mr. Hargrove, opting to give his wife the cute panda one. "And you." My voice is chipper and I owe myself a pat on the back for trying like Taryn asked. "Are you two ready to order or do you need a minute still?"

"We're ready," Mrs. Hargrove replies, her voice gentle and sweet, just as I'd suspected it would be. "I'll have one egg, scrambled, and a wheat toast."

"And I'll have the same," Mr. Hargrove says gingerly as he closes the menu, setting it on top of his wife's.

"You got it. If there's anything else in the meantime, just let me know."

Mrs. Hargrove raises a shaky finger. "Could I please get my water, dear?"

"Oh, shit!" I blurt out, immediately slapping my hand over my mouth, and speaking into my palm. "I'm so sorry."

Mr. Hargrove chuckles. "Don't worry, dear. We don't give a damn if you curse."

I drop my hand, revealing a smile that raises up my heat-infused cheeks. Gathering up the menus, I say, "I'll go grab that ice water."

On my walk back to the waitress station, Taryn bumps her hip to mine. "Rhea Brooks, is that a real smile on your face?"

That's right. She said Brooks. Although I was born a Thorn, I opted to use my mom's birth name just to play it safe. It was a compromise Dexter and I made. I get to be myself while attempting to start a new life in a small town, as I wished, so long as I use a name that doesn't scream *here I am.*

"I said I'd try, didn't I?"

"You've been saying that since you started here three weeks ago. I'm just happy to see you're capable of producing more than a sour-ass look on your face."

"Sour-ass?" I spit out a laugh. "Has anyone ever told you you're insulting?"

"I'm honest, babe. Big difference."

"Well, your honesty is insulting," I mutter under my breath as I flip the hood on the ice machine.

"I heard you," Taryn raises her voice as she pushes through the hung double doors to the kitchen.

"I wanted you to," I shout back.

Holding the glass cup to the waterspout on the fountain drink machine, my eyes wander around the room. I've never had a place to call home, and I certainly wouldn't call the bed-and-breakfast next door home, but if there was ever a place to relate the feeling to, it would be here, oddly enough. A run-down tavern in the middle of nowhere, surrounded by mountains and dirt roads. Who would have thought?

Still sweeping the room, taking in the faces—some familiar, some new—my eyes land on one in particular. A strikingly handsome man who seems out of place. Dark, unkempt hair with a provocative allure. It looks like he's pushed it back with his fingertips, but a few stray strands hang carelessly on his forehead, and he makes no attempt to sweep them away. He's got a scruffy taut jawline that matches his onyx locks with a dash of salt and pepper mixed in. Clad in a pair of black dress pants and a white button-up shirt, he definitely holds all the sex appeal. His sleeves are rolled up to his forearms, exposing a sheen of black ink, but more importantly, a Cosmograph Daytona Rolex. Even used, those watches are worth thousands. Interest piqued, I keep watching. He's older, early forties maybe. He's exactly the type of man I would pursue in my past life—meaning, only a month ago.

Something about him is familiar. Like we've crossed paths before, but I credit the familiarity to the small town. I'm sure I've run into him a time or two and just never paid him any attention. Then again, I'm certain he would've stood out in any crowd. He's not like the others I've met here. Lockhaven is another world, and this man looks like he warped here from another galaxy.

My first couple weeks in Lockhaven are still somewhat of a blur. I was a nervous wreck. My social anxiety was off the charts, considering I've never engaged in small talk for reasons that didn't benefit me. I can't even count how many awkward hugs I got my first day here as I was being welcomed into town with a population of less than a thousand people. I should've known better than to let Gladys bring me to the tavern for dinner. Gladys is the owner of G&C's Guesthouse where I'm staying. G for Gladys, and C for Carlisle, her late husband. I'm learning it's a pattern in this town to name your businesses after yourself—Taryn's Tavern, Jimmy's Quick Stop, Reba's Book Nook.

When Gladys took me out, she showed me off like I was her child who just returned from college. It was unnerving, to say the least. I spent the next three days holed up in the room I'm renting. I didn't even eat out of fear of leaving the room and having someone try to hug me again.

Just thinking about it makes me feral. There are a lot of things I struggle with that are normal day-to-day situations for most people, true affection being one of them. I chalk it up to my childhood, or lack thereof.

The mysterious man's eyes lift from the book he's reading and I'm certain my heart stops beating. A rush of warmth courses through me and suddenly, I'm frozen in time. I can't look away because his hypnotic eyes have locked me under a spell. He doesn't look away either. It's as if I've captivated him in the same way he has me.

Intrigued, he raises a brow. Is he challenging me? Should I walk over to him? After all, flirting is my forte. I might be socially handicapped, but I'm damn good at making men swoon.

So why don't I move? Why do my feet remain stuck to the peeling tile beneath me?

An icy chill runs through me, halting any thought process.

"Jesus, Rhea." Taryn scoffs, grabbing the glass from my hand.

In that instant, my attention is snapped away from the mysterious man and is now focused on the cold trickle running down my arm. Water from the cup I'd been holding sloshed over the edges, but I was so transfixed, I hadn't noticed.

"What the hell happened?" Taryn grabs a bar rag and starts wiping the counter.

I gulp, feeling slightly embarrassed at my mishap. I look over at the reason for my stupor, only he's gone.

"I'm sorry," I tell Taryn. "I...was daydreaming and completely lost track of what I was doing."

"I'd say so." She laughs. "Head in the game, babe. Your shift is almost over."

I look at the clock on the wall and realize she's right. Twenty more minutes and I'm out of here. I should be ecstatic to flee this place. Except, I've only made thirteen dollars in tips. Thirteen fucking dollars and I don't work again until Sunday, which is four days away. How the hell am I supposed to survive on these tips and a nine-dollar-an-hour wage?

"Taryn," I spit out as I drag a bar rag up and down my arm, cleaning up the mess I've made. "When am I gonna get to work a night shift?"

"When you stop flooding my waitress station," she says as she walks away. "And when you can fake a better smile."

My chest rumbles with a low growl. "Smiles. Bah humbug."

The final twenty minutes of my five-hour shift fly by. I close out my two tables and collect another four dollars in tips, ending the day with a whopping seventeen bucks.

"I'm out," I tell Taryn as I head for the door, my greasy waitress apron in hand.

"Hold up, babe." She jabs a finger in the air as she continues to jot down an order from a trio of teenage girls.

I glance at the clock impatiently, the scuffed tips of my black, secondhand sneakers tapping out a beat of annoyance on the welcome mat by the door. Gnawing at the corner of my bottom lip, I rub at a stain on the thigh of my jeans. I make no attempt to mask my irritability, and Taryn glances in my direction a few times, giving me the evil eye. I raise my eyebrows at her, silently urging her to hurry her ass up. All I want is a nice warm shower and a soft pillow to rest my head on.

"Say you're ready to get out of here without saying you're ready to get out of here," Taryn says, stuffing her notepad into her apron as she closes the space between us.

"Sorry. It's just been a long day."

"Don't make me regret this, Rhea, but why don't you swing by Friday around nine and get a feel for the nightlife here. Maybe I'll consider giving you a weekend shift in the near future."

"Really?" I beam with excitement. "Yeah. I'll be here."

"Great. And maybe afterward, you can let your hair down and pull that stick outta your ass. It's starting to show."

"Ha ha. Very funny."

"Wasn't meant to be funny. I'm dead fucking serious."

I shake my head, a smile growing on my face as I leave the tavern. Taryn is a royal pain in my ass, but I kinda like her. She's got spunk and sass, and I think I could use a little of that in my life.

CHAPTER
FIVE
ALARIC

TIME SEEMS to move exceptionally slow when you're waiting for something. Then, when you've finally got it, it moves at lightning speed.

My trip around the States has ended, but my venture around the sun with Rhea has only just begun. My only hope is that time continues to move at a slow pace so that I can savor every moment of what lies ahead.

We've decided to settle into a small town near the mountains of Vermont. If it had been my choice, it would be far more secluded than what we've been given. Nonetheless, beggars can't be choosers. While this stay will be longer than those in the past, it's still only temporary. Once my wildcat returns the favor and gives me her heart, as I've done for her, I'll take her away and she'll never have to run again.

I'm still at a stalemate because my timing has to be impeccable. Everything up to this point has gone according to plan. I knew one day she'd get tired of giving up her body to men for money while conning her way into a bed so she could sleep.

Rhea is staying at a quaint bed-and-breakfast while

working next door at some hole-in-the-wall tavern. It makes me sick to see the strain she's putting on her body for such a small payout, but it beats what she's had to do for less in the past. She's doing well, and from what I've seen, she looks happy. Slightly lonely and maybe a little depressed, but that won't last much longer. Soon, I'll make my move. I just need to garner a little more patience because the next phase of my plan is the most important.

"Your car is ready, Mr. Banks," the valet attendant says as I exit through the revolving doors of the hotel I'm staying at. It's best to keep my distance as much as I can right now while slowly piquing the interest of Rhea. I've allowed her to see me, but only for a brief time. I need to play on her mind, leaving a question mark of who I am and where I go when I leave. She's going to hate it—and me—but much like my stay at this hotel two towns over from Lockhaven, it's only temporary.

Forgoing the option to have Leonard, my driver, accompany me on this venture in Vermont, I've given him some time off and driven my Aston Martin up the eastern part of the U.S.

It's a twenty-minute drive to the ghost town where Rhea is staying. It's not the worst place imaginable, but she deserves so much more than what Lockhaven has to offer. The main street runs straight through the town, lined with quaint storefronts, including the tavern where Rhea is working. There's an old four-way stop sign at the intersection, but there are no traffic lights in sight, which I'm not used to. Beyond the buildings, mountains peak up the horizon until they meet the sky.

When I come to the only stop sign in Lockhaven, I take a right instead of going straight, and make a quick left down the alleyway to park in the small lot behind the tavern. I pull up beside a rusted-out, single cab pickup with a deer carcass in the bed of the truck and a green pine tree air freshener hanging from the rearview mirror. It says a lot about the folks in this town, and I'm not sure how I feel about Rhea getting acquainted with men who walk down the street barefoot, smoking cigarettes while sipping on a longneck bottle of beer.

My girl stands on a pedestal; I know the people in this town don't hold a candle to her worth.

There's no hesitation as I whip open my door and get out, my shoes stirring a cloud of dust from the dirt parking lot. Hurried steps lead me to the back entrance that takes me into a small gift shop. There's a wall of used books for sale on one side, while the other side holds an assortment of various objects from homemade candles and bar soaps to gift cards and wrapping paper.

Passing a rack of secondhand tee shirts, I go through the door with a printed sign taped to it that says, *Taryn's Tavern. Where Friends Meet.* The hours are listed below, but I don't give a damn about those. All I care about are the hours that Rhea will be inside this place. And if my schedule for her is correct, she's here now.

It's confirmed when I step through the door, and I see her beautiful face taking the order of a gingerly couple seated at a small two-person table. Even from here, you can see the adoration on their faces for each other, and I have every intention of having that same kind of relationship with my wildcat one day. I just have to earn it first.

Sticking to the wall, I make my way to an empty seat and I immediately pull out my paperback novel of *The Outsider* by Stephen King.

With the book open in the palm of my hand, I read—or at least, pretend to. I'm not opposed to Rhea knowing I'm here. In fact, I want her to. But I don't want her to notice I'm watching her. This time, I'd rather she watch me while building the intensity of what will soon be our first encounter.

I watch over the frame of the book as she slaps a hand over

her mouth at something she must have said. It has her cheeks turning a pretty shade of dark pink. I find myself smiling along with her, wishing I could feel her degree of humiliation. I want to feel everything she feels—happiness, rawness, sadness. Only then will I be able to relate to her mental state. And let's be honest, her mental health is shit. If I'm going to spend forever with her, I want to know how to help her with that.

Every move she makes stirs a new emotion inside me. My eyes drag down to her tight, round ass as she leans over the table and picks up the menus. She shouldn't be wearing jeans that are so formfitting. I glance around the room, making sure no one else sees what I see. Scanning their faces, I can see them focused on their food or conversation, which means the men in this place quickly receive the all clear to live another day.

Rhea tucks the menus under her arm, holding them with pressure, then she turns to walk away. Taryn, the owner of this place, bumps her side into Rhea's, and I straighten my back, still peering over my book.

"Rhea Brooks, is that a real smile on your face?" I hear Taryn say to her. I'm glad she opted to go with her mother's maiden name. Had she used her given name of Thorn, she might actually be found, and I prefer she remain my secret for at least a while longer. It's why I'm staying so close and monitoring everywhere she goes. Grayson Thorn may be dead, but he wasn't the only threat to my girl. And if anyone else comes for her, we're going to have to run.

A minute later, she's behind the bar filling a glass of ice. Her gaze slides across mine and I casually lower my book, looking down at it as if I'm reading. As hard as I fight myself not to look, I can't help it. My eyes lift, catching hers. In an instant, my soul is set on fire. It's the first time we've made eye contact, and it's everything I hoped it would be.

Like a moth to a flame, she's drawn to me as much as I am

to her. I can't look away, nor can she. My limbs feel like lead, and I hold my breath, unwilling to make any sudden movement that will shift her attention elsewhere.

I slowly arch my eyebrow, mouth pinched into a thin line. There's no doubt she recognizes the meaning of my expression —*do you need something from me, Wildcat?*

Rhea is going to hate me at first, I've made sure of it. Enemies-to-lovers is a very popular trope, after all. Plus, I know her too well at this point. If I gave her everything she wanted right away, she would run, thinking it's too good to be true. So I'll play the long game. I've gotten this far on instinct alone, my plan for her is solid. Before she even realizes what's happening, she's going to trip that line and fall madly in love with *me*.

It's nice to see you, my love. Hang tight. Soon enough, you'll know all my intentions. Good and bad.

Her attention is snapped away by the water overflowing in her glass. It seems I've rattled my wildcat enough for today.

Baby steps. In due time, she will be mine.

Slowly getting to my feet, I slip out the front door when she's not looking. There's no doubt I left an impression on her, just as I expected.

CHAPTER

SIX

RHEA

"Good evening, Rhea." Gladys's brittle, low voice hits my ears in a near-whisper as I pass by the kitchen. I've learned during my short time here that I have to lean in when she's speaking because I can barely hear a word she says.

"Hi, Gladys." I keep my words simple as I backstep to the doorway without entering. If I go in, she'll likely spark up a conversation about the weather, or how I really should let her steam my tops because the wrinkles are *unlovely*. Her words, not mine. I've lived out of a suitcase my entire life; wrinkles don't faze me in the least.

She's whipping a wooden spoon around a large stainless-steel bowl and the smell of garlic floods my senses.

Her eyes lift from the bowl, but her hand doesn't stop as she speedily stirs whatever is inside. "I trust you're enjoying your stay here?"

I nod with a pressed smile. "Very much. Thank you." There's a bit of silence before I say, "Enjoy your night."

One foot steps in front of the other when she grabs my attention again. "You look beautiful. Going out tonight?"

"Umm. Yeah." I shoot a thumb to my right. "Just over to Taryn's."

I decided to doll myself up tonight with a cute sequin blush-colored dress with long sleeves. There's a dipped V in the front that really highlights my hot-as-fuck cleavage. My tits are probably my favorite thing about myself. I'm not petite by any means and I've learned to love my hourglass curves. There's nothing wrong with showing off my goods every now and then. Even if I am just going to a tavern in a one-street town where I'm the outcast.

"Ahh." Gladys's voice bubbles. "Work or pleasure?"

She's a sweet lady, and I'm eternally grateful for her renting me a room for an indefinite amount of time, but she sure is a nosey little thing.

"Neither," I tell her honestly. "I'm not working, but I also doubt I'll enjoy myself much. People, noise—not really my thing. But I can't just sit in my room all day, so I figure," I gesture to my outfit, "why not, right?" It's the truth. My outfit has absolutely nothing to do with the man I saw earlier today. I'm definitely not hoping he's there or that he takes notice. Not even a little bit.

She chuckles airily. "Oh, Rhea. You really need to learn to enjoy the simple things in this life. Before you know it, the highlight of your weekend will be testing out a new garlic mash recipe. Go have yourself some fun."

"Thanks, Gladys," I snicker. "I'll definitely try."

"You know what, dear," she begins as she lets the spoon fall inside of the bowl. "The night is young. Why don't I go with you so you're not all alone." Her soft brown eyes light up as she unties the ropes of her floral-print apron behind her back.

I hold up a hand, halting her. "Oh, Gladys. That's not necessary. You stay here and finish your new recipe. I'm anxious to try it when I get home."

"You sure, dear?" Her face falls slightly, but I don't want to be leaning into her all night just to be able to hear her over all the noise at Taryn's. I do feel a little bit bad, though, because she's been so kind to me.

My tongue clicks on the roof of my mouth. "Absolutely. How about a rain check? We could light up the town another night?"

When you reject an offer from someone, it's always best to lift their spirits with a new invitation. Even if you have zero intentions of following through with the plans. At least that's the way I've always manipulated situations. This time is different, though. I'm not fleeing before sunrise and I'm going to be seeing Gladys often. In this case, I think I might actually mean what I say.

"Sounds like a rocking good time." Gladys throws her fist in the air and I can't help the laugh that slips out of me. She's cute as fuck and I can only hope I'm as cool as her when I'm in my eighties.

"Good night, Gladys." As I move to put one foot in front of the other again, she calls out.

"Oh, and speaking of rain checks. Rent for next month is due Monday, and wouldn't you know it, it's supposed to rain. Be safe tonight, dear."

Fuck. Thanks for crushing my spirits, Gladys.

I keep moving forward, each step feeling heavier than the last.

I'm dead-ass broke and don't get a paycheck again until next Friday. It would be nice if I could count on tips, but the residents in this damn town have proven to be tightwads.

I walk out the front door and down the three cement steps

in front of the large house. It's a six-bedroom place, with five rooms that are rented out. Most of the guests just stay here for a weekend at a time, but Gladys said there are the occasional semi-permanent occupants. Currently, I'm the only one.

Out front is a small lawn full of flowers. There's a worn stone path that leads to a wrought iron gate opening up to the sidewalk. I click the lever and push it open, stepping right onto Main Street. Directly next door is Taryn's Tavern. It's a very convenient location of work for someone who doesn't have a car. It's also a reminder that I need to quit being so damn negative. Sure, I don't have any money. Gladys will probably kick me out on Monday when I tell her I don't have rent, but hey, at least I've got the weekend.

I haven't even closed the gate and I can already hear the honky-tonk music coming from inside. When I stop to listen to the lyrics of "Fancy" by Reba McEntire, they take me back to another time. A time when life felt so easy, but looking back, it was only easy because the hardness of it all didn't touch me. I was too numb to feel anything at all.

"Aren't you a little young to be in a bar this late on a Saturday night?"

"I'm eighteen," I tell the grouchy bartender. "I must've missed the rule about teenagers not being allowed in here."

"Common sense, girl. Why don't you go home and cuddle your teddy bear and get yourself a good night's sleep."

I roll my eyes at his charade. "My civil rights are allowing me to sit my cute ass at the table right over there so I can order some food. Are you refusing my service due to my age?"

"Kitchen's closed, shortcake. Now see yourself out before I put in a call to the town sheriff."

I stick my tongue out at him, snarling like the child he's pegging me as.

"There'll be no need for that, Butch." The voice of a stranger comes over my shoulder right before I feel his arm extend around my waist. His strong hand settles on my hip and a shiver runs through me. "Butch is right, though, it is pretty late. Let's get you home safely."

I look up to see a set of shiny white teeth smiling down at me. It's probably the first full set I've seen in this run-down town. Drawing in a deep breath, I inhale the scent of cologne and the smell alone flashes dollar signs in front of my eyes. He's got a few years on me, I'd say at least fifteen—maybe twenty.

I'm led toward the back of the bar, past the jukebox that is blasting out "Fancy" by Reba McEntire.

"I'm Mayor Sandoval. But you can call me Paul," my new friend says as he continues to usher me out back.

Interesting, my new friend is the mayor? This can either be really good, or really bad.

"Nice to meet you, Paul. I'm Dallas." I turn to face him and extend my hand in the small space between us.

He places his strong, calloused fingers in mine. "Dallas, huh? Pretty name for a pretty girl." The stench of whiskey rolls off his tongue. It's strong enough to make me feel intoxicated from just breathing it in.

"Why, thank you," I say coyly. Is it just me, or is the mayor of this town hitting on me?

I'm certain he is when he doesn't let go of what was supposed to be a swift shake of our hands. Instead, he lowers our clenched hands until they're dangling between our close-knit bodies.

"So what're you doing out this late on a Saturday night?"

I glance up and down the hall we're walking down, pretending to look for a clock. "Is it really that late?"

"Almost two a.m. Bar's closing soon."

I slap a hand over my mouth, pretending to be surprised at the time. *"Didn't realize it was that time already. I was out with some friends and got hungry. Thought I might come get a bite to eat."*

"Tell ya what, I happen to own a restaurant down the road. Why don't you let me get you some food and take you back home. As the mayor of this town, it's my duty to see that pretty girls like you get home safely."

My eyes light up and I bite the corner of my lip. "Aren't you just the sweetest."

What Mayor Paul doesn't know is, I don't want his food. I want so much more than that. Entering a closed restaurant after hours with the mayor? A cash register full of money? Hell yes! This might be my best payday of all, and I barely had to put in any work.

We step out into the night air and Paul points down the alley. "It's just a short walk to the right."

I roll my shoulders, smiling from ear to ear. "Lead the way."

Holding my hand, Paul walks me into the alley. Each step offers less and less light. The music from the bar slowly fades away, and the only sound is the clapping of my red high-heeled shoes against the rocks on the gravel path.

Suddenly, Paul jerks my hand, stopping me from moving any farther. In a swift motion, I'm shoved hard. It isn't until I go flying inside that I realize there was a barn door in the wall. My back hits the ground hard, knocking the wind out of me.

Once the shock of the situation wears off, I lift my head and listen to the sound of the latch locking shut. It's so dark, I can't see anything.

"Paul," I say harshly. "What are you doing?"

The next thing I know, the weight of his body is lying heavily on mine. A hand claps over my mouth, restricting my voice. "That's Mayor Sandoval to you." His voice is so different from a minute ago, my brain struggles to catch up with who he really is.

I squirm and try to wriggle free. "Get off me!" I attempt to shout, but my words sputter into his palm. Did the con artist just get conned by this fat-ass bastard? I really need to step up my game.

In a hurried motion, he pushes his pants down, and I pinch my eyes shut, not willing to see what fate awaits me.

His solid frame presses against mine, forcing my thighs apart, but I dig my heels into the dirt ground and clamp my muscles to keep them together.

"This'll be a lot easier for both of us if you just relax, pretty girl."

I pound my fists into his back, fighting like hell because I refuse to make this easy for him. His hands grab my wrists, pinning them together in a vise I know I'll never break free from. He may be drunk, but his strength and weight are enough to overpower my scrawny ass.

Tears pool in my eyes for the first time in a while and I hate that he's the one pulling them out of me. No one deserves these, only my mother. I bite my lip, refusing to let them fall for a man as worthless as this.

He tries to push his mouth to mine, but I bite his lip until I taste blood and spit it back in his face. I can't see for shit still, but I know the gesture lands when he lets out a stream of curses. The hand that was pushing down my pants moves, and for a moment, I feel like I've won something. Until the sting of a smack meets my cheek.

A sound stuck between a sob and a battle cry escapes me, but I know it's no use. We walked too far back into this alleyway for anyone to be able to hear me.

All hope is lost when he steals the last of my strength and pushes himself inside me. I close my eyes while hopelessness claws at my heart.

I have no choice but to surrender myself to this fate. I've lost this battle, but I sure as fuck plan to never lose another one.

The asshole had his way with me that night, then called me

a dirty whore and told me to get the hell out of his town. Given no choice, I left, but I made damn sure I got something from him in return.

I threw a chair through the window of his restaurant, emptied the cash register after using some condiments to write 'your mayor is a dirty rapist' on as many walls as possible before I fled. I didn't even hide my face. I didn't need to. Dallas no longer existed the moment I left that godforsaken place.

Even if Paul did leave me with something to remember him by.

Things don't always go the way I plan, and memories like that hurt like hell. But it's better to move forward than backward.

My phone vibrates in my clutch purse and my heart immediately jumps into a frenzy, considering only a handful of people have this number. It has to be Dex or Taryn. It's certainly not Gladys, since I literally just walked out the door.

When I pull it out, I see that it's not a message or a call, rather an alert from the Siren's Call app I used to use before I arrived in this town. I downloaded it again just in case I was in a pinch for money. I take a deep breath and set aside the memories of the past, then tap on the app to see a notification from one of the members who sends me private messages on occasion.

We've chatted a couple times, but I've never actually met him. Oddly enough, he's never booked a meetup. My first chat with him was the first real conversation I've had with anyone in a very long time. I quickly became invested and knew I had to put an end to it. I started to rely on his messages when I was feeling down and even went so far as to message him first once.

My mom's words rang heavy in my ears that day, 'never get

attached to the people you encounter in this line of work'. Not that I *worked* with him, or probably ever would now. It would be too weird. Regardless, I click on his message to read it.

HawkEye: I miss talking to you.

I bite back a smile. Knowing someone actually misses me is a novel feeling. What's even more unique is that this man doesn't want anything in return. He just wants to talk and get to know me.

But I never want to go back to the dark places this app took me. I'm free from the pain of my past now and I have to at least try to move on after all the work my uncle and I put into finding this new place.

Without responding, I close out of the app and put my phone in my purse.

In front of the tavern door is a couple passing a cigarette back and forth. Stepping around them, I have no choice but to inhale a cloud of smoke and cough it back out as I pull open the large wooden door.

The aroma of beer and cheap perfume hits me smack-dab in the face. It's quite the change from the smell of coffee and frying bacon I'm used to in the mornings here. The tables have all been pushed to the far back wall, aside from a few that remain with occupants sitting in them. I can only assume the furniture has been rearranged to accommodate a dance floor. Taryn wasn't kidding when she said this place transforms on the weekends.

There's a man onstage on the wall opposite the bar. He taps the microphone before shouting into it. "How the hell is everyone feeling tonight?"

The crowd goes wild, clapping and chanting while raising their drinks in the air. I pause next to the door, taking it all in.

"And she comes to life on the weekends." Taryn's voice hits my ears and I smile at her.

"What's that supposed to mean?" I ask, unsure of whether she's referring to my outfit, or the fact that I actually came.

"I saw that smile on your face, Rhea Brooks. Don't even try to pretend it wasn't there." She grimaces. "Even if it's since been replaced with that sour-ass expression we're used to from you."

"Once again," I scoff, "insulting the staff." I drop my arms that were crossed over my chest and make my way into the open space as the band begins playing a country rock song I've never heard before.

To my delight, Taryn follows me. "You know what you need? A drink."

"Lead the way," I tell her with a wave of my arms.

"Girrrrl," she drags the word, "can't you see we're busy as hell? Make your own damn drink."

I chortle because it's such a Taryn thing to say. As she walks away, she hollers, "First one's on the house. After that, you pay."

A slender man who already appears to be three sheets to the wind throws an arm around Taryn's shoulder, following her as she makes her way to one of the tables. "Did I hear you say drinks are on the house?" His words slur and Taryn tosses his scrawny arm off her.

"Not for you, James. In fact, I think it's time to cut you off."

"Bitch!" he snaps. "The fucking band hasn't even started yet. You ain't cutting shit off."

"I'll cut your dick off if you talk to me like that again." Taryn points a stern finger at the door. "Get your ass outta here."

My eyes widen in surprise as I watch the situation unfold. When James just stands there, swaying back and forth with a scowl on his face, Taryn grabs him by the arm and drags him across the room.

"Out!" she shouts, shoving him toward the now open door. She gives him a push and before anyone can blink, he stumbles onto the sidewalk. "And if I catch you back in here tonight, I will call Sheriff Guthrie." Her attention turns to Stephanie, one of the waitstaff. "Call his brother and make sure he gets home safe." Stephanie nods in response before disappearing behind the bar.

Taryn's gaze catches mine and she shrugs her shoulders as she shouts across the room, "You sure you're ready for this?"

I bite back a smile, not willing to let her see how ready I really am. This town has been boring as fuck, until now. I need some excitement, and this might be the only place I get it.

Making my way to the bar, I offer up a few *his* and *hellos* to the friendly customers who acknowledge me. I feel like an alien dropped in the middle of nowhere. Everyone watches me as if I'm about to perform some out-of-this-world-trick or something. It's an unsettling feeling, especially considering I'm not a fan of attention.

I make myself a drink, consisting of vodka and Red Bull, because God knows I need it, then I find a seat at the end of the bar. I can count on one hand the amount of times I've drank, so it's not going to take much to lighten me up. Living a life on the run requires a clear head. I never knew when I was going to have to flee. The fear of slipping up and making a mistake while under the influence wasn't a risk I was willing to take. But my life is different now. I'm allowed to enjoy these small pleasantries for the first time.

As I sip on this drink and my worries slowly dissipate, I'm more certain than ever that I'm going to shine in this town. A few minutes later, the effects begin taking hold of me. The tension begins to leave my body, and for once in my life, I relax a little, allowing myself to engage in an enlightening conversation with a kind gentleman sitting by me.

"It must've been hard moving away from your family like that," my new friend, Benny, says as he waves a hand in the air, calling the bartender over.

"It was. But I talk to my mom and dad, like every day." It feels good to make up stories sometimes. Almost as if I'm really living in them. It's probably not the best thing for my mental state, but it's better than reliving and sharing the true events of my past.

"Ready for another?" the bartender asks. I'm surprised to see the new face behind the bar. He's a younger guy I've never seen before. Light brown hair with a clean shave on the sides and some shag on the top that's flipped over to the right. He's got hazel eyes and when they land on mine, butterflies flutter through my stomach. He's fucking hot.

"Make it a double," Benny tells him.

"You got it, Mayor Dean."

I gulp when I hear that the guy I've been talking to is the town mayor. Suddenly, the air around me feels restricted. My lungs struggle to inflate and my head feels dizzy.

"Oh, come on, Tyler. You know it's Benny in here."

Tyler chuckles, but the sound slips through my ears as nothing but static noise.

I find myself sliding off the stool, dazed and confused. I don't fully know what's happening, I just know I need to put space between me and this man. It's the drink, it has to be. I'm okay. It's just the drink.

I'm suffocating. My chest feels tight. My vision is blurry.

Am I breathing?

I am. I'm okay.

"You okay, Rhea?" Benny asks as he places a hand on my arm. I jerk it away quickly, my muscles tightening as my defenses kick in.

The next thing I know, I'm making a beeline for the girls'

bathroom. Paying no attention to the elderly ladies who wreak of high-end perfume, I curl over the porcelain sink, staring into the open drain in an attempt to center myself.

Your past is not your future, Rhea. One bad mayor doesn't make them all bad. You're okay!

It helps to give myself little pep talks. It's the only way I've learned to calm my racing thoughts. It's not like I have anyone else to talk me off the ledge. I've only got myself, and that's enough. I've got this. I always do.

"Seems she's had a bit too much to drink," I hear one of the ladies whisper to another.

"She's practically a child," the other says. "The kids in this town sure do need to find some hobbies."

I turn my head, eyeing them both with a heavy scowl on my face, though they don't see me looking. The eldest one is running a comb through her poofy white hair while another is dragging red lipstick across her bottom lip. I don't say anything because I've learned it's a waste of breath to educate nonsense. I have other ways of voicing how I feel.

Once the ladies finish up, I follow them out of the restroom and to the bar. The one who looks like she's got a polar bear sitting on top of her head takes a seat at the bar and her friend joins her.

Forgoing the stool I was on, I join the ladies.

"Mind if I sit here?" I ask politely.

"Sorry, but no," Polar Bear Hair pipes up. "We're saving that for a friend."

Ah. Another gossiper, I imagine. Regardless, I sit down anyway.

"Dear," her friend says, bending forward until her necklace dangles on the bar. "Did you not hear Karen? We're waiting on someone."

Her name is Karen? Why am I not surprised?

"How lovely," I respond coyly. "It's a shame that the bar is filling up quickly. Guess she'll have to sit somewhere else."

The ladies share a look of annoyance while I eyeball the purse hanging from a hook beneath the bar. I slide my leg over, bumping it with my knee, testing the waters. When she doesn't take notice, I know I'm golden.

When Karen turns her entire body to face her friend, specifically so she can avoid me, I dig inside her purse. My fingers graze over a soft leather wallet and I slowly drag the zipper down until I feel cash. Without hesitation, I pluck it out and slide it between my foot and my shoe. I'm not sure how much I got, and it's in no way enough to pay rent, but I'm almost certain it'll aid in me having a hell of a good time tonight.

I slide to the left and peel my sticky ass off the pleather stool before getting to my feet. With my own purse draped over my shoulder, I bump slightly against Karen, getting her attention. "My bad." My words are laced with sarcasm and I know I'm being a bitch, but how dare they judge me. With a wave over my shoulder, I say, "Enjoy your night, ladies." They scoff and tsk, then return to their conversation. My voice drops to an under-the-breath mumble as I widen the space between us. "I know I will."

I make my way to the corner of the bar and scope out the scene before crouching down and taking the cash out of my shoe. Still lowered, I flip through the folded bills and realize they're all ones. Six one-dollar bills. What the fuck am I going to do with six bucks?

Blowing out a breath of frustration, I stand back up, only to be met with familiar eyes across the room. Sitting at a table, all alone, is the mysterious hottie that was in here during my last shift. He's adorned in all black. It's fitting because the vibe I get from this man is pure darkness. The sleeves of his button-up shirt are, once again, rolled up, exposing the tattoos on his arms. I deepen my gaze on them, wondering what sort of artwork it is. With this guy's demeanor, I'd guess something ‚like skulls or crows.

My eyes slide up to find his sultry blue eyes staring vacantly at me. A rush of heat shoots through my core and my knees weaken. No man has ever made me feel so miniscule with just a glance, and no matter how hard I try, I can't look away out of fear of losing his attention.

So instead of trying, I cross the room toward him, really emphasizing the click-clack of my heels against the hardwood floor—even if the sound is drowned out by the band's music blasting through the speakers.

I keep walking, with zero intention of stopping at his table. If I know men like I think I do, he won't let me pass. He'll acknowledge me. Maybe ask if I'd like to join him at the table, or perhaps offer to buy me a drink.

I allow my hips to alternate an evident rise and fall. With a stoic expression, he raises a short glass of caramel-colored liquid and brings it to his mouth while never taking his eyes off me. Fuck. His lips look delicious. What I wouldn't give to be that glass.

And right about now he should speak up. Grab by arm. Something. Anything.

But he doesn't. Instead, he just lets me walk right on by.

Talk about a fucking ego deflater.

Damn. He didn't even blink.

My shoulder's slump in defeat and I slow my steps. Once I'm behind him, I turn around and steal a glance at his left hand. He has to be married. There's no other reason why he'd watch me like that without making a move. Besides, I did the fucking catwalk for this man.

No ring. Un-be-lievable.

He has to be gay. Either that, or that vodka and Red Bull really went to my head and I'm just feeling too damn confident right now.

But hey, I've got six bucks, so I might as well get another and see how much more disappointment I can handle tonight.

CHAPTER
SEVEN
RHEA

"Hey, Rhea." I jolt at the sound of my name. My eyes lift from the money in my hand to the bartender who's got his palms pressed to the bar in front of me. "We haven't had a chance to meet yet." He stretches a hand out. "I'm Tyler."

I return the gesture and place my hand in his. "Oh, yes. Taryn mentioned you. You go to college and work here on the weekends, right?"

Tyler takes a step back, grabs a beige bar rag, and starts wiping the crumbs and spills off the surface in front of me. "That's right." He smiles widely, exposing his perfectly straight, white teeth. He's even better-looking up close. "How about you? Are you in school or anything?"

"No. Not yet, anyways." I hate that there's a bite of shame in my tone when I say that. As if I'm not valuable just because I have zero intentions of going to college. It's not that I haven't considered it, but I need to make sure wherever I go is a place I plan to stay for a while. So far, Lockhaven is feeling pretty comfortable, but things can change in the blink of an eye. I need more time before I can fully trust myself not to flee at the first mishap. Dexter seems to think I won't last a month, and I have every intention of proving him wrong.

Tyler drops the dirty rag in the sink behind the bar. "Nothing wrong with that." He leans as if he's ready to share some big secret. "Between you and me, I don't even know why the hell I'm going."

"Isn't getting a degree the whole purpose of going to college?" There's a bite of sarcasm in my tone, but I'm actually being serious. Why else would someone go to college?

"Well, yeah. But did you know that more than forty percent of college graduates don't even use their degrees?"

I think about that for a moment. It makes sense. Everyone is pressured at a young age to decide what they want to do for the rest of their lives. It makes sense forty percent wouldn't get it right on the first try. In fact, I'm surprised it's not higher than that. "Can't say I did. I guess I've never done my research on college statistics." My head drops in shame as I fidget with the money in my hands. "It's never been an option for me, so I've never looked into it."

"Tyler," Taryn snaps from the end of the bar, stealing his attention from me. "We've got customers down here with empty glasses. Get your ass back to work."

I gulp, while Tyler rolls his eyes, grinning. "Don't let her scare ya. She's the biggest hard-ass with the softest heart."

I laugh. "I've seen the hard-ass, but I have yet to see anything soft when it comes to Taryn."

"You will," he assures me. "Just give it some time. Don't give up so quickly on this place, it will grow on you." He slaps his hand to the bar. "So, did you need another drink?"

"Oh. Yes! Vodka and Red Bull, please."

He gives me an awkward sideways glance. "Are you even old enough to drink? Because I just turned twenty-one and you look years younger than me."

"I'm not sure if I should take that as a compliment or an insult. But yes, I actually turned twenty-one in July."

Tyler raises his eyebrows, and I can hear the sound of his tongue clicking on the roof of his mouth. "Prove it."

I unzip my purse and pull out my wallet. "I swear I'm not lying."

Tyler holds up a hand, lowering it as I push my wallet back into my purse. "I'm just messing with ya." His hazel eyes sparkle and his mouth draws up into a broad smile. I trust you, Rhea."

That's his first mistake. I have yet to know what his second is going to be, but when it comes to trusting a word I say, it's only a matter of time before the dominos all crash down.

He reaches out and grabs the bottle of vodka and a glass, keeping his eyes on me as he mixes it. "How long do you plan on hanging around here?"

"Lockhaven? I dunno." I shrug my shoulders. "Forever, maybe?" I can't believe I just said that, but the possibility is real.

"I meant the bar." He laughs. "But please don't give this town your entire life. Get out once you've gotten what you came for; otherwise, you might actually be stuck forever."

"And you? Are you stuck forever?"

"Nah, I mean, for now I am. But there's a whole world out there I wanna see one day. Just gotta get myself in a position where I can afford it."

"Well, I've seen enough to know that Lockhaven is the safety net I need. It's a mess out there."

"Oh yeah?" His eyes perk up as he slides my drink toward me. "Where have you been?"

"Here. There. Everywhere. But enough about me. You should probably get back to work before Taryn kicks your ass."

"Eh. I could take her." I laugh. After just watching her

throw out that other man, I'm not sure many people want to go up against her.

My eyes trace the curves of his lips as they move upward, and I find myself doing the same. This is exactly what I wanted. Normalcy. A normal night out and normal conversation with a person my age. No ill intentions. No agenda.

"You're probably right, though," he says. "But you didn't answer my first question. You plan on being here for a while?"

My shoulders rise. "I'm not really sure. Taryn asked me to stop in to get an idea of what the weekends are like. So, here I am."

"It gets pretty busy, but Fridays are usually more chill than Saturday nights. If you really wanna see the place get rowdy, come by tomorrow. Say, around eight?" His brow rises and I find myself leaning closer over the bar.

"Are you asking me on a date, Tyler?" It's a joke, and the sound of his laughter proves he knows it.

"A date at the tavern where we both work? Come on now, give me more credit than that?"

"Okay"—closing the gap between us as my drink inches toward him—"let's say you did ask a girl out on a date, where would you take her?"

I've never been on a date, and Tyler seems like a stand-up guy. So I'm genuinely curious what guys his age do with girls like me on a Saturday night out.

"Let's see." He presses his palms to the top of the bar, elbows raised. "Dinner and a movie would be the safest option. I mean, who doesn't like food and movies?"

He's right, but I feel like there's more to him than dinner and a movie. "And the unsafe option?"

"There's a bonfire tomorrow night at the power lines. Music, drinking, college-aged kids raising hell."

I pull my drink toward me, leaning down to let the straw slip between my lips. "I'm listening."

"I get out at ten tomorrow." He leans over the bar until our faces are mere inches from each other's. I catch the scent of his cologne. It's sweet yet musky and I find I really like it. "So, Rhea...do you wanna play it safe, or unsafe?"

I ponder on it for a minute while sucking down half the contents of my glass. Then I let the straw lazily part ways with my mouth. "I've always been a risk-taker." I bite my lip. "So, let's raise some hell."

Tyler snaps his fingers at me with a wink. "I like the way you think." He straightens his back and glances down at Taryn. "I gotta get back to work before Taryn really does kick my ass. I'll see you tomorrow."

I grab my drink, pulling it back toward me as I get comfortable on the stool. "I'll be here."

A few minutes pass and I'm staring into an empty glass, my head swimming only a little. Scouring the area, I look at all the tipsy customers paying no attention to little ol' me. It's a nice change from all the sideways glances I get when I walk into a room in this town.

Knowing no one is watching, I casually lean across the bar and grab a bottle of vodka and quickly pour a shot's worth, or two, into my glass.

"Hey," the man beside me snaps, "you can't do that."

"Sure I can." I slide the vodka back into the holder behind the bar. "I work here." Without hesitation, I grab my glass and scurry away, chuckling to myself before he can get another word out.

Suddenly, someone steps right in my way and I collide full force into him, spilling my stolen drink all over myself. "What the hell!" I seethe, hands out—one holding my now empty glass. I look down at my doused dress and my lips curl into a snarl before I lift my head to meet the eyes of my accomplice to this disaster. "It's you," I say, before realizing the words actually left my mouth.

"And it's you." The words roll off his tongue and into my ears, lingering for a while. His voice is coarse and gravelly, void of any emotion.

Once again, I find myself lost in his gaze. The way his eyes lock on mine is hypnotizing.

"Now if you'll excuse me," he says, moving to go around me.

I spin around, watching him walk away while vodka runs down my leg.

Oh no he didn't.

"Hey," I shout as I go after him. "Hey! Come back here!"

Okay, I might be a little tipsy, but this man walked right into me and spilled my drink, without even so much as an apology or an 'excuse me.' It takes two bodies to collide and his was one of them. He could have been a gentleman and offered to buy me a new drink. Or, at the very least, got me a damn towel.

"Hey, you!" I raise my voice, trying to be heard over the bass that's rattling my bones.

When he doesn't so much as glance over his shoulder, I follow him to the bar. He stops at the end, waiting with an empty glass.

"What the hell was that?" I scoff, slamming my empty glass beside his.

His head turns slowly to face mine, shoulders taut and teeth clenched. "Excuse me?"

"You spilled my drink." I gesture to my dress that is very clearly now carrying said drink.

He chuckles, but the sound lacks any enthusiasm. "You're drunk. Just walk away before you make a scene, little girl."

"Little girl?" I sputter a laugh as my arms fan around me. "Are you kidding me right now? I have just as much right to be here as you do...*old man*."

The jackass grips his empty glass, his knuckles white, jaw clenched. He lifts it slightly, then brings it back down as if he's beckoning Tyler toward him.

"I know you hear me." I get closer to him. So close that I can smell his intoxicating scent. It's a mixture of leather—which is one of my favorite smells—and vanilla. Of course he would smell good on top of being drop-dead gorgeous. His attitude, though, that fucking wreaks of entitled asshole.

Tyler comes over, his questioning eyes dancing from me to the jerk beside me. "Everything okay over here?" he asks hesitantly.

"No," I tell him honestly. "This jerk spilled my drink." I wave my hands in front of my dress, showing him the proof. "It might be hard to see, but I can certainly feel it soaking into my bra."

"You," Jerkface emphasizes as his gaze slowly turns to face me again, "bumped into me."

Tyler's eyebrows rise, lips pursed as he draws in a deep breath. "I'll just get you a new one, Rhea. It's fine."

"It's not fine. He spilled my drink and now he's pretending like nothing even happened." I'm not the least bit surprised Tyler is trying to solve the problem without confrontation. It's obvious he's a good guy, while this prick is an egotistical stuck-up jerk.

Tyler leans in closely and says quietly, "You work here, Rhea. Might be best to just let this go since there's a good chance he'll be your customer one day."

Opting not to embarrass myself, or Tyler, I eat my pride. "Fine." My shoulders drop in defeat. "Fine. Thank you, Tyler. You're a stand-up guy." My eyes roll to my new enemy. "Unlike some of the assholes in this place. I'm good on the drink, though."

"Cute," Jerkface mumbles before his attention shifts to Tyler. "Now, could you return your attention to the paying customers in this establishment?"

I sneer in disbelief while Tyler forces a smile on his face. I hate that I put him in this situation. *Sorry*, I mouth the word.

It seems two drinks is my limit. My emotions are getting the best of me right now, and that's not something that happens often. Not that they aren't warranted with this guy, but regardless, I'm not a fan of making a scene or doing anything that gets people to notice me unless I want them to.

Cutting myself off for the night is wise. I need a clear head if I'm going to show this man how much he underestimated me.

CHAPTER
EIGHT
RHEA

"It seems we've got off on the wrong foot, Mr...." After I ate my pride, I went to the bathroom and cleaned up a little bit. When I came back out, I saw Jerkface sitting in the same spot at the bar and decided to move forward with my mission to 'take him down a peg.'

His eyebrows pinch together as he glances at me sideways, taking care not to give me any more attention than necessary.

"Banks," he says point-blank, fingers tapping softly against his glass. "Alaric Banks."

"Banks, huh? That's a...rich last name." My words are meant to be humorous, but the bleak expression on Alaric's face tells me he probably doesn't have a humorous bone in his body. Not to be confused with the humerus bone.

I laugh out loud at myself and when I'm warranted a scoff of annoyance, my smile drops instantly.

"Nothing?" I ask, and his response is more silence. "Okay." I sigh heavily. "Well, I'm Rhea." I extend my hand to him as he remains seated on the stool.

With his arms resting casually on the surface of the bar,

Alaric picks up his drink and brings it to his mouth, staring off as if I'm not even standing here.

Is this guy fucking serious right now?

"You do know you can be a complete asshole, without ruining other people's nights, in the comfort of your own home, right?"

His scathing glare turns to me and he lowers his glass to the bar with gentle ease, as if he's setting down an egg he doesn't want to crack. "Is this your idea of an apology?"

I begin a slow clap, picking up in intensity as a sardonic grin spreads across my face. "And he speaks."

"If so," he continues, "you're doing a terrible job."

A bout of sarcastic laughter spews from my mouth. "The only apologies being given out in this room should be coming from you."

"You called me an asshole."

"Because you are one, obviously." I gesture to his expensive suit and smug attitude.

"Okay." He turns to face me, his shoes resting on the footrails of his stool. I can't help but notice his shoes—brushed leather Prada. I know expensive things when I see them and this man is a walking dollar sign. "If I'm an asshole, what does that make you?"

"It makes me someone who doesn't tolerate cruel behavior. That's what."

Alaric glances left, then right, using slow and subtle motions before he leans close and whispers, "I might be an asshole, but at least I'm not a thief."

I'm taken aback by his accusation, so much so that my pulse quickens with nervousness. Why would he say that? What does he know? Instead of letting him see that he actually riled me, I scoff. "You're delusional."

"I saw you steal from that sweet lady's purse then use that money to buy the drink I spilled."

There's no way his words are a coincidence. So he saw me, who the fuck cares? No one is going to believe this guy. Besides, it was six fucking dollars that the lady probably didn't even notice was missing.

"So, you admit you're the one who spilled it then?" When he doesn't respond, I lose it. "You know what? Fuck you. You're just a crazy drunk who walked into the wrong bar, in the wrong town. Better watch your back. People get crazy around these parts." I spin on my heel to leave, but I'm halted by a strong hand on my wrist. His fingers tangle around with tenacity, showing that I'm not going anywhere until he lets me.

Alaric tsks, a shit-eating grin on his face. "You do realize that stealing from the mayor's wife was a very bad move for someone trying to find their place in this town?"

My teeth grind as I career forward, our eyes level. "You don't know a thing about me."

"I know you stole."

"Prove it." With his iron grip on me, my pulse begins to race. I don't like being caught off guard, but even more so, I don't like it when I'm touched without consent.

"Don't test me, little girl."

"Quit calling me a little girl, asshole." I try to pull away again, but his grip only tightens. I bite my tongue to prevent the tears that want to well up from springing to life.

"Quit calling me an asshole, *little girl.*"

I don't attempt to break free again; I happen to like the attention of rich older men with cocky attitudes, even if he is pushing the limits. It makes it all the more satisfying when I put them in their place and take what I want. "You're insufferable."

"And you're a pain in the ass."

"So what if I am. What are you gonna do about it?"

The next thing I know, Alaric is on his feet, snatching my purse off the bar and taking my hand. This time, I fight back, jerking my arm to no avail. "What are you doing? Let go of me! And give me my damn purse!"

My heart begins to race as memories of past events infiltrate my mind. I've dealt with aggressive men before, and most of the time, I've come out on top. Other times, I lost the fight. I have a scary feeling in the pit of my stomach that Alaric is the kind of man that doesn't lose. Probably should've just kept my mouth shut.

We hit the hall to the bathrooms and Alaric spins me around, shoving me hard into the wall between the two bathroom doors. His palms plant on either side of my head, caging me in. "You sure do like to run your mouth, don't you?"

I mock him with a grin. "Better than saying nothing at all." I go to duck around him, but he lowers one arm, using it as a barrier to keep me in place. My gaze slides up and down his arm, my lips twitching as I fight the urge to smack it down.

"Is it, though?" He drops his chin, inhaling a deep breath. There's a beat of silence before his eyes flicker back to mine. His finger trails along my bottom lip and he watches each stroke intently. "That pretty mouth is going to get you in trouble one of these days."

My eyebrows rise, challenging him. "Maybe I like trouble."

A shiver runs through me and I drag my tongue along the top of my teeth. Being this close to him is intoxicating. Even more so than the vodka. He's an arrogant jerk, but for some reason, I'm unequivocally drawn to this man. It's a mystery I can't put my finger on. It has to be his strikingly good looks and his wealth. Even not knowing what he does for a living, I'm certain it's a desirable, high-ranking position. Not to mention, I love a challenge and this man has handed me one on a shiny silver platter.

He thrusts his chin out, eyes wide with wonder. "Is that so?"

I've got him right where I want him. All I have to do is say the word and this night will end exactly how I need it to. Men like sex. They like the idea of sex, and the act of it. It's the aftermath they so carefully avoid. Most want a one-night stand, and looking at Alaric, I'm certain he's a no-strings-attached sort of guy. Therefore, I can offer him something he can't refuse.

My eyes drag down to his mouth before my hands rise to cradle the back of his head. "Very much so." My fingers sink into his soft hair and I pull his face closer to mine, tempting him without giving him too much, too soon.

His mouth ghosts over mine in a tantalizing way that has my insides quivering. "How long are you in town for?" he asks, his tone a low rumble.

"Just stopped for the night on my way to bigger and better places. You?"

"I'm not staying in Lockhaven. My hotel is in the city, but I'll be checking out tomorrow morning."

"Perfect."

He quirks a brow. "Why's that?"

"Because after tonight, I never wanna see your face again."

"Such a romantic." His eyes roam over my body and I push my tits out a little more than normal when I take a deep breath.

"A realist," I correct him.

For a sliver of a second, I thought maybe he was different. He's certainly more subdued than most men, but his lack of willpower sits right there along with the rest of the population's. It seems my date for the night is just another statistical male with a boner. Can't say I'm disappointed. It'll make my job much easier. But there is a small part of me that held out hope for him when I didn't grab his attention earlier.

"So, are we gonna do this?" I ask, confidence dominating my tone.

"Do what?"

I slither up to him, lustful eyes on his as my fingers trail down his arm. "Go back to your place. See where the night takes us."

There's an ache in my chest knowing he'll fuck me then send me on my way, never to see me again. The emotional strain this position takes on the human mind is something no one can relate to unless they've been in my shoes. It hurts to know you're not enough. That you will never be anything more than a body in their eyes. In the end, you're just cast aside and forgotten.

I've always tried to look at it from a different angle. Use them, or they'll use you. If I don't allow myself to feel like the victim, then I'm not one.

"I thought you'd never ask." He takes my hand, leading me out the back door of the tavern.

This wasn't my plan, not by any means. I came to Lockhaven to turn over a new leaf and settle down. I just never anticipated it would be this hard. Rent is due on Monday and I have no choice. This will allow me one more month to figure something out until it's due again. Maybe I'll try to get some more hours at Taryn's, or pick up a second job. Either way, it's one night that will not set me back.

The crescent moon offers little help in lighting up the parking lot, but there's a tall flickering lamppost that leads our way.

We cross the parking lot, Alaric's grip on me tight, as if he thinks I'm going to pull away and run. It's apparent he doesn't know me at all.

"This is us," Alaric says, reaching for the passenger handle of his car.

I pull my hand back, and to my surprise, he allows me to free myself. My fingers ghost over the bright red paint on the hood of the Aston Martin as I walk to the passenger side. "Wow. This is your car?"

Alaric pulls open the door and gestures for me to climb in, while saying, "One of them."

"Red happens to be my favorite color. Is this a Chevy or a Ford?" I play dumb when the truth is, I know cars very well. I also know high-end fashion and the presidents on every dollar bill. I have no intention of letting Alaric know I'm aware he's got money. I don't want to acknowledge it or talk about it. It's a manipulation tactic I've learned to use over the years to make men let down their guard.

Alaric chuckles under his breath, fighting hard not to crack a smile. But I know it's threatening to break free and if he weren't such a tight ass, he'd allow it. "Neither," he says as he leans into the car and grabs the seat belt before bringing it across my body. I hold my breath, not allowing my chest to move as I watch him, slightly stupefied.

Once the belt is clicked into place, he pauses with his face just in front of mine. When he doesn't speak, I open my mouth to say something to break the awkward tension, but just as the word, "I..." sputters out of my mouth, he ducks out of the car and closes the door.

It's insane the amount of influence this man has on my body. Every movement, every word, leaves an aching need settling in my core. Sexual acts have always been a way of life, not a pleasurable need. But tonight, I just might enjoy myself.

Alaric walks around to the driver's side and gets in. With

his foot pressed firmly to the brake, he presses the button on the dash to bring the car to life.

Once we're out of the parking lot, Alaric turns onto the main road. His wrist drapes over the steering wheel, his fingers twitching, while his hand lies limply on his leg.

I really am fucking insane. I'm in a car with a complete stranger who obviously has zero compassion for other people, considering our altercation only an hour ago. He belittled me and tried to make it seem as if something he did wrong was my fault.

If this were a story someone was reading, they would absolutely think, *this girl has lost her mind.*

I've never—*never*—put myself in a situation where all of the control is taken away from me. But right now, Alaric has all of it.

"You know, you're pretty brave getting in the car with a stranger you met at a bar."

I gulp. *Are you reading my mind?*

When he looks at me, I raise an eyebrow and a devilish smirk spreads across his face.

Of course he's not reading my mind. He's just stating the obvious. Something we both know to be true. I'm an idiot who can't handle her alcohol. After this experience, one drink is my limit because two, apparently, has me throwing every single rule out the window for a man I don't even fucking know.

"Don't worry, Rhea. You're safe with me."

My body settles slightly, getting comfortable in the seat, even if that's exactly what a serial killer would say.

"You've never killed anyone, have you?

He laughs. "Killed someone? Why?" He steals a glance at me before his eyes return to the road. "You think I'm gonna kill you?"

"I didn't until now."

77

"I just said you're safe with me, didn't I?"

"Isn't that exactly what someone who's trying to kill me would say? Plus, you also answered my question with a question. So, I'll try again. Have you ever killed anyone?"

"Maybe I'm the one who should be worried. After all, I let a girl who stole from an old lady in my car. So tell me this, Rhea," his eyes find mine again, but this time there's a glint of seriousness in them, "have you ever killed anyone?"

Crossing my arms over my chest boldly, I look out the passenger window as the lie seamlessly slips through my lips. "Nope."

In my defense, those men died before I even touched them. However, there's a good possibility it was the excitement of the night that stopped their old hearts. There was another time. That one was self-defense, though. A guy got a little aggressive on the balcony at his mansion in Beverly Hills and I may have pushed him a little too hard. I didn't mean to kill him, but he died nonetheless.

Slowly, I turn my head to look at Alaric. There is no reason why he should ever assume I killed anyone, so his question was just a response to mine. Normal people don't just go around killing for no reason. And I think it's pretty safe to assume that even though he's an asshole, Alaric is a fairly sane person.

"Well, now that we got that out of the way." I reach over to turn the volume up on the stereo, but I'm taken aback when Alaric puts his hand over mine. "What?" I freeze, letting our hands linger for a second longer.

"I don't like listening to music when I drive. It's a distraction from my thoughts, and I have a lot to think about."

I jerk my hand away and put it back in my lap. "That's weird."

"I could argue that listening to music while driving is weird."

"But it's not." I scoff. "It's normal."

"Says who?"

"How about ninety-nine point nine percent of the population. Guess you're the other point one percent."

"Is that a fact?"

"It's more of a fact than your notion of it being weird to listen to music when driving."

"You sure do have a lot to say, you know that?"

"Oh, I'm sorry. Am I distracting you from your thoughts? Were you busy thinking?"

My phone pings in my purse, taking me by surprise. I thought for sure I silenced my notifications. I reach inside, turning over my phone while keeping it hidden, and I see that it's a notification from the Siren's Call app, which is the app I use—or used—to hook up with clients. It says I've got a prospect in the area in search of a 'companion.'

Curiosity gets the best of me, and when I tap the notification, I see that the client is in very close proximity. I'm a bit surprised that anyone in this area even uses the Siren's Call. It's growing in popularity, but it's mostly used in bigger cities. Not small towns like Lockhaven. I'm not able to see an exact location, but rather a radius within twenty miles. I suppose it's possible the user is in one of the larger, nearby cities.

It's nice to know that if I become too desperate...

No! I'm done with that app!

I really am done. It's been a crutch for years, but I don't need it anymore.

"Everything all right?" Alaric asks as he reaches into the back seat and retrieves something.

I quickly shove my phone back in my purse and zip it closed. "Yeah. Everything's fine."

The next thing I know, a sharp object pierces my skin. I look down to see a needle sticking out of my forearm, and when my eyes drag up to Alaric's, I find him looking back at me, expressionless. "You asshole!" I grit out, fighting to free the words from my mouth. "You fucking played me!"

I try to pull out the syringe, but I'm too late. His thumb presses against it, forcing the liquid into my vein. I feel a stinging burn, followed by an icy chill traveling through me.

Then, nothing.

CHAPTER
NINE
ALARIC

"Oh, baby." I yank the needle from her arm. "I didn't play you. There are no games when it comes to matters of the heart."

She stares at me blankly as her thoughts slowly leave her.

My chest expands in excitement, knowing I'm already messing with her emotions.

Rhea stole cash from a lady at the bar tonight. It's proof that she's struggling to get by. If I could, I would give her everything I own, right here and now. But that's not the way this is going to play out. One day, she'll never have to want for anything. Right now, though, I need her desperation as much as I need air.

Rhea told me she was only passing through town, but I know the truth. She just wants me to think I can't find her after she robs me blind. The thing is, my eyes are wide open and I can see her very clearly.

My wildcat thinks she's always one step ahead of everyone, making calculated decisions and executing them flawlessly. Little does she know, I've been running the show from behind the scenes, subtly manipulating her plans so they work in my favor.

Her lashes flutter and her arms go limp. Her head tilts to the left, then back up before falling to the right. She mumbles some words I can't make out as I drag my fingers through her hair. She won't remember any of this.

Pressing the button to bring down the window, I stretch my arm out and toss the syringe, then I roll it back up.

"Oh, Rhea," I mutter as I stroke her soft cheek with my knuckles. "You aren't going to make this easy on me, are you?" My eyes return to the road, then find her sleepy face again. "That's okay, baby. You're worth every second of it."

The remaining fifteen minutes of the drive are quiet. Just the way I like it. Most people prefer noise to drown out their racing thoughts, while I favor sitting with them. It's what helps you get ahead. If you're always thinking, always aware, then no one can outmaneuver you.

Pulling up to the valet at the hotel, Rhea is out cold. Her mouth is agape and her tongue is resting against her lower lip. What I wouldn't give to slip my cock between those lips. My erection grows knowing soon, I will.

Leaving the car running, I swing open my door and move swiftly as I round the hood to the other side. Before the valet attendant can reach the door, I open it and usher him aside. "I've got her. She's had a little too much to drink," I tell him. Rhea's lax body falls into me and I reach across her to unleash the seat belt.

Digging my hands under her body, I scoop one arm under her warm thighs, and the other around her neck as I pull her up in a single swift motion, cradling her delicate body against my chest. Old man, my ass.

Holding her tightly in my arms, I fish out a crisp hundred-dollar bill for the attendant.

Leaving her door ajar for the valet attendant to close, I head toward the revolving doors, taking great caution not to let her head fall. I might have drugged her, but letting her get hurt under my watch will never be part of the plan.

"Good evening, Mr. Banks." The receptionist's lips curl into a smile that stretches across her face, but her gaze doesn't so much as flicker to Rhea as I carry her in my arms.

Ignoring her greeting, I head to the elevators. Carrying deadweight is tiresome, even for a man of my physique.

I've been very short with all the staff here, while they've catered to my every need. When you have money, you have to be careful about the people you let get close. So, instead of making polite conversation with people I don't want to get to know, I pay and tip them well. I'm not egotistical, by any means, but as much as I know Rhea's worth, I know mine as well.

I happen to come from an affluent bloodline, and my family name is well-known around most parts of the country. Being the generational owner of a Fortune 500 tech company, as well as a shareholder for some of the wealthiest businesses around the world, respect is given without a need to ask for it.

I press the button, and when the elevator doors open, I step inside. The attendant takes us up to my floor, already aware that I'm staying in the presidential suite.

"Have a good night, Mr. Banks."

I acknowledge him with a nod, a gesture I find to be repetitive on my part, then I disappear through the elevator. Digging into the front pocket of my pants, I pull out my cell phone and hold it over the keypad on the door. The moment the light flashes green, I push it open. With a heavy sigh, I carry Rhea right to the bed. "It won't always be like this," I tell her, knowing she can't hear me.

I take off one of her high heels, then the other, and I drop them to the floor. Standing over her like this, while she's passed out and unaware, temptation haunts me. I've waited so long for this. Eight months that have felt like a lifetime. I gave up my life and killed countless people for this—for her. For us.

When the corners of her eyes twitch, I softly brush my fingertips over her eyelids to keep them closed, knowing it's the effects of the injection.

Rhea is broke as fuck right now. She's also pissed at me for spilling her drink on her. Therefore, she was going to come back here with me, we'd probably fuck, then she'd take all my money and leave. Which is fine, she can do just that. But not before I finally get a taste of what I've been craving for months.

I'm fully aware that she likely would have fucked me of her own free will; I could see the look she gave me when I got into her personal space, but I could also see the panic. I don't want her to remember our first time as something done out of desperation. I want her to beg for it, for *me*.

My fingers comb through her hair, all the way to the ends. She lies there in perfect form, unaware of what's happening around her. No appreciation for my heart that is growing fonder of her with each passing second. The temptation to kiss every inch of her body haunts me. I'd love more than anything to fuck her pussy raw right here and now. Except, I want to see her eyes staring back at me as she comes around my cock.

"Fuck, Wildcat. You are a force."

Compelling myself to peel my eyes away, I strip out of my clothes, leaving them in a pile on the floor.

I kneel beside her on the bed, fisting my erection as it throbs with an insatiable desire. Her nipples pucker through her dress, and I watch as they rise and fall with each breath she takes. Stroking the shallow end of my engorged cock, I trail my fingers over the bud of her breast. "I always knew this moment would come, Rhea. I knew we'd be together one day."

Moving my fingers slowly down the sequined fabric, I stop at her thigh, then trail upward again, this time bringing the dress with me until her satin red G-string is exposed. "Fuck," I grumble as I touch the wet spot on her panties. "Looks like you've made a mess of yourself." I lick my dry lips as a pant slips through them.

"Don't worry, baby. Daddy will clean you up."

The buildup inside me goes from zero to a hundred in a matter of seconds. My muscles tense and my hand freezes, all the blood in my body rushing to my cock. I'm not ready to come just yet. It can't end this soon when I've waited so long for a moment like this with her.

I drop my hand and position myself between Rhea's legs on all fours. With both hands on either side of her inner thighs, I part her legs and drop my face into her dampened panties. I draw in a deep breath, inhaling her sweet scent. My eyes close and irrational thoughts infiltrate my mind.

"The things I wanna do to you, Wildcat." My words vibrate off her sex and I only wish she could feel the rumble against her pussy. I bet it would feel so good. I imagine her squirming under the movement, pushing into me, begging for more.

Two fingers dip beneath the hem of her panties and I lift my head to get a better look. My heart jumps into a frenzy when I see the stubbled hair on her pussy. Once Rhea and I are finally together, she won't need to take the time out of her days to shave, I'll make sure she has a fresh wax regularly, or she can get lasered, whatever she wants. I never want her to have to lift a finger to do an ounce of work, even if it's her own self-care.

I eagerly run my tongue along the soft ridge of her delicate flesh. Overcome with a dizzy sensation, I fall into a trance, feeling like I could come right now just by tasting her. Pleasure courses through me, overwhelming my thoughts until there's nothing left but *her*.

Savoring each stroke against my taste buds, my tongue keeps moving in lavish circles around the contour of her lips, flicking violently at her sensitive nub. If only she was aware and could feel all the pleasure I'm bringing her.

Pulling her panties more aggressively to the side, I bite my tongue at the sight of her entrance while pushing away the thoughts in my mind that tell me to have patience—I've been patient enough.

Two fingers circle her wet cunt before I push them inside her. A raspy moan rumbles in my chest as I relish how soft and warm she is. I pull them out, dragging my tongue from my fingertips to my knuckles, then stick them back in again.

When I feel her walls contract around my digits, I work harder, knowing that even while she's unconscious, she can still orgasm.

"Come for me, Rhea. You know you want to."

I drop my head again, flicking my tongue against her clit as my fingers delve deeper and deeper until I can't go in any farther. I pump my fingers while rubbing on her G-spot. I know I've found it when she lets out an involuntary gasp.

"Next time it'll be my cock spreading you wide, baby. You just wait."

Suddenly, her breaths quicken, her chest rises and falls more rapidly, and a moan slips through her parted lips.

"That's my girl." I work harder and faster, desperate to feel her come around my fingers. I place my hand just under her belly and add a small amount of pressure so my fingers make her feel even more full, as if I were actually fucking her.

Her inner muscles clench tightly and the next thing I know, she's squirting all over my hand. It's the most beautiful thing I've ever seen. Like a fountain of conviction.

I couldn't be more pleased that my girl is a squirter. I have big plans to dehydrate her in the near future.

I keep going until the liquid stops flowing from her, then I pull my fingers out and push myself onto my knees. Using the wetness of her arousal, I lube my cock. My pulse rapidly fires with anticipation for my own orgasm. "I wanna fuck you so bad, Wildcat. I'd love nothing more than to shove my cock in your juicy pussy, but our first time won't be like this."

Knowing I'm close, I part her slick folds with my fingertips and rub my head against her sensitive nub as I come all over her pussy, marking her.

I pant and tremble, my eyes jerky as I come down from the high. Letting go of my dick, I lower my head again and softly kiss her inner thigh, the warmth of her skin sending shivers through me. Taking a deep breath, I remind myself this isn't the end; it's only the beginning.

"I will worship you, Rhea. You *will* be my queen."

CHAPTER
TEN

RHEA

MY EYES SHOOT open and the first thing I see is the glowing light of a clock that reads 4:20 a.m. I gulp, feeling like I've lost time somehow.

I'm in a horrid state of disorientation. My head feels like it's been stuffed with cotton. My ears are ringing. And I'm almost positive I pissed my pants.

It's fairly dark with only a glint of light coming from the cracked-open door of the adjoined bathroom, but when I roll over, I gasp at the sight of Alaric lying beside me.

No. No. No!

Gently, I lift the corner of the blanket to see that he's got on a pair of boxers, which is gratifying. However, it doesn't excuse the fact that I am in his fucking bed!

I was supposed to come back here, maybe fuck him, then steal all his money and leave! So what the fuck actually happened is beyond me.

Fighting like hell, I try to remember the events of last night...

I stole money from the mayor's wife.

Alaric spilled a drink on me.

I cut myself off.

We were standing in the parking lot. I was planning to leave with him. Which I did, apparently. I can vaguely picture the outside of his car in my head. It was an Aston Martin, I do remember that. Fire red with black rims. An engine that purred.

Did I black out before getting in his car?

Or...

I spring out of the bed, not even attempting to silence my steps as I frantically search for my purse.

What if he drugged me?

"You. Son. Of. A. Bitch," I grumble out each word slowly as I stare at his comatose body lying in the bed. "What the hell did you do to me?"

I'm still in my clothes and I don't feel like I've been violated in any way, aside from the piss in my underwear. I suppose it's not uncommon to lose control of your bladder when you're knocked out.

I rub my arm, noticing a sore spot and when I look at it, I see the tiniest bruise that has me certain he injected me with something.

The thought is terrifying. I was passed out in this room with this stranger, for God knows how long. He could have done anything he wanted to me.

"You don't know who you just fucked with, asshole!" My voice is a low growl as I snatch his wallet off the nightstand. Oddly enough, my phone is lying there, too. Directly in front of the clock on my side of the bed.

Is this a test? Did he plant this here just for me, knowing I'd see it next to my phone? Alaric doesn't know a thing about me, if that even is his real name, so why would he suspect that I'm desperate for money right now? He did see me steal from a lady's purse at Taryn's. Vaguely, I remember him throwing that in my face.

I don't know this man from Adam, though. His intentions could be just as morbid as mine.

I flip open the wallet and quickly extract a wad of cash. My eyes light up when I see that it's all one-hundred-dollar bills. This is a rarity and I won't complain about it. Normally I'd leave some behind, so my heist isn't so obvious, but there's not a doubt in my mind Alaric will know it was me. And you know what? I don't fucking care. As far as he's considered, I'm a tourist leaving town today.

This man...oh, this man! He is in for a rude awakening when he wakes up. I know he drugged me, and if he comes after me for stealing his money, I'll prove it.

I snatch my shoes off the floor, careful to be as quiet as possible. With haste, I scour the room one last time for my purse. There's a good chance he either hid it, or it's in his car. Or it's very possible I left it at the bar. I'm going with that possibility because I don't have time to stick around and search. Shit, my ID. Nope. Not a big deal. Dex can make another ID if needed. I'm not sticking around here a second longer.

Without another thought, I rush out the door, letting it close with a thud. My feet don't stop moving until I'm at the elevator.

The doors open before I can even press the button, and I'm surprised to see an attendant waiting inside at this hour of the night—or morning, rather.

"Good morning," the short man says with his hands folded daintily in front of his chest. "Going down, I assume?"

Before he can unclasp his hands and press the button, I do it myself. "Yes, please. Sorry. I'm in somewhat of a hurry."

"No worries." He cracks a smile. "I hope you're feeling

better this morning?"

"Feeling better?" I spit, my bones rattling with anticipation. "Did you see me last night? Was I awake?"

He lowers his head without a response. When the elevator doors open, he lifts his eyes as if he's expecting me to walk out.

Quickly, I press the button to close the doors and stand in front of the panel, so he can't reopen them. "Answer me. What state of consciousness was I in?"

When he's still silent with sealed lips, as if he's been paid to remain shut, I step forward. "Tell me, dammit!"

Finally, he looks at me, before his eyes trail down to my hand. I look at it, remembering that I'm carrying a handful of cash. I quickly put my hand behind my back.

"Oh?" I say, a revelation hitting me. I bring my hand back, front and center, exposing the money. "You want some of this?"

He shrugs, and I'm certain that's exactly what he wants. I pluck out one of the one-hundred-dollar bills, which is practically millions to me. I hold it in the air, looking sternly in his eyes. "If I give this to you, I want to know everything that is to know about last night." I go to hand it to him and he nods as his hand reaches out. But I pull it back before he can take it. "I also want you to tell me everything you know about Alaric Banks."

Nervousness flashes over his features, a telltale sign that there's much to hear. I dangle the bill in front of his face, giving him a whiff of the crisp paper smell. "Do we have a deal?"

He jerks it from between my fingers and I smirk. "That's what I thought." I snatch it back before he can even attempt to conceal it in his pocket. "But there's one more thing."

His eyes perk up and he waits with bated breath as I relay the final terms of our arrangement.

"I need a ride into Lockhaven..."

"Whoa, lady. You're asking a lot for just a hundred bucks."

"Will you let me finish?" I scoff. "I need a ride into Lockhaven, be it a taxi, or whatever ride services you have around here."

"It's the city. We've got every ride service in existence." He practically rolls his eyes at me.

"Good. Then it shouldn't be a problem." I go to hand him the money but hold it back just enough to finish what I have to say before he can swipe it from me again. "Call me a ride. I'll pay for it. And Alaric can't know about this. I don't even want him to know we spoke."

"Deal. Now, can we hurry this up? We've stopped for almost five minutes. The elevator needs to move or my manager will have my ass."

Exhaling audibly, I give him the hundred bucks. "Now spill."

"I don't know the man well, but my boss told me to make him a priority." He folds the cash precisely in half then sticks it in the breast pocket of his jacket. "Apparently he's very wealthy, and a straight-up asshole who takes vengeance on anyone who double-crosses him. He's been staying here for a couple weeks, but he's due to check out this morning."

I knew he was wealthy. His watch and shoes alone told me that. And the fact that he drugged me last night proves he's an asshole. "Any idea where he's from?"

"Not a clue. That's all I know. Take it or leave it."

"No. This is helpful," I tell him. "We can go down now."

Without a word, he jabs his finger on the button and takes us down.

"I'll wait out front for my car," I tell him. "Name's Brook."

"I hope to see you again soon, Brook." A greedy smile crosses his features.

The doors come open and I step out. "You won't."

CHAPTER
ELEVEN
RHEA

AFTER A LONG, hot shower, I dropped into my bed and haven't moved since. I've been staring at the money in my hand for the past hour. Counted it at least twenty times. Seven-hundred and fifty dollars—and that's after the hundred I gave the elevator attendant, and fifty for the taxi ride home. This is the most cash I've ever taken from anyone since Mom left me. Don't get me wrong, guilt is not eating away at my soul or anything like that. My wheels are just spinning.

Aside from being unconscious half of the night, this is the easiest theft I've ever pulled off. It was almost *too* easy.

He didn't rape me, bind me to his bed, or assault me. He simply put me to sleep and left me there with a loaded wallet on my side of the bed. I'm nobody to him. A complete stranger. All I can confer is that he either trusted me too much, or he set me up.

But why? Why would he trust me? And if he didn't, why would he set me up?

The thought crosses my mind that this could have something to do with my dad, or even the man that was following me prior to his death. I've pushed that paranoia away so many times that I'm hesitant to allow myself to go there again. That threat is gone. There's no way Alaric is connected to my past in any way, shape, or form.

"Ugh," I grumble as I drop my head back on the pillow and close my eyes. Why do I even care? I'm never going to see him again, and I've got enough for rent now.

Setting the money on my nightstand, I grab my phone, wondering if I should just say 'fuck it' and leave this town while I still can. If Alaric does come for me, I should probably ensure that he never finds me.

It's not like I've grown roots in Lockhaven yet. It's really not much of a loss. I can get a job and a place to stay somewhere else. Maybe this time somewhere with dramatically less southern hospitality.

No. Fuck that.

What am I even thinking?

This is *my* town now! I've never run from danger, and I sure as hell won't do it now just because of some tourist.

I swipe open my phone, contemplating a text to Dex, when I see that I've got another message from HawkEye. We've been talking on and off for a couple of months, and while he pushes for me to talk more, I keep my responses short and casual.

Feeling lonely and defeated, I opt to read the kind words he always gives to me.

> HawkEye: Just your weekly reminder that you are stronger than you think. I hope life is treating you well.

I smile at the message. If only all men could be so thoughtful. Bored, I message him back for the first time in weeks.

> Wildcat: It's been a struggle, but I'm still alive.

I'm surprised when his response is immediate.

> HawkEye: I'm here if you want to talk.

I've always been short in my responses to this guy, or girl. Honestly, I'm not sure which it is. I've never asked anything about him. But right now, I could use a friend, and HawkEye is really all I've got.

> Wildcat: You're sweet, but I don't want to bore you with my misery.

> HawkEye: You never bore me. Now, let's hear it. What's got you down?

I get comfortable on the bed, wanting to unleash everything I've held inside for years, but I know I won't. Instead, I type out something more summarized.

> Wildcat: Life, I guess. Moved to a new town. Got a new job. Just trying to start a better life for myself, but it's been harder than I anticipated.

> HawkEye: That's a good choice you've made. Don't give up so easily. But tell me…why are you still on this app if you're trying to start a better life?

He's got a good point, but the true response wouldn't make any sense to him, because it doesn't even make sense to me.

Before I can type out anything, another message comes through.

> HawkEye: Did you keep it just for me?

> Wildcat: Never know when I might need it again. There may come a point when I need to flee this town and go somewhere new.

> HawkEye: You're not going anywhere!

I'm taken aback and quickly type out a response.

> Wildcat: Why do you care?

> HawkEye: I'm sorry. That was brash. I meant to say, don't leave. Give it some time. It's never easy starting over. But you're a strong, beautiful girl. You've got a lot going for you. In the meantime, I'll just pretend that you kept the app just so we could communicate.

> Wildcat: Well, maybe I did.

It's a lie, but flattery is my forte, and I have a knack for telling men what they want to hear.

> HawkEye: Good. Because I like talking to you. I think about you often. Do you think about me, too?

> Wildcat: Of course I do.

Another lie. In fact, the only time this person ever crosses my mind is when I'm reading the messages he sends me.

> HawkEye: I'm already looking forward to seeing you again.

I blink a few times as I reread his message. Then I respond with a critical question.

> Wildcat: Have we met before?

I'm almost positive HawkEye was never a client of mine. Unless he uses multiple aliases. It's not uncommon for married men, but I feel like he would've told me.

I'm on pins and needles waiting for his response. I scoot up on the bed, folding my legs in front of me as I watch the screen impatiently.

I wait and I wait, but two minutes later, nothing has come through.

Tapping hurriedly into the phone, I hope he hasn't left the chat.

Wildcat: Are you there?

Another minute passes, and nothing, so I swipe out of the app and drop my phone into my lap.

I'm losing my mind. I've always been a paranoid person, but lately, my paranoia has gone to extremes. I often remind myself it would be abnormal not to be a little fucked up after all I've been through. Once you travel through the darkness I have, I'm not sure you ever fully walk out of it.

I'm so scared I'll never change. To anyone out there, I'll never be more than a washed-up whore. I'll never be loved again because the only person who ever loved me is my mom, and she's gone. Letting someone else in feels like a betrayal to her memory, and I won't do that if it means I'm at risk of losing the place in my heart that has always been reserved for her.

Doesn't matter. Love is overrated. It never lasts. And if you don't have it, you don't have to feel the pain of losing it.

Three Years Ago

My phone vibrates repeatedly against my knee on the bathroom floor. Pulling my face out of the toilet for a nanosecond, I steal a glance and see that it's Dex, before vomit burns my esophagus again.

I return to the toilet as it climbs up my throat and comes out in heaves. I'm not sure how there's anything left, considering this is my third time throwing up in the past two hours and I haven't eaten anything since breakfast yesterday.

Once the spasms in my stomach stop, and I'm confident I'm getting a break, I sit on my ass and drop my head against the wall.

Taking deep breaths, I control the urge to return to the toilet. Sweat protrudes around my forehead, so I grab the damp towel on the floor from my bath last night and I wipe my face off.

Finally, feeling a tad better, I reach for my phone.

There are four missed calls from Dex, but no messages. It's not uncommon, considering we only leave messages when it's dire.

I tap his name and call him back, and he picks up on the first ring.

"It's about damn time." His tone is stern and forthright, and I'm certain he was getting worried. It's actually a comforting thought, knowing someone cares enough to check in on me.

"I'm sick," I gripe, followed by a bout of lingual groans.

"Sick sick? Or hungover?"

"You know I don't drink, Dex. I'm sick. I feel like complete shit. Can't eat. Been throwing up nonstop." As the nausea creeps back in, I close my eyes with the phone still pressed to my ear. "I think I caught a stomach bug."

"Do you need me to put in a call to Perry?"

Perry is a close friend of Dex's and also a doctor in family medicine. He's the same doctor who cared for my mom in the end. He also lives in Kentucky.

"I'm in Memphis, Dex." He can't see my eye roll, but it's apparent in my tone.

"No shit. But he might be able to recommend someone in the area who can make a house call."

"A house call to a hotel?" My sarcasm is still wildly apparent, but I'm being realistic here.

"Just trying to help."

"I appreciate that. But there's nothing a doc can do. It's just a bug. It'll pass."

"You're probably right. Unless..."

"Unless what?"

"You're not pregnant, are ya?"

My eyes shoot open and I lift my head off the wall. "Hell no, I'm not pregnant. I'm not an idiot, Dex. I'm always safe."

My mind wanders back to the darkest point in my life, when desperation ran hot and I let my guard down.

The night the mayor of Mayville raped me. Which was exactly five weeks ago. Shittttt.

"Dex," I say softly. "I gotta go."

I end the call and return to the toilet, only this time, the only thing that comes up is a mixture of bile and foam. The acidic taste lingers in my throat and causes my stomach to convulse violently.

After dry heaving for a good five minutes, I wipe away the tears and sweat on my forehead and stagger unsteadily to my feet.

Making a beeline to the nearest pharmacy, I use the last of the money I have to figure out if I really am sick or if I have a whole new set of problems to worry about in my godforsaken life.

Twenty minutes later, I'm in the bathroom of the twenty-four-hour drugstore, staring at the pregnancy test in disbelief. Two pink lines stare back at me. Two little dashes that bring the weight of the world crashing to my shoulders as they change everything. A numbness like no other consumes me from the inside out and I crumple to the dirty floor and cry like I haven't allowed myself to since losing my mother.

I can't even take care of myself. How the hell am I supposed to take care of a baby?

That night was a turning point for me—at least, I had hoped it would be. I pulled myself together and made a promise that I was going to do better. In an hour's time, I made plans to get a job and find a room to rent. I was going to do it, all on my own. The baby was the wake-up call I needed to live a better life. Not just for me, but for us.

My heart hurts just thinking about it. For a brief moment in time, I felt like everything I had been through up until that point was worthwhile. I learned to fight for myself, to survive, all for my precious baby.

Before my eyes shut that night, I had fallen in love with the life growing inside me, despite the monstrous nature of its conception. There was a fierce surge of protectiveness that wrapped itself around my soul and I promised I would do everything in my power to keep my innocent baby out of harm's way, out of this life. I was going to find a way to give him or her the world.

Two weeks later, I failed us both.

TEARS STING my cheeks for the first time in a while, and after falling asleep to the sensation of them running down my face, I wake up with my heart still heavy.

I'd hoped a nap would cure the ache in my chest. It's not often I allow my mind to visit that dreadful part of my past. It's best if I try not to think about it at all. I have no time to dwell on the things I can't change. All I can do is hope for a better tomorrow. Even if tomorrow is worse than today, I'll never stop searching for the light at the end of my tunnel.

Forcing myself up, I go over to the antique dresser full of drawers I've never filled. Sitting on top is a Ziploc bag that I put packets of forget-me-not seeds in.

I unzip the seal and pull one of the packets out before wandering quietly to the front lawn of the bed-and-breakfast.

In nothing but a pair of boxer shorts and a tee shirt, the cool air laces my skin, raising goosebumps along my arms.

Ripping the top of the packet off, I whisper into the wind, "Guide me, Mama. I don't know what I'm doing anymore."

Tipping the pack upside down, I sprinkle the seeds on a small mound of dirt beside the stairs directly out front and push them into the ground with my bare toes, making sure they are covered in soil.

"Rhea," a familiar voice calls out. My eyes shoot up and I see Tyler standing in front of the wrought iron gate to the B&B. "Did you miss the memo that it's not summer anymore?" The smile on his face brings back an ounce of the hope I'd lost. It's crazy how just a simple expression has that sort of pull on a person.

I slap my hands to my thighs with a grin. "Seems so."

"You know the frost coming is going to put a damper on your seeds sprouting?"

I giggle, my heart already feeling lighter. "I considered the possibility."

There's a good chance the flowers won't bloom, but there's always a chance one survivor in the pack might. It's sort of a metaphor for my life. Girls like me don't make it big. Hell, we barely make it at all. But I keep moving forward, knowing that there is always a chance for a better tomorrow.

Tyler rests his arms on the gate, the dimples in his cheeks pronounced. "Do you make a habit of planting flowers in your pajamas..." He glances at the invisible watch on his wrist. "...at five o'clock in the evening?"

I press my fist to my thigh and steel my shoulders. "Maybe I do," I shout back with a playful tone. "That a problem?"

He laughs. "You're kinda weird, ya know that?"

"I'm...*sorry*." I shrug my shoulders, but we both know I don't mean it.

"Don't be. I happen to like weird. It matches my personality."

I downcast my eyes, giggling like a teenager, as heat creeps up my neck. Am I actually smitten by him right now?

I'm not usually drawn to boys my age—ever, for that matter. My attraction has always been toward older men because in my line of work, that's where the money is.

While I have found a handful of my clients attractive and I've actually enjoyed my sexual interactions with a few, none of them ever left me with that edge-of-my-seat infatuation. There was never a desire to see any of them again after our nights together.

But right now, I'm surprised to find that I don't want Tyler to walk away. I want him to stick around for a little bit because something about being in his presence makes me feel better.

"I gotta get going," Tyler says. "Still down for playing it unsafe tonight?"

My eyes go wide. "Tonight?"

"The bonfire. Don't tell me you forgot." He tilts his head, smirking.

I actually did, until now. The butterflies in my stomach are urging me to tell him I'll be there, but there's another part of me that thinks I should lie low until I'm certain Alaric Banks is long gone.

I'm not going to pretend there isn't a fear instilled inside me that Alaric might come looking for me after last night. The elevator attendant said Alaric has no problem seeking vengeance for anyone who double-crosses him. But he also said he was checking out this morning.

After the way he turned the tables on me last night and knocked me out cold, I can't trust he's not lurking around town right now, waiting for the opportunity to exact his revenge for my thievery.

It seems I'm forgetting who I am as I all but crumble to pieces at this moment. I've outrun men with enough power to cripple an entire nation. Fuck Alaric. If he's as rich as I think he is, he doesn't give a damn about the nine hundred dollars I stole from him. Hell, he might have wanted me to take it because he felt sorry for what he did. Regardless, I refuse to cower.

"Actually," I flash him a smile, "I'm very much looking forward to it."

"Happy to hear." He shoots a thumb to his right. "I'm already late for work, so I better go. I'll see you soon."

"See ya." I watch him leave with my arms crossed over my chest. His strides are wide and determined. I'd hate to be him, walking into work late. Taryn's probably cursing under her breath at this very moment. After about five feet, Tyler stops and looks back at me briefly before giving a faint wave.

I quickly wave back, smiling from ear to ear as he disappears around a lamppost and into the tavern.

When my nipples pucker against my crossed arms, I remember I'm not wearing a bra. I bet I look like good ole white trash out here in my pajamas with no bra. Hey, maybe I do fit in here after all.

CHAPTER

TWELVE

RHEA

"I'M LEAVING, GLADYS," I holler from the door before pulling it open. A gust of cold wind whirls inside, mixing with the aroma of Gladys's apple pie that's in the oven. When she doesn't respond, I credit it to the sound of the mixer going. Probably for the best, considering she'll want to chat, and I'm already running late. I told Tyler I'd be there at ten when his shift ends, and it's already a quarter after.

I step outside and close the door behind me, thankful I'm somewhat warm in these clothes. I'm not exactly dressed to impress in a pair of worn jeans, my work shoes, a borrowed black Lockhaven football hoodie with yellow lettering, and a white beanie that Gladys found for me to wear out of a box of things from past guests. I won't be getting frostbite, so there's that.

Tyler is already standing outside the front door of the tavern. He's wearing a gray down jacket with a hoodie underneath that's pulled over his head and a pair of blue jeans. His hands are cupped around his mouth and a cloud of steam rolls out. The minute he sees me, he begins to walk my way, quickly eating up the space between us.

"Sorry I'm late," I tell him regretfully.

"No worries." He gives me one of those genuine smiles and I instantly feel comforted. "I literally just walked out the door. Taryn forced me to make up for the ten minutes I was late at the start of my shift."

"Why am I not surprised?" I chuckle.

"Because it's Taryn." Tyler nods to the right and I follow him around the building. "I get it, though. She's running a business and she has high expectations of her staff. I'd probably be the same way."

I find myself feeling extra awkward tonight for some reason. Lately it's like I'm a stray cat who's been brought into a home for the first time and doesn't know how to behave. My social skills are excellent when I'm working hard for something, but Tyler is different than most men I encounter. He's genuine and down-to-earth, and I truly want nothing more than friendship from him. Never thought I'd see the day where I'd be seeking friendship from a boy who lives in the same town as me.

Wow. It hits me. I'm really here. Right where I've always wanted to be. A smile creeps across my face and a warm rush of contentment swirls in my stomach.

If only my mom could be here to enjoy this simplicity by my side. Not right now, of course. I wouldn't want her anywhere near me while I'm with Tyler, or any boy for that matter. She always had a knack for embarrassing me in social situations.

I remember when I was thirteen and we were eating the continental breakfast at a hotel we were at. Mom caught me making eye contact with a cute boy and brought it upon herself to invite his family to sit with us. Thankfully, they didn't join us. They probably just thought we were a couple of weirdos, but she said it was because she didn't want me to miss out on feeling the giddiness of a crush.

Even when her timing was off, and it wasn't realistic for us, my mom always sought out ways to make me feel like a normal teenager. That's the reason I loved her when our life was shit. She tried; I saw it every day. Our circumstances were crap, but my mother loved me.

We cross the back parking lot and Tyler stops at a beat-up, blue cab pickup truck with rust spots scattered all over it. Pulling open the passenger-side door, he sweeps his arm toward it, gesturing for me to get inside.

"Thank you," I tell him as I climb inside. A musty scent wafts out as I sit down on the bench seat.

This is definitely an old truck, late nineties at least, maybe even older. There's a small hole in the floorboard, where cold air is creeping up, and I put my foot on it to keep what little warmth there is inside.

Tyler gets in and immediately turns the key, holding it in place as the engine sputters before finally coming to life.

"You cold?" he asks, and I immediately nod as I wrap my arms around myself.

Reaching deep into the back seat, he retrieves a baby blue crochet blanket. "The heat takes a bit to get going," he says as he lays it on my lap. The woven texture feels heavy and warm while the faint smell of hay fills the air.

"Thank you," I tell him, looking down at the blanket for signs of an eight-legged insect, or maybe a wild critter. "Did you grow up on a farm, by any chance?" I immediately eat my words, knowing that was probably an insensitive question considering I asked because of the smell.

"I did. I actually live on a farm about five miles outta town."

"Your parents' farm, I presume?"

"Nah, it's mine. Started collecting animals for my barnyard when I was four, and by the time I was five, I was butchering chickens and cows."

I side-eye him, searching for a sign that he's joking. "Are you messing with me?"

"Very much so." He throws an arm across the seat as I shake my head laughing. His hand rests directly behind my head, as he backs out of the parking space. "It's my parents' farm. I live on their property in a small two-bedroom cabin with my older brother. How'd you guess?"

"Just...a good guess." I shrug, paying close attention to where we are going. I'm usually good at reading people and situations, but I've been wrong before and needed an escape plan.

"How about you?" he asks. "I assume you didn't grow up on a farm in a small town like Lockhaven?"

Heat rises from my neck to my cheeks as I sweat beneath the layers I've got on. Conversations about my upbringing always make me tense. "No farm," I tell him truthfully. "I moved around a lot. Never really settled anywhere or made many friends."

"Military parents?"

"Something like that," I say, leaving it at that while quickly shifting the subject to one that's more comfortable. "So, what can I expect at this party?"

"Ohhh," he drawls. "Little of this. Little of that. Few cows, some chickens running around, and maybe even a hayride under the stars."

My eyebrows pinch together as I look at him skeptically. "You're messing with me again, right?"

"You're catching on, and I have to apologize. My sense of

humor is often used to hide my nervousness." A shy smile pulls at his lips as he looks back at me.

"Nervousness?" I sputter. "Why would *you* be nervous?"

Tyler gives me one more fleeting glance before his eyes return to the road. "It's not often a cute girl like you walks into town and hops in the passenger seat of my pickup truck."

I bite the corner of my lip, blushing. "I don't buy that for a second. I bet you've got a new girl in this seat every weekend."

"Hardly. Truth is, I haven't hung out with many girls outside of a social setting in a couple months."

"Oh?" I say, hoping he'll elaborate.

"I moved back to Lockhaven at the end of the summer after my ex-girlfriend and I split up. We had an apartment in the city and we were both attending Harmond University. Came home from a late class and found my best friend in my bed with her. Haven't talked to either of them since."

My heart hurts for him. "Shit, Tyler. I'm so sorry."

These are the things I'm thankful I missed out on. The sting of a heartbreak. The pain of losing friends. I've put a shield around myself for that very reason.

"Don't be. I'm not. I'm just glad I found out before I proposed to her."

"Proposed." I gasp. "You're only twenty-one years old."

His shoulders rise, caging in his neck. "We were together since I was sixteen. I loved her. She was all I really knew, so keeping her made sense. We grew up together and learned about life away from our family together. It just made sense at the time."

Hearing Tyler talk about his ex proves just how virtuous he is. I've never in my life met someone so real. I've traveled to every state in the U.S. and of all the people I've met, Tyler is probably the sincerest.

It's proof that he's too good for me. I shouldn't even be

sitting in this truck with him right now—he shouldn't want me here. I'm a fraud. A common whore. And Tyler is everything that is good in this world.

"If you ask me," I say faintly. "You're better off without a girl like that in your life."

My lips press into a thin line as I gaze out the passenger window at the passing fields. The next thing I know, Tyler's hand is resting over mine on my lap. When I turn to look at him, I see the cracked smile on his face. "Thanks, Rhea."

I let my hand sit beneath his as eagerness dampens my palms. My heart swells and warmth travels through my veins. It's a new feeling, but one I think I kinda like. Is this what it's like to have a crush?

We drive in a comfortable sort of silence with me fearful to move because I want him to keep holding my hand. It makes me feel safe and adored, and it's the sort of affection I didn't know I ever wanted. I guess it's normal; everyone wants to feel wanted at some point. It's a human instinct. We crave that powerful force inside us that says we are good enough.

That's how Tyler makes me feel. Like I could open up to him, tell him all my secrets. And he would still hold my hand.

Maybe it's just wishful thinking—hoping that one day someone would know the real me and still want to know more.

An array of headlights come into view, just before I see the blaze of a fire stretching to the sky. I straighten my back and Tyler pulls his hand away to steady the wheel. My hand feels cold without his presence, but I'm glad he's getting us down this narrow dirt road safely.

Cars come and go as we travel down over the rough terrain of the road. There's a wide-open space surrounded by woods and a fire smack-dab in the middle, where a crowd is gathered.

"What is this place?" I ask in awe, looking out at the array of people and cars.

"Cedar Hills. It's part of the national forest in the middle of nowhere, where we can be as loud and as obnoxious as we want." The grin that splits his face is full of joy and just a touch of mischievousness.

"I've never seen anything like it." Adrenaline races through my veins as I take in all the possibilities for the night.

It's wondrous and exciting. People my age dancing and laughing, not a care in the world. There are couples holding hands and friends dancing, all while laughing and having the time of their lives. It's funny how you don't know what you're missing until it sits right in front of you, lighting up the night sky like a beacon for your soul.

I've watched a lot of television and read many books. I know what people my age do for fun, but it was something I pretended was make-believe. As I look at the crowd and their unending joy, the realization that I could have experienced so much more in life hits me like a ton of bricks.

I sit there in stunned silence, even after Tyler opens the door for me. He tilts his head in question then looks to the party.

"You still feel like playing it unsafe?"

I look from him to the fire. Every instinct in my body tells me not to do it. This feels like a place for the lawless. A place where anything could happen, but also anything could go wrong. I should shut the door and ask him to drive me back to the thing I know will keep me safe. Hiding.

But that's not what I do. When Tyler raises his hand, I take it and leap from the truck, landing on a bed of raised dirt. My sneakers dig into the rigid grooves of the trail, and instantly, I'm hit with the thump of the bass blasting from some speakers on the back of a tailgate.

Like a child on Christmas morning, my eyes light up as they dance in amazement from one scene to the next. Some girls dream of fairy tales, where the knight comes to save them and fairies fly around. But me, this is what I think I've craved since I was a child. Freedom in the chaos.

I follow, my hand still settled firmly in Tyler's, as we walk toward the crowd. Every few people we pass, he gets a high five, or "What's up, man?" It's the small-town attention I'd expect him to get in a place like Lockhaven.

"Are you nervous?" Tyler asks, placing a hand on the small of my back as he leads me toward wherever we're headed.

"No," I tell him truthfully. "Should I be?"

"Nah. Not even a little bit. I guess you're probably used to meeting new people often with all the moving you did growing up, huh?"

"Oh, you have no idea." He doesn't know how sarcastic I'm being, but I play along. Once you start a story about your past, you have to sell it.

A minute later, we're standing in line at a keg. I try not to let my nervousness about so many people show. I don't normally drink and if the other night was a warning for me, I probably shouldn't, but I need a buffer to handle this crowd.

"Tyler fucking Jarman." A guy's voice comes from behind me and I whip around to see who it is.

"Hey, Nelson." Tyler beams as he slaps his hand into the guy's open palm. "How you been?"

"Not bad. Not bad. I heard you moved back. What the hell, man? You were so fucking excited to get out of this shithole." As the words leave his mouth, his eyes land on me. The guy named Nelson shoots a thumb toward me, now looking at Tyler with questioning eyes.

"And who do we have here?" He seems a little drunk as he looks between Tyler and me.

Tyler laughs. "Nelson, meet Rhea. Rhea, meet Nelson."

Nelson extends his hand to me, and after looking at it for a good thirty seconds as I read his demeanor, I lay mine in it and shake.

"It's nice to meet you." He seems like another nice country boy like Tyler. I hate that I'm so skeptical with people, but it comes with my upbringing.

"Likewise."

We're joined in the line by a girl, probably about the same height as me, maybe half an inch shorter. She's got long blonde hair, crystal blue eyes, and she's wearing a solid white fur coat. A little different than what I'd expect out here, but it does look very warm.

"Christine," Nelson says, "this is Tyler's friend, Rhea."

Christine, taken aback by the introduction, looks at Tyler, dumbfounded, while paying me zero attention. "Does Tamara know about this?"

Tyler scoffs. "Why would she?"

"Oh, I dunno," Christine grumbles. "Maybe because you were sleeping at her house three days ago."

My eyes widen, face drawn back, and it's apparent there's a lot I don't know, or care to know. "Look," I say point-blank. "Tyler and I are just friends. We work together. There is absolutely nothing going on between us."

"Sleeping at her house doesn't mean I was sleeping with her," Tyler snaps back. "There are twenty other girls that live in that house. They threw a party and I had too much to drink—"

I grab Tyler's arm, cutting him off. He sure as shit doesn't have to explain himself for my sake, and I won't let this girl bully him into thinking he owes her anything. "You don't have to explain yourself to these people. Let's just get our drinks and have some fun." I push myself up on my tiptoes and whisper in his ear, "Unsafe, remember?"

He nods, awareness washing over his features. He shakes his head, as if to banish the excuses floating around his brain. "Yeah. You're right."

"These people?" Christine stammers. "We happen to be Tyler's friends, unlike you, who claims to just be a co-worker. And his ex, Tamara, is my best friend."

"Congratulations," I deadpan as I tug Tyler in the appropriate direction toward the keg and away from these naysayers.

"Excuse me!" Christine huffs as she trails behind us. "I don't like your attitude."

I spin around, the toes of my shoes digging into the dirt. "Oh yeah? Seems like you're asking for more of it. Why are you following me?"

I'm not a fighter, but I've fought, and I'm sure as fuck not opposed to wiping that smug look off this bitch's face with my fist.

"Because you walked away when I'm still talking, which is not only disrespectful, it's also cowardly."

I laugh airily. "Cowardly? Girl, you don't know a damn thing about me."

"Probably best." She looks at her freshly-painted nails. "Because I'm sure if I did, I wouldn't like you much."

I step up to her, nose to nose. "Well, I don't know you and I already think less of you than the dirt everyone here is walking on."

"Whoa, whoa, whoa," Tyler singsongs as he pulls me down a peg. "Let's just part ways and have a good time."

I glower at Christine, challenging her to say one more word, as my fists ball into tight knots at my sides. Her eyes travel to them, taking note of my offensive stance. "Oh, you wanna fight?"

"Just say the word," I growl back at her.

"Wow, Tyler," Christine sneers. "Never expected you to downgrade to pure trash."

Oh, hell no. Did she seriously just say that?

"You bitch!" I charge at her, but I'm immediately pulled back by Tyler. His arms wrap around my lower torso as I stretch my hands out, trying to get a grip on any part of her I can.

Christine jumps back as if she's surprised I'd actually come at her. "You're a fucking psycho. Go the hell back to wherever you came from." She flips her hair over her shoulder as she spins around.

After a few steps, she glances over her shoulder with a devious smirk on her face as if she planned this to a T. She wanted to make me look bad. She pushed every button perfectly and set me off.

"I'm good," I tell Tyler, and he lets me go. I rub my temples, disappointed that I allowed that girl to get me so worked up. "I'm sorry," I tell him regretfully.

"You're sorry?" He chuckles. "I'm the one who should be apologizing. I really should've let you beat her ass."

A smile draws on my face. "Then why didn't you?"

"She's not worth it. That girl has been a pain in my ass for years and I would love nothing more than to watch someone shut her up for a while. But she's also known for spreading rumors and creating drama. I'd hate for you to be dragged into that shit so soon after moving here."

"Well, I think it's a little too late for that. But don't worry about me. Stuck-up little bitches don't intimidate me in the least."

We move up the line and a guy at the front hands us each a cup. When it's our turn, Tyler fills us both up and we part ways from the crowd, finding an empty space by the large fire.

"Cheers," Tyler says, holding his cup in the air.

"And what is it we're cheersing to?"

"You. Being a total badass."

I laugh as some of the weight I've been carrying for as long as I remember starts to subside. I never wanted love, but I didn't realize just how much I truly wanted friendship. "What makes you say that?"

"I pretty much could tell the minute I first saw you. I was certain when you called that guy out for spilling your drink. And now, after that stunt with Christine, I'm positive that I *do not* want to get on your bad side."

I knock my cup against his and waggle my brows. "I'd say that's a good call." I take a small sip, remembering last night and how only two drinks led to poor choices.

"So, tell me about yourself, Rhea. What do you like to do for fun? Who's your favorite band? And most importantly, are you a pumpkin spice fanatic?"

"That's most important?" I laugh. "No to the pumpkin spice. I like the smell but not the taste. I don't have a favorite band, and for fun, this is slowly topping the charts."

"Drinking beer at a fire in the middle of nowhere tops the charts?"

"Well, it does for tonight anyways."

Tyler flashes a smile over the rim of his cup. "I'm happy to hear that."

"How about you? Favorite band, and all that jazz?"

"Man, I knew I shouldn't have asked that because I had a feeling you'd ask the same." He taps his chin with one finger exaggeratedly, and I think my face actually hurts from smiling at this point. "That's a tough one. I'm a sucker for Luke Combs, Morgan Wallen, and pretty much any country guy or gal. Hell no to the pumpkin spice, and as for what I like to do for fun, this is quickly topping the charts."

My cheeks flush with heat and a giddy feeling rises in the

pit of my stomach as I repeat his words. "I'm happy to hear that."

Tyler continues to peg me with questions, trying to get to know me, and each one has me feeling more and more uncomfortable because most of them are answered with a lie. After an hour, I've become another carefully crafted character I've created—a cheerleader in middle school, a member of the drama club in high school, and an average student with a passion for photography. I've never even owned a camera aside from the one on my phone.

I had a boyfriend for a year, then moved, and the long-distance relationship didn't work, so we called it quits. How the ever-loving fuck do I let these lies slip so seamlessly past my lips?

Tyler, who is nothing short of a holy being, has only had one serious relationship. He was the quarterback of his football team all through high school, and is now attending college on a four-year scholarship. Oh, and he attends church every Sunday and asked me to go with him tomorrow.

I currently feel three feet tall standing next to him.

I lied again and told him I had to help Gladys prep dinner because a new guest is arriving tonight.

A new guest really is arriving, but she never asked for my help. I suppose I could turn my words into the truth and offer a helping hand. Either way, I'm certain I will burst into flames if I step foot into a church, so I had to tell him something.

"You need another drink?" Tyler asks, peering over my cup. I give it a whirl, showing him that it's still half full.

"I'm good, but thank you. And I'm fine here if you wanna go get another."

"One's my limit when I'm driving." He tosses his cup into the fire and I watch as the red plastic slowly melts into a pool of nothingness.

"So what now?" I ask him, curious about what else happens at these sorts of parties.

"We can mingle, or we can get outta here. It's your call."

"As exciting as all this is, I'm not sure I'm wanted here." I nod toward the eyes glaring at me from across the fire.

Tyler follows my stare to find Christine laughing with her friends as she watches us intently. I don't doubt for a second she's talking about me.

"Forget about them," he says as he wraps an arm around my waist. "They wanna talk, let's give them something to talk about."

In a fluid motion, he pulls my body flush to his and his mouth lands softly on mine.

It takes me a second to comprehend what's happening, but once I snap out of the confusion, it's actually really nice. My hands move to the back of his head, cradling it against my palms as I bring him closer, deepening the kiss.

When his tongue slithers into my mouth, my legs go weak and my pulse jumps into a frenzy.

His lips are like satin against mine and his gentleness is something I'm not used to. For a moment, I forget that we have an audience. But when Tyler breaks the kiss, I'm reminded of why it happened in the first place.

Still holding me close, I look up at him. "Was that to make someone jealous?"

"I'm here with you, Rhea. Everyone's jealous."

I can't even begin to explain the feeling inside my chest. It's warm and fuzzy, as well as satisfying. No man has ever made me feel so seen before. This is the feeling I've been chasing my entire life.

It's also the one I've fought so hard to avoid.

I take a step back, remembering how devastating it is to

have something so special jerked away from you. One minute they're there, and the next minute they're gone.

As happy as I feel when I'm with Tyler, it can never go beyond friendship, and even that's a risk.

"You okay?" Tyler asks, noticing my apprehension.

Just as I open my mouth to speak, my eyes catch a glimpse of someone standing in the woods behind Tyler, staring right at me. Those eyes. Though the rest of his face is behind a black ski mask, there's something so familiar about them. The way they watch me, as if they're piercing my skin and cutting me open, just to get a glimpse of my soul.

I step around Tyler and begin toward the black shadowy figure. But just as he realizes I'm coming closer, he turns around and walks deeper into the woods, disappearing into the night.

"Did you see that?" I ask Tyler, pointing toward the trees.

"Probably just a lame-ass high schooler fucking around. After all, Halloween is just around the corner."

"Yeah." I nod. "You're probably right."

Still, there was something unsettling about the way he was watching only me. And those eyes don't lie. I've seen them before.

This moment is all too familiar. Months of being followed and watched. Back then, I didn't care. There wasn't a fear of this person capturing me because he never tried, and it was just proof that it was time for me to keep moving. But here? This is supposed to be my safety net. The place I plan to call home. The threat is gone. My father is dead. So who is this man?

Unless...

Could it be Alaric? Would he really follow me to the woods and taunt me over nine hundred dollars? Or am I just being paranoid again?

Tyler has a good point—Halloween is coming. Not that this person was wearing a costume. But it's cold, too. And high school kids do dumb shit. Hell, even college kids do dumb shit.

I'm overthinking this, but either way, something feels off.

"We should go," I tell Tyler as the unease in my stomach spreads like wildfire.

"I agree. I think we've seen all we need to see here tonight." He takes my cup and tosses it into the fire as he takes my hand. "These types of parties used to be fun back in high school. Now, they're just the same thing every weekend. It gets old. Ya know?"

"Yeah," I tell him in response, unsure what he even said. I keep looking over my shoulder, waiting for the masked man to appear again. The high from arriving and seeing something so new to me fades quickly.

When the masked man doesn't make another appearance, I chalk it up to nerves. I want to slap myself for even thinking it was someone here for me.

One of these days, I'm going to get over myself and stop thinking the world is out to get me. I just hope I do it soon because I'm tired of living a life where I feel like I need to keep running.

CHAPTER

THIRTEEN

RHEA

I'm laughing at myself this morning as I get ready for work. The level of distrust I have in the human race is unreal.

Last night I was certain someone was watching me from the woods at that party. Tyler drove me home and I had convinced myself the masked man would be waiting for me behind my bedroom door when I opened it. To my surprise, the room was empty and all was well.

Passing by my bedroom window to grab my apron, I notice a flock of people on the streets decorating for Halloween. There's a group of elderly ladies who seem to be bickering while one swings a witch's broom in the air and the other points at a lamppost. In front of the hardware store, there's a man hanging a string of plastic skulls around the entrance.

My chest swells as I watch the community gather together. I've never had the privilege of living in a town like this before.

For the first time ever, I feel like this could be my home.

With a smile on my face, I grab my cash that's in an envelope. I gave up on seeing my purse again, so I need to talk to Gladys about getting new keys made.

"Gladys," I shout as I pass by the bathroom in the hall, "are you home?"

When I make it to the kitchen, I can see that she's on the phone. She holds up a finger and I mouth the words, *I've gotta go. Here's rent.* I set the envelope on the counter, walking away with a smile on my face. I did it. I paid rent for the month. I'm not even going to let the guilt of how I came about the money bring me down, because there is none. What I took from that man is pennies compared to what I'm sure he's got in his accounts. Not only that, he fucking drugged me. If anything, he owed me, and now we're even.

As for the keys, I'll have to talk to Gladys about them later.

I step outside and the cool wind brushes against my bare arms. It seems the vibrant sunshine beaming through my window was deceiving.

"Good morning, Rhea," a kind lady says, and while I don't know her name, I've seen her at Taryn's a few times.

I respond with a chipper, "It sure is."

Everyone I pass is smiling and it's strange, but I feel like I actually belong in this town as people wave and say hello, like I'm one of them.

Man, I wish Mom was here to live this life with me.

I walk into Taryn's, and I'm immediately halted by a very loud, "Stop!"

Not moving an inch farther, with the door still held open, I freeze with a ladder smack-dab in front of my face.

"Carefully go around," Tyler says, and I'm surprised to see him here, considering he generally only works Friday and Saturday nights.

With gentle ease, I step around the ladder, taking care not to bump it because he's at the very top.

Once I'm in, the door closes, and I look up to see Tyler hanging orange lights from the high beams on the ceiling.

He pauses, hands pinned to the wall, and looks down at me. "Good morning." His cheery, perfect smile looks down at me and my face heats like a damn schoolgirl looking at her first crush.

"Better hurry that up. We open in five minutes," I tell him. "Wouldn't want you getting knocked down by a herd of hungry senior citizens."

"As long as you catch me, I'll be fine." He winks.

I laugh as I tie my apron around my waist. "If that's your game plan, then we're both in trouble."

Returning to the lights, he hooks the cord on the string then descends the ladder. Face to face, he says, "Maybe I wanna get into trouble with you."

I'm not sure how this guy manages to make me blush so often, but once again, I feel the heat in my cheeks. "I don't think you're capable."

"Oh yeah?" He lifts his chin. "Why's that?"

"Easy. You're too good. I don't think there's a rebellious bone in your body."

"In case you've forgotten," he steps closer, and his voice drops to a near whisper, "I did kiss you in front of everyone last night."

My legs tremble just thinking about that kiss and the way Tyler's hands gripped my hips. It was everything I always hoped a kiss could feel like.

"I do remember that. Very well, actually. And now that I think about it, you probably started a whole lot of rumors we'll both need to clear up."

Tyler grabs the sides of the ladder and pushes it together. "Or we could leave them guessing." Grinning, he carries it away and I shake my head, trying desperately to push down the excitement in my chest.

Getting involved with Tyler is the last thing I need. Not

only do we work together, but he's far too good for me. Not to mention, I barely know him. It would be insane for me to jump into something with the first guy in this town to pay me any attention. The best thing I can do for both of us is keep this relationship in the friend zone, even if my lips do still burn with the memory of his kiss.

The morning goes quickly, and before I know it, we're jumping into the lunch menu. Tyler is still here decorating for Halloween, and he's even gone out to help on Main Street a few times when his muscles were needed by a couple ladies.

I'm pleasantly surprised when my shift ends and I've made forty-three dollars in tips. It's not great, but it definitely could be worse.

As I'm leaving out the front door to walk home, I'm stopped by Tyler. "Wait up," he hollers as he jogs to the door where I'm standing. My eyebrows rise and the corner of his mouth lifts. "I was wondering if you'd like to come over for dinner tonight?"

Taken aback by his offer, the first word out of my mouth is, "Dinner?"

"Yeah. You do eat, right?" That damn grin stretches across his lips.

I chuckle. "Of course I eat."

"Good. Then it's settled. I'll pick you up at G&C at six?"

I'm hesitant to respond, unsure what this dinner is going to entail. "If this dinner is with your family, I'm just not sure..."

"Hell no. Just you and me."

I breathe a sigh of relief. I'm definitely not ready to meet anyone's parents. The thought has me wondering if maybe Tyler and I should talk about *us*. If there's even the slightest chance he's getting attached in a way that I'm not, I should probably let him know now that I'm not interested in starting up a relationship.

"Okay," I tell him, knowing tonight will be the perfect opportunity to do just that.

"Great." He leans in and places a chaste kiss on my cheek before walking past me. His hand slides across my hip and goosebumps break out on my arms.

Yeah. We definitely need to talk. My body might crave his kiss and melt at his touch, but love isn't something I will ever hurt for again.

"I'M HOME," I holler as I walk through the door, taking one shoe off then the other. My feet are fucking killing me and I need a nap.

"Rhea," Gladys says from the living room. She's in her recliner, knitting something fluffy and pink. "I'm glad to see you. Will you be around this evening? There's someone I'd like you to meet."

With my shoes in one hand and my apron in the other, I walk into the cozy room. "Actually, I've got dinner plans at six."

Her eyes light up. "Dinner plans, hmm? Anyone I know?"

I bite back on the smile trying to grow on my face. "Tyler, from Taryn's."

"Oh, Tyler!" she gushes. "He's such a nice boy."

"Yeah, he is." I shoot a thumb over my shoulder. "I'm gonna go lie down for a bit. Let me know if you need anything. Otherwise, I'll find you before I leave in a couple hours and you can introduce me to this mystery person."

Gladys returns to her crocheting. "Okay, dear. You go relax. Rest well."

Dragging my feet down the hall, my mouth opens and a big yawn comes out. Once I get settled in this town and back on my feet, I need to search for an office job where I can sit all day.

I push open the door to my room, ready to plop down on my bed for a good two hours, but I stop in the doorway, stunned by the sight in front of me.

"What the hell?" I mumble as I cross the room to my shattered window. The whole center is missing and all that's left are frayed, pointed edges along the trim. I poke my head out and look around the area, but see nothing out of the ordinary.

"Gladys!" I holler as I turn back toward the door, but just as I go to leave, a note on my bed catches my eye. I backstep, picking it up quickly.

Flipping the page open, I read the handwritten message.

You can keep what you stole, but I get you in return.

I gasp at the words in front of me. There's no signature, nothing else. Just those twelve words.

It takes me less than a second to realize this note is from Alaric. It has to be. I haven't duped, conned, or slept with any men in this town. I haven't been using the Siren's Call app. I barely know anyone. The only person I've stolen from who knows where I am is Alaric.

Pinching the note between my fingers, I sit down on the bed, reading it over and over again as the masked man from last night comes to mind.

I knew I wasn't losing it. That man was definitely watching me, and this note along with the broken window proves that Alaric hasn't left town.

He's still very much here. And he's after me.

CHAPTER
FOURTEEN
RHEA

I TOLD Gladys about the window and she was very understanding. She called the hardware store and was able to get the owner's son to come out and put some plastic over the broken glass. A replacement should be delivered in a couple days. According to Gladys, this is the second time they've had to replace a window due to the kids playing football on Main Street. If only I could tell her this definitely wasn't a case of careless child's play.

My nap still hasn't come. I've been lying in bed, tossing and turning, for the last hour, but my thoughts are intrusive. It's obvious what needs to be done—I have to leave Lockhaven.

I grab my phone with a sigh. I was just starting to like this place. Just starting to make friends and settle down. For the first time in forever, I don't really *want* to leave.

"It's me," I say to Dex when he picks up after the third ring.

"Long time no talk. How ya doing, Doll?"

"You were right," I say, tone loaded with remorse. "A small town was a bad choice."

Dex sighs. "Damn, Rhea. Sorry it didn't work out. Why don't you just come to Atlanta? You can have a nice life here."

"It's not the town, or the people. It's me, Dex. I'm broken. I'll never change."

"There's nothing wrong with you, Doll. You just...don't know any better."

"But I do." I laugh mockingly. "I'm twenty-one years old. I know right from wrong. So why do I continuously make the wrong choices?"

"Well, if you think you're always making the wrong choices, maybe running again is one of them. Do you *have* to leave?"

I don't want to tell him what I did. We agreed that if I started new here, I was going to stop the stealing thing. But, I had no choice. I throw my arm over my eyes as I tell him, as if I could hide from the words as they leave my mouth. "I fucked up. I stole from a rich asshole and he's making threats now. He's gonna blow me out of the water if I don't get out of here fast."

He chuckles dryly. "Sounds to me like you're giving him the power."

I scoff. "What the hell am I supposed to do? He's probably some big name I don't know about, and I'm just...a nobody."

"You're Rhea fucking Thorn."

"Brooks," I correct him.

"No. You're a Thorn by blood. And from what I've come to know about the Thorns, they hold power too."

"Power that does me no good."

There's a beat of silence as I toy with the idea of staying and standing up to Alaric. The note says I can keep what I stole, but he gets me in return. Obviously that isn't going to happen. You don't get to just *keep* people. I'm not even sure why he'd want me anyway.

And another thought...I could be totally off base. This might not be Alaric at all. It could just be some prank. Hell, it could be the mayor's wife for all I know. Or someone else who saw me steal that six bucks from her purse.

"Sleep on it, Rhea," Dex says, breaking the silence. "Don't make any rash decisions. I'll call in the morning to see what you've decided."

We end the call in an agreement, and I decide to get out of bed. I've still got plans with Tyler tonight, and I have every intention of standing by them. But before I go, Gladys wants to introduce me to the new guest at G&C.

Using the bathroom in the hall that is shared with other guests, I run a comb through my hair and brush my teeth, then change into a very casual black tee shirt dress and a pair of black flip-flops. Adding a zip-up hoodie for warmth, I call it good.

With winter coming soon, I'm going to need to set aside some extra cash for warmer clothes. Just another thing added to my endless list of expenses.

After one more glance in the mirror, and a fluff of my hair, I leave the bathroom in search of Gladys.

I find her a minute later at the eight-person oblong table in the dining room. There are three seated guests—two of which I've seen before.

"Rhea," Gladys beams. "I'm so glad you could make it." She pulls out a chair, gesturing for me to sit down.

"I can't stay. As I mentioned, I have dinner plans tonight."

"Oh, but just for a moment, please?"

I nod reluctantly. "Okay. Just for a minute."

I take a seat, my eyes wandering from person to person. There's a middle-aged man with dark hair and a matching mustache, dressed nicely in a pair of khakis and a blue button-up shirt.

Beside him is a woman I take to be his wife, and when I see them holding hands on top of the table, I'm certain of it. I've seen them around before, but never had a chance to officially meet them.

Finally, my gaze lands on the girl seated right beside me. She looks to be about my age, and she seems unsettled. She's got shoulder-length red hair, cute freckles sprinkled on her face, and she's fighting to make eye contact as she stares aimlessly at the empty plate in front of her.

When I get a better look at her, I notice her legs bouncing up and down in a nervous manner.

"Hi," I say quietly to her. "I'm Rhea."

Without looking at me, she grabs the fabric napkin and begins fidgeting with it. "It's nice to meet you, Rhea. I'm Heather."

"I'm so happy you could all be here," Gladys says, clapping her hands together gleefully. "I know you're all just here temporarily, but I want you to feel like this house is your home while you're staying. Whether it's a week, a weekend, or a couple of months like our dear Rhea."

My mouth curves into a smile. Gladys is so kind and warm, like the grandparent I never knew I wanted. She's got a way of making all my worries dissipate in her presence.

"With that said," she continues. "We have a couple new guests staying with us." She waves her hand in the air toward the girl beside me. "Heather and—" Her words trail off as she sputters and looks behind her. "Well, he was here a minute ago."

All of the air escapes from my lungs in one hefty exhale when the new guest walks into the dining room. His eyes land on mine, and time stands still. "Sorry I'm late, I had to take a call."

"Everyone, this is Alaric."

An icy chill falls over the room as he steps in farther, his dark gaze never leaving mine. The large glass chandelier overhead flickers, almost as if it's my mother's ghost warning me to run like hell.

My thoughts elude me as I slide my chair back, the legs scraping abrasively against the hardwood floor.

"Rhea dear. Is everything okay?" Gladys asks with a concerned expression on her face.

"Yeah. I...I have to go," I stammer as my mind spins out of control. I fumble for words and my hand shakes as I push the chair back in against the table. "It was nice meeting you, Heather." As for Alaric, it's certainly not a pleasure and if I never see him again, it'll be too soon.

My legs feel like lead, but I force them to keep moving until I'm out of the room. Once I'm in the living room, and out of eyesight, I press my back to the wall.

What the hell is he up to?

I don't panic often. For the most part, I can remain level-headed in intense situations, and I usually come up with a plan to get myself out of them quickly. But this time, I'm not sure what I can possibly do other than run like hell.

Tyler is waiting for me to have dinner with him, but there is just no way I can go to his house and pretend like nothing is wrong.

As I walk back to my room, I retrieve my phone from the pocket of my hoodie.

With a shaky hand, I dial Dex. "Pick up," I mutter under my breath as I turn the hall to my room. "Come on, Dex."

Thinking nothing else could come as a surprise tonight, I'm proven wrong when I see Alaric standing at the end of the hall near my room.

"What the hell are you doing?" I bark, not allowing myself to display the level of fear he's instilled in me.

"It's nice to see you again, Rhea."

I walk toward him, shoulders taut as I stick my phone back in my pocket. "Get away from my room."

"But this is my room." He nods toward the door beside him. "Looks like we're going to be neighbors."

"Have you lost your fucking mind? Why are you even here?" I whisper-yell, putting all of my anger into my words but not wanting anyone to overhear us at the same time.

"Same reason you are. I needed a place to stay."

I put on a tough facade while my heart is literally trying to flee from my chest. "You had a place to stay at the hotel. I thought you were leaving town."

"Technically, I did leave town. Besides, I found a reason to stay."

"Let me guess. That reason is me?"

"Smart and beautiful, I see." His cocksure grin makes me want to punch him in his perfectly-chiseled jaw.

"Well, enjoy the room." I go to walk around him to get to my door. To my surprise, he allows it. "I'll be checking out immediately."

Suddenly, I'm captured by his hand wrapped around my wrist in a vise. "The hell you are."

"What do you think you're doing?" I snort in disbelief, attempting to pull out of his grasp. My voice sharpens when he doesn't budge. "Let go of me!"

"You're not going anywhere, Rhea. You stole from me, and now you're forever in my debt."

"You're fucking delusional."

"Actually," he sneers. "I'm quite realistic." He leans in close, his breath hot against my face. "And realistically, I can tell you that if you think you're going in that room to pack up your bag and run again, you're sadly mistaken, *little girl*." He puts extra emphasis on those two words and they chill me to the core.

"Why would you say that? What makes you think I've done this before?"

Saying I'm not going to run makes sense. But he said *again*.

The smirk on his face is telling. He's a lot smarter than I'm giving him credit for.

"Are you really that naive to think this was a chance encounter, Rhea?"

"Of course not," I tell him with another jerk of my wrist. "We met the other night. And yes, I stole from you. But you deserved it. You fucking drugged me!"

His grip on me tightens to the point that I can feel the blood draining from my hand. "Don't pretend like you weren't going to use that drug on me to rob me blind for the way I treated you. I pride myself on being intellectual, Rhea. I'm not here to play games. When I saw your plan, I merely put you down for a nap, so I could get a peek at what I've been missing."

A shiver runs through me. If he's insinuating what I think he is, then this man is more depraved than I could have ever imagined. "Did you touch me?"

He slithers closer, lips drawn back in a sinister grin. "How could I not?"

My stomach lurches as I gag on the rising vomit. "Oh my God!" I shout in revulsion. "You're fucking sick!"

"If I'm sick, it's because you've made me this way. The moment I saw you, I fell ill."

One more swift tug and I'm finally free of his grip. I hurriedly grab the handle of my door and turn it. With a forceful push, I shove it open and throw myself inside. Only, I don't enter alone.

"Get out!" I shout with a stern finger pointed down the hall. "Get out now or I will scream at the top of my lungs!"

"No, you won't," Alaric retorts coyly, closing the door

behind him. "You scream, I'll tell everyone in this house who you really are—a lying thief. You try to run, I'll follow you. If you so much as open that pretty mouth and mention a single word of this, I will take you somewhere no one will ever find you." His hand pinches my chin as I try to force my body not to fold into a ball under his intense gaze. "Do you understand?"

Fear isn't something that happens to me naturally. I've been in countless situations where I should have been scared but wasn't. I've always considered myself a warrior because I'm able to walk into the darkness and come out unscathed without an ounce of worry for what could happen to me. I guess when you feel like you don't have anything to live for, you're not afraid of dying. Therefore, panic is a waste of time.

But right now, I am terrified. It's as if I'm staring down a black tunnel and there is no way out. Maybe it's because for the first time ever, this town has made me feel alive. It's nothing special. Just a dot on the map. But the people here make me feel welcome and part of their community. I've never had that before.

"I said," he begins slowly. "Do. You. Understand?"

I could nod and be compliant. Give him a polite, 'yes, sir.' But that's not me and I don't care how scared I am, I will never again cower to a man or let him overpower me—physically or mentally.

"Fuck you," I grit out in a venomous hiss, just before a ball of spit flies from my mouth, landing directly on his cheek. He doesn't so much as flinch, but his eyes remain deadlocked on mine in a stone-cold stare.

Slowly, he raises his hand to his face, dragging his fingers down my saliva on his cheek. And when he shoves those same fingers in his mouth, sucking my spit off them, I wince.

Then in a fluid motion, he grabs my face with an iron grip, clenching as his fingertips pry my mouth open. Raising his wet fingers, he shoves them into my mouth, past my teeth, and pushes against my throat.

Relentlessly, he tips my head back, practically choking me with his fist.

I sputter and gag while my nails claw into his wrist, trying to free my airway. I attempt to clamp my teeth down on his fingers, but he only squeezes my cheeks harder.

My heart races as I frantically swing my hands, slapping at his arms to try and get his attention. My breaths come in ragged gasps as I try to decipher if I'm choking, suffocating, or merely having a panic attack.

"Say you're sorry," he grits out in a demanding tone.

I ball my fists, trembling and pounding at any part of him I can reach.

"Apologize, dammit!" he snaps at me, and I'm left with no choice but to do exactly what he asks.

"Sorry," I say in a hoarse whisper. It really sounds like more of a muffled gag and I probably could have said anything else, but he would have known regardless. My tongue pushes against his fingers and I taste the saltiness of sweat on his skin as his eyes peer down at me until they break through all of my walls and tear into my soul.

Finally, he pulls his fingers out of my mouth, and I stifle a groan. "You fucking psycho!" I curl over, spitting out the taste of him.

Alaric places a hand on my back as if to try and comfort me, when really, it just makes me want to vomit on his sleek black shoes.

"It won't always be this way, Rhea. Your defiance will eventually turn to compliance, and I won't need to punish you for your cruel behavior. But, mark my words, I will punish you if you step out of line. Just remember," he bends down until his face is beside mine, "it's better to obey than to sacrifice."

He pats my ass before straightening his back. In an instant, I shoot up, profanities spewing from my mouth as I pound my fists to his chest, walking him backward until he's against the wall. "You fucking psycho! I don't know what the hell you think you're going to get from me, but you're not getting anything! I will never obey you. And this *will* be the last time you ever see me!"

Suddenly, his fingers are wrapped around my throat and I'm the one being backed into the wall. He lifts with slight pressure, bringing me to the tips of my toes. "If you try to leave Lockhaven, I will hunt you down, Rhea. I will find you, and I will cage you so that you never run again. Is that really what you want?"

I shake my head no, knowing now is not the time to get argumentative. I just need to bide my time and get away from this crazy man so I can call the cops. They'll help me. They have to.

"Good," he says matter-of-factly. "And if you tell anyone about this, me, or us, I will punish you twice as hard. Do I make myself clear?"

I gulp, unable to mutter a word with the limited air supply I have. Instead, I just nod my head.

A smile grows on his face, widening with each passing second. "That's my good girl." His mouth moves toward mine and I try to turn my head, not wanting his lips anywhere near mine. Holding me in place, he kisses my cheek so hard, I can feel his teeth grind against my cheekbone.

Finally, he lets me go and I curl back over again, gasping for air.

"We're going to have a nice life together, Rhea. I promise you that." He opens the door but doesn't bother to shut it as he walks away.

With my hands on my knees, I watch as he walks down the

hall, disappearing around the corner. Then I drop to the floor and break down. Tears fall carelessly down my cheeks as I think of ways I can try and outmaneuver this man, but I have nothing. I don't take Alaric to be a liar, and I certainly don't find him to be forgiving.

I crawl to my door and lock it as my body folds in on itself, still sitting on the floor. Reaching into my pocket, I pull out my phone to call Dex while Alaric's words replay in my mind. *If you tell anyone about this, me, or us, I will punish you twice as hard.*

Instead of calling Dex, I dial the tavern.

"Taryn's Tavern, how can I help you?"

"Hey, Taryn. It's Rhea."

"Hi, hun. Everything okay?"

"Yeah. Everything's fine. I'm just trying to reach Tyler. We have plans tonight, but I have to cancel and I don't have his number."

"Actually," she says. "He's been waiting for you here."

There's a beat of silence before Tyler comes on the line. "Canceling on me?"

"I'm so sorry, Tyler. I think I'm coming down with something." I cough a few times into the phone for added emphasis.

"Shit, Rhea. Sorry to hear that. Of course, it's no problem. We'll just reschedule for another time. Get some rest."

"Thank you for understanding."

"No worries. We'll talk soon, okay?"

A mixture of regret and guilt floods through me as I say, "Okay."

I end the call and drop my phone beside me before completely falling apart. It's been years since I've cried this hard.

Three years, to be exact...

"Hey, baby. You lost?"

I keep walking, not daring to give this scumbag a moment of my time. I just need to get back to my hotel room with this bag of food, because I'm fucking starving. It's the first time I've had an appetite in weeks and I was able to scrape up enough money for a burger and fries.

The man continues to stumble drunkenly behind me, clutching a crumpled brown paper bag wound around a bottle of liquor.

"I just wanna talk," he calls out as I pick up my pace, trying to get away from him.

My stomach turns and I'm not sure if it's the all-day morning sickness I've been having, or the overpowering scent of stale beer and cigarettes coming off this guy. His thick beard holds scraps of food and God knows what else. I clench my nose just thinking of how rancid his breath probably is.

He's been following me down the alley for five minutes. All I need is two more and I can turn out of here and onto the main road, where he'll get spooked by witnesses and leave me the fuck alone.

"I'm fucking talking to you, bitch!" he stutters as the smell of him draws closer.

The next thing I know, two men step out from beside a dumpster, but these ones are much better put together than the one behind me.

Both are wearing matching black leather jackets with baseball caps that obscure their features. One of them towers over the other, and he's holding something in his hand at his side that glints briefly in the light from a nearby window. It's not until he steps forward that I see it's a gun.

My heart leaps into my throat and I quickly turn around, bumping into the old man who is following.

"Earl, my friend," one of the guys singsongs. "You always bring us the best snacks."

I look the man, who I take to be Earl, in the eye. A sly smirk spreads across his face as his laughter echoes off the surrounding buildings. It's a coarse, throaty sound that carries the strong scent of stale beer. His snake-like tongue slips out of his mouth as he curls over in laughter, sloshing some of the liquid from the bottle he's still clutching.

I cringe at the sight, but find the courage to whisper, "Please help me."

"Did you guys hear that," he spits. "She thinks I'm gonna help her."

I swallow hard, turning back around slowly to face my oppressors, knowing pleading with them is my only hope.

"I'll give you whatever you want. Just please don't touch me."

The taller of the two circles around me, his side brushing my body as his eyes drink me up. Then, he approaches Earl, smacks something into his hand, and tells him to scram.

The shorter one bites at the corner of his lip and that's when I notice he's missing one of his front teeth. My stomach twists into tight knots. "Please," I say again, hopeful for even an ounce of humanity in these two.

Suddenly, a hand strikes me across the face so hard that my bag of food goes flying, and I'm forced to the ground. "Help!" I shout, before that same hand slaps to my mouth, stifling my screams. "Don't hurt me," I cry into the damp palm that's trying to silence me.

Pinned with both hands over my head, I squirm and fight, pinching my eyes shut because if I can't see it, it's not really happening. Or at least, that's what I tell myself.

"Hey!" I hear someone shout from the end of the alley. I open my eyes to see a flashlight pointed in our direction, but I can't make out the handler. "Police. What's going on down there?"

By the grace of God, the guys let me go. "You're gonna keep your fucking mouth shut, bitch! And I'm gonna make damn sure of it!"

I feel a boot connect with my jaw, and I taste the warmth of my own blood. A sharp pain sparks through my arms as I'm hit again and again. My stomach twists painfully with every kick and an overwhelming ache settles into my limbs.

The men disappear and I lie there helpless, worthless. Nothing and nobody to everyone, in desperate need of medical attention.

But that attention never comes, and I'm grateful for that. The last thing I need is to be plagued with questions about who I am, or where I'm from. I've done a good job staying away from the law, and I'm not about to give up now.

I push myself off the ground, grunting and groaning with each move I make.

Somehow I manage to stumble out of the alley, my heart pounding and my legs threatening to give out from beneath me. I catch my balance and slam against a red brick wall. Glancing down at my jeans, I see a bright red spot slowly spreading across my crotch. I shakily touch it then raise my fingers. "No!" I cry out as my breath catches in my throat. "Please, God! No!"

I never felt pain like that before. Even losing my mom doesn't touch the unwavering ache in my chest that I carry with me day in and day out from that loss. It's indescribable. But I keep on living. Because that's what I do. I survived that, and I'll survive this.

FIFTEEN

ALARIC

"Fuuuuck!" I growl under my breath as my fist meets the mattress of the bed. I punch it over and over again, alternating fists while releasing as much aggression as I can without making a sound.

She will come around, Alaric. It's only day one. You knew this would be hard at first.

I don't like having to punish Rhea. I especially don't like having to be forceful with her, but it's the only way to show her that I'm the one in control. She needs to understand who is calling the shots here. If I let my guard down for even a minute, she'll think she holds the power and she'll run. Or worse, she will use it against me. There isn't a doubt in my mind.

If she wants to run again, that's fine. But this time, I'll be coming with her; right by her side the whole time to protect her the way she deserves. I'm done playing this idiotic game where I keep her safe from the sidelines and she has no idea who I am or all I do for her.

Pulling myself together, I run my hands down my shirt, take in a deep breath, and exit my bedroom.

I move slowly toward Rhea's door, only stopping once my ear is pressed to it. There's a lot of shuffling going around. There's also the sound of sniffles and moans and it hurts me to know I've made her cry.

I wish I knew what she's thinking. Is she plotting an escape? Or is the reality settling in that she isn't going anywhere?

My only hope is I've instilled enough fear in her to stick around.

Lockhaven is growing on me. I could see us being very happy here for the time being. I'd hate to leave so soon. Not to mention we're safe here, living off the grid without worry of someone finding us.

When the sounds on the other side grow louder—banging, thrashing, and sobbing—I know I need to give her some space.

Returning to the dining room table, I apologize for my swift exit. "I'm sorry for the interruption, I had to take that call."

"Oh, that's okay," Gladys says in her sweet, old voice. "Go ahead and have a seat beside Heather and we can dig into this lovely feast she and I prepared."

I do as I'm told, taking the seat I was instructed to, next to a pale-skinned girl who shivers nervously as I sit down. "Hello," I quip. Unhurriedly, I undo the buttons on the sleeves of my shirt, slowly rolling them just below my elbows. With a crisp snap, I open the neatly folded fabric napkin and spread it across my lap. "This does smell lovely." I wink at Gladys.

She smiles coyly before sticking a wooden spoon into a large stainless-steel bowl of mashed potatoes.

It's been months since I've had a nice home-cooked meal. Following Rhea came with sacrifices, but I'd gladly make them all over again.

Hit with many questions, such as where I'm from, how

long I'll be staying, and where I'm going next, I answer them truthfully. I'll be here as long as it takes and I'm going wherever my future wife wants to go once our time in Lockhaven is done.

Heather, another guest that came in today, was asked the same questions. But her responses were simple nods and shrugs. There's something off with this girl.

We finish eating and I offer to help Gladys clear the table.

"You are the sweetest man to stay here in a while, Alaric. We're happy to have you."

I set a stack of dirty dishes in the sink, then place a calming hand on Gladys's shoulder. "I'm always happy to help. Just holler whenever a hand is needed."

Her smile is soft and sweet and it's proof I've got her right where I want her. Before long, every person in this house, every soul in this town, will be doing my bidding. That power will open the gates for Rhea and me. Before long, she'll see who I am, and she will be begging for a place at my side.

"Do you know many people in Lockhaven?" Gladys asks as she squirts some dish soap onto a rag. There's a dishwasher right beside the sink, but something tells me Gladys is very old school when it comes to washing her dishes.

"Not many," I tell her truthfully. "Rhea and I have bumped into each other a couple times. She seems like a very...sweet girl."

"Oh, she certainly is. And that boy she's been running around with, he's as sweet as sugar."

My eyes narrow, teeth grinding. "Boy?"

"Tyler Jarman," Gladys says as she scrubs at a casserole pan. "Rhea seems quite smitten with him. Can't say I blame her. He reminds me of my late husband, Carlisle."

My nails dig into palms as my fists curl tightly. "Tell me more," I demand, anger bubbling inside me.

She doesn't pick up on any of that, though, as she continues to wash the plates. "There really isn't much to say about them, but I get the feeling she's quite taken by him. Always going next door when he's working. She actually had dinner plans with him tonight." Her gaze shifts to the hallway, following the sound of footsteps, and she taps a sudsy finger to her chin.

"That might be her now. I'm surprised she hasn't left yet."

I walk to the hallway and look left to find the old man from dinner walking into his room. Returning to Gladys, I say, "It wasn't her." These dinner plans she's got are news to me. If Rhea thinks for a second she's going to meet up with this fucking kid tonight, she's sadly mistaken.

"Well, Tyler is a very sweet boy. He grew up on a farm not far from town and has always been a helper to those in need. Much like you, Alaric." Her smile is gentle and soft and I have to remind myself not to hurt the poor old lady just because I don't like her words. Tyler and I are *nothing* alike.

As for Rhea being 'taken by him,' over my dead fucking body. She will not be smitten or taken. The only thing she will ever be, from this point forward, is mine.

The doorbell chimes and Gladys drops a spatula in the sink. "Who could that be at this time?"

It's six o'clock in the evening and she acts like it's the middle of the night with her hurried steps to the door.

After shutting off the water Gladys left running, I walk to the doorway in the kitchen, looking into the living room as she pulls open the door.

"Tyler," Gladys gushes as she strokes her cheek with her wrinkly fingers. "It's so nice to see you again. Are you here for Rhea?"

I size him up, knowing it won't be hard at all to break his

scrawny neck. If he lays a finger on my girl, that's exactly what I'll do.

"I am. She called and said she wasn't feeling well." He holds up a brown paper bag. "So I brought her soup and tea."

My heart pounds fiercely in my chest, eyes nearly bulging out of their sockets. "I'll take that to her," I tell him as I approach him and Gladys. I reach for the bag, but Tyler holds it back.

"I'd actually prefer to give it to her myself, but thank you." He eyes me skeptically, as if I'm just some random man and not Rhea's future husband.

Nostrils flaring, I try to steady the rage brewing inside me. "Fine," I say point-blankly while glowering at our guest. "Gladys," I place a calming hand on her back, "why don't you return to the kitchen and I'll show *Tyler* to Rhea's room? Assuming she wants company."

Gladys nods and steps back. "Come again soon, Tyler. A friend of Rhea's is a friend of ours."

If Gladys and Tyler knew Rhea at all, they'd know she doesn't have friends, nor does she want any. Much like me, Rhea only has relationships that benefit her. This punk-ass farm boy has nothing to offer Rhea; therefore, he's a waste of fucking air.

Walking down the hallway, Tyler follows, and I keep my eyes on Rhea's door. "There's a good chance she's probably sleeping."

"Eh. That's all right. I'd just like to sit with her for a bit. Make sure she's feeling okay."

I spin around, chest inflated. "If she's sleeping, you'll need to leave. There will be no sitting with her. Rhea needs her rest."

He slowly shakes his head, eyes wide in confusion. "I'm

sorry," he says, searching my face for familiarity. "We haven't met before, have we?"

"We have not. I'm new in town."

Chewing on his bottom lip, he continues to gawk. "I swear I've seen you somewhere before."

"I must have one of those faces. I've never seen you a day in my life." It's a lie. I remember Tyler very well. However, it wasn't until now that I put two and two together. I should've guessed when Gladys mentioned they work together, but my mind was elsewhere, and I was in no way trying to figure out who Tyler was. I'm more concerned with how I'm going to keep Rhea away from him.

"And Rhea? Do you know her well?" Tyler asks as he continues to question me like he actually deserves answers.

"I know her well enough. Is that a problem?"

Tyler shakes his head again. "No problem at all. I'm just surprised with you being so protective over her that Rhea's never mentioned you before."

"Rhea prefers to keep her life private." I knock my knuckles to her door while glowering at Tyler. "Rhea, darling. You have company."

A second later, the door opens and there she is. Red, tear-stained eyes, sniffling nose, but still the face of an angel.

"I was telling your friend, Tyler here, that you need your rest." I snatch the bag from his hand before he can dispute it.

Tyler grumbles and rolls his eyes. "How are you feeling?"

Like a deer in the headlights, Rhea's gaze dances from me to Tyler. "I'm...umm. I'm okay."

I smirk mischievously at my girl as I hand her the paper bag. "Why don't you tell Tyler good night so you can rest? You need it if you're going to be well enough to work tomorrow."

She looks at me, puzzled, wondering how I know she has to

work. Soon, she will realize that I know every move she's going to make before she makes it.

"Actually." Rhea straightens her back, mirroring my wide grin. "Would you like to come inside, Tyler? I'd really enjoy the company." She holds up the bag of food. "And this was so sweet of you. I don't know how I'll ever repay you." Her expression drops instantly as she looks at me. "But I have some ideas. I've been known to compensate for kind gestures very well."

If she's insinuating what I think she is...

I can't allow my mind to go there.

"Yeah. Of course," Tyler says, stepping into the doorway. He looks back at me, grinning. *Bastard.*

Jaw ticking, I take a deep breath. "I just remembered," I tap the side of my head like I stupidly forgot, "didn't you tell Gladys you'd help her in the kitchen?"

"She's sick." Tyler scoffs.

Rhea grabs Tyler by the sleeve and pulls him into the room. "Goodbye, Alaric." She slams the door closed and I raise my fist, ready to pound it into the wood frame. But I stop myself because this is nothing. Tyler is just her friend. It's not like she's really gonna have sex with him as a thank-you for fucking soup.

"What's with that guy?" I hear Tyler ask, his voice somewhat muffled by the crumpling sound of the paper bag.

"Ignore him. He's a fucking weirdo."

"No kidding. He acts like he's your dad. It's sorta creepy."

"He's harmless."

Her response brings a smile to my face. I know she's well aware that's not true.

I go to my room, leaving the door wide open, so I'm able to hear when Tyler leaves. Minutes turn into an hour and I've paced from my suite to the hall and back countless times, waiting with anticipation.

Finally, the voices in my head have become too loud and I find myself back at her door, pounding with an iron fist. "Rhea. Open the door."

"Go away, Alaric!"

I lean closer, my lips practically touching the surface as I grit out, "Open the fucking door!"

It flies open and I step back, but when I see Tyler, I stomp past him into Rhea's room. "We need a minute," I tell Tyler with my eyes deadlocked on Rhea's.

"Get the hell out!" Rhea shouts as she points toward the doorway.

The next thing I know, I feel a hand on my shoulder, but I quickly spin around, slapping it down. "Are you fucking touching me?" Tyler's eyes go wide as he withdraws his hand and takes a step back.

What the hell is the matter with kids these days?

Rhea crosses the room and steps between us, arms spread wide. "Alaric, you need to leave."

I take Tyler in, noticing his shoes are now off and his jacket is laying across the end of Rhea's bed. He's made himself much too comfortable here.

"Give me one minute. That's all I ask."

She sighs heavily before looking at Tyler. "Can you just give us one minute?"

"You don't have to listen to him, Rhea. I can go get Gladys."

His words make me laugh out loud, because what the fuck is an eighty-year-old lady going to do? It's comical that he thinks she can remedy this situation when he can't do it himself. Fucking pussy.

"It's fine," Rhea assures him. "It'll only take a minute."

I walk over to the bed and snatch up Tyler's jacket, then

grab his shoes from beside her dresser. I shove them into his chest and walk him out the doorway.

"Like she said, it'll only take a minute." I push him out the door, then slam it closed so hard a painting of a majestic castle rattles against the wall.

When I turn back around, Rhea's palm flies across my face.

"What the hell do you think you're doing?" She pushes two hands into my chest as I cradle the print of her fingers on my cheek. She walks me backward until I'm slammed into her dresser, knocking an empty paper cup to the floor. "This is *my* room! *My* space! You have no right to make *my* friends leave!"

"Friend?" I laugh. "Tyler isn't your friend. I know boys, Rhea. He only wants one thing from you and I can promise you, it's not friendship."

"So what?" She huffs. "Maybe I want the same thing. Maybe." She smirks. "Maybe I've already given it to him."

My muscles quiver, pulse rapid firing. "You're lying."

"Am I?"

In a knee-jerk reaction, I grab her by the throat, demanding the truth. "Don't you dare lie to me! Have you fucked him?"

"Yeah." She drags out the word, grinning maniacally. "Yeah, I fucked him. His dick slid into my pussy with such ease, as if it was molded just for him. Then, as we came together, our cries of ecstasy created a beautiful symphony that I'll never forget."

"You take that back right now or I'll go into that hall and slit that boy's throat. I'm not fucking around, Rhea." I reach into my pocket, keeping my fingers still loosely wrapped around her throat. Pulling my hand out, I show her the pocketknife I'm holding. "I *will* kill him."

Her eyes widen and she gasps as she breaks free from my hold. Walking swiftly to the other side of her bed, her jerky eyes drag from my hand to my face. "Are you insane?"

"I am," I tell her honestly. "And you've got three seconds to tell me the truth about you and Tyler or I'm going to show you just how insane I really am." I flip the knife open, watching as she stumbles backward a few steps.

"Okay." She holds her hands up in surrender. "Okay. I lied. Tyler and I have only kissed and it was just to make some people jealous. That's it."

"Good." I close the knife and stick it back in my front pocket. "Let's keep it that way."

I eat up the space between us. "Go out there and tell him good night." My hands drag down her shivering arms. "Then I'll give you real sounds of ecstasy instead of the fake ones you speak of."

"No." She shakes her head. "Fuck no. I don't want to be anywhere near you. But I do want my damn purse back."

Ignoring her request for her purse, which I do have, I say, "That's a shame because I'm not going anywhere. Now go tell your *friend* good night, or I'll be forced to tell him who Rhea Brooks really is."

"Alaric." Her voice cracks. "Please don't do this."

"Trust me, Rhea. It's for Tyler's own good. If you care about him at all, you'll stay far away from him, and any other guys for that matter."

She swallows hard before lifting her eyes to mine. "This won't last. Eventually, I will free myself from the hold you have over me. No one tries to control me and gets away with it." Her defiant eyes remind me I have limited time to make this plan work. If I can't convince her that she was made for me soon, she will find a way to run.

Walking past me, she goes to the door and pulls it open. Once it's closed behind her, I take a seat on her bed and smile, pleased with myself. "I've been controlling your movements for a while now; you just didn't know it then."

SIXTEEN

RHEA

AFTER A LOT of convincing that Alaric wasn't a threat, Tyler left. I lied and told him I was tired and planned to go to sleep. I also kicked Alaric out of my room—literally. I had to force him out using all my strength. In the end, he blew me a kiss as I shoved the door closed in his face.

I didn't sleep well. I'm almost positive he sat outside my door all night. I could see his shadow and hear the sounds of him walking. Then, it would grow silent, and there would be a pressure against my door, making it look like it was about to cave in on itself, which led me to believe he was leaning against it.

To say I'm freaked out is an understatement. I've been trying to reach Dex, but I get no answer. I've left him a dozen whispered messages because I knew Alaric was listening. I'm starting to get worried that something's wrong with him. It's not like him to ignore my calls.

Regardless of what's going on with Alaric, I still have to go to work today. It's not fair to Taryn if I call in, and I can't hide away forever. Or at all, for that matter. Besides, I said I wouldn't let him control me. I can't let him win.

Instead, I'm going to face this shithead head-on and bide my time until Dex tells me where the hell I should go next. The idea of fleeing this town hurts more than it should. When I do leave, I can never be myself again. I'll forever live in hiding because I have no doubt Alaric will never stop trying to find me. With the money and resources he must have, I'm scared running might not even be enough at this point.

I grab my apron off my dresser and freeze when I see my purse lying beside it. Taking a step back, I pick it up while pinching the zipper with the tips of my fingers, inspecting it like it's coated in fentanyl.

This wasn't here last night when I laid down, and my door was locked all night. So how the hell did Alaric get into my room to leave it on my dresser?

Does he have a key to my room? Of course he does! Son of a bitch!

I quickly unzip my purse and shuffle around the few items inside. Not the least bit surprised, my keys are gone. There were only two—one for the front door and one for my room. I've been leaving my room door unlocked the last couple days, and I've been fortunate enough to not need it to get into the house itself by making sure to come and go when Gladys is knitting.

That asshole! Now I'm going to have to ask Gladys to change the lock on my door.

With my purse and apron in hand, I storm out of my room, smacking face first into, none other than, Alaric.

"Good morning, beautiful."

"Move it, Jerkface! I need to go to work."

"No 'thank you' for returning your purse?" he coos, as if I should be bowing at his feet for returning something he took.

"You stole my purse. Then you stole my damn keys. Then you broke into my room last night. I'm not thanking you for shit."

"Actually," he begins, pointing a finger in the air like some sort of pompous asshole. "You left your purse in my car. My car that you willingly got into. Anything after that was your fault."

"My fault?" I wheeze. "My fucking fault? You drugged me!"

He shrugs his shoulders causally. "You shouldn't have gotten in a car with a stranger. Let it be a lesson."

"The only lesson I'm learning in all of this is self-restraint."

"Why's that?" He slithers up to me, his side brushing against mine as I try to leave for work. "Is the temptation as real for you as it is for me?"

I scoff, lip curled in disgust. "If by temptation you mean the urge to murder you, then yes."

"That's not very nice, Rhea. After everything I've done for you, you should show a little more gratitude."

"What the hell have you possibly done for me?"

"Easy. I've saved you, and I continue to save you each day." He stops, folding his hands behind his back.

"You really are delusional, aren't you?" I walk around him, thankful that he isn't grabbing me or trying to cage me in again.

"I see quite clearly, actually. And when I'm with you, I like what I see."

Gagging, I keep walking, putting as much space as I can between us. Except Alaric doesn't know the concept of personal space and he seems to insist on following me—down the hall, out the door, and right into Taryn's.

"I have to work, Alaric. Will you please just go?"

"How can I keep you safe if I'm not around?" The surety in his voice is unnerving. For some reason, I think this guy really thinks he is helping me.

I clock in and go about my day, pretending he's not there while he just stares. Waiting, watching, observing my every move.

Taryn forces me to wait on his table, and I'm shocked when he leaves me a one-hundred-dollar bill for a tip. However, the note he left I could go without...

You will never want for anything else in this life as long as we're together.

I crumple up the paper and make sure he's watching as I throw it in the trash. Then, I flip him my middle finger.

With a book open in his palm, he shakes his head, grinning as he crosses his legs and sinks into the chair. I have to force myself not to stare at him.

It's just my luck that the psychopath harassing me looks like a fucking Adonis. Why couldn't he be repulsive? Instead, he's probably the most attractive man I've ever crossed paths with. One I would one hundred percent give the time of day— if he wasn't such a whacko.

In fact, I did give him the time of day. I did everything in my power without throwing myself into his lap the other night. But look where it got me. I gained myself a stalker, who just so happens to be a gorgeous sociopath who loves to read.

Customers come and go, making the day go by quickly. I move from one table to the next, and I couldn't be happier that we're actually busy this morning. Not only am I making a good amount of tips, it's also a distraction from Alaric, who's still here—four hours into my shift.

When he closes his book and sets it on the table, my heart jumps into my throat. Maybe he's *finally* leaving. I stop punching an order into the computer at the waitress station and watch him over the top of the screen. His chair slides back, his eyes gander around the room, and he stands.

Yes. Go. Leave me alone!

With his book down and his iced tea still half full, he walks around the table and my pulse pounds with anticipation. Hopefully he's realizing I'm not as exciting as he wants me to be and he's giving up.

Not even giving me a slow sweep, he walks past all the tables to the back of the room.

I step out from the waitress station, not taking my eyes off him. But when he pushes open the door to the men's bathroom, my shoulders slump in defeat.

He just had to take a piss. Guess four glasses of iced tea will do that to ya.

A minute later, I'm carrying a tray of hot food from the kitchen and I see him emerge from the bathroom.

With my palm in the air and the tray resting on top, I head for the table. But Alaric wants to be a smart-ass and he stops right in my path.

"Excuse you." I go to walk around him, but he sidesteps, blocking my way. "Would you move?"

"Have dinner with me tonight." The casualty in his tone makes me laugh internally. It's as if he really thinks I'm going to say yes.

My lip curls in disgust as I steady the tray on my hand. "Fuck off." I walk around him again, and once again, he steps in my way. "Move, Alaric!"

"Not until you agree."

"Move now or I'll shove this entire tray of food in your face."

He snickers. "You wouldn't dare."

"Bet."

"It's just dinner. One hour, tops. There are some things we need to discuss."

"The only thing we need to discuss is your lack of boundaries."

"Fine." He shrugs his shoulders. "We can discuss boundaries. I think that's a great idea."

"Now, will you move?" I two-step again, and finally he moves out of my way. He's sadly mistaken if he thought that meant I was agreeing to dinner with him.

With a wave of his hand, he clears a path. As I walk past him, I'm so damn tempted to fling one of these sizzling pieces of bacon at his face. But that would not only upset my customers, but would be a waste of perfectly good bacon.

Tray still in hand, I unload at the small round table where Mr. And Mrs. Hargrove are seated. As usual, they ordered the exact same meal with a glass of ice water for Mrs. Hargrove.

"Thank you so much, Rhea," Mrs. Hargrove says, her voice as sweet as honey.

"You're very welcome. Can I get you two anything else?"

"This will do, dear," Mr. Hargrove responds.

As I'm walking back to the waitress station, awaiting more customers, the door chimes and a group of younger guys come in—probably high school aged. There's three of them, all loud and boisterous.

Taryn seats them and comes over to where I'm standing. "You want them?" she asks with a click of her tongue and a nod in their direction.

"I could use the tips."

"Good luck with that." She shields her mouth and leans in to whisper, "Those assholes don't tip for shit."

I raise my eyebrows and roll my lips before patting her on the shoulder. "In that case, they're all yours."

"Nah," she drawls. "I'm going on break, hun. Be back in fifteen."

"Jerk," I mutter under my breath.

Dragging my feet, I approach the table of guys. Notepad out and pen pressed to it, I prepare to deal with even more bullshit in my day. "How are you guys doing today?"

"Pitcher of Diet Coke and three glasses," one of the guys, wearing a Lockhaven letter jacket, barks without lifting his eyes from the menu.

"Okay, then," I say, not bothering to write it down.

This should be fun.

I grab their drink order and return to the table. Their laughter halts when I approach and pinch my eyebrows, wondering what's so funny.

Setting a sweating glass full of ice in front of each of them, I can feel the tension like a thick blanket. I could be nosey and ask, but I probably don't wanna know anyways. Instead, I force a fake smile on my face and do my job. "Do you need a few minutes, or are you ready to order?"

Out of nowhere, the one in the letter jacket sputters out a laugh before breaking into full-blown hysterics. One of his friends, a scrawny guy, with blond—nearly white—hair follows suit and is now laughing his ass off too.

I look from one guy to the next, confused as hell as to what's going on. "Am I missing something?"

"Tell her, man." Unable to refrain from laughing, the letter jacket guy drops his head into his folded arms on the table.

"You fucking tell her," the blond guy says.

"Come on, guys. Knock it off," the final guy says, shaking his head in embarrassment of his friends. I take him to be the mature one of the trio.

Letter Jacket Guy lifts his head, letting out a small snort with his lips pressed together. It's obvious he's struggling not to laugh again. "Uh." He averts his gaze. "You've got blood on the back of your pants. Might wanna go check that out."

The color drains from my face, my body frozen in shock. A jolt of adrenaline floods through my veins as I make a beeline for the bathroom.

Once I'm in the bathroom, I know I don't have long before the panic attack sets in. I go into a stall and close the door before falling to pieces on the dirty, cold floor.

Three Years Ago

The weight of the world presses heavily on my chest, suffocating me from the inside out. Like a thick fog that refuses to lift. If there was ever a time to call it quits on this life, it would be now, because this life is ready to quit on me.

My soul has turned to ash, and the only thoughts that now circle through my mind are morbid ones. Each day I tell myself I'm going to try harder, but how can I when each day is harder than the last?

This life is unfair.

This life hurts.

I'd love nothing more than to die and be born again. But chances are, I'd fuck that up too.

Laughter fills the streets of the city. Couples holding hands. Families taking pictures together.

And here I am...

My body aches and my eyes burn with hot tears.

My shoes are barely on my feet. The soles peeled off, leaving me with just a sliver of rubber. Every step feels like I'm walking on the cold hard concrete.

My pants are stained with a rusty hue of blood. The kind woman at Planned Parenthood said I was likely early on in my pregnancy—six weeks at most. She offered me a fresh pair of pants but I couldn't bring myself to take them. I did this. It's all my fault. I should have to live with the memory of what I did. I break things.

It's only been twelve hours since those men attacked me, but something in my brain seems to have shifted. In less than a day I went from wanting to do everything I could to survive and protect my baby, to this. Hollow and worthless.

I didn't tell Dex about the baby, and I don't plan to tell him, or anyone for that matter. It's so shameful and humiliating that I couldn't even protect a life growing inside me.

I scratch at my head, feeling tiny particles of rock against my scalp. My hair is caked in debris and dust from the construction going on near the bench where I fell asleep last night.

The roar of my stomach is a reminder that I haven't eaten since yesterday morning. I went out and got food, ready to feed myself and give my baby some nutrients. Only, my food was trashed, and my baby...is gone.

Why is everyone I love always taken from me?

Am I being punished?

My back slides down the wall, feeling the roughness of the brick against my spine. Sitting on the cold, damp ground, I hunch over and let the tears silently stream down my face.

"I miss you so much, Mama." I cry into my chest. "I need you."

I'm not sure how much time has passed when my head shoots up at the sound of something being thrown my way. I blink in shock as a greasy, half-eaten chicken leg smacks against my knee. It drops to the ground and I look at it, noticing there is still some meat on the bone. I'm about to reach for it when a heavy boot stomps down on it, crushing it into the ground. The man scoffs as he shakes the leftovers off his boot, sending them to the curb.

I look up and my gaze is caught with sneers and laughter from a group of teenagers passing by. Every few steps, they turn and whisper. They probably threw it at me just to be cruel.

I swallow down the urge to chase after them and shove them into oncoming traffic.

What's the point?

There will be another who'll throw something at me, laugh at my misfortunes, pity my life. I can't fight them all, especially when I can barely muster the strength to get off the ground.

So I stay. Minutes. Hours. An entire day.

The sun sets, and I'm still here. Three bucks richer because a lady felt sorry for me. At least I'll be able to buy a cheap meal, possibly my last. I still haven't decided yet.

These are the constant battles in my head lately. To live, or to die?

It's crazy how quickly things can change. Yesterday I felt alive, even if morning sickness was kicking my ass. I had something to live for.

Today, I don't want to feel at all. So, I do what I do best.

"Hey," I holler, grabbing the attention of a couple guys walking by. I've seen 'em around and know what their business is on this street.

The taller, slender one wearing a bomber jacket stops. His hand on his chest. "You talking to me?"

"Yeah, you." I curl my fingers, calling him over. "Come here."

The two guys share a look then backtrack to me. "What do you want"?" the shorter of the duo says in an annoyed manner. As if I'm wasting their time.

"I need something from the two of you."

Their eyes perk up, another quick glance between the two of them. Then they crouch down to where I'm sitting.

"What exactly are you looking for?"

I shrug my shoulders, unsure really. "Make me forget."

It's as simple as that. It's all I really want.

The taller of the two laughs. "That's quite a stretch. How forgetful are we talking here?"

With no fight left in me, I sulk. "Just make me fucking forget it all."

"Come with us."

Already feeling numb to the world, I push myself off the ground and follow the guys into an alley two blocks down.

Casting a suspicious glance up and down the alley, the guy then turns to face me. "How much do you got?"

Biting the corner of my lip, I bat my lashes. "How much do you want?" My hand runs down my dirty shirt and over my puckered nipples.

"Girl," he sweeps his hand in the air, "get the fuck outta here. You're broke as shit."

They begin to walk away, but desperation seeps in and I grab the shorter guy by the sleeve of his jacket because he's within reach. "Wait. Please."

"Word of advice," the guy's eyes slide up from my hold on him to my eyes, "find a different outlet. You don't want the high you think you do. It's not worth it."

Tears prick the corners of my eyes. "It's just for today."

"And what happens tomorrow?"

"I fight like hell to survive another day."

The shorter guy blows out a whistle at his friend, who's still walking away. His friend pivots around and heads back toward us.

They share some unspoken words as the guy I'm holding tips his chin.

Tall Guy pulls at the lapels of his jacket, then unzips it with a heavy sigh. "Sit down," he demands of me.

I gulp, then do as I'm told, right in the middle of the alley.

"Not there." He growls. "Against the wall. You're gonna need the support after this."

He pulls a pre-filled syringe and tourniquet out of his pocket, and I don't even question what's in the syringe, because I don't care.

When he kneels down, he looks me right in the eyes. "This is a one-time favor for a girl who needs a wake-up call. This isn't an invitation into a life of addiction. Today sucks. But tomorrow is a new day." He pulls up my sleeve, ties the tourniquet around my arm, and taps his finger to the syringe. After carefully selecting a vein, he threads the needle into my arm. Before I can back out or even register the choice I'm making, he pushes the plunger.

I'm not sure where they went. When they left. Where I'm even at.

I don't know anything, and I finally care about nothing.

This is what my life has become.

Mom would be so disappointed.

I laugh out loud as tears continue to ride down my cheeks.

No wonder I'm all alone. I wouldn't want to be near me either. I'm a conniving, ruthless, manipulative whore. The only blessing I can accept at this moment is that I didn't have to suck two dicks to get high. Seems there's some kindness left in the world, after all.

My limp body is lifted away and I'm patiently waiting to see the angels—to see my mom.

Did I make it to heaven? Or will I burn in hell?

As long as I'm out of the life I was living, I'll take either.

My heart begins to beat slower and slower, its rhythm lulling me. I'm ready to accept whatever fate awaits me.

Wherever I am, it's warm—comfortable, cozy. It smells sweet like pumpkin pie. Just like the one Mom cooked in a vacant house we broke into for Thanksgiving when I was seven.

"Mom," I mutter, feeling a scratch in my throat. "Are you here?"

"Shhh," I hear. But it's not Mom's voice.

My eyes flutter open and I see a shadowy figure standing over me. Everything is so hazy. I see his form, but I can't see his face.

It's not until I blink away the grogginess that I'm able to see he's wearing a mask, one you'd see a doctor or a nurse wearing. He's got a baseball cap on and a sweatshirt. I look down at his hand that's resting gently on my shoulder. His nails are clean and he smells really fucking good. Not like pumpkin pie, but like sage and spice— an expensive cologne.

"Who are you?" I gasp, heart pounding.

"It's okay. You're safe."

161

"Are you...an angel?"

"Oh no." He chuckles dryly. "I'm far from good. But, I'm not here to hurt you. I'm here to help you."

No one has ever wanted to help me before. It's only natural that I struggle to trust his words. Everyone always has an agenda.

"Where am I?" I choke out. "Am I dead?" I go to sit up, but he pushes me back down.

"No. You're very much alive. Thank God. I found you in an alley. You were blue in the lips, barely breathing."

"Why?" I shout, a lump lodged in my throat. "Why didn't you leave me?"

"It was below freezing. I saved you." His brows pinch in confusion.

"I didn't want to be saved. You wasted your time." I turn to my side, unable to look at the man who stole my chance at escaping this world. "You should have left me there." I close my eyes, hoping that maybe I won't ever have to open them again.

When I do, he's gone.

I wake back up to an empty hotel room with nothing but a note.

The room is yours for the week. There's an envelope of money for you on the night-stand, and some new clothes in the bath-room. Use room service at your discretion. The pain you've endured does not go unnoticed. One day your struggles will be worth it. You'll see.

A spark of light was rekindled inside me that day. That man denied being an angel, but he sure as hell felt like one.

If only that flame still burned. As I sit on this bathroom floor, still alone and curled into a ball as panic seizes my chest, I can't help but wonder if it ever truly will all be worth it.

CHAPTER

SEVENTEEN

ALARIC

TEETH GRINDING AND CHEST HEAVING, my palms slam to the table, rattling the glasses filled with cola and ice. "Do we have a problem over here, boys?"

Three pairs of eyes shoot to me. One scoffs, the other laughs, because that's what he likes to do apparently. And the third, well, he just stares down with trembling hands gripping the page of a menu.

"Dude," says the one wearing a high school football jacket, "do we know you?"

"Not yet. But you're about to."

"Get lost," his loudmouth friend sneers as he reaches for his drink.

I intercept it, snatching the glass up and squeezing it in my hard so hard, I'm surprised it hasn't shattered yet. My knuckles turn white and the veins in my arms bulge. "I see we've got some comedians over here. You think it's fun to humiliate girls? Make them upset? Make them cry?"

"It was pretty fucking funny to us," the one in the jacket

says, shrugging as if he didn't just hurt the one person on this planet I would kill for.

I slam the glass down on the table, the liquid sloshing over the top. My fingers like claws, I grab the asshole by the throat, cutting off his air supply.

I'm well aware that I'm drawing the attention of the other guests, but I do not fucking care. My goal is to make them see me, admire me. Well, they should admire me for taking out the trash for free. "When she comes out of the bathroom—if she comes out—you're gonna apologize to her. Then, you're gonna get the fuck out of this tavern and never step foot in it again. Do I make myself clear?"

Suddenly, it's not so funny to him anymore as he nods what little I allow him to under my grip. His Adam's apple bobs against my fingers as he gulps.

The others just sit there, knowing it would be a bad move to try and defend their friend's honor.

I give his head a swift shove and drop my hold on him. "If I ever see any of you three assholes speak to that girl again," I lean close, my voice a whisper, "I'll slit all your goddamn throats."

Three pair of eyes widen in shock, and I'm certain the threat has dissolved. But when I turn to walk away and I hear the chuckle of laughter coming from the one I had in a choke-hold, I'm even more certain that he hasn't learned his lesson. He will, though. In due time, he'll pay for hurting my girl.

My adrenaline is pumping fiercely as I walk to the bathrooms. An elderly couple flinches as I pass by them, but I force a smile on my face, trying to alleviate the intense situation. "Good afternoon," I say with a gentle nod.

They don't respond. Not that I expected them to. I'll have to work to earn back the favor of the people currently in here.

Bypassing the men's restroom, I go straight for the ladies'.

Fist balled, I knock on the door. When it doesn't open, and no one responds, I crack it open.

"Rhea, I'm coming in."

"Go away!" she sniffles, and it's a sound that breaks my heart. She's in pain. Rightfully so. Those guys were complete assholes to her.

Ignoring the desperation in her voice telling me to leave, I push the door open farther and step inside. It's a shared bathroom with three stalls, but the main door has a lock, so I click it to give us some privacy.

Crouching over, I find her in the middle stall sitting on the floor with her legs bent. I drop down with my back to the door. "You okay?" I ask, genuinely concerned for her mental state.

"Like you care. Just go, Alaric!"

"I care more than you will ever know. If I could absorb all the pain they made you feel, I would do it in a heartbeat."

"You don't even know me!"

"I know you more than I know myself, Rhea. I've watched you and waited for you. And the first time you saw me, I knew it was all worth it. I saw the look in your eyes that first day. You were as mesmerized by me as I was by you."

"Yeah," she grunts. "Until you showed me your true colors."

"But aren't we all an assortment of colors and moods and personalities? Wouldn't it be boring if we were only one shade?"

The next thing I know, the stall door is being pulled open and I'm toppling backward into Rhea's legs. She pushes me with her shoe, trying to get me away from her. "Move, nutcase!" She steps around me and leaves the stall. "I can't believe you came in here. You really are a psycho."

I push myself off the floor and onto my feet, then stand behind her as she washes her hands. Looking down, I see the spot of blood. I begin unbuttoning my shirt, watching her reflection in the mirror.

"What are you doing?" she asks skeptically while her eyes stay fixated on me.

I don't respond. Instead, I finish undoing the last button and slide my arms out, leaving me in only a white tee shirt.

Rhea goes to turn around, but I put a hand on her shoulder. "Stay still."

"What the hell are you doing? Don't touch me!" She tries to shove me away, but it's weak.

I shake my head at her armored behavior before wrapping the sleeves of my shirt around her waist. I tie them in a knot in front of her, tugging tightly to keep it in place.

"Why are you doing that?"

"Because you've bled through your pants."

"Ugh," she grumbles under her breath, but I hear her very clearly. "I hope that fuckwad dies a slow and painful death." Her voice rises as she appears to shake away the thought. "You're something else."

"Why? Because I'm tying my shirt around the waist of the girl I love to hide that she's got her period unexpectedly?"

"Yes!" She huffs. "That and the fact that you think you love me. Add to it that you haven't taken your eyes off me during my entire shift. All of it. Yes! You're fucking blackmailing me. You've staked some sort of sick claim on me and I don't even know you."

"Give it some time, baby." I rest my chin on her shoulder, inhaling her scent. It's a mixture of her and the greasy food in the tavern, but it's still her nonetheless. "Before long, we're going to know each other very well."

She jolts to the left and I straighten my back, her aroma still floating in the air around me.

"It's obvious you know nothing about me because if you

did, you'd know that I can disappear in the blink of an eye. I have the ability to be anyone I want to be."

"I won't deny you're very good at running away. However, your hiding skills could use some work. If you were as good as you think you are, I wouldn't be here right now."

She quirks a brow. "Are you saying you followed me to Lockhaven?"

"As I've said before, this wasn't a chance encounter, Rhea."

Mouth dropped open, she takes a step back. "It was you." Her voice shakes and cracks. "You're the man in the black car." Her hands fly to the sides of her head and she grips her hair, pulling strands from her ponytail. "How did I not see this? Why didn't I put two and two together?"

"You're a smart girl. I knew it would all click eventually."

A terrified look crosses her features as she takes another step back. "But why? Did my father send you?""

"As I'm sure you already know, your father is dead, Rhea."

"I know he's dead, which makes this all the more unbelievable. What do you want from me? Are you..." She blinks rapidly, collecting her thoughts. "Are you the man I'm supposed to marry?"

She begins pacing erratically, fisting her hair. I grab her by the shoulders and hold her in place. "I wasn't sent by your father. If anything, I've been keeping you safe from the men who were. I'm only here because I love you."

"Love?" She chuckles dryly. "You don't know me enough to love me."

"Rhea, baby. I loved you at first sight and every sight since then. I don't have to know everything about you to know that I want to know everything about you. I want to know what makes you smile. What makes you laugh. What makes you cry. I want you to tell me about every person you've encountered who has done you wrong, so I can make them pay. I want you. All of you. Forever."

Her eyes widen, neck craned back as her head shakes in slow and subtle movements. "You don't know what love is." Her words are a whisper, but ones I hear, and feel, deep inside my soul. "You're not in love, Alaric. You're obsessed. Those are very different things."

Stepping closer, I refrain from touching her because I know she'll only move away. "I know what love is because of you. It's the very emotion we fight to avoid, but also the one that heals the darkest parts of ourselves. You healed me, Rhea. And I'm going to return the favor."

I notice her hands resting over her stomach. With her chin down, she closes her eyes momentarily. "I never want to feel an emotion so strong again. So if you think you're going to make me love you, you're wrong. I'm no longer capable." She lifts her sad eyes to the mirror, looking into mine. "Run while you still can. Before your heart is too invested in someone who can't even take care of her own."

My eyes slide to her hands again, cradling her stomach as memories infiltrate her mind. Memories I know to be some of the most painful she holds. "If my heart breaks, I'll gladly use the pieces to mend yours. I know I haven't always gotten to you in time, Rhea." I move my hand over hers and I'm surprised when she lets me. I need her to know the truth, to see it for herself. "But I've always been there. I won't make the mistake of getting to you too late ever again."

Her eyes hold me in place as she tries to make sense of my words. Her gaze carries a warmth that rekindles a flame deep within me. One that I felt was slowly sizzling out as hope for a future with Rhea began to seem so bleak. I knew this wouldn't be easy, but I never anticipated it would be so hard. The look she's giving me now reassures me that everything I've done, and continue to do, is worthwhile. For the briefest of moments, I feel seen by her.

She takes a step back and I allow her that space. "I...I have to go home and change."

Stumbling over her feet, she goes to the door and attempts to rip it open, only to be halted by the lock. With a trembling hand, she clicks the latch and yanks the door with so much force, I'm surprised it's still on its hinges. When I step out behind her, I watch as she leaves—wearing my shirt around her waist. Fuck if that image will not be etched in my memory for an eternity.

CHAPTER
EIGHTEEN
RHEA

I NEVER WENT BACK to work. After I got back to my room, the panic flared again, and with it came a whole new set of emotions I wasn't prepared for. I called and told Taryn I still wasn't feeling well, so I'm currently sitting in a hot bath while Alaric waits outside the bathroom door because, apparently, that's what sociopaths do. He hasn't said anything, but much like last night when I slept, I know he's out there.

Taryn was super understanding about the situation and said I could make up the hours Saturday night. I was pretty ecstatic because weekend nights are where the money's at. Before we hung up the phone, she asked me about Alaric and I was honest in telling her that I don't know anything about him and he's just some guy staying here at Gladys's.

She also mentioned that if he pulls a stunt like he did earlier, he's not welcome at the tavern anymore. I had no idea what he did until she told me about it and I have even more conflicting feelings where he's involved. On one hand, he's insane. But on the other hand, he swore he would protect me, and he kept that promise. Even if it was just from getting my feelings hurt. Which is more than I can say for any guy I've ever known.

I sigh heavily, sinking deeper into the water. I'm almost hoping he does something like that again so I can work without constantly being watched. Except, he's Alaric, I'm sure he'd find a way to keep his eyes on me. And for some insane reason, I think I like knowing I have a bodyguard out there.

Ever since he alluded to being the guy in the black car who was following me, I can't help but feel this strange connection to him. It's crazy. I know. He's obsessed with me. Not to mention he's got some serious sociopathic tendencies. But he's been on this ride with me for a while now and he's still here.

Over the months, before coming to Lockhaven, there were times when I would feel lost or alone and I'd look out a window and see that car. In some strange way, it made me feel less forsaken. Like I was actually in someone's thoughts, or maybe even worthy of being cared about. I can't begin to understand my thought process because I'm not normal either. I guess Alaric and I do have that in common.

My eyes catch his white shirt lying on the floor and I stretch my arm out of the bathtub to grab it. Maybe I'm insane too, because I haven't left his shirt out of my sight since yesterday. Having it makes me feel the same comfort I felt when I would see that black car.

Balling it up in my hand, I take care not to let it dip in the water. Slowly, I bring it to my nose and inhale deeply. Of course he'd smell like a fucking dream.

Gorgeous. Rich. Built like a god. Smells good. Have I mentioned his body?

He's got all the qualities I would quite literally kill for in a man. But he's also got all the ones I don't want.

He's depraved. Then again, so am I.

He's violent when he doesn't get his way. Kinda like me, although I'd say I'm more manipulative.

He's overprotective. Which is actually sort of flattering.

No! What the hell am I doing?

Am I actually making excuses for this man? He drugged me. He's been stalking me. Not only that, he's threatened me.

You scream, I'll tell everyone in this house who you really are— a lying thief. You try to run, I'll follow you. If you so much as open that pretty mouth and mention a single word of this, I will take you somewhere no one will ever find you.

Those were his words right before he pulled out a knife and threatened to kill Tyler. He's unhinged. I've crossed paths with many different personalities, but Alaric's is by far the most unsound.

My phone beeps from on top of the toilet lid, and I jump so hard, Alaric's shirt tumbles out of my hands and into the bathtub.

"Goddammit!" I curse, quickly fishing it out and wringing out as much water as I can before flopping it onto the bathroom rug.

Sitting up, I stretch my neck to try and look at my phone to see what the notification was. God, I hope it's Dex. I'm really starting to worry about him. I hope he didn't go and do something stupid that got him locked up, or killed even. Dex does dealings with some shady-ass people, so there's no telling why he's ghosting me.

Not wanting my phone to have the same fate as Alaric's shirt, I lean out of the tub and swipe the screen to find that it wasn't a call or text from Dex, it's a text from Tyler.

> Tyler: Just checking in to see how you're feeling. Taryn said you left work early because you still weren't feeling well.

If only that were true. I wish I came home because of some virus that I could actually get over. Instead, I'm here because of sheer humiliation.

I still can't believe that fuckwad jock at Taryn's. I sincerely feel bad for the woman he marries one day. Instead of being a man and pulling me aside, he made a mockery of me just to get a few laughs from his friend. I say friend because the other one wasn't laughing at all.

Still leaning over the edge of the tub, I type out a quick response to Tyler.

> Me: I'm feeling a lot better. Thank you for asking.

> Tyler: Glad to hear that. Let me know when you'd like to reschedule our dinner plans. Was looking forward to hanging out.

My fingers tremble as I type out a lie. I don't want to lead him on, but I don't want to hurt him either. The truth is, I'm not sure I will reschedule my date with Tyler. Alaric's threat rings in my ears and fear of what he'd do to Tyler clenches at my gut.

But that's not the only reason—I'm also hopeful Dex will respond soon and I can leave this town. Not because I want to, but because I have to get away from Alaric. And Tyler. He's too good for me and the drama that comes with my life.

> Me: I'll definitely let you know. And I'm sorry, again, that I had to cancel.

> Tyler: No worries. Shit happens.

I leave our conversation on that note, and when I swipe out of our text exchange, I see a notification from the Siren's Call app. Considering I've disabled alerts for prospective clients, I know it's a message, and I know exactly who it's from—the only person I talk to on the app.

Sinking back in the tub, I cautiously hold my phone in the air above the water. A smile spreads across my face as I read the kind words sent early this morning from the friend I've never met.

> HawkEye: I've been slacking with daily reminders, but here is one for today: Your strength is untouchable, and your beauty can be seen by the blind.

I'm not sure who this guy is, but no one has ever said such romantic words to me before. If his goal is to really just make me smile and feel better about life, it's working.

> Wildcat: You always say the right things at the right time. Thank you for that.

Considering he sent the message this morning, I'm surprised when his response is immediate.

> HawkEye: I'm only speaking the truth. How are you doing? Have you settled into your new home?

> Wildcat: Barely. But I don't want to burden you with my misfortunes. How are you?

> HawkEye: I'm doing well. Also just moved. I'm finding the new town to be...inviting. But, please. Talk to me about what's going on. Everyone needs someone to vent to. Who better than a complete stranger? LOL

The fact that he used the abbreviation LOL makes me feel so much more at ease. It's proof that he's not a total robot and there is a human behind these messages. Sometimes it's hard to tell if I'm just talking to a horny old man or, worse, a teenager. Which he very well could be.

I don't know HawkEye, and as far as I know, he's never been a client of mine. But there's no harm in talking if it makes me feel better. He's right when he said everyone needs someone to vent to. I've never had that someone, until now.

So I let it all out in one very detailed message...

> Wildcat: Life is just really hard. Then again, I don't remember a time when it was easy. I want nothing more than to leave the past behind me and start a new life as someone worthy of actually living. I moved to this town hoping it would be the place to do just that. But my past followed me here in the form of an obsessed man who is threatening and stalking me. I've finally made a friend, and this psycho has basically forbidden me to see him. He says if I leave, he'll find me. But I have to at least try to get away from him. Right? I can't just roll over and let him win. Even if that means I'll live in fear of him showing up everywhere I go.

After I hit send, I set the phone back on the lid of the toilet because I need a second to clear my head. I can't believe I just told him all that. I've never opened up to anyone about anything in my life. Especially nothing that *real*.

My heart is pounding with nervousness as I contemplate what his response will be. Does he think I want pity? That's the furthest thing from the truth. Will he think I'm asking him for help? That's not the case either.

I don't know why I told him what's going on. As I sit here, soaking in the water that's turned cold, I wish like hell I could take it back.

My phone beeps and I jolt with anticipation. Staring at my device for a minute, I finally decide to get out of the bathtub so

I don't drown myself out of sheer disgrace. This sort of stuff doesn't happen to normal people.

Stepping one foot out on the plush bath mat, then the other, I grab a towel off the rack behind the toilet and wrap it around my body, tucking in the corner to hold it in place. With my head held back, I wring the excess water from my hair then roll it up and secure it with a clip. I take my time, scared with every move I make that when I look at that message, another person in my life will disappoint me.

Then, after one deep breath, I pick up my phone.

> HawkEye: Have you ever considered the possibility that running away will only make matters worse? Maybe it's time to stop running and face your troubles head-on. You might be surprised to find that life is more peaceful when you don't leave behind unfinished business.

I'm not sure why his message irritates me the way it does. It's not insensitive, but it is at the same time.

> Wildcat: Are you saying I should stay and allow this man to dictate my life?

> HawkEye: Is that truly what he's doing, or is he trying to protect you from something that is out of your control? Maybe you should try asking him before jumping to conclusions, and/or running.

> Wildcat: I can't believe you're siding with this psycho!

Before I can rethink my response, I hit send, immediately wishing I could take it back. I really need to stop making rash decisions.

HawkEye: Don't get upset. I'm always on your side. How about we talk about something else to get your mind off all the stress around you? Tell me one attainable thing you want right now.

Wildcat: That's a loaded question. It's impossible to narrow it down to one thing. I'd love to get an education of some sort. Even if it's just my GED to start with.

HawkEye: I like that. I think you should do it.

Wildcat: That would require settling down in one spot with absolutely no chance of running.

HawkEye: And where you're at is definitely not that spot?

I sit down on the bathroom floor, still wrapped in a towel. I'm feeling good about the direction our conversation is heading. I don't dream often because everything I want seems so far out of reach. But maybe this one thing isn't as far out of reach as I think.

Wildcat: I thought it was. I suppose it still could be.

HawkEye: There's the strong girl I've come to know. Don't let one mishap scare you off. You're a fighter. Keep on fighting.

Wildcat: You're right. Maybe I will. Now, it's your turn. What is one attainable thing you want right now?

When his response doesn't come right away, I get impatient and swipe out of the conversation to check my text messages and calls to see if I missed anything from Dex. I'm not surprised to see there's nothing. My gut wretches at the thought of what could be going on. This isn't like him at all. I don't know much about Dex; therefore, I don't know who I could even call to go check on him. But I feel like it's getting to that point.

A notification from the Siren's Call app pings, so I go back to my conversation with HawkEye to read his response to my question.

> HawkEye: You.

I'm taken aback, not sure how to reply to that. What is with these men thinking they want me when they don't know anything about me? I'm a mess. A broken fucking mess. No one should want anything to do with me.

> Wildcat: You don't even know me.

> HawkEye: Then let me get to know you. Tell me everything. The good, the bad, and the ugly.

I'd love more than anything to talk to someone like they were my therapist, but I'm not there yet. Especially with this guy.

> Wildcat: In time, maybe you will know it all. And once you do, you'll wish you didn't.

> HawkEye: Impossible. I have a feeling I'm only going to admire you more once I know who you really are.

I can't help the smile on my face. There's something so enlightening about talking with this guy. It's harmless, and it brings me comfort. Therefore, it can't be a bad thing.

> Wildcat: Let's hope you're right. I have to get dressed now. I just got out of the bathtub. Talk later?

> HawkEye: I'd love that. Take care, Wildcat.

> Wildcat: You too, HawkEye.

I close out of the app, still grinning from ear to ear as I slip into a plush robe. Flipping my head down, I wrap the towel around my hair and fasten it. My hand runs over the mirror, wiping away some of the fog. The reflection looking back at me is one I could get used to, and it's all thanks to one short-lived conversation with a man I'll probably never meet.

I walk out of the bathroom, completely shocked to see that Alaric isn't there. Though the sound of his bedroom door closing tells me he was. He must have bolted when he heard me click the lock. Either way, I'm not going to acknowledge him, or even give him a second of my time, because I have some serious living to do.

CHAPTER

NINETEEN

RHEA

It's been five days since I worked. The last time I set foot in Taryn's was the same day I left because I got my period unexpectedly. In those five days, my encounters with Alaric have been brief and surprisingly uneventful. The only thing I can ascertain is that he's grown bored with me.

Then there's the total fucked-up part of me that wonders why. Am I no longer good enough for him? Is he interested in someone else? I saw him chatting it up with the new girl in the house, Heather. They looked like they were having an in-depth conversation and when I tried to eavesdrop, I knocked over a ceramic pumpkin, shattering it to pieces on the floor. I played it off by pretending I'd just entered the room. Heather jumped up to help clean while Alaric turned a blind eye and went into the kitchen to help Gladys with dinner.

That evening, I sat across from him, waiting for him to nudge my foot or ask where I was the night before. I had gone for a late-night walk to clear my head and not once did I see him following me.

At this point, I'm not really sure what to make of his behavior. I should be relieved, but instead, it's unsettling.

It's Saturday morning, and I'm working the night shift tonight. I thought I might pop into Taryn's early and say hey to Tyler since we haven't talked much. I've been avoiding him for obvious reasons, but if Alaric is backing off, maybe that means his threat about staying away from Tyler no longer holds true. I guess I'm about to find out. It may be a risk, but I really don't think Alaric cares at this point.

I roll out of bed, stretching my arms to the ceiling while letting out a big yawn. The sun is shining brightly and I'm determined to make today a productive one.

Walking over to my dresser, I pull out a pair of denim jeans and a black long-sleeved tee shirt with a white skull on it. On top of the skull is a stack of books. I figure it's fitting since Halloween is in just three days.

Taryn mentioned there will be a masquerade party on Halloween night at the tavern. Since I'm not working, I might run over to the thrift store this afternoon to see what I can find. I've been there a couple times this week, picking up random articles of clothing to add to my collection. I even put said clothes in my dresser. Which is a big step for me.

I still haven't heard from Dex and I've garnered that it's a good thing. Had he answered my hundreds of calls and messages, I probably wouldn't be in Lockhaven anymore. I would have ran before trying to work through my problems here, and that would have been a big mistake.

I'm beginning to learn that for every problem, there *is* a solution. Look at me being an adult and solving them all on my own. Who would have thought?

Feeling optimistic, I walk toward the door to go to the bathroom, new-ish clothes in hand. I'm halted by the sight of a strange black jacket hanging on the doorknob. I walk closer, realizing I've seen this jacket before. It's got a large, yellow L and H on the sleeve—short for Lockhaven. This is the same jacket that the asshole at the tavern was wearing. In fact, I even nicknamed him 'Letter Jacket Guy' in my head.

I pull the jacket off the knob and wince when I notice it's damp. When I look down and see the streak of blood on my hand, I gasp, tossing it to the floor along with the clothes I was holding.

My heart races as my mind swirls with irrational thoughts. I rub my fingertips together, smearing what is definitely blood. But whose blood?

Frantically, I search the pockets, looking for any sign of the jacket's owner. I come up empty-handed, but it doesn't matter. I know damn well who it belongs to.

I quickly toss the jacket into my room and slam the door shut then run to the bathroom to scrub off any evidence of what I just touched.

Someone left that jacket waiting for me, and I don't even have to think twice about who that someone is.

Just when I thought I was out of danger, this happens. I have no idea what it means. Is it another threat, or did he do something to that boy?

Either way, I'm in possession of what could be evidence, and my fingerprints are now all over it.

I scrub for minutes, watching until the water runs clear. And when it does, I scrub more, lathering up the soap until my hands are nothing but skin and bones beneath sudsy bubbles.

My eyes stare back at me in horror as I contemplate the possibility that Alaric killed that guy. I gulp, unsure of whether he did it to set me up, to prove a point, or to simply end his life for hurting my feelings.

Who the fuck kills someone over hurt feelings? Or for any of those reasons for that matter?

I slam my hand down on the faucet handle, without drying my hands. With a new mission in mind, I tear open the bathroom door, going straight to Alaric's room.

Without knocking, I turn the handle to find that the door is locked. I heave a frustrated sigh. Of course, the psycho would ignore my privacy and steal my key but lock his door when he's here. I pound my fist to the wood, over and over while shouting, "Open the damn door!"

My chest tightens and my eyes prick with tears. "Alaric!" I scream. "I know you're in there. Open the door! Now!"

Another door comes open, and I take a step away from Alaric's. My eyes travel down the hall to see Heather coming toward me. "He's not there, hun. Alaric is next door. I'm on my way to meet him for breakfast. Would you like me to tell him you're looking for him?"

"No!" My voice rises, warranting a stunned expression from Heather. "I'll tell him my-damn-self." I storm back to my room in a rage. Stepping over the bloodied jacket on my floor, I give it a kick, noticing some of the blood has smeared onto the hardwood floor.

I don't want to risk damaging the evidence further, so I slide my feet into a pair of flip flops then go back out, closing my bedroom door behind me.

I walk hurriedly down the hall toward the front door, regretting my outburst. None of this is Heather's fault and I shouldn't be taking it out on her. If anything, I should be warning her to stay far away from that crazed man.

Still in my pajamas, my feet pad in my flip-flops as I practically jog to the tavern. In a swift motion, I jerk open the door, making a grand entrance that pins all eyes on me. I stand there with my back to the door, and when it closes, it nudges me farther into the room.

Suddenly, I realize I didn't think this through. So here I am, standing in a pair of black-and-red plaid pajama pants and an oversized black hoodie with yellow lettering on it. My hair is a mess, my gaze as wild as my soul, and my heart is thumping violently in my chest. My eyes dance from face to face, and widen in surprise when I see Sheriff Guthrie seated at a table with two of his deputies.

I walk toward them slowly, knowing the risk I'm taking. But I can't let Alaric get away with this. If I do, he could later use it against me. I'll forever be at his mercy with the fear of him outing me for all the mistakes I made in the past, as well as the possibility that I've been framed for that guy's murder—assuming he's dead. This could all be a ploy to get a rise out of me.

I have no idea what I'm doing, or what the consequences might be, but when I approach the table, I have the sheriff's and the deputies' attention, and I just freeze. My eyes dead-locked on Alaric's as he walks through the revolving doors of the kitchen.

"Thanks again, Alaric," Taryn says gleefully. "It would have been days before they got someone out here to fix that pipe. I owe you one."

"What the hell?" I mumble under my breath, but it's loud enough to draw attention to myself again.

Since when are Alaric and Taryn on speaking terms?

"Everything okay, hun?" one of the deputies asks as he takes a bite of his Belgian waffle.

Frazzled, I open my mouth to speak, but the words get lodged in my throat.

"Mr. Banks," Sheriff Guthrie says, his eyes on Alaric. "I can't thank you enough for your generous donation to the town's annual Christmas Tree Lighting ceremony. Without it, we may have had to cancel this year."

Alaric approaches the table, his eyes on me as he pats Sheriff Guthrie on the shoulder, and says, "I'm happy to help. Everyone in this town deserves to feel the spirit of Christmas." His eyebrows lift and a devilish smirk spreads across his face.

Am I dreaming right now? No. I can't be, because even in my wildest dreams, this wouldn't happen. This is a nightmare, but one I fear I'll never wake up from.

I swallow hard. My hands are tied. Alaric is playing everyone in this town. They'll never believe me over him.

"By the way," Alaric continues, now looking at Sheriff Guthrie, "any word on that boy that was hit last night? Such a terrible tragedy." His gaze narrows on mine while my chest rises and falls rapidly.

"Nothing yet, but we won't rest until we find out who did it. Mayor Dean's grandson, Nick, was a staple in this community. Always lending a helping hand when needed. Brought a smile to everyone's faces. Not to mention he was one of the best damn football players Lockhaven has ever seen."

Mayor Dean's grandson?

I feel lightheaded.

The door chimes, but the sound slips through my ears as I'm flooded with a thousand different emotions, ranging from anger to hurt to terror.

I take a step back, bumping into someone. "I'm so sorry." I spin around to see Heather smiling widely.

"Oh, good. You found Alaric. You seemed upset at the house. I hope you two were able to clear the air."

"I...umm." I take a few backward steps to the door before shooting my thumb over my shoulder. "I have to go."

"Hold up." Alaric rushes toward me, placing a gentle hand on my arm. I jerk it away abruptly, still speechless. "Was there

185

something you wanted to say?" He ganders around the room while curious eyes watch us. "We're all ears."

I give the customers a slow sweep before returning my glaring gaze to him. "You..." I whisper a hiss, "You won't get away with this."

He leans close, his breath hot against my ear. "It looks like I already have."

TWENTY

ALARIC

"Is she okay?" Heather asks as she takes a seat in the chair I pulled out for her, genuinely concerned for Rhea.

"She'll be fine." I give her chair a push, sliding her in.

I'd rather not discuss Rhea with Heather. It's tough juggling these two ladies. Rhea is the one I have to keep in check. She needs to realize how serious I am. I'm not going to just give up on her and disappear. I meant it when I said I won't make the mistake of getting to her too late ever again.

Then I have Heather, an enigma. There is something suspicious about her, but I can't put my finger on it. I caught her lurking around the house in the middle of the night a few days ago and I've made it my mission to find out why. So far, I've come up empty-handed.

"So," I say, taking a seat in the chair across from her, "tell me about yourself, *Heather*." I put an emphasis on her name because I'm not even sure it really is her name. I find it nearly impossible to trust people, and even harder to see the good in others in a world that is ruled by greed and hate.

I've noticed she averts her gaze often, as if carefully

avoiding eye contact. She fidgets with the napkin in front of her. Unrolling it, she pulls out the silverware, lining them precisely in front of her. "As I told you yesterday, there really isn't much to tell."

My fingers drum against my glass of ice water, the dew coating my fingers. "Everyone has a story to tell. Where are you from? Why are you here?"

She chuckles nervously. "I'm here because you invited me, silly."

She's acting just like Rhea would if she felt backed into a corner with a question. I don't like it. "Not here as in the tavern, here as in Lockhaven. Do you have family in town?"

"No family. I was simply just passing through and I liked the small-town vibe Lockhaven had to offer." Her eyes finally lift to mine. "I've never had that before, and it's comforting."

"Hmm." My fingers tap faster. "Seems to be a common denominator among new arrivals."

"Do you mean Rhea?"

My eyebrows shoot up. "Why would you say that?"

"Because she's a new arrival. And it seems there is some tension between you two. I just assumed—"

"Word of advice, Heather," I lean into the table as it presses hard against my rib cage, "don't ever assume anything when it comes to Rhea. Better yet, don't even acknowledge her existence."

"Why?" She snorts, bringing her glass of water to her lips. "Is she crazy or something?" She takes a small sip then sets her glass back down. "I sort of get the sense she is."

I bite the corner of my lip, observing her nervous behavior. Yet, her words are so bold and the confidence behind them is baffling. "For such a quiet girl, you sure do have a lot to say."

"I'm a private person, Alaric. But I notice things. I watch people. I observe them. Then I draw my own conclusions."

"And once you've drawn those conclusions, then what? Do you relay this information to anyone?"

Surprised by my question, she cranes her neck. "Like who?" She laughs, though I know it's a tactic to hide what's really going on here. I know how the criminal mind works. I've kept my guard up my entire life for reasons such as this. Heather came to Lockhaven with a purpose, and I intend to find out what that purpose is. If it has anything to do with Rhea, or myself, she won't live to relay the information to whoever she was sent by.

"Be careful, Heather." I scoot by chair back, ending this breakfast before it's even begun. "You wouldn't want to draw the wrong conclusions about the wrong people."

IT'S HALF past midnight when I hear Rhea's bedroom door screech across the hardwood floor. I spring out of my bed, tossing my book down on the mattress. I go to the door, ear pressed to it, as I listen for the soft sound of her footsteps in the hall.

Sure enough, I hear them. Once she's passed, I slowly turn the handle and crack my door open, watching with one eye as she fades into the darkness, wearing her work sneakers and a black hoodie with the hood pulled up. In her hand is a plastic grocery bag, holding something that seems to be weighted down.

I bolt to my window, snatching up my tennis shoes in case I need to leave quickly. I slide one on, then the other, my eyes never leaving the side of the house where the front door is.

I watch, and I wait. As suspected, she comes out the door, looking around before bolting. In one breath, I cross the room and pull open my door, then I inch open the entryway and slide out.

Once the door latches with little sound, I give it a good thirty seconds, then I start to track my wildcat.

Keeping a safe distance, I stay close behind her as she walks down Main Street. I take notice of her glancing at her phone that's held out in her hand. If I had to guess, I'd imagine she's looking at a map.

Rhea hasn't lived in Lockhaven very long so she doesn't know the area well. Although, she did go for a nice long walk yesterday. At one point while I was following her—in the same manner I am now—I'm certain she got lost. I watched her spin around in circles a few times then backtrack to read the street names. A couple minutes later, she just turned around. I hid behind a tree until she passed, then I followed her back home.

Right now, she doesn't seem lost. It's as if she knows exactly where she wants to go. She's just using the phone to double check her movements in the dark.

Once she's reached a point where there are no more street-lights, she turns on the flashlight on her phone.

We walk for another five minutes or so, then she takes a left into the cemetery. I've always known Rhea was tough as nails, but I never pegged her to be a nighttime cemetery walker. No. She's here for a reason and I think I know what that reason is.

I follow her past some headstones, then she stops, leans over, and says, "Rest in peace, Lucy." As if she knows who this Lucy person is, or was.

One of the things I love about Rhea is her uniqueness. She's her own person and does what she wants to do without fear of what people will think of her. At least, that's the way she used to live. The longer I watch her in Lockhaven, the more I'm starting to realize she's putting on a facade, and the less I like it. One day, she won't have to pretend for the people in this town. She's too good for them anyway.

We trek a few more steps, then suddenly she stops and drops the plastic bag on the ground.

Hiding myself, I duck behind a tree and peer around it with my phone held up. I snap a few pictures then lower it to my side.

Rhea squats down and shuffles nervously through the bag. It's hard to see with the only light coming from the half-moon and her shaking phone light, but it looks like she's pulled out a pair of gardening gloves.

I watch intently as she pulls out what appears to be a small garden spade. I'm not sure where she got it, but it has to be Gladys's. She must have snuck into her garden shed out back and stolen it.

I watch as she wrestles with the hard-packed dirt, her arms quivering with the effort. Every once in a while, she growls in annoyance. At one point, she tosses down the spade and throws her hands in the air in defeat. Then she picks it up and goes right back to work.

Part of me wants to laugh at the sight of her determination to dig such a large hole with such a small tool, but the other part is really fucking proud of her. She's working with what she's got, just like she always does. Rhea is resilient, and it's one of the many things I admire about her.

I snap a few more pictures. When she finally retrieves Nick's jacket, I hold my finger on the center button, making sure to capture every moment.

Oh, Rhea. Don't you know hiding evidence is a felony?

My girl is smart, but oftentimes, her pride gets in the way and she makes decisions that could really get her in a lot of trouble. Much like now. She could have easily tossed that jacket in my room and asked me about it. I would have told her the truth—that I killed that asshole Nick. Instead, she wanted to avoid confrontation and took matters into her own hands.

Big mistake, Wildcat.

She pulls off the gloves and tosses them in the hole, along with the spade, and plastic bag. A smart move, I might add.

Then using her shoe, she begins filling the hole back up with dirt. When everything is buried and nothing is left but a mound of dirt, she packs it down with both feet until it's flat.

I click a few more shots, then turn around to leave the same way we came. Long strides lead me out of the cemetery, and I'm confident I've put enough distance between us.

The element of surprise is in my favor when I use the key I had copied to enter Rhea's room.

Then, I sit on her bed and wait with the proof I've just captured.

Rhea thinks she's going to leave Lockhaven, but I've just ensured she stays a little longer.

I've been waiting in the parking lot for over an hour while the little prick lifts weights. My patience is wearing thin. I've gotta get back to Rhea to make sure she isn't packing a bag or running her mouth, so he needs to wrap this shit up.

A couple days ago, I found out the name of the fucker who made Rhea cry at the tavern. I spent the days that followed learning Nick's routine. Every day after school, he has football practice, then he goes to the gym and works out for another hour. And after that, he jogs home for the exercise. His house is only a half mile away, so there isn't much distance between here and there to do what needs to be done.

I contemplated different ways of taking him out, but this is the cleanest, quickest way.

More time passes and when I see the side doors to the high school gym open, I straighten my back in the seat of my car. Once I see that it's him, wearing that same jacket with a backpack pulled over his shoulders, I start the engine, keeping my headlights off.

I give him a head start and when he's on the road running, I creep slowly out of the parking lot.

Stealing a glance in my rearview mirror, I make sure there are no witnesses before flooring the gas pedal. The tires squeal with excitement as my car lurches forward at full speed and his body slams against the bumper with an echoing boom. It's a beautiful symphony that sends a wave of energy through me.

I slam on the brakes and spin the steering wheel so fast my tires screech. I floor it again, riding over his body for safe measure.

I bring the car to a screeching halt and jump out of the driver's door. Moving quickly, I go to where he's lying on the street, a pool of blood surrounding him while more continues to flow like a river down the asphalt.

Kicking his body over with the toe of my boot, it's confirmed that he's dead. Vacant eyes stare up at me and I only wish they could see the sickening smile on my face.

I crouch down beside him, grab the sleeve of his thick jacket, and rip it away. A wallet falls out of the pocket and I leave it lying there as I roll him onto his side and pull the other sleeve off.

"No one makes my girl cry and gets away with it."

Standing up, I square my shoulders, a newfound rage pumping through my veins. In one swift movement, I bring my boot up and stomp it into his face, feeling the crunch of bone as his nose flattens.

Satisfied, I leave him there to rot until someone finds him. Unfortunately, it won't be long enough.

TWENTY-ONE

RHEA

IT's DONE. Not even a speck of dirt under my nails. Alaric thinks he can use a murder he committed to try and sway me, but he's fucking with the wrong girl.

He's all but admitted, without even speaking to me, that he's the one who hit and killed Nick. Now he's fooling Taryn, Gladys, Sheriff Guthrie, and probably everyone else in this town. Before long, they'll all be wrapped around his finger.

It's okay, though. They can feel however they want about Alaric. I know the truth and with that knowledge, I plan to walk the straight and narrow, steering clear of his path to self-destruction.

Feeling a bit better now that the jacket is out of my possession, I walk down the hall to my room. I pull my key out of my pocket and stick it in the lock. Only, when I turn the handle, I find that it's not locked at all.

Holding my breath, I push the door open, coming face to face with Alaric sitting on my bed. I release all the air from my lungs in one hefty exhale as I try to convince myself not to rip out my hair in frustration.

"Seriously?" I scoff, walking into the room and slamming the door behind me. "Don't you have anything better to do than torment me?"

He leans back on the bed, his elbows pressed to the mattress and a grin on his face. "Not really."

I shake my head, taking slow and steady breaths to keep myself calm. "Get out."

"But you just got here, and we have so much to talk about." The confidence in his tone is unnerving to say the least.

At some point between crossing the room and those slow and steady breaths getting lodged in my lungs, I begin fuming. My hand swings out then flies back, landing my open palm on his face. "Are you trying to ruin my life?" I shout. "Murder, Alaric! Really? You killed that poor boy, and for what?"

"That *boy* was anything but poor." He cradles his wounded cheek in his palm, but the smile on his face never falters. "I did it for you."

"For me?" My voice rises even louder. "He used me to try and get a few laughs from his friends. Maybe it hurt my feelings a little bit, but I've dealt with worse. I handled the situation just fine on my own. You had no business—"

Suddenly, he springs off the bed, anger now crippling his features. "When you ran to the bathroom and cried on the *fucking* floor, it became my business."

"You don't get to dictate other people's lives just to fit your own agenda, Alaric." I grip the sides of my head, feeling like I'm going to combust with rage. "This is fucking insane!"

"I don't understand why you're so upset about this. You said you hope he dies a slow and painful death. I was simply giving you what you wanted."

My head draws back quickly, palms sweating profusely. "Are you serious right now? I said that out of hurt and anger. I didn't actually want the kid dead. He was just a kid, Alaric."

"I tailed that kid for a week and watched him try to take advantage of girls, do drug deals on the side outside his school, then go home to the woods to torture animals. I did you and the world a fucking favor."

"Maybe he just needed help. Just because I say something out of anger doesn't mean I want it to come to reality!"

Casually, he lifts one shoulder in a half shrug and his mouth curves downward in a scowl. "I guess you should make yourself more clear next time."

There are so many things I want to say and do to this man. I'm half tempted to dig a bigger hole with that jacket so I can curl Alaric's dead body up and bury him with it. Then again, burying him alive sounds pretty satisfying too.

My voice drops a few octaves, my defensiveness wearing thin. "Why are you here? What do you want from me?"

"I'm here for you. To protect you and love you as long as I live. Every time I watched you struggle, I got closer, but I knew better than to come in and save you because you never needed a white knight."

"And I don't need one now. I'll never love you, Alaric. Ever. So if you think for a second that you're going to manipulate this entire situation and I'm going to fall head over heels for you, you're wrong."

"If I'm manipulating you, it's only because I see everything you can become. I know your potential, Rhea. But let me make one thing clear, I could have taken you long ago and forced you to live a life with me, but I allowed you to spread your wings first."

"Bullshit. I was just too fast for you. I saw you everywhere, and each time I did, I ran somewhere else. You may have always found me, but I was two steps ahead of you, knowing you'd come eventually."

"Did you know I'd come here to Lockhaven?"

"I knew it was a possibility, but I assumed since my father was dead, you didn't need to."

"This isn't about your father. At least, not anymore. Yes, there was a time when I agreed to help him find you, but that reasoning ended the minute I laid eyes on you. I'm here because I could no longer stand the distance between your heart and mine."

"So you want a life with me? What?" I chortle. "You want me to marry you?"

"Eventually, yes."

"Well, I hate to break it to you, Mr. Banks, but that's never going to happen."

He digs his fingers into the pocket of his jeans and pulls out his phone, a sense of assurance radiating from him. Tapping away at the screen with purpose, he then looks up, a smug smile on his face. "I beg to differ. It's going to happen, and much sooner than you think."

Holding his phone in the air, he shows me a picture he took —of me burying Nick's jacket.

Each swipe of his thumb against the screen has my heart pounding faster. He scrolls through them all, dozens of them.

Mouth hung open in disbelief, I stumble backward until my legs hit the edge of the bed. I sit down abruptly, feeling like I might pass out. My breathing comes in shallow gasps and my words are nothing but a strained whisper. "You followed me?"

Alaric sits down beside me, a picture of me still on display on his phone in his hand. "Don't you know by now, baby? I'm always following you."

His hand moves to my upper thigh and while I see that it's there, I'm too stunned to react. I swallow hard as I turn to look at him. "What do you plan to do with those?"

He clicks a button on the side of the phone, turning it off before stretching back and stuffing the phone in his pocket.

"You don't have to worry, Rhea. Your secret is safe with me, as long as you do everything I ask of you. It's that easy."

"Easy?" I snicker. "Nothing about any of this is easy. You killed Nick and now you're blackmailing me. You knew exactly what you were doing the entire time, didn't you?"

Moving his fingers in slow strokes over my leg, he says, "Of course I did."

I can't even begin to wrap my head around what's happening. Of all the situations I've endured in my life, this sits next to the most terrifying. I've done a lot of bad things, but I always did a very good job at covering my tracks. At least, I thought I did. Alaric is probably holding all my secrets in his dark and depraved mind, ready to unleash them the second I don't do what he asks.

"Okay," I tell him. "You got me. Now tell me what it is you want me to do."

A knowing smirk tugs at the corner of his lips while his fingers slide between my legs. His gaze meets mine and an unwanted heat rolls through me as he leans closer. "There is so much I want you to do, but first..." He pauses, inches away from my mouth. "Kiss me."

Tears prick at the corners of my eyes as I nod in slow movements. "Fine."

His lips press against mine, but I keep my mouth firmly closed. He moves his lips gently back and forth, trying to coax me into kissing him, but I remain unresponsive.

There's no doubt in my mind that Alaric wants more than just a kiss. He wants to fuck me, right here and now. A hundred different options flow through my mind, ranging from murdering him to just doing what he asks. I settle with the only plausible option: I have to do this.

I've had sex more times than I can count with various men I don't even know. To me, sex is not sacred, it's an act of passion that is one-sided more times than not. At least, in my case it is. I've given myself up for less, so for my freedom I can do this.

I fall into the kiss, hating myself more and more with each passing second. For someone who was so desperate to stay away, I sure have fucked myself over because this is the most passionate kiss I've ever felt in my life.

Alaric's mouth is surprisingly warm and soft for such a cold man. His tongue moves gently against mine and it doesn't feel like a crazy stalker is kissing me. It feels like I'm cared for, for once.

The hairs on my arms stand tall as our mouths melt together. Every nerve in my body lights up like a firework. It's a feeling I never anticipated when Alaric told me to kiss him.

Desire runs down my wobbly legs and straight to the pit of my stomach. I want more of it—of him.

Alaric pulls back and I already miss the way his lips feel against mine. Maybe it isn't sex he wants, after all. Perhaps he really only wanted a kiss.

"Okay," I tell him. "I did what you asked. Now I need you to answer some questions for me."

Make me kiss you again. Please. Oh no, you don't! I dig my nails into my hand to get rid of that thought.

The back of his fingers glide across my cheek. "You're a good kisser, Rhea. Is that because of all the practice you had with random men?"

Nothing he says surprises me anymore. Therefore, I don't react. "Yep. And kissing those strangers was far more satisfying than any kiss I'll ever share with you."

Okay. I reacted, but with a lie. I have no intention of making it easier for this asshole, no matter how warm and comforting his lips are. I never want him to know what that kiss did to me. It'll only inflate his ego and lead him to believe we actually have a future together.

His lips press together in a thin white line. "We'll see about that." He grabs my face with both hands and pulls my mouth to his once again, and I'm entranced. This time, it's not soft and gentle, it's harsh and eager. My hands move to the back of his head, holding him in place as I return the gesture.

With a strong hold on me, he forces the kiss deeper until our teeth are clanking and my heart is pounding out a brutal rhythm against his. I know he can feel it, and the thing is, I can feel his too. Alaric is damn near *trembling*. His palms are sweaty against my cheeks, and his tongue quivers in my mouth. I have to force myself not to gasp at just how good he feels.

Finally, he relents. As he leans back, I lick my lips, tasting the sweetness of lemonade that rolled off his tongue.

Taking the upper hand, I jump off the bed and say, "You're not touching me again until you answer my questions." I can't allow him too much leeway here. His touch is doing things to me; I need distance if I'm going to get anything out of this situation. Alaric wants me, and I want the truth.

He rolls his neck, cracking the tense bones. "Fine. For every question I answer, you give me something in return."

I scoff. "Spoken like a true man."

"Oh no, Rhea. I'm not like other men. I'm not using you by any means. I don't want just one night with you. I want forever. So don't compare me to your clients. I'm here because I love you."

"Whatever." I roll my eyes. "Who do you work for?"

"I work for myself. I happen to run a very successful business."

"Okay." I nod, satisfied with his response. "Did you know my father?"

"I knew Grayson very well. In fact, we were best friends for many years."

"So it's safe to assume you knew about the contract?"

"For a while I didn't, but recently, it fell into my hands."

Finally, I might get some answers about that damn contract and what it entailed. Not that it matters anymore, now that my father is dead.

"Tell me about it. I need to know everything. I know it's void now because my father is dead, but—"

His eyebrows shoot to his forehead. "What makes you think the contract is void?"

"Well, it has to be. Grayson died."

"That's true, Rhea. But his fortune didn't. Much like his assets and his estate, that contract still very much exists. I'm not sure where you got your information from, but that contract is still active. It's another reason why I couldn't stay away any longer. You need real protection."

I feel like I've been punched in the gut as I drop back down on the bed beside Alaric. I keep a good distance between us, so he doesn't try and kiss me again, but I'm feeling too overwhelmed to stand. "That doesn't make any sense. How can that be if he's not alive to fulfill his part of the deal?"

"He's not alive, but you are. You were the deal. You and his money are the only part of the contract that matters."

"Well, it's easy then. I'll just never meet the terms of it, obviously. What's the worst that can happen?"

"Damn straight you're never going to meet the terms of it, because we're going to marry first. Once we get married, then the contract no longer exists."

I rub viciously at my temples. "I don't understand any of this."

Alaric stands up, positioning himself right in front of me as he explains. "Your father gave away your hand in marriage to someone who turned out to be a very dangerous man. He's a crime lord down in Mexico and he wants *you*, Rhea. You're indebted to him, and once the two of you are married, he will own a share in Grayson's fortune, making him all the more powerful." He grabs my shoulders eagerly and raises his voice to make himself clear.

"This man will hurt you, Rhea. He'll sell your body to his minions for the right price. He'll dress you up and use you as his arm candy, only to go home at night and beat you bloody. He'll tear you down until you are nothing but a bag of bones. And when you're no longer of use to him, he'll throw you out." He shakes his head, eyes closed. "You think your body has been abused before? Well, this guy will make your past feel like a blessing."

My hand flies to my mouth as I gasp. I knew it was bad, but I had no idea how bad it could be. Alaric, noticing the terror in my eyes, crouches down in front of me.

"Hey. He's never gonna get near you. Ever. I'd die first."

I close my eyes as tears slip through them and roll down my cheeks. "And what happens when he kills you and I'm left to my own devices?"

Two hands rest on my legs while hopeful eyes look back at me. "It's not going to happen. I can promise you that. As long as you do what I say, you'll be safe."

I laugh loudly, though the sound is more grueling than humorous. "You expect me to believe that after everything you've done?"

"Everything I've done was with purpose. I didn't take those pictures tonight to turn you in. I took them so you could see that you can be easily followed. You need me. None of this was ever to hurt you. I need you to trust me." He stands up again and clears his throat.

"The contract states that you cannot marry prior to your

twenty-first birthday, which you haven't. Up until you turned twenty-one, you've been useless to him. But now that you're of age, he's ready to collect. Unless..."

"Unless what?" I spring to my feet. "Tell me. Is there a loophole?"

"Ian can't make you his wife if you're already someone else's."

My hands fly in the air. "Fine. Whatever. Then I'll get married. To someone. Anyone. Hell, I'll marry Tyler."

I swear I can hear the sound of his knuckles cracking as he clenches his fists. "You marry Tyler, or anyone else for that matter, and I'll make you a widow before your wedding night. No one else has the money and resources to protect you. Much less, the wits. But more importantly, no one else could ever love you like I do." His words are stern and I take them seriously. I believe Alaric would do just that. He's already proven how far he'll go for me.

My fists dig into my hips and I raise a brow. "And I assume this is the part where you tell me I'm going to marry *you*?"

When he drops to his knee and reaches into his pocket, my first reaction is to knock him over the head and run. Man, I'd love more than anything to do just that. But if what Alaric says is true, I might need him more than I think. My life begins once the threat of that contract is gone.

Alaric pulls out a black velvet box and flips the top, exposing the biggest diamond I've ever seen in my life. It's four, maybe five, double-squared carats sitting on a white gold band. It's stunning. So much so that it literally takes my breath away.

"This isn't the conventional way to do it, Rhea. I'd love more than anything to ask you this question with confidence in what your response will be. But time is of the essence, so Rhea Thorn, will you be my wife?"

"No," I blurt out on impulse. "I won't marry you, Alaric." I gulp, feeling the thickness of regret in my throat because there is a good chance I'll soon wish I'd said yes. "I've made it this far on my own, and I'm going to continue to take my chances. So thanks, but no thanks."

Alaric stands up and grabs my left hand savagely. He separates my fingers and slides the band on my ring finger. "You can take all the chances you want, but I'm not willing to take any when it's your life on the line. You will marry me, or I'll bring all the evidence I have to Sheriff Guthrie and have him lock you up where I *know* you'll be safe."

The ring fits perfectly and I hold my hand up, admiring how beautiful it is.

"Did you hear me, Rhea? Those are your options. Pick one."

Snapping out of the trance I fell in, I lift my eyes to his. "I pick neither. But thanks for the ring."

I could sell this baby for a pretty penny and go wherever the hell I wanna go. Alaric says this Ian guy is in Mexico, then I'll go on the other side of the world just to hide from him.

I spin on my heel and walk to the door. Pulling it open, I step to the side. "You can leave now."

"For fuck's sake, Rhea," Alaric shouts, storming toward me. I jolt, taking a step back. When he slams the door, I press my back to the wall. "Have you heard a goddamn word I've said to you?"

Once the shock of his outburst wears off, I trudge slowly toward him. "I heard you very clearly and I'm not okay with the options you gave me. I don't need your help and I'm certainly not marrying you."

"Fine." He shrugs his shoulders. "Have it your way. But when you end up in a body bag at the age of twenty-five because you've been used and abused so badly, don't say I didn't warn you."

"Oh," I sneer, "I thought you were gonna go to Sheriff Guthrie."

Seems Alaric barks a lot, but his bite is weak. He won't follow through with turning me in. He cares too much about me to turn over evidence of my wrongdoings.

"Is that what you want? Would you prefer to live a life in prison?"

"I dunno. Is that what you want? Because if I go down, you're going down with me. You killed Nick, not me."

"Didn't you have clients that would turn up dead, Rhea? And let's not forget about the man who flew off his balcony in New York City."

"Prove it!" I snap back.

"I can prove a lot of things," he grits out. "Don't test me."

"Oh yeah. Like what?"

"I can prove that you killed your father."

In an instant, all the blood drains from my face. I put a hand on the door, bracing myself. "What did you just say?"

"You heard me. I followed you to his house. I watched as you slowly dragged that knife across his throat while he was sleeping. You thought by killing him you were voiding that contract, didn't you?"

"Shut up!" I howl. "You're lying!"

"Am I, though? You murdered your own father in cold blood and never even batted an eye as you were doing it. You call me crazy, but it takes a psycho to know one."

Nostrils flared and fists balled, I lunge at him. "You don't know what you're talking about!" I bring my fists to his chest, alternating hands as I pound on him over and over again. "He wasn't a good man," I cry out, tears falling down my face. "There's no excuse for him giving me away like that. No reason will suffice. I was his daughter, dammit! He was supposed to love and protect me, but he failed me. He failed me, and he failed my mom."

Alaric grabs me by the wrists, squeezing them as his knuckles turn white. "I'm not judging you, Rhea. I'm just stating what we both know to be the truth. All I ask is that you please stop judging me."

I jerk one of my hands from him and aggressively swipe away the tears on my face. "How do you even know all of this?"

"That's not important. None of this is. What's done is done. All that matters is what you're going to do now."

"Oh, yeah." I sniffle. "And what is that?"

"Marry me."

"Fuck you!"

In one swift motion, Alaric pulls me to his chest. One arm wraps around my waist while the other grabs the back of my neck. "If that's an invitation, then I accept."

CHAPTER

TWENTY-TWO

ALARIC

OUR MOUTHS COLLIDE together like a violent train wreck. I can feel the resistance on Rhea's end, but she doesn't try to fight me off for long. Instead, she pours all of her agony into this tantalizing kiss.

It's everything I hoped it would be. Our first kiss was intense, but this is like nothing I've ever experienced before. I've never been so hungry in all my forty-two years of life. My body has met many women, but my soul has never connected with another the way it has with her. For that reason, I never want to be with anyone else ever again.

My hand glides beneath her sweatshirt, fingertips dancing over her ribs. Rhea arches her back as I creep higher, ghosting my hand down the soft fabric of her bra until I reach the clasp. Inching it open, I cup her breast in my palm, savoring the warmth of her skin against mine. I tease her nipple with light brushes of my thumb then give it a soft pinch. I nearly groan when I'm rewarded with a slight moan against my mouth.

My cock twitches in response to the sound, the desperation for her touch almost unbearable. I move my hand back down, caressing her supple curves. "I'm gonna fuck you, Rhea. Then I'm gonna marry you."

"Seems a little ass-backward, don't ya think?" Her words are breathless, in no way is she trying to push me away. *Finally.*

She's being compliant right now, even though her words are worth a grain of salt. Rhea isn't going to willingly marry me right away. It's going to take some work. But right now, things are definitely looking up. After all, she's still wearing my ring and she looks fucking stunning with it on.

"We're both rule breakers." I hum into the crease of her neck. "I think we'll get away with it." I grip the bottom of her sweatshirt and lift up to remove it. Once it's free, I toss it on the floor and throw her bra on top of it.

When I've got my shirt off, I press my chest to Rhea's and lower her to the bed. My face hovers over hers while I unsnap the button on her jeans between our tightly pressed bodies. "Do you have any idea how long I've waited for this?"

She sneers. "Not very long considering you drugged me and took advantage of me two weeks ago." Her fingers trail down my chest and she gives a gentle tug at the hair coating it.

"I didn't fuck you then."

The heat of her grip on my chest hair burns into my skin as she uses it to tug me closer. She holds me there, suspended in time with my lips just inches away from hers. "Then shut up and fucking do it," she breathes before finally pressing her mouth hard against mine.

I lift off her momentarily to remove her pants, bringing her panties down with them. I toss them all carelessly to the floor.

I'm surprised to see that she's clean-shaven this time. My fingers run down her folds and I tsk. "I sure hope you cleaned up for me and not for someone else."

"Maybe it was just for myself." She shrugs and I actually believe her.

"That I'll allow." I growl deep in my throat as I lower my head between her thighs "You like touching yourself, baby?" Her eyes meet mine, and I see the heat there as she nods. Taking her hand, I place it over her slick folds and murmur on her core as she begins massaging her clit with the pads of her fingers. "That's right. Show me how you do it."

The sound of pleasure that slips between her lips drives me fucking wild. I watch in rapture as she circles her sensitive nub, only to dip down between her folds ever so slightly. I bite my lip, dying for that sweet cunt to be on my mouth again. I can't resist lifting her fingers and tasting them on my tongue.

"Fuck. You taste so good." I growl in satisfaction as I put them back in place. Her heated gaze meets mine and arousal floods through me as I watch her work her clit.

My hand reaches up, feeling the slope of her breast. I spread my palm flat and apply gentle pressure as I massage in a circular motion.

She whimpers in response so I move to the other breast and caress that one, too.

When my tongue glides upward between her folds, she lifts her hips. I remove her hand and take over the action of stimulating her sensitive nub with the pad of my tongue, then I press two fingers at the entrance of her wet cunt.

Starting slow, I push against her entrance in soft circles. When her body opens up to me, I increase my pressure and speed, until my knuckles brush against her inner walls. In a repetitive motion, I suck on her clit while my fingers fuck her.

"Fuck," she cries, and it's a beautiful sound that I'm desperate to hear again.

I move harder and faster, my fingers drumming a beat against her G-spot while my mouth holds suction and my tongue dances with her dripping core. She follows the rhythm with her hips as I move faster and faster. When my eyes lift slightly to steal a peek at her, I see her watching me with a lustful stare. Captured by the intensity of her gaze, my soul catches fire.

Suddenly, her expression shifts to a heated glare and she pushes my head down. "Don't watch me. Just get me off."

I pop off of her center and she whimpers. *Yeah, not so tough when you're so close, huh?* "We're going to have to adjust that attitude before we get married."

Ignoring my words, she grabs a fistful of my hair, slamming my face into her sex. "Shut up."

My lips twitch with a smile as I continue to work for her orgasm. She's such a mouthy little thing.

Her hands move to her sides, gripping the blanket. The fabric bunches between her fingers and her hips move quicker, desperate for release.

"Come for me, baby. Come on Daddy's face."

I suck hard on her sensitive nub while my fingers delve in and out of her, stimulating every inch of her cunt.

Her moans grow louder and I keep up my relentless pace, knowing she's about to soak this bed.

Her muscles contract around my fingers, the heat radiating from her skin as her body tenses up and she explodes. Juices flow out of her, splashing me in the face. I drag my tongue up and down her, slurping every drop of her sweet arousal.

"That's my girl." I swipe my tongue up the length of her pussy one more time before lifting my head.

She drops her head down, relaxing into the mattress while I take off my pants. "I'm not your girl. And you're not my daddy."

"That's where you're wrong. You." I slide up her body, lining my hard cock with her entrance. "Are." I shove it in deep and hard, her tight cunt clenching around me. "Mine."

She gasps at the intense bout of pressure inside her, eyes wide in surprise.

I lunge again and again, riding her body up on the bed until the top of her head is flush with the wooden headboard. She's soaked, but still so tight and hot around me. As if she were made to take my dick.

"Jesus Christ, Rhea," I grumble. "You feel so fucking good."

Her walls clench, gripping my cock with a mixture of pleasure and pain, as if she's trying to force me out of her while also begging me to stay. It's a failed attempt and only arouses me further. My arms slip under each of her legs, pulling them upward as I bring her knees to her chest. I pound into her sopping cunt, forcing out a guttural groan. Deep waves of pleasure ripple through my core.

"This is just the beginning, Rhea. The start of a beautiful fucking life together."

She turns her head, not willing to look at me. But I see her. I see the space between her lips and I hear the moans that slip through them. She loves this as much as I do.

My eyes focus on her chest as it rises and falls with a steady rhythm. Her breasts sway in tandem with the motion of each forceful thrust. I can feel the tension inside me build up to the point of explosion.

"Fuck." I growl in one ragged breath. "I never want this to end."

She lies there motionless, but her fingers are, once again, tangled in the blanket. Her eyes pinch closed to hide the pleasure I'm bringing her. It's just like my girl to deny me seeing her unwavering rapture. Though, she did show me moments ago when it was only to satisfy herself.

Her breathing grows more audible and labored, her chest rising and falling more rapidly. "Come for me again, Rhea. Don't fight it. Let me feel you come around my cock."

In an instant, her hands fly to my back, nails digging deep into my skin as she drags them beneath the surface. "That's right. Hurt me. Bring me pain while I bring you pleasure."

I drop one of her legs and use my free hand to grab a fistful of her hair. Jerking her head up, I expose her neck, then clamp down on the sensitive skin. With each scratch of her nails, I suck harder, bruising her. Leaving my mark.

It's a silent war between us. Who will surrender first?

I delve deeper, thrusting a whimper out of her. "Don't make me punish you again, little girl."

Her nails dig deeper and I'm certain she's peeling away my skin. "Maybe I like to be punished. Or *maybe*, I'm the one who's going to punish you."

My teeth sink into her neck and she winces. "Give it your best shot, baby."

We rip into each other like wild animals and I'm aroused more than I ever knew possible. I fuck her hard and fast, watching her face to memorize every little expression she gives me.

"Look at me." My fingers press against her jawline until she's forced to meet my gaze. "Every time your eyes leave mine, I'm gonna fuck you harder."

Her lips part and her nostrils flare. Her breaths turn frantic and it's enough to put me damn near over the edge.

Keeping her eyes on mine, she watches me. My cock swells inside her, my veins engorged and thumping to their own beat. "Damn, baby. I'm gonna come."

"Pull out," she demands in an instant, knowing I didn't slip on a condom.

From what I've noticed, Rhea was always safe with her clients. She also said so herself. But even if she wasn't, I'd still fuck her with a naked cock because I couldn't bear the thought of never feeling her insides swell against me.

Ignoring her demand, I plunge deep inside her, releasing as my body shudders in delight.

"Pull out, Alaric!"

I watch her face, observing the desperation in her eyes, and once I've filled her up, my mouth tugs up in a grin. "My bad."

"You asshole!" She slaps her hands on my back, then scratches me even deeper than before.

"This punishing game is sort of fun."

"You punished me by coming inside me?" She pushes me up, and I lift the weight of my body off hers. "What the hell is the matter with you? I'm not on birth control. As you well know, I can't afford it."

Real panic seems to flood her body as my slippery dick slides out and I roll onto my back. "That wasn't a punishment. I just wanted to feel you from start to finish."

Rhea grumbles a few inaudible sounds mixed with some curse words as she climbs out of her bed. "Get up." She lifts her hands in the air. "You will go straight to the pharmacy and buy me the morning-after pill. We're done here."

I fold my arms under my head, making myself comfortable while the mixture of our arousals slides down my dick. I'll buy her the pill. After all, I know how much she was hurt after she lost the baby. If I can't convince her to marry me, I sure as fuck won't be able to convince her that her child, our child, would be safe with me.

"What?" I snicker. "No snuggles?"

"Ha! Not a chance in hell."

"Come on, baby." I pat the side of the bed next to me. "Pull the stick out of your ass for a few minutes and just lie down with me."

She shakes her head in annoyance and grips the end of the comforter beneath me. "Get off my bed or I'll pull you off."

I smirk. "I'm two hundred and fifteen pounds of solid

muscle. But go ahead and give it a try."

She jerks the blanket, only dragging me down an inch, and I laugh. The sound sends her into a fit of rage. Her fists plant firmly on her hips. "Why are you so fucking insufferable?"

"I actually thought I was being pretty sweet. Name one guy you've fucked who wanted to snuggle after."

"Easy. Daniel. Martin. Craig. Mr. Lyons, who happens to be the senator of an entire fucking state."

"Huh. Well done. Which state was that?"

"Hell if I remember. A big one. Texas, maybe." Rhea snatches up a dirty towel from the floor and tosses it at me. "Cover your junk. I'd prefer to never look at it again."

The towel lands on my stomach and I push it back on the floor. "All right. So I guess I don't win on the romantic front. Doesn't mean I won't stop trying."

"That's a shame." Her voice is a whisper that I hear very clearly.

With a robe now wrapped around her, she pulls the bedroom door open. "I have to use the bathroom. Be a gem and disappear before I return."

I sink deeper into the mattress when her phone catches my eye from beside the bed. I reach for it, knowing my girl is too smart to leave her phone unlocked. It's attached to a cord so I turn on my side and tap the screen, just to see if she's got any notifications.

My jaw clicks when I see a message from Farm Boy. I can't read the entire thing, but I can see the first sentence.

> Tyler: Looking forward to seeing you at work Saturday. How cool that we finally get to...

It ends there, but if I had to guess it read: 'How cool that we finally get to work together.' How cheesy is this guy? Rhea likes this?

I slam the phone down and lie back with my head resting on Rhea's pillow. I turn slightly, drawing in a deep breath of the scent of her hair.

Rhea is working a Saturday night shift at Taryn's, which means many more drunk men than what she's used to. It also means working closely beside my new nemesis, *Tyler*. My plans are never open because I'm always watching Rhea, but Saturday night just filled up. I swear over everything that is holy in this world, if one guy so much as looks at her wrong, he'll be the next unsolved case in Lockhaven.

"For the love of God, Alaric." Rhea comes storming back into the room, slamming the door behind her.

"Easy, killer. Don't you know people are trying to sleep in this house?"

She scoffs at my sarcasm. "Why are you still here? And why the fuck are you still naked? Get your old ass dressed."

"You know," I scoot up until my back is against the headboard, "calling me old doesn't hurt me the way you probably want it to. If anything, it makes me that much prouder to have a young bombshell like you as my future wife." I wink at her, loving when she gets all tousled like this.

"You could only be so lucky." Rhea pulls open her drawer and retrieves a pair of boxer shorts and a tee shirt. Leaving it open, because she has terrible housekeeping skills, she unties her robe and lets it slide off her silky smooth skin.

I can't take my eyes off her. She's fucking gorgeous and she knows it. One of the many things I love about Rhea is that she's not shy with her body. She knows she has all the right curves and isn't afraid to show it.

Now I just need to guarantee no one else sees it again but me. The thought of another man touching her makes my skin crawl. Knowing that so many already have makes me feel crazy. I can't think about it because I'll snap and I don't want to take my jealousy out on the only person I care about in the world.

"What now?" Rhea says, fully clothed. "Do you have some diabolical plan that is going to save me? One that doesn't involve forced nuptials?" She crosses her arms.

I pat the mattress in another attempt to call her over, and when her eyes trail from my hand to my eyes, there's a glint of temptation behind them. She wants to lie down with me. If she'd stop being so damn stubborn, this could be a good evening for both of us. What I wouldn't give to sleep beside my girl tonight.

"I think it's best if we sleep on it. Come up with a solid plan tomorrow. We still have some time."

"Fine." She huffs. "Now get out of my bed so I can get some sleep."

She's not going to budge. As much as I'd love to push the matter, or even give her no choice, we've made enough progress tonight that I'm feeling confident with the way things are going. I said I don't want to manipulate her unless it's to protect her, so I'm going to keep my word on that.

I exhale heavily and fling my feet over the bed. Crossing the room to where she's standing with her arms pushing up her perfect chest, I press a chaste kiss on her cheek and she snarls. "Sleep well, my love."

"Mmhmm."

I laugh at her smugness as I walk out the door. "By the way, you got a message from Tyler. Might want to respond, or delete it rather."

"Good night, Alaric." She shoves me out the door and slams it shut.

I trail my fingers down the door and whisper into the empty hall. "Good night, Wildcat."

That girl is a firecracker—and she's all *mine*.

TWENTY-THREE

I WAKE up and immediately see a diamond glistening in front of my face. *Why am I still wearing this thing?*

Shooting up, I pull it off, though it takes some effort. Once my finger is free of it, I hold it up in the beam of light coming through my curtains. It really is a beautiful ring. Alaric did an exceptional job picking it out. Unfortunately for him, I'm not accepting it. At least, not as an engagement ring. I'll gladly keep it, but it won't ever be because I'm marrying him—or any man at all for that matter.

Marriage isn't in the cards for me. Statistics show that fifty percent of first marriages end in divorce. That's a coin flip. A very big risk at enduring *another* broken heart. I've had mine sliced open enough to know I don't want that pain again. I won't survive it.

It's not that I'm incapable of loving someone, or being loved, I simply don't want *love* in my life. I always end up losing it.

Opting not to pawn the ring just yet, I pull open my nightstand and take out the envelope that holds a few packets of forget-me-not seeds. I tuck the ring inside the envelope for safekeeping, then I put it back in the drawer.

Getting out of bed is a bit of a struggle. My body aches fiercely, which is proof that it's been a while since I've gotten laid.

Last night was so much more than that, though. It was brutally beautiful. The way my body connected with Alaric's was magical. Everyone says sex is this amazing, life-changing thing, but that hasn't been my case. Once, I actually fell asleep —and I was the one on *top*. How the fuck that happened is beyond me, but it did.

However, sex with Alaric was nothing short of amazing. He certainly knows how to work his fingers and his tongue. And don't get me started on that dick. Not only is it practically the size of my forearm—I may be exaggerating a bit, but not much —it's got the optimal curve that hits all the right spots.

Fuck. I'm getting wet just thinking about it.

His dick. Not him. Of course not him. I don't think about Alaric in that way. Never will. He's a pain in my ass and doesn't know when to back off or shut up.

No. I only want his appendages.

Dragging my feet, I gather up some fresh clothes and head to my door, backtracking when I realize I can't keep my hormones in check.

It's been a while since I've used Bob—the nickname I gave my rabbit dildo. And all this thinking about the way Alaric made me feel last night really has me worked up. Another release will do me some good. I've been so stressed lately. So many things are happening that I can't control and I *hate* not being in control.

Pulling open my nightstand drawer again, I take out Bob and roll him up in my clothes—yes, him. He's the one constant in my life. One of the only objects I possess that has traveled with me to many different states. I don't keep things that aren't of use to me, or don't hold any meaning, but Bob is a *necessity*.

Feeling anxious, I move quickly to the bathroom and close the door behind me, making sure to turn the lock on the handle.

I set my clothes on the small space of the vanity and undress. I reach behind the curtain to turn on the shower, letting it get nice and steamy for me. While I wait for it to get to the right temperature, I unravel my clothes and pull Bob out.

With one foot on the toilet, and the other on the floor, I press the button on the end, putting it on medium speed. Moving slowly, I glide it in, resting the curved tip on my clit. My body jolts under the pressure, my legs already trembling from how worked up I got thinking about last night.

I move the toy back and forth, relishing in how good it feels. My head rests back and I close my eyes, driving the dildo deeper inside me. My back arches and it doesn't take long before I'm soaring to the tempo of the vibration. "Fuck," I mutter under my breath, now looking down and watching as it slides in and out of my wet pussy.

It's not Alaric, but it sure as hell feels good.

I reach the height of my orgasm after only a minute, gasping as I come around the pink toy. My body quivers and I immediately have to pull it out because my clit is too sensitive to handle any more.

The next thing I know, the bathroom door flies open and I'm too stunned to speak. Alaric comes charging in with a bottle of water and something else in his hand, then slams the door behind him. He's too quick to join my side and I'm not able to see what he's holding.

"What the fuck!" I growl. "How did you even get in here?" I

219

point a stern finger at the door he must have somehow unlocked. "Get the hell outta here!"

His expression is stern and serious, and it's obvious he came in here with intent.

He doesn't listen to my demand. Instead, he grabs a fistful of my hair, jerks my head back, then he uses the tips of his fingers and presses them so hard against my cheeks that my mouth is forced open. I swing Bob around, smacking him in the head a couple times, but it doesn't faze him in the least.

Suddenly, he puts something in my mouth. It rolls around and the chalky bitterness coats my tongue. I try to spit it out, but Alaric clamps my jaw closed with a forceful thrust under my chin.

"Swallow," he demands.

I try to open my mouth to spit it out, gagging on whatever it is he just fed me, but I fail miserably.

"Swallow, dammit!"

Given no choice, I swallow the pill down. It gets lodged somewhere in my throat and I manage to choke out the word, "Water."

Quickly, he twists the top off with one hand then brings the bottle to my lips. Pulling my hair again, he forces my head back and I swallow down the water, along with the pill.

"You son of a bitch!" I howl, still under his hold. I attempt to pull away, but he tugs my hair harder.

In a swift motion, Alaric raises his hand to his mouth, holding a syringe.

"No. No. No," I beg. "Please don't."

Using his teeth, he pulls the cap off, then he jabs a needle into my outer thigh. I wince in response, on the verge of tears. But I'm too angry to cry.

When he lets go of my hair and takes a step back, I throw Bob at him, hitting him smack-dab in the face.

"Did you just throw a fucking dildo at me?"

"Yes, I did!" I bend down and pick it up and smack his arm with it over and over again. "What the hell was that?" I look down, rubbing my bare thigh. "Are you knocking me out again?"

I feel dizzy. Lightheaded. My heart is racing. I toss Bob in the sink, grasp my chest, then sit on the cold toilet lid. "Am I going to pass out?"

"Calm down." He casually screws the top back on the bottle of water. "It was just a morning-after pill and a shot of birth control. You're protected for three months, at which time, we'll have to do this again. Minus the pill."

"Are you fucking kidding me?!"

"Nope. Not kidding. I hate to break it to you, baby, but if you dreamed of being a mother, your dreams will undoubtedly be shattered. Once we're married—and we will marry—we will not procreate. I have absolutely no desire to share you with another human."

"Then get a fucking vasectomy, you misogynistic pig!" I push at his chest as I stand, and he stumbles back, slightly stunned. *Point for Rhea.*

"Get out!" I scream at the top of my lungs as I charge at him. "Get the fuck out!"

He moves backward toward the door with each shove on my part.

Once he's out of the doorway, I slam it closed. My whole body slides down the door until I'm sitting butt-ass naked on the cold floor. I'm happy he got me the pill but that shot only gives him more power over me. I have to find a way to even this playing field.

Who the hell does this guy think he is?

I HAVEN'T LEFT my room since I returned from the shower. My anxiety can't decide if Alaric was lying or not. I feel okay one moment, then I don't the next. I know it's my irrational thoughts getting the best of me. He probably was just shooting me up with birth control and feeding me the morning-after pill. I didn't ask for it, the birth control at least, but I got it nonetheless.

Back to feeling pissed off, I'm desperate for a distraction. I grab my phone and respond to Tyler's message from yesterday.

> Tyler: Looking forward to seeing you at work Saturday. How cool that we finally get to work together. There's another party after since it's Devil's Night. You should come. I promise to make it more exciting than the last one.

Feeling devious, I glower as I type back a response.

> Me: Count me in. I'd love to go to the party with you. And what's more exciting than a first kiss? I'm curious to find out.

> Tyler: I guess I'm going to have to get creative ;)

I smile at his reply. Tyler is such a good guy, yet here I am knowingly dragging him into my mess. I'm not sure why I just agreed to go. I think part of me just wants to piss Alaric off. I need to show him I'm my own person, which means that only I will decide my future.

I close out the messages and go into the Siren's Call app. It's been a couple days since I've talked to HawkEye. Usually he sends me a daily, or every other day, message with some sweet words that always cheer me up. He must be busy lately.

So, I figure I'll try to make his day instead.

> Wildcat: Just a daily reminder that your life could be worse. At least your day job isn't to power wash portable toilets.

I hit send, wondering if that was actually funny, encouraging, or insensitive.

> HawkEye: But that is my day job and it pays well.

I laugh out loud as I tug my comforter up to my chest, getting comfortable in my bed.

> Wildcat: In that case, I hope you're not having a shitty day.

> HawkEye: Well, no one has pissed me off yet so it's a good start.

> Wildcat: Happy to hear.

> HawkEye: How is your day going?

> Wildcat: Just got jabbed with a needle near my ass so I can't say it's great, but it could be worse.

> HawkEye: Ouch! What was the shot for?

> Wildcat: Birth control.

> HawkEye: Ahh. Can't be too safe.

> Wildcat: Exactly.

I won't go into detail about the shot, because it's not

important. I'm not sure why I told him in the first place. I guess I'm just starting to feel more comfortable chatting with this guy.

> HawkEye: I assume you decided to stay where you're at and not move away again?

> Wildcat: For now. Don't really have a choice.

> HawkEye: Have you looked into enrollment in a GED program yet?

> Wildcat: Not yet. But it's on my list of things to do.

> HawkEye: I'm glad. You deserve to chase your dreams.

> Wildcat: I think so, too. Thank you.

> HawkEye: Is it safe to assume you've met someone if you got a shot of birth control? You're not meeting clients anymore, right?

> Wildcat: Not exactly. Well. Sort of, I guess. There is this guy...

> HawkEye: Go on.

Dammit, I should have just said no. I could tell him about Alaric, but that conversation would never end. Instead, I lie a little.

> Wildcat: He's super sweet. Probably one of the kindest people I've ever met. But we work together.

I expect his response to be immediate, but when it doesn't come, I type out another message.

> Wildcat: Are you there?

He doesn't respond so I set my phone down, only to pick it right back up. Curiosity gets the best of me and I go to my search engine and type in 'Alaric Banks.'

I hit enter, and watch as the screen loads with different articles about him ranging from business deals to accomplishments, and one with the headline: **2021 Top 50 Most Successful Entrepreneurs.**

I have to read it again just to make sure my eyes aren't deceiving me. Alaric was selected as one of 2021's top fifty most successful entrepreneurs. That's fucking insane! It was two years ago, but still. It's amazing. I had no idea he was so influential. And it's not just his business, *it's him.*

I click into the article and scroll to find out more about him, but there isn't much to read. There's a picture of him that gives my pussy a pulse because my God the guy is fucking gorgeous.

He's the owner of a tech business called A to Z Technology, which is compared to some of the biggest companies in the world, such as Apple and Microsoft. I don't read what they specialize in because I don't really care. All I know is, Alaric has more money than I could have ever imagined. Not just that, he's successful as fuck.

So what the hell does he want with little ol' me? It's baffling, to say the least. I'm a nobody and I'm worth nothing.

I close the article and click a few more, finding nothing interesting. Until one in particular catches my eye.

Planned Business Merger between A to Z Technology and Thorn Enterprise.

It's not the headline that grabs my attention, it's the photo.

Two men, one being Alaric, and the other being my dad. They're shaking hands and smiling for the camera.

I look at the date and it's the same year as the other article —2021.

Alaric wasn't kidding when he said he knew my father very well. I click the link and read the caption beneath the photo.

Lifetime friends, Alaric Banks and Grayson Thorn, have announced an agreement to bring global technology and natural resources together and create, what they hope will be, the nation's largest solar assisted energy source. Acquisition to be finalized in late 2023.

Oh, shit. I guess I really fucked that up for Alaric. I guess there's nothing I can do about it now. I turn off my phone and set it back on my nightstand, memories of that day flooding my mind.

Darkness looms as I enter the mansion that could have been my home. It's large and beautiful and full of expensive things, but it's also hollow and empty at the same time. It doesn't give off the comforting feel that one might expect for such a gorgeous place.

The smoky scent of a cherry lingers in the air and I follow the aroma, knowing exactly who's holding the lit cigar.

This isn't my first time in the house. I came here earlier to disarm the security systems and erase all the footage while Grayson was at his office. When he got home, I watched his red face from the window while he screamed at the baffled security company to fix the problem.

Now, luck seems to be on my side because the power has completely gone out at the Thorn estate.

I'd like to think it's my mom looking out for me, but I get the feeling it's something more practical.

I saw the mystery man's car earlier today. I know he's here in Redwood. Perhaps it was him. A stalker, but a savior at the same time. I'm not sure why I feel a sort of companionship with the stranger, chalk it up to being alone for the better part of my life and fighting tooth and nail for the other parts. This person doesn't seem to want to hurt me. It almost feels like everywhere I go that they follow, I'm protected somehow.

Creeping slowly down the hall to Grayson's study, where he's likely puffing out smoke while rubbing his big fat belly, I take care not to make a sound. It's a difficult feat considering the ceilings are so high in this house that every movement has an echo, but I'm a professional and memorized the route earlier.

Once I'm at the door, I take a deep breath and slowly push it open. The hinges creak and a wall of smoke wafts out. I refrain from choking on it, not wanting to give him the satisfaction of a single reaction.

Grayson's silhouette is cast in an eerie light from a lantern on the desk and he's hiding behind the glow of an orange ember, as I suspected. His dark, emotionless eyes lift and he looks at me, though he can't really see me. I'm clad from head to toe in black, with a ski mask hiding my face.

"Who the hell are you?" he grumbles as he snubs his cigar in the metal ashtray. The moon casts an eerie glow of light around us.

"Hi, Dad," I quip, crossing the room to where he's sitting behind the desk.

His eyes widen in surprise at my greeting and it's apparent he wasn't expecting me anytime soon. "No. It can't be. Rhea?"

"Surprised to see me?" I take out the hunting knife I brought with me.

"I can't see you. Take off the mask. Let me see your beautiful face." He goes to stand but I push him back down in the chair, holding a firm hand on his shoulder. I hold the leather-clad knife to his neck in warning.

"No," I tell him. "You haven't earned the right to see my face and I have no intention of wasting another breath talking to you."

My fingers drag across the leather as I slide the knife out, exposing the freshly sharpened blade. It reflects the moonlight and I feel a sense of rightness in my chest.

"Wha—what are you doing?" His voice is thick and raspy and laced with a fear that has my adrenaline pumping fiercely. He deserves this, he deserves so much worse but this is all I'm capable of right now.

Stepping behind him, I wrap one arm around his neck in a tight bear hug. "You thought you could steal my future and give it to a stranger? Well, now I'm going to steal yours and send you to hell."

I'm not a trained killer, but as my arm helps to pull up his head, thoroughly exposing his neck to me, I reflect on all of the struggles Mom endured because of this man. She was terrified of him. Then I think about all of the nights we went without food while this man stuffed his face in his ivory tower.

Flashes of every painful memory come right to the surface because they are all his fault. If he could have just been a decent human being and loved his daughter and wife I could have grown up happy, loved, fed. Instead, my reality has been hell. So it's only fitting that I see to it that's his reality too.

Grasping the hilt of the knife, I press the cold metal blade against his pale throat. He lets out a strangled gurgle, struggling to breathe as I drag it slowly, delivering him only a slice of the pain that was my life. Warm liquid hits my arm as I make the final life-ending cut to his jugular. Blood begins to pool across his neck, trickling down to his desk and dripping to the floor.

Eyes wide and vacant, his head lolls back, revealing the gaping wound on his throat. Blood gushes from the jagged edges of flesh and my stomach curls at the sight.

I turn and sprint out the open door, fighting to keep down whatever wants to come up. As I mentioned, I don't do this often, so my response is much less put together than I would have preferred, but I keep my head on straight. With the knife still clutched in my hand, I race out of the house, leaving a trail of bloody footprints.

The only advantage to leaving a trail of evidence is that it will only confuse people in the end. My small footprints will look as if a child were here and snuck past all this security all on their own..

Once I'm outside, I go around the house and retrieve the bag I left there, forcing myself to keep choking down the wave of nausea that hits me. I take my shoes off and put another pair I brought on and I stuff the bloody ones in the bag, along with the knife and my blood-soaked black jacket.

The sound of leaves crunching has my gaze shooting to the edge of the woods.

I have to get the hell out of here. Running frantically, I don't stop until I'm off Grayson's property. Even then, my feet move quickly. As if my body is forcing itself into a state of panic and shock all at once.

When I approach the ride-share car that's waiting for me, I slow my pace and peel off the ski mask.

Act cool, Rhea. You've got this. The unknowing driver gets out and opens the door for me with a greeting of some sort that I can't process right now. I simply nod and get in the back seat of the car, telling him to take me to the nearest bus station. Once I get there, I'll dispose of the bag, leave this town, and never look back.

The contract should be void. I should be free.

Little did I know how wrong I was, that I only made things more complicated for myself. Maybe if I had stayed and talked to him, I could have gotten him to drop the contract. Maybe if he saw how much of an asset I could be, he would have chosen me over the stupid deal he made.

But those are all what-ifs. Dreams someone like me doesn't have the luxury of even thinking about.

I just don't understand how Alaric can be so forgiving. I killed a good friend of his. Does he really love me enough to let that slide so easily?

What if he doesn't love me at all? What if this is all an act of revenge for taking Grayson's life and destroying what could have been one of the greatest mergers in the history of time. Okay, that's a little far-fetched, but it sounds like a really big deal.

And I blew that deal to hell.

CHAPTER
TWENTY-FOUR
RHEA

"RHEA DARLING," Gladys sings from outside my door, her relentless knocks growing louder and louder. "Are you awake?"

"Uh-huh," I grumble into my mattress with my pillow held tightly over my head.

She knocks again, this time even louder. "Rhea, you've got mail."

I toss the pillow off me, lifting my head with my tired eyes still closed. "You can leave it outside the door." I drop my head back down and add, "Please and thank you."

I have manners when I want to. I'm actually learning to use them more. Not that I feel it's necessary at... I open one eye to look at the clock on my nightstand. "Twelve p.m."

I'm not sure how I slept so late. Guess I needed it. Knowing I'm sneaking off to a party with Tyler this evening, I decide to close my eyes again and get even more sleep. There's no saying what time I'll be strolling in tonight.

Except my brain has other plans. It wants to start analyzing every situation and person in my life again.

Six days ago, I did a search on Alaric and found out there is a lot more to him than just an obsessed stalker. It was actually intriguing. I went to bed that night feeling worthless and intimidated by his presence. He's gold, and I'm paper.

Now when I talk to him, I feel myself tense up. I haven't been acting like my bratty self lately. My responses have been short and I've made it a point to keep our interactions to a minimum.

The only thing I can assume is that I feel immense guilt for destroying his business deal. But that's ludicrous. I shouldn't care. I don't give a damn about Alaric. Do I?

Why is he even on my mind...again!?

I roll sluggishly off the bed, shoulders sagging, and in my best Eeyore voice, I grumble, "Why bother?"

Pulling open my door, my eyes immediately drop, landing on a large envelope and package at my feet. Who the hell would send me mail, let alone a package? No one even knows I'm here. I guess it could be something about my taxes since I had to fill out a W-something or other for Taryn. I was even able to give her a legit social security number once Dex finally found it. Had I known my stalker would follow me here, I might have taken a different approach.

Regardless, I'm here now and so is he and I'm making the best of a situation I have no control over.

I bend down and swipe up the package and envelope, surprised at how heavy the box is. Then I return to my room, closing the door behind me.

Starting with the envelope, I read the text on the front. The sender is a business called Newport Online Education, and when I see the recipient's name, I gasp. *My wildcat.*

My heart feels like it's going to explode from my chest. Every second that passes only adds to my anxiousness. How does he know where I am? Is he following me, too?

I slide my finger under the flap of the envelope and peel it open. Inside is a packet about my current enrollment at Newport Online Education. Inside there is also a paper receipt for my payment into the GED program for...

"Six hundred dollars!"

This is crazy! He doesn't even know me, and he certainly shouldn't know the address of where I'm staying. There is no personal information about me on that app.

A wave of emotion surges through me as I read over the details. Classes begin the first week of December and run for six weeks. Once they conclude, I have to take a test. If I pass it, I get my GED.

I should be in awe of his kind gesture. I can't believe HawkEye did this for me. But it's hard to get excited when this guy has details about me that he shouldn't.

Laying the envelope on my bed, I grab the package, giving it a shake to try and guess what's inside. It sounds like a large book. Maybe something that will help me with the classes I'll be taking?

I don't have any tools or scissors on hand, so I tear into the box, ripping the top completely off. When I see what's inside, tears well in my eyes.

My first ever computer—or laptop, rather.

It's beautiful.

I've never even used a laptop before. I've only ever used the hotel computers that are in a small room for guests. When I was a kid, I loved typing stories on them. Only to delete them once I finished. I remember one story in particular about a ten-year-old girl named Jasmine who lived on a horse farm. She had three sisters who were her best friends and every day they'd go riding together. I didn't grow up playing with baby dolls or babies, so writing stories was my favorite way to pretend.

I set the box back down, my new laptop still inside, and I grab my phone to message HawkEye.

> Wildcat: How did you get my address?

> HawkEye: I'm very resourceful.

> Wildcat: I'm not going to lie, this is a little creepy.

> HawkEye: You don't need to fear me, Wildcat. I simply did a little research and found the address.

> Wildcat: I don't even know what to say. You have no idea how much I appreciate this, but it's weird. You shouldn't have.

> HawkEye: It's the first step in your fresh start. You can do this. I know you can.

My crippling fear is slowly replaced with elation. I'm not sure why, but I truly think he just wants to help me.

> Wildcat: Thank you for that. No one has ever believed in me the way you do. It means more to me than you'll ever know.

> HawkEye: My only hope is that eventually you'll believe in yourself, too.

> Wildcat: I think I'm on the right track.

> HawkEye: I think so, too.

Excitement about the laptop ripples through me, so I leave our conversation at that and tear into the packaging.

The next three hours are spent setting it up and scrolling aimlessly on TikTok. I've never had social media, and I still don't. I'm currently viewing as a guest. But I watched some of the most fucked-up, most hilarious, and most emotional videos. I just have to ensure I don't fall down this rabbit hole daily because I could lie in bed all day watching this shit.

Before I know it, it's eight o'clock and time to get ready for work. My nerves are at an all-time high, considering it's my first weekend and night shift.

I decide on a pair of blue jeans and a cute baby blue crop top that shows a sliver of my stomach. Then I destroy my whole ensemble with my worn shoes that have the backs pressed down. I'm currently saving money for next month's rent, but once that's paid, I'm investing in some new shoes. *Brand new.* Not smelly used ones from the thrift store.

My hair is thrown up in a high ponytail and I brush a few strokes of mascara on my lashes. Feeling pretty confident in the way I look, I blow myself a kiss in the mirror and head to Taryn's.

THE VIBE at Taryn's is crazy. People are chatting with friends, dancing to the band, eating delicious fried food. Everyone is in good spirits and the tips have been insane. I've been here three hours, with only an hour to go, and I've already made a hundred and thirty dollars. That's more tips than I make during the day shift in a week. If I could do this every Friday and Saturday night, I'd be able to pay rent without a problem.

I look around at the crowd of over fifty people, searching for the one person I shouldn't want to see.

I've been so busy since I arrived, pouring drinks left and right, slinging cash, and making money, but he's been in the back of my mind the entire time.

It's odd that I haven't seen him yet. He claims to always be watching, so where is he now?

"How's it going?" Tyler asks, sliding up beside me and snapping me from my thoughts. He sticks a frosted glass under a beer nozzle and tilts it slightly to decrease the amount of foam. It's a trick he taught me when I first got here. He's also had to help me with almost every mixed drink, and I'm sure he feels like I'm more hassle than help.

"It's going," I tell him, lifting a brow. "Scotch on the rocks?"

He chuckles. "That's an easy one. Rocks means ice. Just pour some scotch. If they didn't specify," he grabs a bottle of dark liquor and he sets it on the bar, "then they get bottom-shelf scotch and it's five bucks."

I reach out a hand, wrap it around his arm, and squeeze. "Thank you, Tyler."

"Welcome. Holler if you need anything else." He tops off the mug of beer and heads to the other end of the bar.

My eyes lift slowly and I find Alaric standing directly in front of me on the other side of the bar. His blue eyes flash with anger and his jaw is set tight. There's no question that he's livid.

"You look like you could use a drink," I say to him casually as I pour a shot's worth of scotch in a small glass over ice. Well, it was more like two and a half shots, but I did the best with the pressure I'm under.

Alaric rests his arms on the bartop and leans in, beckoning me with a curl of his fingers.

"I don't have time for this, Alaric. Do you want a drink or not?"

"What I want," he grits out, speaking each word slowly. "Is for you to stop throwing yourself at your fucking co-worker."

"Throwing myself at him?" I laugh as I sweep my hand in the air. "Get the hell away from me."

As I'm walking away with the drink I just made in my hand

to deliver it to the guy who ordered it, I hear Alaric holler, "And pull your fucking shirt down."

Feeling the urge to piss him off, I raise my hands in the air, forcing my shirt to ride up even farther. Then I look over my shoulder and smirk before flipping him off.

The next thing I know, Alaric is maneuvering his way through the crowd at the bar, his scathing glare deadlocked on me.

I quickly bring the customer his drink. Not even waiting for him to slap down a tip, I walk over to the bathroom, quickly trying to get away from people. There's no doubt in my mind Alaric is about to make a scene, and I need to find a way to control it.

I'm making my way across the room, moving through the crowd, when I trip over someone's foot. "I'm sorry," I say to the person I stumbled into. When I look up, I see that the strong arms holding me belong to Alaric.

"Don't start." I sigh heavily. "I'm working."

There's a slackness in his face as he grips my arm and pulls me the rest of the way across the room. I look around, making sure Taryn isn't watching because if she sees this, she'll definitely throw him out, or worse, call the cops.

I shouldn't care. I should want her to see the way he's manhandling me right now. But for some strange reason, I feel this urge of protectiveness. I've always felt a little insane, and this just reaffirms that I am. *I'm protecting my stalker, who's also a psycho.*

Alaric shouts over the music, not caring who hears him. "Do you have any idea how it makes me feel when I see you with your hands on another man, or vice versa?"

I don't respond because it's not actually a question and he's going to tell me how it makes him feel anyways.

"It's similar to the feeling of having your entire body

engulfed in flames. Do you know what that feels like?" His face is red, and dammit, I actually feel a little bit bad. A *little* bit.

"Can't say that I do," I tell him honestly. "I assume you do if you're making the comparison. I must say, you look pretty damn good for someone who's had their entire body burned." I smirk.

"Do you think this is a joke?" Alaric pushes me against the wall, planting one hand on the left side of my head while his other holds me in place with a firm grip on my hip. "We're not playing games here, Rhea. I don't fucking like it." His voice rises to a near shout. "So quit fucking doing it. Stay the hell away from Tyler, and every other man for that matter."

"Tyler is my friend," I bite back. "If I want to talk to him or hug him, then I will."

"Since when do you have friends, or want them for that matter?" He looks genuinely confused, as if it's weird that I want someone in my life for something other than a con.

"Since now!" I try to throw my hands up, desperate for him to see that this isn't a game I'm playing either. I might have lifted my shirt to mess with him, but with Tyler, I want him as a friend.

"Since I decided to stay in Lockhaven and turn over a new leaf. I want to be normal, Alaric, but you're making it really fucking hard for me." A lump lodges in my throat and I wish he could just see what all of this is doing to me. "You say you love me, so please, just let me finally enjoy my life."

Eyebrows drawn together, he peers down at me. His hand slackens against the wall and he bends his elbow to lean close. "Do you want more than friendship with that boy?"

"No!" I blurt out honestly. "I really don't."

"You know if you fuck him, then you better plan to meet me in the backyard next to Gladys's garden shed so I can watch while you dig his fucking grave." His hand tightens on my waist, showing me just how serious he is.

My eyes roll and I draw in a deep breath of annoyance. "Jesus. I'm not going to fuck him, or anyone else for that matter. Now, will you move so I can get back to work?"

His voice softens in a way that makes me swoon. "You mean that?"

"Yeah. I do. But don't let it go to your head. Doesn't mean I'm planning to fuck you either." I feel myself starting to sweat, so I attempt to duck under his arms, to no avail.

Why is he so damn hypnotic? The man above really likes to throw wrenches in all my plans. He could have sent me some short, stubby, old man as a stalker. Instead he sends me this Adonis with a temper problem and an obsession for only me. I wish I could run away, but I'm beginning to realize the reason I haven't is because I don't really want to at all.

Alaric's vehement personality is growing on me like an invasive weed. I find myself searching crowds for him when he's not in sight. I think of him when I go to bed and when I wake up. I'm completely and utterly fucked up beyond recognition because of this man.

He tips his chin, the corner of his lips tugged up. "Why are you such a pain in the ass, Rhea?"

"You know, if you don't like it, you can just leave this town and forget me, right? You have that option." My chest constricts. I don't want to lose him, but it's more because I hate being abandoned once people find out I'm not worth their time. Not because I like him or anything.

"Leaving is not an option. And forgetting you is impossible. I think the same can be said for you. It's been my mission to ensure you never forget me, and I think I've succeeded. Am I right?" His fingers trace the outline of my forget-me-not flowers as if he's trying to tell me something.

I lift my shoulders, locked under the spell that is Alaric Banks. "Maybe."

"I can work with 'maybe'...for now."

My eyes travel to his mouth and I find myself licking my lips when his tongue drags across his bottom teeth. "Go ahead," he says. "You know you want to."

I gulp, eyes shooting to his hot gaze. "Want to what?"

"Kiss me. I saw the way you were looking at my lips." He leans closer and my heart jumps into a frenzy. "Do it."

I avert my gaze, unable to look at him out of fear I will melt into a puddle at his feet. One damn orgasm and I'm already like this? "I...I have to get back to work, assuming I still have a job after going MIA for so long when we're this busy."

Alaric drops his arm, setting me free, but I'm frozen. Why am I having such a hard time walking away? I despise this man. He's gone out of his way to prove he can destroy my life through schemes and blackmail. He's cold and ruthless, yet mysterious and alluring. And my God, his mouth looks delicious. *Fuck my life.* I grab him by the face and pull his mouth to mine in a searing kiss.

He sucks my bottom lip between his teeth. Pushing me against the wall, he molds his body to mine. I feel my nipples harden against the soft cotton of my tee shirt. Warmth creeps up my neck when his stiff cock presses against me. Throwing temptation to the wind, I push into him, wanting to feel every damn inch of him that had me going wild the other night.

The harsh sound of someone clearing their throat has me jumping out of the kiss. I look to my left, my hands still frozen in place on either side of Alaric's head. There stands Tyler, a stern look of disapproval painted across his face.

I feel like a teenager getting caught making out in my bedroom. If only I knew what that truly felt like.

Sorry to interrupt." He looks from Alaric to me. "But we're slammed."

The disappointment in his tone crushes me. I quickly drop my hands and move away from Alaric. "Yeah. I'll be right there." Tyler walks away shaking his head and I cover my face with my hands. "Fuuuuck."

"So he saw us kissing. What's the big deal?"

"What's the big deal? Well, let's see here." I hold up a finger in the air, adding another with each point I make. "You threatened him in my room. You're twenty years older than me—"

"Twenty-one years older," he corrects me.

"Even worse."

"Age is just a number, baby." He slithers up to me again and I'm half tempted to reach for his embrace.

"No." I drop my hands to my sides. "I have to get back to work before I get fired."

"Let her fire you. I'll take care of you."

I take a deep breath, wanting to say so many things about how I need my independence and how this will never work, but I keep it to myself for now. "We'll talk about this later," I say before trekking quickly back to the bar.

TWENTY-FIVE

"Are you sure you know what you're doing?" Tyler asks as he mixes a drink beside me.

I can't bring myself to look him in the eye. I'm not sure why I'm so ashamed of myself. It was just a kiss. Last year I would have fucked a guy in a bar if the price was right.

I'm a whore. A dirty whore who is horny for a crazed, sexy, much older man. It's not just about the sex, though. He's rubbing off on me. I've never had someone fight for me before. I've never had someone stay when I made things difficult. And I sure as fuck have never had someone kill for me. As much as I want to wash him away, I think I'm stained by him.

I'm so dizzy from that kiss that my thoughts don't even make sense.

"Probably not," I respond honestly. "I never really know what I'm doing."

"Look," Tyler turns to me, "I'm not going to judge you. I don't know your history with Alaric, but just be careful, okay?"

I nod, lips pressed tightly. "I will."

Tyler tips his head slightly to the right. "You like him, don't you?"

"No." I blurt out before immediately recanting my response. "I mean, yes. Fuck. I don't know."

Placing a comforting hand on my arm, he looks into my eyes and I can see he really cares. "You can't walk away from him and hold on at the same time, Rhea. You'll break yourself."

"I know," I whisper softly.

Whatever I thought might have been there between Tyler and me is gone. I've ensured that after getting caught kissing Alaric. It's best this way, though. Tyler and I connect on a friendship level and it's actually really nice to have someone I can call a friend, if he even wants that.

"Whoa. Whoa. Whoa." He laughs, grabbing the bottle of liquor from my hand. "That's a rare and expensive bottle. Did someone specifically order that?"

"No." I shrug. "They ordered a whiskey sour so I just found a bottle that said whiskey on it. Is that wrong?"

He chuckles again, turning around and putting back the bottle and retrieving a different one. "Little secret. Mixed drinks get the cheapest booze."

"Well, that's a little devious." I feel some of our usual banter coming back and he starts to relax. Maybe he will be okay with us just being friends.

"That's business." He waggles his brows and grabs the drink he just poured. "Stephanie will be here in five, then we can clock out. You're still coming tonight, right?"

I look around the room, subconsciously looking for Alaric. "Um. Yeah. Of course."

As much as I know I shouldn't do this, I can't blow Tyler off again. He is my friend now, after all. I don't have many and I certainly don't want to lose the one I've got.

"Good," he quips. "Because I invited someone to go with us."

"Oh, really? Who's that?" I ask as I put the whisky sour in front of the man who ordered it.

"Heather. I think you know her. She's staying over at Gladys's guesthouse."

"Yeah. I know Heather. Well, sort of. We've met but never really talked."

"She's a cool girl. Same age as us. I think you two would get along great."

It's strange to me that Tyler thinks we'd get along great because from what I've seen of Heather, she's very quiet and reserved, whereas I'm boisterous and loud.

"Oh, look." His voice lifts and he's grinning from ear to ear. "She's here now." Tyler stretches his hand in the air and waves. I follow his line of sight and see Heather with her hands clasped in front of her, wearing a navy blue down coat that reaches her knees, a pair of blue jeans, and black ankle boots.

She looks cute...and warm.

Tyler walks away, likely going to say hi, and I can't help but feel hopeful for him, and a little nervous too. He's such a good guy and deserves to find someone who makes his heart skip a beat. Someone he searches the crowd for and thinks about first thing in the morning. Maybe Heather could be that girl.

Another man orders and I'm able to fill it without having to ask Tyler for help, which makes me feel like I'm actually getting the hang of this. I hand the man his drink and he lays down a five-dollar bill with a smile. "Thank you very much." I tuck the bill into my apron pocket then check the time.

Stephanie is behind the bar now, which means it's time for me and Tyler to clock out. Excitement buzzes through me as I untie my apron and fold it up, keeping my tips intact.

As I'm walking toward the kitchen to the time clock

machine, I find myself looking for Alaric again. Not only am I curious what he's doing and where he's at, I sort of need to know. There is no way he's going to let me walk out of this bar with Tyler and go to a party with a bunch of strangers.

"Hey," I tell Tyler when he comes into the kitchen with Heather right behind him. "I'm gonna go out the back kitchen door, run my tips home really quick, and grab a coat. Wanna meet in the back parking lot in ten?"

"Works for me."

I do as I said and pass through the kitchen, right behind Jerry the cook. "Have a good night," I tell him.

"You, too, Rhea."

I slip out the back door, the cold air hitting me hard in the face. It's definitely a coat and hat sort of night. The young crowd in Lockhaven are savages—throwing parties outdoors when it's only forty degrees out. I guess that makes me savage, too, since I'm attending.

I'm not even sure why I'm going tonight. I think part of me didn't want to let Tyler down again after standing him up last week. But he has Heather now and they looked cozy together in the kitchen. I doubt he'd care if I bailed.

Creeping slowly, taking in all my surroundings, I go around the building to Gladys's front door. I look left, then right, before pushing it open and going inside quickly. Once I'm in, I breathe a sigh of relief, a devilish grin on my face.

"Gladys," I call out as I turn down the hall to my room. "It's just me. I'm heading out again. Just grabbing my—" My words are cut short when I crash into someone in the dimly lit hall. "Oh, shit. Sorry..." I look up and see that it's Alaric and my shoulders drop in defeat.

His hand lands on my hip as he peers down at me. "Going somewhere?"

"Nope. Just to my room." I go to step around him, but he sidesteps in my way.

"Are you sure about that?"

My head tilts slightly to the left. "Seriously, Alaric?"

"Yes, seriously. You're lying to me. I just heard you hollering to Gladys that you were heading out again. Do you think I'm fucking stupid?" He tightens his grip on my hip and I grit my teeth.

"No, I don't think you're stupid." Giving up, I just tell him the truth. "Look. I didn't tell you because I knew you'd do this." I look at his hand that's gripping my side. "It's just a party."

His eyes perk up. "*Just* a party?"

"Yes, just a party. It's no big deal. I'll be back in a couple hours."

"And who's going to be at this *party*?"

I shrug my shoulders. "I don't know, *Dad*. Probably people my age, and..."

"And Tyler?"

I roll my eyes and cross my arms. "Plus Heather."

"Heather from two rooms down, Heather?"

"Yes," I stammer. "That one. Now, will you please not make a big deal out of this? They're waiting for me next door and I have to go."

"I'm not making a big deal out of anything. It sounds like a good time. You should definitely go." He releases me immediately and a strange sort of cold creeps over the place his hand just was. As if I want him to put it back.

"Really?"

I'm speechless. I can't believe it was this easy. I thought for sure I'd stand here all night defending my right to go.

He grazes my cheek with the backs of his fingers, warmth radiating from his touch. "Of course, baby. You want friends and you want to live your life. Go live it."

I find myself leaning into his touch. "Thank you." I lift a smile, placing my hand over his on my cheek. For once in this messed-up thing that's going on between us, I feel like he actually heard me. Not just heard me, but listened and took it to heart.

"You don't need to thank me. I want you to have fun. You've missed out on so much and you deserve to live a normal life."

I give a subtle nod and our eyes meet. Time seems to pause and for a moment, I forget that I'm even in a hurry to leave. Lately, Alaric's presence has a way of drowning out the rest of the world, until it's just the two of us, with nowhere else to be.

Only, there is somewhere I need to be. "I should go," I tell him regretfully.

"I agree," he says, his hand slowly dropping. I step around him, clutching my apron and the money inside. "It's going to be a cold night," he muses. "Why don't you go grab your coat and we can leave?"

I stop walking and spin around, my eyebrows practically hitting my forehead. "We?"

"Well, yeah," he says confidently. "I'm going with you."

I narrow my eyes and tilt my head. "What?" When he stands there with a stone-faced expression, I snort with laughter. "Oh, you're kidding?"

Behind his blue eyes is no trace of humor.

Of course. I should have fucking known! Just when I thought he heard me, that maybe he would let me have a say and maybe something between us could work, the band snaps, hitting me in the face. *Point for Alaric.*

The sound of the front door opening, followed by chatter, has my eyes shooting wide. "That's probably them," I tell him, my voice strained because I'm not ready to explain Alaric's behavior to Tyler and Heather. Hell, I can't even explain him to myself.

Heather and Tyler come walking down the hall and I step around Alaric, who spins to face the same direction as me with a smile on his face. "Good to see you again, Heather," he says before I can even get any words out to *my* friends for the night. "And Tyler, it's always a pleasure."

"Mmmhmm," Tyler grumbles as he looks at me quizzically.

"Umm. I'm just gonna go grab my coat and then we can leave." I shoot a nervous thumb over my shoulder before going to my room. My heart is thumping violently in my chest. Alaric isn't going to back down. But I also *really* don't want to have a conversation with Alaric about this in front of them.

It's fine. Everything will be fine.

I could just lock my door and not go out at all, but Alaric is right. I want to be out living my life. I deserve it. The only reason I'm even playing this game with him is because I can't deny he's keeping me safe from whoever is out there after me. And I have zero doubts that he would jump in front of a bullet for me.

Oh, and his dick. But I'm not going to acknowledge that one.

I put my apron in my top drawer, then grab my coat that's on the bed, while giving myself a mental pep talk. Taking a deep breath, I leave the room, ready to face whatever mess is out there waiting for me.

"All set?" Alaric asks, his own jacket now draped over his forearm as he reaches his hand out to me. I ignore it.

I nod silently, looking at Tyler's questioning gaze. He doesn't believe a damn word of this.

"Oh," Tyler says, stretching his neck. "Is Alaric going?"

I join the circle and Alaric puts an arm around my shoulders. "Of course I am. Rhea invited me."

I wanna slap him. No. I want to wrap my fingers around his throat and squeeze.

Alaric continues, "Isn't that right, baby?"

No. He. Didn't. My cheeks flush with heat and beads of sweat form on my forehead. "Yup," I quip as I grind my teeth abrasively.

"Hmm." Tyler nods, looking between us and observing the situation. He saw us kiss earlier, so it shouldn't be that much of a surprise. Not that Alaric and I are a thing, but Tyler has no idea what's going on between us.

He's just being a concerned friend. I know it has nothing to do with the way he feels about me because I'm positive any potential feelings disintegrated the moment he saw Alaric and I kiss at the tavern.

"That's great," Heather pipes up, eyes on Alaric. "I'm glad you're going with us."

I don't know the girl, but I wanna grab her by the face and kiss her on the cheek. Her words offer a bit of encouragement that the night might not be so bad.

"Shall we go?" Alaric asks, taking my hand. "Rhea and I will just follow behind the two of you in my car."

I squeeze his hand back tightly, letting him know just how irritated I am with him. I wasn't given an opportunity to fight him on coming, but I sure as hell plan to tell him how I feel about him jumping into my plans.

We walk out the front door and Tyler's car is parked along the street, right behind Alaric's.

"It's not too far," Tyler hollers as he opens his passenger door for Heather. It's a sweet gesture, and when I see that Alaric has his car door open for me, I feel this strange rush of gratification. I find myself looking to see if Tyler noticed Alaric's gesture.

Why I seek his approval is beyond me. I guess I just care about Tyler and I don't want him to be disappointed in me. Another thing I can't begin to understand about myself. I'm finding that relationships with people can be confusing and I'm still learning how to navigate the ones I've formed. I've never been a people pleaser, but as I continue to learn new things about myself, I'm finding that I don't want to hurt the people I've come to care about. If they can worm their way into my heart, they deserve to be fought for.

"After you, baby," Alaric says, a smug look on his face.

I roll my eyes as I drop into the car, ready to give him a piece of my mind once these car doors are closed.

The second he sets his foot on the floorboard of the driver's side, I begin, "I can't believe you! I seriously thought for a sliver of a second you had an ounce of compassion running through your veins. You made me think you're happy that I'm going out with my friends, *like a normal person my age*, I might add. This is so fucking embarrassing!"

The engine roars to life and he drapes his wrist over the steering wheel. Glancing in his side mirror, his eyes are vacant and distant. He eases slowly off of the brake and pulls out onto the road without a single word.

"Dammit, Alaric! Say something!"

"I'm sorry," he says, eyes on the road ahead. "Was there a question?"

"Yes! Well, technically no. But explain yourself, dammit!"

"You lied to me and told me you weren't going anywhere. I caught you in said lie, and here we are." His tone is low and forthright. "What else is there to explain?"

"Why?" I shout over the purr of the engine.

"Because I don't trust people and I have to protect the most important thing in the world to me."

"Me?"

"Absolutely you." As if there was no question in the matter.

He turns to face me for a moment, eyebrows pinched together tightly. "Is it my age that embarrasses you?"

Rubbing my temples aggressively, I think of the best way to answer that question. "Alaric," I say plain and simply. "I've never had friends, especially not friends my age, and I want to make a good impression on them. It's not your age that's embarrassing, it's your *behavior*."

"What?" He huffs. "I think I've been more than kind to everyone in this town. Well, except Tyler. And Nick. And some asshole who parked in my space in front of Gladys's last week."

"Oh God." I sigh. "I don't even want to know what happened to that guy."

"Nothing. But his car is sitting somewhere at the bottom of Meyers Lake."

I shake my head in disappointment. "See. This is what I mean. You can't do that shit."

"Sure I can."

"It's not normal."

"Well, I'm not normal. And neither are you, Rhea. We're the same, you and I. Venomous snakes slithering our way through life, ready to bite anyone who steps on our path."

"No, we're not. My bite barely pierces the skin, yours kills on impact."

The corner of his mouth lifts. "You're so dramatic. Tyler's still very much alive."

"Only because I think part of you knows that if you hurt him, I'll never forgive you."

I hate that Alaric has the ability to turn everything I say about him into some sort of praise on his part. In the end, I always lose, and I'm left swooning over him for reasons unbeknownst to me.

"Does my age really bother you?" he asks, tone low and soft. When I look at him, I see a glint of worry in his features.

I feel a sharp tug at my heart as I watch Alaric. His lips are pressed together in a thin line and his eyes have a lost, almost desperate look to them. This is the first time I've ever seen Alaric question my feelings toward something he can't change about himself.

He's always so confident that one day I will choose him without a second thought, never questioning whether or not we would have a future together. And yet here he is, holding his breath as he waits for my response.

"No," I finally say. "Age is just a number."

He keeps his eyes fixed on the road, but I see the smile playing on his lips. Then I find myself biting back a smile of my own.

We are so dysfunctional.

After a moment of silence, Alaric breaks it with an almost chipper voice. "What do you say we blow off this party and you let me take you somewhere else?"

"No." I shake my head reluctantly. "I can't do that."

"Sure you can. You don't know any of these twatwaffle college kids. Fuck them."

"It's not about them. It's about Tyler. I have to make an appearance at the very least."

"*Tyler,*" he mocks me in a low growl. "Fuck that kid."

"As I've told you at least a *dozen* times, that kid is my friend."

"Fine. Whatever. We'll make an appearance, watch a bunch of drunk idiots make fools of themselves. Then, let's do something actually worth our time."

"And what would we do that is worthy of our time?"

"Be together. Just you and me. Anywhere but there." He reaches over and places his hand on my lap, wearing a gorgeous smile on his face.

I bat my eyelashes, trying to cover up the fact that I'm falling for all the little things that make him, him. His smile, his urgency to keep me safe, the way he makes me forget all my worries. No matter how hard I try to fight it, I gravitate toward him. His words are kind yet demanding, and his actions are both selfish and self-sacrificing. Alaric has become a complete enigma to me.

I'm not sure why my stubbornness is so strong. He is growing on me fast, but for some reason, I don't want him to know it. He'll assume everything he's been doing is okay, and it definitely isn't. He'll think that his tactics are luring me in, but they're not. It's not what he does that has me so captivated by him, it's *who* he is.

No one has ever made me feel so many different emotions at once. No one has ever looked at me the way this man does. And I'm positive I've never looked at anyone the way I look at him, either. Totally and completely entranced.

"Okay," I tell him.

His eyes shoot to mine, wide and surprised. "Really?"

"Sure." I shrug my shoulders. "Why not?"

He gives my leg a tight squeeze, showing me how pleased he is with my response. I look down on it, contemplating my reaction, then finally, I lay my hand over his. I can feel the electricity between us. This warm tingle in my palm.

When I look over at Alaric, and see him stealing a glance at me, I know he feels it too. I have no idea what it means, and I'm terrified to find out because it's definitely nothing I've ever felt before in my life.

CHAPTER
TWENTY-SIX
ALARIC

RHEA'S FINGERS intertwine with mine, melding together as if they'd been designed for no other purpose than to fit in this moment. It's the touch I've been waiting to feel for a very long time. It's not forced or demanded. I didn't steal it or beg for it. Out of her own free will, she chose to hold my hand. Even though she's staring out the side window as if she could care less.

She's coming around, as I knew she would. The walls she's put up around her heart are crumbling more and more each day. I can feel the distance between us shorten as she gets closer and closer to me.

We're almost there, Wildcat.

The threat out there is still strong, and I don't foresee it going away anytime soon. But I've got some men searching for Ian and they're fully prepared to take him out once they're close enough. It's not an easy feat capturing a man of his power, but I have faith the job will get done.

Until then, my focus is my girl. Keeping her safe while deepening the bond between us.

I'm actually glad we're making an appearance at this party. Heather will be there and this gives me the opportunity to watch her actions while attempting to pick up on anything she does out of the ordinary. I still don't trust that girl. The timing of her arrival in Lockhaven, a small town no one gives a damn about, is just a little too convenient.

Trailing behind Tyler down a narrow dirt road, I press on my brakes when his brake lights come on. He pulls off slowly to the side, parking behind a row of cars, so I do the same.

"Guess this is it?" I say to Rhea, reluctantly taking my hand from hers so I can hold the steering wheel with two hands.

"Yep. It's nothing special. Just a party in the woods. I guess this is what people in Lockhaven like to do for fun." She unbuckles her seat belt and looks over at me.

"It's not just Lockhaven. Parties like this are common in small towns. Seems like yesterday I was spending my weekends on top of a keg in the middle of nowhere after football games on Friday nights. Granted, I didn't grow up in a place as desolate as Lockhaven, but it wasn't the city either."

I watch as Rhea's features tense. She wraps her fingers around the door handle, but hesitates to push it open. "I wouldn't know about any of that. I didn't have a normal upbringing, and didn't visit many small towns."

Fuck. I inwardly curse myself for being such an insensitive prick. I know Rhea didn't have the luxury of a traditional childhood. My life is a stark contrast to the struggles she's faced throughout hers.

"I'm sorry," I say to her, my words laced with an emotion that burns my throat.

"Don't be. It's not your fault." She shrugs, pretending it doesn't matter to her. She tries to be so strong all the time when all I want is to shoulder the weight for her. Eventually, maybe I can earn that from her too.

I can't help but feel like I'm partially to blame. I knew Rhea's mom took her away and I should have helped Grayson find her sooner. He didn't care to find her, though. Never once mentioned her until she was of age and he was ready to pay his debt.

If I'd known a monster lurked beneath Grayson's facade, I may have reacted sooner. Looking back, I realize he enjoyed the suffering of innocent people. In his mind, Rhea's mom was getting exactly what she deserved, living a life of turmoil on the run, and Rhea was just collateral damage.

It breaks my heart to think about all she endured. One day, I want her to tell me all about it so I can seek revenge on every living soul that has hurt her. Killing the mayor of that town, the one that raped her and knocked her up, was just the beginning for me. But I saw the way she looked that night. She'd been through hell already; I was just arriving to the train wreck that was her life.

"You know," I begin, but before I can finish my sentence, Rhea pushes open her door.

She leans down and says, "Don't think too much into it, Alaric. I'm fine. The past is in the past." She closes the door and I slap my hands to the steering wheel, hating that I've trudged up painful memories for her. She might not have said anything, but I know she's thinking about all she's missed out on.

Someday and somehow, I'm going to make it up to her. She's going to experience everything she's missed. I might not be able to give her back her youth, or her teenage years, but I can make her twenties the best possible years of her life.

I get out of the car and meet her where she's leaning against the front bumper. Placing a hand on the small of her back, I tug her forward until her chest is flush with mine. I peer down into her eyes, searching for a sign that she's been crying, or is about to. But my girl's tough as nails and does a damn good job at hiding her emotions. I hate that for her.

"You okay?" I ask, fingers grazing softly over her coat.

"Fine. Why?" Her brows pinch, genuinely confused about my concern for her.

"Just making sure. If you ever wanna talk about—"

"I don't. I'm fine, Alaric." She tries to push away from me, but I don't let her get far.

No, you're not. I don't say it, but it's evident. One day Rhea is going to have to talk about the pain she's endured. Maybe not to me, but hopefully to me. She can't hold that shit in forever; it'll destroy her.

"Let's just go to the party for a bit, so we can leave." She was so excited to get here, willing to fight me on it. And now? Now she looks like she can't wait to leave.

My hand slides down and I intertwine our fingers, giving her silent support in the only way I know how. "I like the way you think."

We walk a few feet forward to where Tyler and Heather are waiting and Tyler looks at Rhea, then shoots me a look of disdain. "What the hell did you do to her?"

"Back off, kid, I didn't do shit." Maybe he is a good friend if he can see Rhea is hurting as easily as I can.

"You must have said or done something. She was happy and now she looks miserable." He looks ready to fight me.

"Tyler," Rhea snaps. "Alaric didn't do anything. I'm fine."

He gives me a once-over and tips his chin as if he's threatening me. Farm Boy is lucky as fuck that Rhea cares about him so much. It's the only reason he's still standing right now.

She's never had friends and I'm letting her keep this one because it's important to her. However, if he doesn't learn to mind his own damn business, I might rethink my willingness to let him live.

We head toward the blazing fire that has a crowd gathered around it. Heather seems to be extra quiet tonight, which is odd considering she had so much to say last time I saw her.

"How are you doing tonight, Heather?" I ask, striking up conversation on our walk to the party.

"Doing well, Alaric, thank you." She tilts her head down, as if she doesn't really want to talk.

"Have you decided when you're leaving Lockhaven yet? Or did you still plan to stay for a while?"

"That's still to be determined."

I nod slowly. "I see."

This girl is sketchy as fuck and I don't like her one bit. She's up to something and I need to find out what that something is...fast.

There are about fifty or sixty young idiots prancing around with drinks in their hands, acting a fool. Oh to be young again.

But now that I'm not, I don't enjoy this shit one bit. I'd rather be anywhere than here. I'd really like to be somewhere alone with my girl. At least I've got her on my arm where she's safe. That's the only perk of being at this dumpster fire party.

"More new friends," a guy asks Tyler as he approaches us with a couple of girls. His eyes move from one of us to the next, and his shoulders are far too taut and his chest is much too puffed out for a dipshit with such a small frame. "Where the fuck do you find all these people?"

"Chill out, Nelson. They're friends from Taryn's," Tyler responds before his gaze slides to me. "Well, *some* of them, anyways."

"Rhea," a blonde girl whistles with an upturned face, "I wish you'd told us you were bringing your dad to the party. We would have taken the booze from all the minors." She begins laughing and then nudges her friend at her side until she follows suit with her childish antics.

I step forward, ready to say something smart-mouthed to the girl, but Rhea puts a hand on my chest, holding me back.

She's got this.

"That's okay, sweetie. My daddy doesn't care. Maybe next time I'll bring yours and see how he feels about it...after I suck his dick."

"Ohhh snap," the guy, who Tyler called Nelson, sings. He raises his hand in the air at Rhea and she slaps him a high five.

Normally, I'd be bitten with jealousy hearing Rhea mention sucking another man's dick, but I know it was just a jab at this little bitch. Instead of being shaken, I smirk in response as the girl turns red-faced.

Rhea curls under my arm like she's suddenly proud to have me at her side. I place my hand loosely on her hip, ready to take on the whole crowd if necessary. Together we are dynamite.

"Tyler," one of the girls says, "can we talk?"

He shakes his head, moving close to Heather. "Not now, Tamara. I'm busy."

She sneers. "Busy with her?"

Heather grabs Tyler's hand, holding it with her head held high. "Is that a problem?"

The mouthy bitch, standing with an air of superiority, plants her hands on her hips and snickers. "Last party you were with the chick with the old man, and now it's her. You sure do get around lately, Ty."

To Tyler's credit, he only shrugs. "Maybe I learned from you. Except I happen to make sure I'm single before I go out with anyone else."

A cloud of malice hangs between Tyler and Tamara, and it's obvious they have history. But Heather relentlessly holds tight to Tyler's hand and even goes as far to rest her head on his shoulder.

"Come on," Rhea says quietly, tugging my arm. "Let's go anywhere but here."

"Gladly."

We walk away from the group and we're suddenly in the midst of another, but this one just gives us a few sly glances as we pass through. Everyone we walk by stops what they're doing to check us out, but Rhea keeps her chin up and holds on to me tightly.

I tilt my head down and whisper, "Having fun yet?"

"Hardly. But it is amusing giving all these naysayers a show. Everyone's looking at us."

"Not us, baby. You. You're the most beautiful girl in this town. How can they not stop and look?"

We come across a fallen tree near the edge of the woods, and we sit down on it, our fingers still locked.

"Tell me something," Rhea says, grazing my knuckles.

"Tell me something, she says. Hmm..." I tap my chin. "A unicorn is the national animal in Scotland."

Rhea laughs and it's the most beautiful sound in the world. One I started to believe I would never earn from her in a non-sarcastic manner. "Not exactly what I meant, but that's good to know. Is it true?"

"It is. I don't know the story behind it, but it's very true." I lick my lips, lifting my eyes to hers. "What did you actually mean?"

"I meant something about you. You mentioned coming to parties like this when you were younger. Tell me more."

"You sure?" I search her gaze, not wanting to upset her.

"Yeah. Why not?"

"Okay. Well. You know those girls that were trying to create drama a few minutes ago?"

She sighs. "Yeah."

"Every group has them. My party crew was no different.

When the sun would set behind the trees, bonfires were a must. Beer was constantly flowing and shots were taken. The music was always loud and..."

I look over at her and stop talking when I see that she's looking at the sky with her eyes closed. When she realizes I've stopped, her daydreaming eyes open and land on mine. "And, what? Keep going."

So I do, and she closes her eyes while facing the sky again. Once I realize what she's doing, I go into more detail. Helping her relive the experience through my words.

"I'd always ride to the parties with my buddies, Dan and Travis. Back then, we did everything together. I remember one night in particular during my senior year. We had just won the homecoming football game and the forecast was calling for a severe thunderstorm. Dan's older brother got us a keg. We sure as hell were not going to let that go to waste at our age. We loaded that baby in the trunk of Trav's car, not letting any weather stop us." I smile at the memory and so does Rhea.

"Me and the guys got a small fire going just before the rain hit. Those flames took hold of the decaying logs in the blink of an eye, dancing wildly under the gray clouds. It was the biggest fire I'd ever seen. For a moment, I was concerned we might start a wildfire. But I was young and immature, so I quickly let that thought fall to the wayside." I chuckle to myself, thinking about how reckless I once was.

"Everyone stood around it in sheer amazement at the sight. It rained ashes onto all of us. I still remember the smell of the burning wood—sweet and pungent, much like the one out there. We chanted our school fight song, then lifted Trav in the air in victory because he'd scored the final point that won us the game." I get so lost in the memory I can feel his weight on my shoulders again, the joy of being young flooding my veins as if I'm reliving the moment.

"Then the rain started. With it came hail and thunder. Bolts of lightning that almost touched the tip of the blazing fire. We stayed out there all night, soaked from head to toe. It was the best rainstorm of my life."

Man, those were some good days.

I go silent and Rhea lowers her head and opens her eyes. "Thank you." She smiles back at me.

I always wondered what was going on in her mind when she would tilt her head back while at a hotel computer. I would watch her for hours as she typed, then she would close her eyes and a smile would touch her face. It was one of the only times she seemed happy, and I think I understand what was happening now. She was rewriting her story.

Rhea wants to be the star of her own destiny. I'm determined to make that happen for her while being the luckiest man alive to be part of her story.

"Tell me something," I say, my fingers doing laps on her upper thigh.

Her features soften and her eyes light up under the dim moonlit sky. "When I was nine years old, my mom and I were staying at this hotel outside of Nashville. Rumor had it, Shania Twain was staying on the same floor as us."

A smile creeps across her face as she turns to me. "Well, my mom went out for the evening with the man who got us the room, and I made it my mission to meet Shania Twain. In a pair of Barbie doll pajamas, I walked the hall knocking on every door until I found her. The minute she opened her door, I was starstruck. I held out a notepad and a pen, ya know, the ones that housekeeping leaves in the rooms." I nod, and she continues.

"I couldn't even get out a word, no matter how hard I tried. A security guard started coming down the hall toward me and I tried so hard to talk, to ask her to sign my paper. One of the other guests must have called and reported me knocking on the doors. Shania, being the doll she is, shooed the guard away and knelt down to my level. I can still hear her voice in my head as she said, 'Take your time, sweetie. If there's something you want to say, I'll wait all night to hear it.'" She giggles and it's so damn cute I want to grab her face and kiss her.

"Finally, I was able to squeak out a couple words, asking her to sign the paper. Then she asked where my mom was and I lied and said she was in our room. I went back to the room and sang every song on her *The Woman in Me* album while dancing around with that piece of paper."

The light in her eyes is so warm, I can feel it deep in my soul. "That's incredible. I can imagine you being a determined kid. Always going after what you wanted."

"I was a sneaky little shit, that's for sure."

We both laugh, then Rhea's expression falls. She turns to face me, folding one leg under the other. "Can I ask you something?""

"Anything. Always."

"Do you resent me for what I did to Grayson?"

Not expecting a question like that after the memories we just shared, my eyes widen. "Not at all. Why would you even think that?"

"You and Grayson had a merger planned that was said to be one of the biggest acquisitions of the year. How could you not hate me for ruining that for you?"

"Rhea, baby." I cup her cheeks with my hands. "That was business. It was a measly deal that I planned to pull the plug on long before Grayson died."

"It was a *huge* deal." I can see she doesn't believe me, not that she thinks I'm a liar. I think she just doesn't want me to say what she wants to hear because she doesn't believe someone could really love her as much as I do.

"Listen," I say seriously, because this is serious and she needs to hear it. "Grayson sent me to find you. Once I learned why he wanted you found, everything changed. As your godfather, it didn't sit right with me. I didn't know until after his death who the guy he planned to marry you off to was. But once I found out it was evil in human form, I knew I'd made the right call to keep you hidden from him."

I let my thumb rub across her cheek and she closes her eyes. "The minute I found you, I knew there was no way I could bring you back to him. The baby I held on the day of her birth was all grown up. Now standing before me is a beautiful woman who stole my heart."

"Whoa." Her eyes shoot open and her hands come to my chest, pushing to create distance between us. "Wait a minute. Did you say *godfather*?"

"I did." My voice is nearly a growl as she forces my hand to break contact with her.

"Jesus Christ." She laughs, a mixture of disbelief and amusement. "I fucked my godfather." She shakes her head back and forth. "This just keeps getting more and more insane."

"You think that's insane." I lean in to whisper in her ear and hum in approval when she lets me get close. "Wait until you fuck him again."

She rolls her lips as her eyes narrow. "A little overly confident, are we?"

"Oh, it's gonna happen." My hand slides up her leg, cupping her crotch. "Don't pretend you haven't thought about fucking me again."

"I won't. I'll admit, you've been on my mind more than you should be."

"In what ways?"

I watch as her chest rises and falls rapidly and she bites her lip. She's temptation personified. "All of them." Her voice is breathless. "Sexually. Emotionally. Mentally. You've taken up a space in my head and I'm not sure how to get you out. I don't know what to think about that."

"Then don't think about it." I lean close, my mouth ghosting hers. "Just think about me."

She falls into me, our mouths connect instantaneously. My thumb presses to her chin, tilting her head up while she puts a hand on the back of my head, holding me in place.

"Let's get the hell outta here," I mumble into her mouth. When she nods against mine, a shiver of excitement races through my veins.

I feel like I'm back to the eighteen-year-old version of myself as I fling Rhea on my back and piggyback ride her to the car. We pass by groups of people, not giving a damn about a single one of them. Rhea laughs as I pick up my pace, until I'm full-on running.

"You're gonna drop me!" she shouts into the air. Just before we make it to the car, it starts to rain. Not just some simple rain either. It's soaking-clothes, sky-roaring, lightning-striking, pouring-down rain.

"Ahhh," she cries excitedly with her head turned up to the sky. "This is amazing."

I lean down and let her slide off my back, then I just stand back and watch her live her best life as she dances to her own tune in the drenching downpour.

She throws her arms out wide and spins around with her face to the sky, allowing the water to pelt every inch of her beautiful body. Every couple seconds, she opens her mouth and sticks out her tongue catching droplets. Her laughter is contagious, bouncing off trees and echoing through the open space. People stop and stare, but in my mind, they're just jealous.

My girl is a wild one. A little crazy. Ruthless at heart. She keeps me on my fucking toes. And I don't think I could love her any more than I do right now.

Everything about Rhea is perfect. And *this* is now etched into my memory as the best rainstorm of my life.

WE'RE DRENCHED. Completely fucking soaked as we laugh our way into the house. I lead the way to Rhea's room, confident she's going to allow me in this time.

But when she stops and pulls me in the direction we came, I foresee an argument in the future. I can't allow us to end a perfect night apart. I *have* to be with her.

"I wanna see your room," she says sheepishly. "See your things. See what makes you, you. Do you make your bed? Fold your clothes? I wanna know. It's only fair since you already know everything about me." She gives me a pointed look, clearly knowing I went through every inch of her living quarters.

"My room it is."

She tugs my arm, jerking us in the direction of my door as I reach into my pocket for the key.

The second it opens, I push her inside and cup her ass as I lift her up. Her legs wrap around mine as I carry her to my bed —that's made perfectly, I might add. Not a wrinkle in sight.

I lay her down gently, my eyes dragging downward from her eyes to her toes. "You're perfect, Rhea Brooks."

"I'm wet."

"You're stunning." I bend down, my knees pressing into the mattress between her legs. "And you're about to be a whole lot wetter." I kiss her mouth passionately. The effects of her mouth on mine make me woozy and I collapse on top of her.

Pushing myself up slightly, I allow our chests to stay flush so I can feel the thumping of her heart. It's beating just for me.

"I need you," I grumble. "Right now."

"I need you, too." Her breaths are ragged and unfulfilled and her words are music to my ears. "I wanna touch you. Taste you."

My cock twitches against my briefs. "You have my permission to do whatever you want to me."

Rhea presses her hands to my chest gently and I lift off her. Eyebrows dancing, I say, "What exactly did you have in mind?"

She wriggles out from beneath me, biting the corner of her lip, and the action drives me wild.

I lie down on my back, hands folded under my head, and I let her take the lead. She's in her element, having complete control, and my mind begins to wander to places it shouldn't. Rhea has been with many men. But all the ones before me are nothing but shadows in her past. I wasn't her first, but I damn sure will be her last.

TWENTY-SEVEN

RHEA

THERE'S an insatiable urgency inside me to touch Alaric. We've had sex once, but I never got to wrap my fingers around his girth, or stroke my hand up and down his length. I want to see just how perfectly he fits in my palm. Then, I want to feel him pressed against my tongue as he fucks my mouth.

Thoughts about my past infiltrate my mind. How any blowjobs I gave in the past were for money and I never enjoyed them much. I mean, what's to enjoy about sucking a stranger off? But it's different with Alaric. I want to pleasure him because I have no doubt my actions will earn his praise. And even better, his determination to please me right back.

"Go ahead and take me out, baby. Look at my dick. Touch it. Taste it. Memorize it. Because mine is the last one you'll ever see."

I lift my brows, a smirk tugging at my lips. "A little cock-sure, are we?"

He growls headily. "Damn straight I am."

I'm on my knees, sitting between his legs as I slowly drag down the zipper on his pants while peering up at his lustful eyes. The way he watches every move I make is gratifying. I find myself behaving seductively as I arch my back, squeeze my tits together to expose my cleavage, and trail the tip of my tongue across my upper lip. Alaric pays attention to the small details and to him, I'm more than just damaged goods.

He kicks out of his pants, and as I go to reach for it, desperate to feel it in my hand, Alaric lifts up and grips the bottom of my shirt. I raise my arms and he peels it off me. Before lying back down, he takes his own shirt off and tosses it on the floor. "Pants," he orders, and I strip them off faster than I've ever done before.

He curls his fingers, summoning me.

My eyebrows arch in response as I stretch upward until we're face to face.

I'm met with cold fingers on my back as he fumbles with the clasp of my bra. "Let's get rid of this." The fabric slides off my shoulders and I help remove it the rest of the way.

His gaze softens and I press my body closer. Tilting my head, I meet his lips in a teasing kiss before I quickly slide back down. He may think he's in charge, but I'm a lady on a mission. And I'm very used to getting my way.

Without hesitation, I take the shallow end of his dick in my hand. His skin is like velvet against my fingertips, his veins raised as I stroke him from base to tip.

Leaning my head down, I lap my tongue around his shaft, then suck his head into my mouth, tasting a bead of precum.

Slowly, I take in more of him, inch by inch until he's pressed against the back of my throat. I can hear his breathing pick up and his legs shake ever so slightly. It makes me feel powerful, like I'm in charge, and I love every second of it.

I hum around him, causing a vibration that has him shifting beneath me. The old bed creaks against the floorboards as he circles his hips, seeking friction from my mouth. I can feel the warmth of his body radiating beneath me and my heart races with excitement when he lets out a subtle moan.

Continuing to stroke the base of his dick, I suck harder and faster, flicking my tongue feverishly against him.

Laying a hand on my head, his fingers tangle in my hair as he subtly guides my movements. "Jesus, Rhea. Your mouth feels fucking amazing."

His words appease me and give me the confidence I seek to take it a step further. Dragging my tongue down his length, I cup his balls in my hand before sucking his left nut into my mouth.

"Fuck, baby." He growls, raising his hips into me. I smile around him in satisfaction.

Stroking him steadily, I move to the next one, sucking it between my teeth and circling my tongue around his smooth sack.

A sweet bitterness hits my taste buds as I trail my tongue upward until I'm at his head again, then I take all of him in my mouth, sucking hard and fast. My head bobs up and down while his cock pulsates against my tongue, growing even thicker.

Suddenly, his hand is on my cheek and he's lifting me up. "I'm not ready for this to be over yet."

In a swift motion, he grabs my waist and flips me over until my back is pressed to the bed. His body shifts down until his face is snug between my legs. His tongue trails a path from side to side, never touching where I really want. He follows up with soft kisses until my body starts to shake with need.

Finally, his fingers massage my core before he pushes two inside me, delving so deep I gasp. He twists and turns, hitting my inner walls before he's submerged against my G-spot. A moan escapes my lips and the hungry look he gives my pussy has me quivering in anticipation.

Pulsating the tips of his fingers, he kisses my clit, then laps his tongue around it until I begin panting. When my hips buck up, begging for more, he gives it to me. Sucking my clit between his teeth, he nips with gentle pressure.

I wince in response and when he repeats the motion, I cry out in pleasure.

He lifts his head momentarily, looking into my lustful eyes. "You like that, baby? You like when Daddy kisses your cunt?"

Fuck me. I swear every time he refers to himself as Daddy, I feel like I'm going to come on the spot.

A heady moan parts my lips and I nod. "Yes."

He works his fingers inside me and it's like nothing I've ever felt before. Electricity surges through me and every muscle tightens, gripping him as I exhale a whimper.

I grab a fistful of his hair, forcing the pressure of his mouth against my sensitive nub, and when I get what I wanted, I come undone.

The sounds that escape me are feral and unmasked. I make no attempt to silence myself as I all but scream in ecstasy.

"Oh, God, Alaric. I'm gonna come."

"That's my girl. Come around my fingers, baby. Make a mess so I can clean you up."

His voice is a flame that engulfs my entire body. My breath hitches and my toes curl into the mattress as I feel the rising tide of pleasure inside me. I tremble and shake and my eyes roll back as I'm shocked with a million little lightning bolts.

My fingers twist tightly in his hair, using it to calm the urgency inside me so I don't completely combust.

In one heavy exhale, I release all the pent-up air in my lungs. "Holy shit," I croak, feeling dizzy and weak.

"That feel good, baby?"

All I can do is nod because my vocal cords feel dried out.

Once I've come down completely, I feel the wetness of the mess I made on the bed.

Alaric does exactly what he said and he cleans me up. His tongue drags up and down my inner thigh, taking every last drop of my arousal.

In the blink of an eye, I'm flipped onto my stomach, lying in my own juices. Alaric grabs my hips, then forcefully jerks them up until I'm on my elbows and knees.

I twist my neck to look at him as he clenches his fist around his cock, the veins on his length bulging. He drags the tip between my ass cheeks and growls in a thick and raspy voice. "You want this, baby?"

My body trembles in response and I whisper an affirmative, "Yes."

He teasingly presses firmly against my entrance without entering, and when I scoot back to try and take him, he slaps his palm hard against my ass cheek, forcing a whimper out of me.

"Tell me you want Daddy's cock," he commands, and his authoritative voice sends an electric thrill through my body.

"I want it, Daddy."

"That's my girl." With his calloused hands gripping my hips, he pushes his cock inside me, and I thrust forward, all the air leaving my lungs.

My head lolls to the side and my eyes close as he pummels into me over and over. Gripping the plushness of the comforter with both my hands, I cry out in ecstasy.

He drives into me with intensity, the bed creaking as it bounces and shifts beneath us. I have no doubt everyone in this house can hear us, but I'm too lost in the moment to care.

My body quivers and a rush of heat floods every inch of me. I moan loudly, the sounds of my pleasure echoing off the walls.

Alaric's hands come forward, roaming over my body. He

cups my breasts, pinching the bud of my nipple, then returns to digging his fingers deep in my hips.

I bend my back further, rolling myself to his rhythm. Sweat beads and trickles along our connected bodies, and the smell of our arousal coats the air.

Alaric hums through a heady breath and slaps a hand on my ass, halting his movements. I wiggle back, pushing for more, but he holds me still. "Tell me this cunt is mine and no one else's."

"It's yours." I moan in the heat of the moment. What scares me a little is that I believe the words that leave my mouth. I believe he won't let anyone else have me. And I believe that Alaric Banks isn't going to leave me. "All yours."

Pleased with my response, he resumes fucking me. "Damn straight it is."

Alaric works his dick feverishly inside me, his breath heavy as he grinds out a groan with each lunge.

Tension ripples through my body, filling me with a dire need to release. I find myself clenching my inner walls, clinging to his length as he drives into me.

I cry out in pleasure, breath held, as I come around him. "Oh, God, Alaric."

He lets out a guttural growl, shuddering as he pushes deep in my core before giving me a couple more pulsating thrusts. I can feel his hot seed fill me up so much it nearly drips out, making me feel so full and so sated.

His sweaty chest rests on my back, his breath hot and heavy. "I love hearing you say my name."

I drop down, letting him collapse on top of me. We lie there for a few minutes while Alaric strokes his fingers through my hair. "I love you, Rhea. More than you'll ever know."

My heart swells and I find comfort in his words, but then I remember that the one person who told me they loved me is gone. The only people I love in this world are no longer here.

"You shouldn't," I finally say. "The more you love, the more you suffer when it's gone."

Alaric rolls off me until he's lying by my side. I turn to look at him and he puts a thumb under my chin.

"Hey," he says in a forthright tone. "Love is more than just a feeling to mourn because you've loved and lost." He strokes a hand through my hair, as if he can fathom the amount I've lost in my life and wants to make up for it.

"It's more than just the good times too, Rhea. It's a lot of sacrifices, a thousand arguments with no resolution. It's rough days and good days. Storms and sunshine. Love is about trust and compromise, even though you'll always be right and I'll always be wrong. And I'm okay with that."

A small smile tugs at my lips while tears sting the corners of my eyes and I swallow hard, fighting like hell not to break down into a blubbery mess.

His warm fingers graze my cheek as his penetrating eyes gaze deeply at me. "Just because the people you love are no longer here, doesn't mean you don't still feel the emotions they gave you. I love you, Rhea, and I'll love you until the day I die. My only hope is that I'll be reborn into the same universe as you so I can love you all over again."

"It hurts, Alaric. It hurts so much that I don't want to feel it again. I've lost so much," I tell him through strained vocal cords.

"And you still have so much more to gain. Don't let the past scare you away from your future. I'm not going anywhere, Rhea. I think I've made that very clear. I am someone you can trust to fight at your side."

There's a beat of silence before I finally smile and say, "Who the hell are you and where did you come from?" Alaric is such an enigma. This man has put me through hell. Yet, the same hands that pushed me, pulled me out of the fire and led me into the light. I've never felt so adored. So safe. So loved.

He chuckles before his expression grows serious. "I'm your HawkEye, and you're my Wildcat."

My body jerks upright as my elbow digs into the softness of the mattress. My mouth falls open while my breath catches in my throat.

"What did you just say?" I tumble over my words in confusion and shock. "You're...HawkEye?"

How did I not see this?

In less than a second I go from sated bliss to utter confusion. I'm second-guessing everything about myself. I've always considered myself to be a very intuitive person. You have to be to survive the shit I did. But, this...this is something I *never* saw coming.

"I wanted to tell you that first night at Taryn's, but I couldn't bring myself to do it." He looks at me like this is a simple conversation. As if he didn't just flip some fundamental part of me upside down. I should have known when I got that damn computer.

I sit all the way up, staring off at the wall as I wrap my head around this. I'm not angry, surprisingly. I'm almost relieved because I was starting to worry that HawkEye was following me after he sent that package.

"You should have just told me," I tell him with a disappointed shake of my head.

"Believe me, I wanted to. But HawkEye was my way of talking to you without aggression and judgment. I know I come off strong in person and you didn't trust me—you couldn't. But you trusted him, you felt safe with him. He was my alter ego that gained access to your life and your thoughts."

My face drops in my hands and Alaric sits up to trail his fingers up and down my back. "How pissed are you?" he asks, a bite of worry in his tone.

I drop my hands and turn around on the bed until I'm facing him. "I'm not pissed," I say honestly. "I'm actually glad it was you."

His eyebrows shoot to his forehead. "Seriously? I thought for sure I'd be eating my teeth the minute you found out."

"That's still up for debate, but not over this. So the GED enrollment and the laptop, that was you?"

He nods and I immediately throw my arms around his neck, feeling the scratch of his chest hair against my breasts. "Thank you."

"You don't have to thank me. It's just the beginning of making all your dreams come true." I can feel the way he believes in me to the depths of my soul. It might be strange to think that in only a week or so this man changed me, but it's been so much longer than that.

HawkEye wormed his way into my life a long time ago. And I'm starting to see all the ways Alaric has been there for me. He never ran away, even when things got hard.

I take his face in my trembling hands and press my lips to his while a flood of emotions consumes me. I can feel it all— everything I fought not to feel for so long stirs in my chest like a violent storm just before the rainbow.

CHAPTER
TWENTY-EIGHT

RHEA

ALARIC and I stayed up nearly all night talking. I curled under his arm and fell asleep, listening to the sound of his heartbeat. It's strange the amount of peace you can find in one sound with one man.

Alaric caught me by surprise in so many ways and my life seems to be changing so quickly. But I actually like the changes. I feel safe in this small town that I now want to call home. For the first time in my life, I actually have a place to call home.

I plan to go to school and get my GED and who knows, maybe after that, I can find something I love to do. Maybe there's a position in Alaric's company I might want to try out and actually earn my place in the world. While it's great he has money, I also want to know I'm good enough to earn my own.

We talked about that and so much more. He supported me in every dream I confessed to him. Even something as insane as wanting to ride a damn unicorn. He only laughed and said he would find a way to put a horn on a horse so I could live that dream.

We talked about him being HawkEye and when he first saw me. He confessed to being the man in the black car and I confessed that I always thought of him as some sort of guardian angel. It was nice to have a constant in my world, even if it was creepy as hell. I also drew the conclusion that he was the one who saved me after I lost the baby.

That was the hardest talk of the evening. I cried and let it all out about my dreams of being a mother and making that baby's life the best it could be. We both agreed we didn't want children in the end, but getting to tell him about that part of my life helped me heal in ways I didn't know I still needed today.

I asked him why he never came to me, especially that night, and he was honest in telling me he was afraid.

"I didn't want to be your knight in shining armor. I just wanted to be there for you. I watched you enough to know that if you knew who saved you, you would have thought I did it out of wanting something back. But the truth is, Rhea. All I want is your love, and I'm desperate to earn it."

Little does he know, he's earned it a thousand times over. I just don't know how to reciprocate it. Or even accept it. But as I fell asleep in his arms, feeling safe for the first time in who knows how long, I think my heart began to let him in through some of the cracks.

Then I woke up to him bringing me breakfast in bed. A delicious plate of pancakes, bacon, and scrambled eggs. He said he helped Gladys make it, but after a long debate, he fessed up to only buttering the pancakes, which was still super sweet of him. Even if he was trying to take credit for the sweet lady's work.

I always assumed Alaric was only getting in Gladys's good graces because it was a zip-line to me, considering we live in her house. But when he told me she reminds him of his late grandma, whom he spent most of his weekends with as a child, I realized he actually enjoys her company.

It's hard to imagine Alaric being anything but abrasive, but I'm beginning to see who he is beneath his hard exterior. There's a gentleness inside him. He's kind and attentive and protective as hell, but that part of him is saved only for the people he cares about.

I never wanted to fall for anyone, ever. But I'm falling fast and it's scary as hell.

A knock at my door has me setting the breakfast tray to my side. I pick up my napkin and dab my lips as I holler, "Come in," knowing it's Alaric. He went out after bringing me breakfast, saying he had some business to take care of. I suppose his work life doesn't stop just because he's in Lockhaven with me.

The door opens and I'm surprised to see that it's Heather. "Good morning," I say as I set my napkin on top of the tray.

"Good morning, Rhea. Gladys sent me in to collect your dirty dishes." She eyes the tray beside me. "That was really sweet of Alaric."

My cheeks lift with a wide smile. "It was. He just keeps surprising me." I grab the tray and get off the bed to carry it to where she's standing in the doorway.

"Where is Alaric, anyways? I wanted to talk to him about something."

"Oh, he had to go out for a bit. He should be back soon." Feeling nosey, I press on the matter. "Is everything okay?"

"Yeah. Everything's fine." She sweeps the air with her hand. "It's nothing important. I'll just catch him later." Something about the way she says it puts my nerves on edge.

She reaches for the tray, but I hold it back. "I can bring this to the kitchen. You really don't have to."

"No. I insist. Gladys and I are just cleaning up the mess from breakfast. It's no big deal."

"You're sure?" I don't like it when people go out of their way for me, it makes me feel helpless. I know I should be doing more around the house to help Gladys and the guests, but I've just been so consumed by work and Alaric.

"Absolutely," Heather insists, taking the tray from my hand.

She turns to leave, but I stop her. "Heather, wait. How are things going with you and Tyler?"

Spinning back around, I can see that the mention of Tyler has brought a smile to her face. "Really good, actually. He's so sweet. We're kind of going to the party at Taryn's together tonight."

I clutch my chest, feeling so much happiness for Tyler. "I'm so glad. He really is a good guy." I shake my finger at her, grinning. "Don't you go breaking his heart or I'll come for you."

Her shoulders slump and a look of remorse flashes over her features. "I wouldn't dream of it. I just hope I don't break my own heart."

The look on her face is all too familiar. It's the same one that stared back at me in every mirror I've looked into since I lost my mother. "Hey." I lay a hand on her shoulder. "Is everything okay?"

Heather always appears so timid and fragile. Like she's hiding from someone or something.

She nods, forcing a smile on her face. "I'm fine."

"My two favorite words." I take the tray from her and set it on my dresser while she stands back watching in confusion. "Come in," I wave my hand, gesturing her into the room. Once she's stepped out of the doorway, I close the door.

"You can talk to me, Heather. Whatever you're going through, I've likely been there."

She drops her chin to her chest, avoiding eye contact while her hands tremble at her sides. "I'm in trouble."

My heart jumps a beat and my eyes shoot wide open as I take her by the arm and lead her to my unmade bed. "What kind of trouble?"

She sits down, still averting her gaze as she twiddles her thumbs nervously in her lap. "I can't go too much into detail, but I got mixed up with the wrong people. Did some things I'm not proud of, and now I'm indebted to a very bad man."

"Oh, Heather." I softly pat her back, not used to the emotions but trying for her. "You're singing to the choir. Let me help you. There has to be something I can do."

After another long beat of silence, Heather jumps up frantically. "It's fine. I shouldn't have said anything." She hurries to the door, and before I can reach her, she's out, slamming it closed behind her.

My heart aches for her. I know that feeling of hopelessness and regret all too well. My only hope is that she'll find the courage to open up about her troubles and let someone in, because keeping it all inside and trying to take on the world alone is a loneliness like no other.

I walk toward my bed to grab my phone, stopping in amusement when I see a black box with a gold bow on the nightstand. How I missed it is beyond me. Anxiously, I grab it and untie the bow, then set the box on my bed. Lifting the lid of the box, I see a notecard.

I pick it up and flip the card open to read the handwritten note from Alaric.

For tonight. I'm prepared to be left breathless,
as I always am when I'm with you.

My body flushes with heat and my heart leaps into my

throat. And when I look down to see what was beneath the note, my jaw nearly hits the floor.

I grab the smooth velvet fabric and lift it from the box, revealing a beautiful, formfitting, long-sleeved dress. I hold it up to my body and sway slightly with it, knowing the smile on my face won't be leaving anytime soon.

"THANK YOU SO MUCH FOR BREAKFAST," I tell Gladys as I join her in the living room. She's in her rocking chair, knitting a baby pink blanket. Or at least, I think it's a blanket.

"Of course, darling," she says, pushing her feet off the floor in a steady tempo. "Will you be here for dinner tonight?"

"I'll probably just grab something at Taryn's." I take a seat on the sofa, stretching my arm to hand her an envelope of money. "Here's my rent for November."

Gladys looks at the envelope, and without taking it, her eyes lift. "Rhea, honey. You're paid up for the next six months."

I shake my head. "No. That's not right. I haven't paid since the beginning of *this* month."

"Sure you have. Alaric gave me your envelope last week with six months' rent paid in full."

My eyebrows cave in. "I never gave Alaric any money, and I certainly can't afford to pay six months in advance."

"Well, if you didn't give him the money, that means—"

"He paid it." I shake my head in confusion. "Why would he do that?"

Gladys simpers, her eyes twinkling. "That man cares for you deeply, darling."

"Yeah," I mumble. "I think he really does."

She cocks a brow, searching for a reaction from me. "Is it safe to assume the feeling is mutual?"

I start nodding slowly, picking up the intensity of my movements. "It is." I gaze at the wall as I speak of him. "Alaric is...confusing, annoying, and overbearing. But he's also gentle and kind, and he does things like this that totally take me by surprise."

"That's men for you." Gladys sets her ball of yarn to the side and shifts slightly to face me. "He reminds me so much of my Carlisle. Such a grouch, but as gentle as can be with me." Her eyes light up and I can see the love she holds for her late husband as she speaks of him. "Did you know that Carlisle was sixteen years older than me?"

"I didn't know that." I'm kind of shocked, but I don't know why.

"It's true. My parents despised the idea of us marrying. The world was against us. But our hearts knew that being apart wasn't an option, so we ran away and we got married. A year later, we returned to Lockhaven and showed the people in this town that love has no boundaries."

I rest a hand over my heart, feeling its warmth. "That's beautiful, Gladys."

"Don't let him go, darling. I see the way he looks at you, and I don't think he has any plans of letting you go."

I chuckle. "I don't think he'd let me if I tried." I stand up, my heart full of so much happiness. Before I leave, I lean down and give Gladys a soft hug. "Thank you for this little chat. I needed it."

"Anytime." She pats my arm. "Be safe out there. We've got a snowstorm on the way."

I lift a foot in the air. "I've got my boots and my coat."

As I approach the door, all I can see is the ghosting of fog on the glass. But when I pull the door open, I gasp at the sight. Gladys mentioned a snowstorm in the forecast, but I never expected to step outside in a foot of snow, and it's still coming down. Thick snowflakes fall in abundance, coating everything in sight.

I can't say that I've ever seen snow on Halloween. At least I'll be warm inside Taryn's for the masquerade party.

Alaric ended up taking longer than planned handling whatever it was he had to handle, so he's meeting me next door with the masks we'll be wearing to the party.

The sidewalk is lined with people waiting to get inside the tavern, and all I can think about is the tips I could be making.

I'm walking down the sidewalk when an odd feeling overcomes me. A chill runs down my spine and I look to my left, unknowingly, when I see someone in particular standing across the street. I stop walking, taking in his appearance. He's dressed in all black, wearing a black ski mask—the same mask I saw at the first party I attended with Tyler.

I squint as snow coats my lashes, looking at him as he just stands there, watching me through the holes in his mask. Snowflakes fall down on him, glistening like diamonds on his black apparel.

Normally I'd be fearful, wondering who it was, but now I know it was Alaric at the party. He's either messing with me now, or he's still being a creep without making it known. He told me he's always watching me, and even though we've gotten much closer, it appears he hasn't made an exception.

I step onto the road, looking both ways before beginning to cross, but he turns around and heads down the narrow alley between a row of buildings.

"Alaric," I call out, stopping in the middle of the road. He doesn't stop; instead, he picks up his pace until he disappears from my sight. I sigh heavily, then turn around and go back to the sidewalk.

One more glance over my shoulder proves he's gone. Something in my gut tells me that wasn't Alaric at all. It's an unsettling feeling that I can't shake.

Pushing it down, I go on with my plans and follow the line of people into Taryn's.

I wasn't prepared for the tavern to be even busier than it is on the weekends, which is surprising since it's Sunday night. But it's Halloween, so I guess I shouldn't be that surprised.

Everyone is wearing masks of all shapes and sizes. From colorful to black and white. Some with intricate details, and some that are a simple cloth. There are even people wearing regular Halloween costumes—a witch, a skeleton, and a vampire. Then we have a handful who have found more creative ways to cover their faces, like ski masks.

I chuckle inwardly at myself. That probably wasn't even Alaric. More than likely it was someone leaving here. After all this time, I still get myself worked up for no reason.

"Rhea," Taryn beams as she rushes toward me with a stick-held mask to her eyes. It's silver and black with beautiful gems all over it. She takes hers away from her face and cocks a brow. "Girl, where is your mask?"

"It's on its way." I skim the crowd, seeing if Alaric is here yet, but even if he were, I probably wouldn't find him. "I can't believe how busy it is. It's amazing, Taryn."

"You have no idea. People eat up Halloween in this town, and I don't mean the candy. It's about to be a wild night." She tips her head back. "I have to get behind the bar and serve customers. Have fun, okay?"

"I will, and holler if you need a hand."

She vanishes into the crowd while I try to push my way to the bar for a drink. I'm halfway there when two hands land on my face, covering my eyes. Everything goes black and my first instinct is to panic—until I hear the voice behind the hands.

"Guess who?"

I peel his fingers away and spin around to see Alaric. One hand lands firmly on my waist, holding on to me like he's never going to let go.

I run my hands down the sleeves of his jacket, keeping him at arm's length as I take him in.

He looks sexy as hell with his hair gelled back and he smells like a dream. Wearing a sleek black suit, he's adorned with a black venetian mask strapped to his face. The details in it are stunning. Embossed vines running throughout with diamonds circling the left eye. But what's even more appealing is the sultry blue eyes behind it, staring back at me like I'm the only person in the room.

Alaric raises his hand, revealing another mask. "For you, my lady."

My eyes shoot wide open when I see it. "It's beautiful." Matching his, mine has the same details, with diamonds around the right eye, and a pointed top that looks like the spikes on a crown.

"Turn around," he quips, holding the mask out.

I do as I'm told and he slides it down on my face. I spin back around and this time, he's the one taking me in. "This dress is stunning on you, Rhea."

I grab the sides of the black velvet gown he surprised me with and I do a little curtsey. "Why, thank you. Someone pretty awesome picked it out."

His tongue drags across his teeth and he jerks my body against his. "Well, he did a fine job."

"He certainly did. And I must say, that mask looks much better on you than the ski mask you were wearing before."

Alaric lifts the mask from his eyes and lets it rest on his forehead. "Ski mask?"

"Yeah. Well, I thought it was you because you wore it to the party I went to with Tyler a couple weeks ago. But then I realized it could have been anyone since it's snowing so hard."

"Rhea," Alaric says sternly. "I've never once worn a ski mask. I was at that party, but I watched you from my car with no mask on my face."

"That doesn't make any sense. Someone was definitely watching me there. They stood in the woods, wearing all black, just like the person I saw today."

Alaric brings his hands to his face and rubs his temples aggressively. "It wasn't me, baby."

"It's fine." I sweep my hand in the air. "It's fall in Vermont. It's cold as fuck. It's probably nothing."

"Probably isn't good enough when it comes to your safety. If I had to guess, this was no coincidence. Especially after what I learned today."

My eyes bug out and the noise behind us drowns out. "What do you mean?"

"Let's get a drink and sit down. I have to tell you something. But from here on out, I'm not letting you out of my sight." He takes my hand and leads me to the bar, where he orders each of us a drink. We find a small table at the back of the room and sit across from one another.

"So," I begin, taking a long sip of my strawberry martini while willing my hands not to shake. "What's going on? Is this about the business you had to handle today?"

"Actually, yes." He takes a deep breath, looks around the room, then holds his gaze on something, or someone rather. I follow his line of sight and see Heather sitting at a table with a lady who is staying at Gladys's for the week.

"Alaric," I say, grabbing his attention. He looks back at me, eyebrows raised. "What is it?"

He leans into the table slightly and lowers his voice. "It's about Heather."

I tilt my head slightly toward where she's sitting. "That Heather?"

"That's the one." He takes another sip of his drink then sets it back down, keeping his fingers wrapped around the glass. "I got a strange vibe from her when she first appeared at Gladys's, so I was keeping a close eye on her. Last week I took her out for lunch because I wanted to see her reaction to some of my questions."

"And," I press for him to go on. "Did she pass your test?"

This is asinine to me. Heather is a little weird, but I highly doubt she's the devious person Alaric has created her to be in his mind.

"Not at all. Which led me to digging deeper. Today I went to meet with my PI who's been doing a search on our housemate, Heather. Turns out, her name isn't Heather at all. It's Chloe Blackburn, and she's got herself in a world of trouble."

"Oh my God," I blurt out, remembering my conversation with Heather earlier. "She told me she did something bad. I tried to get her to talk about it, but she clammed up and ran out of my room. So what did she do?"

"Gambled herself into a six-figure debt. I'm still waiting for Arnold, my PI to find out who she's indebted to, but we've got a pretty good idea who it is. Anyways, we're certain she's here to settle what she owes."

My heart sinks deep in my stomach, connecting the pieces quickly. "Do you think it's that Ian guy?"

Alaric shrugs his shoulders. "It's hard to say. But Lockhaven, Rhea? I mean, seriously. Who the fuck comes here just to come here? No family connection. No friends. It has to be him."

"Well," I tilt my head from side to side, slapping my hands to my chest, "I sort of just came here."

"Exactly. It's too much of a coincidence that you'd both arrive within such a short time frame."

"But if Ian did send her here, then why haven't they made a move?"

"All I can assume is he's biding his time for some reason. Scoping things out. Deciding what he's going to do with you. There's no saying what that man is up to."

Suddenly, I feel very seen in such a crowded space. Like eyes are on me, watching my every move. A shiver runs down my spine and I hug myself. "I'm scared."

I've never admitted that out loud before, but the things he told me about Ian threaten to let the bile loose that's sitting in my throat.

The legs on Alaric's chair scrape against the hardwood floor and in one breath he's at my side. "Don't be scared, baby. I've got a plan." He bends down and kisses my cheek as he whispers, "Early tomorrow morning, I'm taking you away from here. We're going somewhere no one will ever find us. It's only temporary until Ian is captured, and if you want to return to Lockhaven, we can come back. No matter where you want to go when this is over, I'll be right there with you." He kisses my cheek again and hugs my shoulders, making me feel safe, even if it's just for a moment.

I gulp, feeling an array of emotions rise inside me. I don't want to leave this town I call home, but I can't stay when the threat is so strong. Like Alaric said, it's only temporary.

Alaric's hand threads into mine and lifts until I'm on my feet. "Until then," he continues in a low voice, "we have to act normal. Like we don't have a care in the world."

With his other hand on my lower back, he leads me to the dance floor where couples are moving slowly to "Wish You the Best" by Lewis Capaldi. "Dance with me." He spins me around then pulls my chest flush to his.

I laugh, pushing down the thoughts that are trying to consume me. "Seems like you haven't given me much of a choice."

Our hands interlock at my shoulder and I lean into him, resting my head on his chest as we sway to the song. His tight hold on me has all my worries dissipating, as if they don't exist, and it's just him and me in this room.

I never wanted to fall in love. I'm not even sure I'd know what it feels like if I did. But if I had to compare it to anything I've felt before, I think this would be it.

I've lost so much in my short years of life, but I'm beginning to believe that sometimes we have to lose in order to gain.

I place my hand on Alaric's chest, feeling the *thump-thump* of his heart, and I'm convinced it truly is beating just for me. We were destined to find one another. Only, he came into my life when I was much too young and it wasn't our time. Fate did what it always does and it brought us together when the timing was right.

The song ends and I take a small step back, grinning up at Alaric. "Thank you," I tell him.

"For what?" He cranes his neck in confusion because, to him, this was just a dance. But to me, it was so much more.

"My first dance." At least one that wasn't in a crowded club where I was only trying to con people for money. My first slow dance, with a man who truly cares about me. Loves *me*.

He leans forward and presses his lips to my forehead, holding them in place. "The first of many."

We walk off the dance floor, hand in hand, and I take a seat at our table while Alaric goes and gets us another drink. Every step he takes has him shooting his eyes over his shoulder to make sure I'm safe, and each time I smile and wave awkwardly.

When he reaches the bar, he presses one elbow to it and turns to his side, watching me the entire time.

All of a sudden, the lights begin flickering and the music skips a few beats. I look around the room, noticing the constant flicker, much like everyone else.

"Must be the snowstorm," I hear someone say. "It's really coming down out there."

The next thing we know, we're all standing in pitch-blackness.

"Stay calm, everyone," Taryn shouts. "It's the weather and I'm sure the power will be back on soon. I'm going to the back room to look for some lanterns."

I'm about to stand up when a cold damp cloth presses against my face, covering my mouth and nose. My head lolls to the side like a heavy bowling ball, and I try to blink through the fog, but it only thickens.

Then pitch-black gets a whole lot darker.

CHAPTER
TWENTY-NINE
ALARIC

"Rhea," I scream over the chatter and noise as I push my way through the crowd. I can't see anything, but it's a straight line from where I was standing to her.

Just a few more steps. "Rhea," I shout again, waiting to hear her call back, but I can't hear a damn thing over these fucking drunk assholes. "I'm coming, baby."

It's so dark and I can't see a damn thing. I reach the table, desperately reaching my hand out, expecting to grab her, but she's not there. I swing my arm, knocking our dirty glasses to the floor. They hit with a thud, likely shattering at my feet. Panic rises inside me when I don't feel her or hear her voice. "Dammit, Rhea! Answer me!"

I shouldn't have left her, but I wanted to grab her a drink like a gentleman and I could see she needed to sit for a minute to collect her thoughts.

Finally, the lights come on and everyone hoots and hollers, but just when I think I'm going to feel relief and find her, I only panic more when I see her mask lying on the floor next to the broken glasses.

"Rhea!" I scream at the top of my lungs, frantically searching the room for her. My eyes land on Heather sitting on a stool at the bar, chatting it up with Tyler. I head straight for her, pushing bodies left and right as I keep my eyes locked on her.

My hand reaches out like a claw as I grab her by the back of the neck, lifting her off the stool as I spin her around. I take her by the arm, holding her in place with my forceful fingers that dig into her skin. "Where is she?" I shout, my face red hot. "Don't act like you don't know."

She tries to push me away, while I'm being pulled back by a group of men behind me, but I don't let up.

"Who?" Heather asks, eyes wide in confusion. But I see behind the facade.

"Rhea! Where the fuck is she!?"

Playing dumb, she lifts her shoulders. "I have no idea where Rhea is. Last time I saw—"

"Shut up!" I screech. "Shut the fuck up and quit lying."

Tyler flies over the bar like Superman and tries to position himself between Heather and me. "Get the fuck off her!"

"You," I emphasize, "better mind your own fucking business. This is between me and Chloe." Heather, or Chloe rather, tenses up, eyes wide in fear. "Yeah," I scoff, leaning in and whispering the gritted words into her ear, "that's right. I know your real name. I know everything about you. So you better talk or I'll go to the police and tell them everything."

"Okay," she says, no longer fighting me off. She looks at the guys behind me, then to Tyler. "It's okay. It's just a misunderstanding."

Pulling her by the arm, we move around tables and people until I bring her to a stop in the hall by the bathrooms. With a jerk of her arm, I push her against the wall. "Talk. Now," I demand in an authoritative tone.

"How...how do you know?" she chokes out when she realizes she's under my thumb and her cover has been blown.

"Doesn't matter. What matters is Rhea. Tell me where he took her."

Tyler approaches us and I roll my neck, cracking my tense muscles. "Back the fuck off," I sneer at him, speaking each word as if it is its own sentence. "You don't want to fuck with me right now, Farm Boy."

"Let her go!" Tyler shouts. "Now!"

Ignoring him, I return to Chloe. "You've got thirty seconds to tell me why the hell he sent you, and where the hell he took her, or so help me God. I will destroy you," my voice rises to an ear-splitting scream, "and everyone else in this fucking place."

Chloe looks at Tyler with a downturned mouth before her fearful gaze returns to mine. "All I had to do was watch her and report everything back to him." Her voice is a low whisper as she realizes she's lost all her power. "I'm not a bad person, Alaric. I swear. I had no other choice."

"I don't give a fuck about who you are or what you've done. Tell. Me. Where. She's. At!"

"He's staying at a cabin in the mountains about thirty minutes from here. I've only been there once..."

I don't give her the opportunity to finish her sentence as I drag her out the back door like a rag doll.

Tyler barks a few demands, but I turn to him, knowing he will understand. "Chloe here sold Rhea out to some really bad people and now she's missing. Want to keep yelling at me and slow down the process of me getting to her in time?"

Tyler looks from Chloe to me. When she drops her head, refusing to meet his gaze, his face hardens, and he nods. "Go find her. Call if you need help or backup."

Now that's a friend I don't mind for Rhea. Although his offer of help is quite hilarious for a farm boy.

Chloe cries like a fucking baby as I pull her through the parking lot to my car. She stumbles and loses her footing as we reach the passenger side, but my hold on her is relentless as I pull open the door and throw her ass inside. Slamming the door closed, I waste no time getting to the other side. I jump behind the wheel, start the engine, and peel out of the parking lot.

Once we're on Main Street, I begin my interrogation. "Look. I don't give a damn about you. You're nothing to me. So don't give me a sob story about how good of a person you are and how you didn't want to do this, because I don't fucking care."

"But it's true. I—"

"Shut the fuck up! I told you I don't care." I hit the steering wheel in pure frustration. "All I care about is Rhea. Was it Ian who took her?"

She nods slowly. "Yes."

My jaw tics furiously as I grind out the words, "Did you know he was going to take her?"

"Yes," she says regretfully. "All I had to do was watch her and relay information. I told him about the party tonight and said she'd be there. He said he was going to shut down the electricity to the tavern at nine o'clock and I couldn't speak a word of it. I'm just trying to pay off my debt. I don't want anyone to get hurt."

"But she could get hurt, dammit! Do you have any idea how powerful this man is? He could be taking her out of the country right now, for all we know."

"When I first arrived at the cabin he's staying in, I over-heard him talking and he said he's going to marry her there, then they'll leave immediately for Mexico."

"Jesus Christ!" I slam my hand into the steering wheel. "And you thought he wasn't going to hurt her? You still thought throwing an innocent girl at the feet of a monster was what good people do?"

I have to hurry. If Ian makes Rhea his wife, I may never see her again. I've been looking for this guy for months. I've had the best of the best searching high and low. Getting to the cabin before they leave is my only hope at saving her.

I tap on the dash screen, bringing up the navigation map. "Type in the address," I demand.

"Okay. I have to get it from my phone." She reaches into her purse, but before she can pull her phone out, I slam on my brakes, the back end of my car fishtailing on the ice before we come to a rolling stop in the middle of the road.

I lay my open palm out, scowling. "Give me the fucking phone."

"But, I..."

"Now!" I howl. She finally takes it from her purse and lays it in my hand. "Do you think I'm fucking stupid. You were going to text Ian and tell him we were coming, weren't you?"

"No. I swear."

Holding the phone in front of her face, I unlock it. "Where's the address?"

"In the text messages. Under John."

Once I'm in the text exchange with John, I start reading quickly, finally coming upon the address.

I tap it into the navigation, then press the call button on my dashboard. I shift into drive and slam on the gas.

The tires spin incessantly, but once they've got traction on the road, we cruise at high speed.

"Good evening, Mr. Banks," Arnold says through the car speakers.

I speak loudly and clearly, so he can hear every word I say without a need for me to repeat myself. "I found him. He's at a cabin in Hackley, Vermont. 1789 Staple Drive." I clear my throat and take a deep breath before saying, "He's got her."

"Fuck," Arnold grumbles. "All right. I'm sending out a message as we speak. I've got a group on it. They're about forty minutes east of Hackley. The weather is shit, but they'll get there as soon as they can. Listen to me, Alaric. You need to hold back when you arrive. I'll let you know when it's safe to go inside."

"I'll try, but I can't make any promises."

"We don't need you getting yourself killed. We'll get her back. And we'll bring him down. Don't you worry."

"Remember the plan, Arnold. I want him alive."

"I can't begin to understand why, but you've got it, boss."

I end the call on that note. It's easier said than done. I'll do nothing but worry until Rhea is safe in my arms.

Arnold is a PI, but he's so much more than that. He's my go-to man for everything I need. With connections all over the world, he gets things done with the snap of his fingers. He'll get a group out there, I have no doubt about it, because I pay him a shit ton of money to do exactly what I want.

"For fuck's sake, Arnold," I snap. "I've been sitting on this dirt road for thirty minutes. What the hell is going on in there?"

Chloe's boredom is apparent as she rests her head against the door, humming the same Christmas tune over and over again. If she doesn't knock that shit off soon, I swear my head is going to explode.

"I'm waiting for an update. They're inside and they have him surrounded. Still no visual on Rhea."

He stays on the line, though it's silent as he waits for information to be relayed to him. Arnold is sitting in the comforts of his own home while barking orders at his henchmen, while I bark orders at him.

I hear the tap of his fingers while Chloe continues to hum, and I lose it. "Would you stop fucking humming!"

Her head shoots up, eyebrows knitted. "Can I leave yet?"

"Someone needs to come get this girl, Arnold. If she's not out of my car within the next thirty seconds, I might just bury her in a snowbank and leave her ass there."

"Shouldn't be much longer." Arnold's voice comes through the speaker. "Keep that girl safe. We might need her as a bargaining chip."

Chloe rolls her eyes and lays her head back down as she sighs heavily. "It won't do you any good. Those men don't give a shit about me. No one does."

I slowly turn my head to look at her, watching while she draws a flower in the fog on the window, and something shifts inside me.

This girl, while annoying as fuck and a big wrench in my plans, could be someone else's Rhea.

She didn't want the task she got, but she had no choice. Much like Rhea had no choice when she did some of the crazy shit she did throughout her life.

So I keep my mouth shut and let the little brat sing her goddamn song. Even though it's like nails on a chalkboard to my ears.

"All right," Arnold says, and I instantly straighten my back. "We've got a visual on Rhea. She's safe. Bound and gagged, but safe."

My heart pangs with agony at his words. While I'm glad she's safe, she's got to be terrified.

"I'm going in," I tell him as I push open my door and step one foot out into the snowbank.

"They're still searching for Ian. You need to stay back."

Arnold's words are a demanding plea, but I can't wait any longer.

"Keep the car running," I say to Chloe. "If I don't return, then good fucking luck getting this car unstuck."

I was in such a hurry, I drove right into a snowbank and got myself packed into the white powder. Unfortunately, that means I have to walk a good quarter mile down the driveway to the cabin Rhea's being held in. But a half mile is nothing when it means getting to the woman I love.

I move quickly, determined to get to Rhea as fast as I can. My feet never stop moving, even as snow rides up my pant legs and into my socks.

Ten minutes later, I'm creeping on the outskirts of the driveway near a row of trees. If this were anyone but Rhea, I wouldn't care enough to step foot on this property. I hire people to do this shit for me. But it *is* Rhea, and I can't wait any longer for someone to save the woman who is my entire world.

There are dozens of footprints in the snow, going in every direction, but I pay no attention to them as I walk around the house to the back.

I pull out my phone, shooting a quick text to Arnold.

> Me: Tell your men I'm coming in through the back door and to stand down.

> Arnold: I've already made them aware. You can use any door, though. They've got Ian.

My legs nearly give out from beneath me as I let out a big sigh of relief. I curl over, pressing my hands to my knees, and I close my eyes for a second because this is the moment my life with Rhea truly begins. *We got him, and Rhea's finally safe.*

> Me: Thank fuck. Put in a call to James Duncan with the Auburn field office for the FBI. He's been waiting for this day.

I stand up, straighten my back, and run like hell to the nearest door. Bursting inside, I immediately call out for her. "Rhea!"

Three guys decked head to toe in protective armor come around a corner, waving me in their direction. "She's in here."

I hear her before I see her and my lips lift in a huge smile.

"You. Can't. Own. People." As I turn the corner I watch as each word is followed up with a kick to the gut. Ian is bound on the floor, two men standing over him while my girl goes feral. It really is a sight.

She rips a band from her finger and I glance at the dead priest on the floor beside her. Throwing the ring in Ian's face, she keeps going. "You have to ask a girl to marry you, dickface. And when she says NO, she fucking means it! Or did the kick to the balls mean something else to you?"

Ian just stares up at her with a mixture of shock and anger written on his face. If he's been here watching her for as long as we were thinking, he should know she isn't a girl to be messed with. She's a wildcat.

"And another thing!" she yells, getting down in his face. "Alaric is TWICE the man you will ever be. So don't you dare go insulting him in my presence."

I clear my throat, loving how defensive she is of me now. Two weeks ago, she would have gone running from both of us, but when her head shoots up to see me standing there, she rushes toward me. Tears streaming down her beautiful face.

I move to her, closing the space between us even faster. Once she's in my arms, I hold her tightly, stroking the back of her head. "Did he hurt you?"

She sobs into my shoulder and I hope like hell they're happy tears. I can feel the anxiety and tension leaving her body as she lets it all out. "He didn't hurt me."

I relax a bit as tears of my own prick the corners of my eyes. I take a step back, hands on her hips as I look at her for any sign of injury. Then I take her hand and rub over where the too tight band had been sitting before she ripped it off. "I wasn't too late?"

She shakes her head, sniffling. "They got here just in time." She cracks a small smile. "Right after I kicked him in the balls mid-vows."

A laugh rumbles in my throat. "That's my girl." I pull her into me and press my lips to hers. "I was so scared."

"Alaric Banks, scared?" she teases.

"Nothing scares me more than the thought of losing you, Rhea. I hope you believe that now." Her heat against me helps calm the anxiety that makes me want to fall to my knees. I didn't lose her. She's okay.

"I do. And...I don't wanna lose you either, Alaric." I let out the breath I've been holding since I saw this fierce woman for the first time. She wants to be mine.

"Alaric," a man says, stepping out of the shadows while holding a large rifle across his chest. He looks around before his eyes land on mine. "You care to see this fucker before Duncan gets here?"

Sometime while we were talking, they must have removed Ian from the room.

I take Rhea's face in my hands, sweeping my thumbs under her eyes to wipe away her tears. "Are you okay for a minute?"

"Yes," she says insistently. "I've given him a piece of my mind already. Go. Give him hell."

I kiss her again, this time letting our mouths linger for a second. Then I walk away, knowing she's finally safe.

301

I've waited a long time for the day I come face to face with the man who threatened my future. Sad thing is, if it weren't for me, this guy wouldn't even have a life to begin with.

I push open the door and find Ian tied to a chair, surrounded by men with guns pointed at him.

He lifts his head and I take notice of the bruises all over his face.

"Damn," I scoff, "they really did a number on you."

"Good to see you, too, *Dad*. Have you been enjoying yourself while you fuck my future wife?"

"So now I'm Dad," I say to him, my finger tapping my chin. He won't get a reaction out of me on this. "The one time I was able to reach you by phone, you told me I wasn't and never would be your dad."

"No, you're not my fucking dad! I have a dad and he's more of a man than you'll ever be." Spit falls from his bruised mouth as he speaks.

"Your ignorant stepfather corrupted you. I'd hardly call him a man."

He leans forward, straining himself against the chains as he shouts, "My stepfather made me the man I am today! Which is more than I can say for the coward who never fought for me."

I walk toward him slowly, keeping my tone low. "Your mother didn't give me the opportunity to fight for you because she never told me you existed. It wasn't until early this year I knew I even had a son. I called you, wanting to try and make it up to you, and you lost your shit like the spoiled brat you are. Then I learned of your deal with Rhea's father, and I've been trying to hunt you down ever since."

"Grayson fucking Thorn," Ian sings as he shakes his head. "That man really fucked me. Made a deal with my mom and Lenny that I was to marry that girl one day and gain half of his fortune. Then the asshole died and never fucking paid up. I could take over a country with that kind of money."

"That wasn't the only deal, and you know it. Grayson helped hide your paternity from me. Never once gave me the slightest notion that I had a son. It's the reason I didn't save him when death came knocking at his door. It was the least he deserved."

"I think it's safe to say we're all a little thankful for him hiding me from you, though." Ian laughs. "I mean, I sure as fuck don't want you as my dad, and I can guarantee you don't want me for a son."

"That's not true. When I first found out about you, I did want that. It's the reason you're still alive right now. Once I learned Lenny and your mom were killed and you took over their legacy, I knew I would never get the chance to be the dad I could have been." I bend down in front of him, so many of his features mirroring mine.

"Fucking right you won't. You're nothing to me. Never will be."

I nod, accepting that fate, for now. "You're going away for life; therefore, you'll have a lot of time to think about what could have been. If you ever want to talk, you know how to reach me."

Being raised by a crime lord his entire life, I've learned that Ian is a cold and calloused young man with no empathy for others. His only goal in life is to rule. There isn't a doubt in my mind he would end my life at this very moment if he had the chance. But given the opportunity, I wouldn't do the same to him. He's my blood, and for that reason, I can only hope one day he's able to change. Though, I'm not holding my breath.

"We'll see about that," he snickers. "Never know, I might just make a grand escape."

I fold my hands behind my back, expression stoic. "In that

case, I wish you the best." I leave the room, knowing there's a good chance I'll never see Ian again. He'll be in solitary confinement with no access to the outside world, and that's assuming he's not given the death penalty. The list of crimes he's committed are a mile long, ranging from multiple rapes and murders to money laundering and extortion.

I may be what some would refer to as morally gray, but I am nowhere near the sadist Ian is. It breaks my heart that the chance to know my son was stripped from me. I hated Grayson for that and planned to screw him out of our deal the minute it was finalized. But then Rhea came in and sent him straight to hell for me instead.

The detective asks Rhea questions, but I find out she was knocked out and doesn't remember much. Luckily, my girl is a proficient liar and con artist, so even when the detective asks questions that would have had his brow lifting at the truth, my girl lies through her teeth like the professional she is.

She plays the part of a woman held captive so well, it actually has a knot in my throat. It isn't until the detective looks away and she winks at me that I catch on to her game. She is playing them, and damn, do I love seeing her at work.

Once all our statements have been given, I take my girl's hand and lead her to the door. There's a tow truck waiting for us at the car, ready to pull me out of the bank. That's all assuming Chloe hasn't hijacked it and taken off.

"I heard your conversation with Ian," Rhea says softly. "Why didn't you tell me he's your son?"

My back stiffens a little, not wanting her to know that I was responsible for the life of the man that hunted her.

"That's a tough question and I'm not really sure how to answer it. I've never told anyone but Arnold. Finding out you have a child should be elating, and it was at first. There was hopefulness inside me that Ian would be excited to learn he was my son. I tried the best I could, but it wasn't enough for him and I've accepted that now."

Rhea presses her head against my chest when we stop, holding on to me tightly. "I'm sorry."

I wrap my arms around her, soaking in the fact that she's really okay and letting my body finally relax. "Don't be. Ian's going to get the help he needs. Or at least, that's what I keep telling myself."

"So, it's really over?" Rhea asks, still skeptical that the threat is completely gone.

I pull her closer, surrounding her with my body like a shield but also giving her the confirmation I know she needs. "It's really over, baby. It's time to start living."

We step outside and I exhale a heavy steam-infused breath when I see Chloe running toward us. She trips over her own feet, face-planting right into the snow.

"Oh my God," Rhea huffs, running toward her. "What the hell are you doing here?" She grabs Chloe by the hand and helps her up.

I can't help but laugh because she looks like a fucking train wreck.

"We'll fill you in on the ride home, baby." I look at Chloe as I point at my vehicle, now pulled out to the road safely. "Back to the car."

She slumps her shoulders, pouting. "Seriously? It took me, like, twenty minutes to get up here to try and help and now I have to walk back?"

"I'm so confused," Rhea says as I wrap an arm around her waist, leading her through the snow.

"It's a long story. But, Rhea, meet Chloe."

CHAPTER

THIRTY

RHEA

Two Weeks Later

I THROW my arms around Alaric's shoulders as I pepper his neck with kisses. "You are the absolute sweetest."

He closes his laptop on the desk in his room and spins around in his chair, immediately pulling me onto his lap. "And why is that?"

My arms envelop his neck and I narrow my eyes. "I just talked to Chloe. She told me all about how you paid off her debts. She was beside herself."

Alaric told me what happened and Chloe filled me in on how Ian manipulated her and threatened her life. While it wasn't fun to hear, I also understood her. How many people had I thrown under the bus in my life in order to get ahead?

That's the reason I went to Tyler for her. He knew a little bit, thanks to Alaric, but I filled him in on a bit more, giving him the actual truth about who I was. He was shocked, but in the end, he hugged me and said he was happy for me that I found Alaric. He agreed to start fresh with Chloe and they have a date tonight.

Alaric shrugs his shoulders casually. "It was no big deal. I guess I just saw a little bit of you in her and I had to help where I could."

"Well, I think it's pretty amazing." My face lights up under his gaze, it's insane how much I've fallen for this man.

His lips press to mine in a soft kiss. "I think you're pretty amazing."

Butterflies flutter though my stomach. It's a feeling I'm getting used to with Alaric. People say over time you stop getting those flutters as relationships grow old, but I don't see that happening with us anytime soon. Every day Alaric finds some way to totally sweep me off my feet.

I know the newness of our relationship will wear off and we'll have our good days and bad days, but I don't think for a second I'll ever stop missing him when we're not in the same room.

"Speaking of amazing," he begins. "I'm pretty sure we have some amazing reservations in twenty minutes, so we better get going."

My phone buzzes in my pocket and I quickly stretch my legs to pull it out. "One sec," I say to Alaric. One glance at the screen and I literally scream out loud when I see who's calling, making Alaric jump. I hold out my hand to him with a smile and he relaxes.

"Dex!" I shout into the phone. "You're alive!"

"Of course I'm alive. I'm fucking Dex Brooks. What? Did you think I was dead?" I roll my eyes because *yes*, that's exactly what I was getting worried about.

"Yes, I did. Why the hell haven't you returned my calls and text messages?"

"Oh right. That. Well, I got locked up for a bit. But I'm free now and all is well."

"Locked up?" I gasp. "What the hell did you do?"

"It was nothing. Just a petty misdemeanor. I sold a fake ID to an undercover cop and got twenty-one days. I felt bad after our conversation, but I knew you were tough and could figure it out."

I exhale a breath of relief. "That really sucks. I'm just so glad you're okay."

"I'm fine, baby girl. But tell me, what's new with you? How's the small-town life you wanted? I'm assuming things got better if the joy in your tone is anything to go by. You sound happier than I've ever heard, Doll."

I look at Alaric, grinning from ear to ear. "I have so much to tell you, Dex. You're not going to believe the shit I've been through." Alaric taps his wristwatch, making note of the time, so I say, "But it has to wait. I have a date with my boyfriend."

"Boyfriend? Wow, girl. I take it things are looking up for you?"

"Life is amazing. And I owe a big thanks to you. You helped me along the way and it got me to where I'm at. I owe you one...Uncle Dex." Tears burn the backs of my eyes, but I won't let them fall.

"Look at you getting all sentimental and calling me Uncle. It was my pleasure, Doll. You've got a fight in you like nothing I've ever seen before. You just needed to get where you were going. But on another note," he pauses briefly before continuing, "I found some people who want to meet you."

I crane my neck in confusion. "You did?"

"A couple cousins on Grayson's side. Axel and Marni Thorn. Their dad, Grayson's brother, was a dickwad just like Grayson. He passed away a couple years ago. Well, apparently there is something huge they need to share with you and I think it has to do with Grayson's estate."

Chills dance down my entire body as I jump to my feet. "You're kidding me? I've got actual family?"

"Ouch, kid."

"Oh, don't be like that, Dex. You know how I feel about you."

Alaric follows my antics and jumps up too. "What?" he huffs, hands in the air.

I shush him with a finger over my mouth and keep listening to Dex.

"I can't say for certain, but being his only child, I'm almost positive that's what it is. With your permission, I'll shoot your number over to Marni and Axel and they can give you a call."

"Yes," I beam with excitement. "Absolutely."

"All right, baby girl. We'll talk soon so you can fill me in on this boyfriend and all the chaos that is your life."

"No more chaos, Dex. It's smooth sailing from here."

I end the call and do a happy dance, tapping my feet up and down on the floor. "I have cousins!"

"Well, yeah," Alaric gloats. "I could have told you that. Marni and Axel Thorn. Pretty good kids. Got caught up in some weird shit a couple years ago, but they're doing well. Married. Kids."

I swat him playfully on the arm, my eyes wide. "You knew and you didn't tell me?"

"I haven't had the chance and I figured it might be too soon to start talking about Grayson. But yeah, you've got living blood relatives."

"Dex also mentioned something about Grayson's estate and how Marni and Axel have some *huge* news to share with me."

"It's probably all yours," Alaric says ever so casually with a shrug. How is he acting so nonchalant? This is insane.

"Well, if it is, then I have some big plans. The merger. The acquisition. We're doing it."

"Stop it," Alaric sweeps his hand in the air. "First of all, that ship has sailed. Second, you don't even know for sure it's yours." He slides up to me, wrapping his arms around my waist with his hands resting on my ass. "Third, you don't need that dirtbag's money. I plan to take care of you for the rest of your life."

I rest my hands on his chest, peering up at him so he knows just how much this means to me. "I've never had anything that was mine, Alaric. After I finish my GED, I could do something great. Like open a women's shelter, or a nonprofit that feeds the homeless."

"The possibilities are endless." He kisses me on the forehead. "And we've got a lot of time to think about it. Until then, we're late for our reservation."

"Shit. I completely forgot about that. I guess I just got too caught up in that call and everything Dex had to share."

Grinning at me, he grabs my coat. "I know you're excited, baby. And we'll return to the subject. We're late." He kisses me on the forehead again and then grabs my purse off his dresser. Taking my hand, he walks me out of his room.

No man has ever carried my purse for me before, but Alaric has made it a habit. He also opens doors for me and runs my baths. He makes me feel like I'm the luckiest girl alive.

We walk out the front door and when Alaric keeps going, past his car, I tug on his hand. "Where are you going? Aren't we late?"

"Just need to run into Taryn's for a minute. Is that all right?" There's a glint in his eyes; he's up to something.

"You said we're already late for our reservation. Can't it wait?"

"No." He shakes his head as he starts walking again. "Not really."

I'm completely dumbfounded. Alaric has been acting strange all day, and now this. I side-eye him, trying to read his expression, but I get nothing.

We walk into Taryn's and my tightly knitted eyebrows immediately jump to my forehead when I see the sight in front of us.

The space is completely empty, not a person in sight, and all the tables and chairs have been pushed to the wall. All but one. In the center of the room is a small table with a candle lit in the center, and on the floor surrounding it are hundreds of pressed forget-me-not petals.

I look to my left at Alaric, tears forming in the corners of my eyes. "You did this for me?"

He takes my hand and I can feel a slight tremble in his touch. Then again, it could be me shaking because I'm completely shocked right now.

Leading me to the table, he pulls out a chair and gestures for me to sit down. "What's going on?" I ask, though I have an idea.

Alaric takes a deep breath and the second he drops to his knee, my hands fly to my mouth.

"Rhea," he begins, a huge grin on his face. "Life hasn't always been easy, and it's not supposed to be. It won't always be easy, but I promise to make it worth it. I can't imagine a life without you in it. You're the rainbow after a storm, and the sunshine after a cloudy day. I need you like I need air."

Reaching into his jacket pocket, he plucks out a small velvet box I know too well. "Please allow me the honor of doing everything in my power to make you the happiest woman alive."

Tears stream down my cheeks when he flips open the box. I gasp at the sight of the ring, though I've seen it before. "I'm going to try this again with the hope you'll answer differently this time. Rhea Brooks, will you marry me?"

My head nods repeatedly as I shout out, "Yes!" I jump into his arms, nearly making us tumble to the floor as my arms wrap around him. "Yes, I will marry you."

Alaric slides the ring on my finger, then grabs my waist and jerks me closer to him. "I love you more than you'll ever know."

"And I love you just as much, plus some." It's the first time those words have passed my lips since my mother, but I mean them with a sincerity I don't think I've ever felt. My mother did her best for me, but it was still a hard life for a child. Alaric fights for my heart every single day and giving it to him is as easy as breathing because I know he will protect it with his life.

EPILOGUE

RHEA

Six Months Later

"Hey, Rhea, need a hand with those?" Tyler asks as he sees me walking to Gladys's with a plate.

"I've got it, thanks for asking, though. Still need me to cover tomorrow night for you to take Chloe out?" His cheeks pinken as he approaches and I love it.

"Yeah, actually, I wanted to talk to you about that." He puts his hands in his pockets, acting shy.

"What is it? Oh God, you're not breaking up with her, right?" My eyes are wide as he grins at me.

"No, I was actually thinking about asking her to move in with me. My brother moved out a few weeks ago and I feel like it's time. But I needed your opinion first. Is it too fast?"

My heart bursts with happiness for him. "It's been six months, Tyler. I guarantee you, as much as I loved living with Gladys, Chloe would love to move in with you. In fact, she was talking about saving up for her own place the other week when we had coffee."

His boyish smile makes me want to laugh. "Yeah, she mentioned that. I thought it was crazy for her to spend that money, but my brother wasn't gone yet, so I didn't want to ask, and you've been too busy to talk to since then with the new house and all."

"Sorry about that," I say honestly. "Speaking of the new house, I meant to text you about the house-warming party. I'll tell you more about it at our weekly brunch." Tyler and I usually meet up for brunch once a week, and the past two weeks, Alaric and I have been trying to decide between houses. "My treat."

"Don't you mean your sugar daddy's treat?" Tyler teases and I nearly throw my plate at him. He laughs, backing away like he knows it too.

"Just kidding, Rhea. See you Sunday." He jogs back to the other side of the street with a wave and I wave back. His friendship has meant the world to me these past six months. It's so crazy to think I have friends now. A whole life to call my own.

Since I'm no longer a guest at Gladys's, I knock on the door with my free hand, the other holding a plate of homemade cookies—cookies *I* baked. They actually turned out better than I expected, considering I've never baked anything before. Oatmeal raisin with chocolate chips. Gladys gave me the recipe, so it's only right that I bring her some. Besides, I've sort of missed our little chats.

The door swings open and the smile on her face instantly warms me.

"Rhea, darling. Why on earth are you knocking?" She steps aside and waves her arm. "Come in. Come in."

I walk inside and I'm immediately embraced in a hug. Gladys's hugs always feel like home.

The house smells delicious as always, like homemade

apple pie. It's a scent I've missed as much as I've missed this place. In a weird way, this house built me. In my short time here, I learned so much about myself. My whole existence I felt like I was standing still while life went on around me. It turns out, I was never standing still, but simply taking the small steps I needed to at the time. Some days I barely moved, while others I jumped.

I lost so much during those years, felt so much deep pain, some of which I continue to feel and probably always will. But it's that pain that reminds me how far I've come, and how far I still have to go. I'm learning to embrace the past, live in the present, and look forward to the future.

"These are for you and your guests," I tell Gladys as I hand her the plate of cookies.

"You baked the cookies." Gladys beams. "They look tasty. I can't wait to try one, I just know our new guests will love them, too."

We walk into the kitchen and Gladys sets the plate down, returning to a pot of boiling pasta on the stove. "I was just preparing dinner. Would you and Alaric like to join us? Chloe invited Tyler over before they go out tonight."

"Oh no, but thank you for the offer. Unfortunately I can't stay long because we have furniture arriving at the house today, but I actually wanted to invite you over for dinner this weekend. If you're not busy."

"That would be lovely, darling. How are you liking the new house?" Her wrinkly hands wrap around the spoon as she stirs the pasta.

I rest my arms on the kitchen counter, grinning like a teenager. "It's amazing. It's right on Meyers Lake with the most beautiful view. Alaric and I have been sitting on the back porch every night since we've moved in, watching the sunset."

Gladys claps her hands together, a twinkle in her eye. "I'm so happy for you. You deserve all the happiness in the world."

"Well, I don't know if I'm deserving of it, but I am pretty happy."

Taking my face in her hands, she looks me in the eye. "You *are* deserving. You're a good person, Rhea. No one is perfect. We all make mistakes. But I've seen the growth in you since you arrived in Lockhaven. Your strength is admirable and you should be very proud of how far you've come."

Gladys doesn't know about my past, but even if she did, I don't doubt her words would be the same.

"Thank you. That truly means a lot."

"It means a lot to me that you still stop by and visit. I sure hope I'll be getting an invitation to your wedding."

"Well, of course you will, silly. But it's not going to be for a while. Alaric and I really want to get settled into the new house and enjoy the simplicity in life before we begin the chaos of planning a wedding. Not to mention I've got the opening of my new non-profit organization in a couple months."

After learning I inherited all of Grayson's estate, I did what I always dreamed of doing, I began the process of starting up a business that will provide relief to the homeless, such as food, blankets, and medical equipment. Of course, that was all after I finished my GED.

Gladys pats her hand over mine. "I think that's a wonderful plan. And I'm so proud of you. I have no doubt the organization will be a great success. Be sure to let me know if you need anything at all."

"I definitely will. We might need a special wedding cake just from you." I grin, remembering how she talked about baking cakes for weddings back in the day. She used to love it, but the B&B began to take priority after a while.

We sit and talk for a little bit while Gladys finishes dinner. I tell her about meeting my cousins, Axel and Marni, as well their spouses and kids. We've made plans to get together again this summer and I'm already looking forward to it.

Before I know it, an hour has passed, so I tell Gladys I have to go with plans to stop in tomorrow after work. I'm still working at Taryn's one night a week just because I enjoy it so much. Chloe picked up my other shifts, which worked out well because she needed a job. Not to mention it gives me a chance to see some of my favorite people—Tyler and Chloe, as well as the sass and spunk of the town, Taryn.

Alaric has been fortunate enough to be able to work from home, with only the occasional need to travel, at which point, I travel with him. His protectiveness has not let up much, or at all for that matter. At first it was suffocating, especially when I didn't fully understand it in the beginning. But now I find it comforting, even though it's no longer necessary with the threat of Ian gone.

I step out of the house and into the warmth of the sun. The light is blinding, but when I squint and look down at my arm, I see a single ray of light dancing over my skin. As I shift my gaze to the left, I see that the sun isn't shining on me—it's actually highlighting a beautiful cluster of flowers.

Not just any flowers, forget-me-not flowers. A lump rises in my throat as I watch a blue butterfly land on one of the petals. I know without a doubt it's a sign from my mom. Its vibrant wings flutter lightly, and I kneel down to get a closer look. With a shaky hand, I graze my fingertips over the flower petal next to it, tears of happiness forming in the corners of my eyes. "I think I made it, Mama," I whisper. "I'm going to be all right."

"I'm home," I holler as I close the front door behind me.

"In here, baby," Alaric responds from our bedroom. I follow the sound of his voice and see him across the room in our master bath, brushing his teeth, butt naked. My eyes land on his firm, round ass and I have an overwhelming urge to sink my teeth into it.

I walk up behind him, wrapping my arms around his torso. "How was your afternoon?"

Bending over, he spits in the sink, then rinses his toothbrush and sticks it in the holder. When he spins around, I'm instantly enveloped in a warm embrace. "Not nearly as good as it could have been if you were here. I missed you."

I push myself up on my tiptoes and press my lips to his. "I missed you, too."

His hands slide down, cupping my ass in his palms, and he squeezes. "Oh yeah? Prove it."

I waggle my brows, the corner of my mouth lifted. "What did you have in mind?"

Gripping the hem of my top, he lifts it up. His eyes rake over me as he tosses my shirt to the side, then his warm fingers reach behind me, unclasping my bra.

I tremble in response when his head drops low and he takes the bud of one of my nipples between his teeth. "Mmm. I like the way you think, Mr. Banks."

He moves to the left and his eyes lift to mine. "I'm only getting started, future Mrs. Banks."

"I love the sound of that. *Rhea Banks*." A groan escapes him and I love that I make him as ravenous as he makes me.

He gets on his knees, eyes full of desire as he eagerly undresses me from the waist down. He sinks his teeth into my thigh with gentle pressure, then he kisses his way up while the pads of his fingers circle my clit. I step my legs out farther, granting him access while a moan escapes my lips.

He slips two fingers inside my dripping center, pushing deeper and deeper with each stroke. My hips chase his hand as I brace myself against the counter.

Moving his fingers faster, he sucks feverishly on my clit, pausing the suction in time with his tongue flicking out. It's a mixture of pain and pleasure that has me crying out.

Alaric looks up at me, while I peer down at him. "Does that feel good, baby."

Mouth agape, I nod as I roll my hips to his movements.

Fingers curled, he pulsates the tips, the action driving me wild. My muscles tense and I hold my breath as I release and my legs begin to shake. My body floods with bliss while proof of my arousal spills onto the floor, turning Alaric on even more. He loves when I make a mess for him.

Before I've even come down from my orgasm, Alaric is on his feet, spinning around. He presses his palm to my lower back until my chest is against the vanity. His fingers thread into my hair at the base of my neck, and he pulls, forcing me to look at myself in the mirror. As soon as my eyes meet his, he grabs my hips and drives his dick inside me from behind. I lift my head, encouraging him to pull harder, so I can watch us chase our pleasure together.

He gives me exactly what I wanted, making me cry out in pure ecstasy. He watches me with adoration and a need so deep, I feel it in my soul.

"You're so fucking sexy," he croaks, his voice thick and his breathing labored.

Alaric gapes at me through the reflection, his eyes on my breasts that bounce to the rhythm of his urgent movements. He reaches both hands beneath me, cupping my breasts and using them to aid his forceful thrusts. It puts him at just the right angle.

I feel myself grasping at the peak of another orgasm as I whimper and moan. "Faster."

Instead, the bastard slows down. "What was that, Wildcat?"

Barley pumping in and out, I know what he wants to hear, but I love to make him wait for it.

"I said, faster." I punctuate my words by pushing back into him, only for him to stop completely.

I groan and a firm hand smacks me on the ass, making my walls clench around him. "Try again, baby girl," he says as he rubs a soothing circle around the tender flesh.

I give in to him because it's what we both want. "Faster, Daddy."

He grins back at me in the mirror, filling me up then setting a punishing pace. One that has my toes curling as I all but fall into the vanity under his movements.

His hands move back to my hips, pinching them with tenacity. I feel his hot breath on my back while beads of sweat slide between our melded bodies.

He picks up his pace, his pelvic bone slamming against my ass cheeks like a collision. His rhythm has me quivering as I gasp for air. "Yes, Daddy," I cry out as I clench around his cock and come again.

I feel his head swell inside me as he thrusts once, twice more. His breaths come in quick gasps and he shudders against me before his body goes still, overtaken by pleasure as he fills me up with his release.

I straighten my back and he slips out of me. Chin on my shoulder, he whispers the words I melt for every damn time, "I love you."

I smile back at his reflection before resting my head back on him. "I love you, too."

The End.

I hope you enjoyed Rhea and Alaric's story! I'll be sharing the link to the bonus epilogue soon so you can get a glimpse at these two in the future! Sign up to my newsletter for the link once it's ready: CLICK HERE
http://bit.ly/rl_news

If you enjoyed Alaric's OTT Obsessive tendencies, you'll love Ridge from We Will Reign, a dark stalker why-choose romance, and book one in the Wicked Boys of BCU Series!

Also by Rachel Leigh

Bastards of Boulder Cove

Book One: Savage Games

Book Two: Vicious Lies

Book Three: Twisted Secrets

Wicked Boys of BCU (Coming March 2023)

Book One: We Will Reign

Book Two: You Will Bow

Book Three: They Will Fall

Redwood Rebels Series

Book One: Striker

Book Two: Heathen

Book Three: Vandal

Book Four: Reaper

Redwood High Series

Book One: Like Gravity

Book Two: Like You

Book Three: Like Hate

Fallen Kingdom Duet

His Hollow Heart & Her Broken Pieces

Black Heart Duet

Four & Five

Standalones

Forget Me Not

Guarded

Ruthless Rookie

Devil Heir

All The Little Things

Claim your FREE copy of Her Undoing!

ACKNOWLEDGMENTS

Thank you so much for reading Forget Me Not. I hope you enjoyed it!

A special thanks to my wonderful team for all the hard work you put into helping me create this book: My dedicated PA, Carolina Leon. All my girls for your support, friendship, and advice. My Street Team, the Rebel Readers for your help in getting the word out.

A an extra special thanks to...

Taylor and Amanda for being the true MVP's and the most amazing Alpha and Beta readers around! Love you, ladies!

Lori Jackson for the stunning cover!

Fairest Reviews Editing Service for the beautiful edit!

Rumi Khan for proofreading and being so flexible!.

Valentine PR for spectacular PR Services.

XOXO Rachel

ABOUT THE AUTHOR

Rachel Leigh is a USA Today and International bestselling author of new adult and contemporary romances. She loves to write—and read—flawed bad-boys and strong heroines. You can expect dark elements, a dash of suspense, and a lot of steam.

Her goal is to take readers on an adventure with her words, while showing them that even on the darkest days, love conquers all.

Rachel lives in Michigan with her husband, three little monsters (who aren't so little anymore) and a couple fur babies. When she's not writing or reading, she's likely lounging in leggings, with coffee in her hand, while binge watching her favorite reality tv shows.

Join My Reader's Group: Rachel's Ramblers

f facebook.com/rachelleighauthor

⊙ instagram.com/rachelleighauthor

BB bookbub.com/profile/rachel-leigh

g goodreads.com/rachelleigh

a amazon.com/author/rachelleighauthor

℗ pinterest.com/rachelleighauthor

Made in the USA
Columbia, SC
28 November 2023

27314714R00202